T0274138

The Search for
the Dragon's Dagger

www.mascotbooks.com

The Search for the Dragon's Dagger

For more information, please contact:
Mascot Books, an imprint of Amplify Publishing Group
620 Herndon Parkway, Suite 320
Herndon, VA 20170
info@mascotbooks.com

Library of Congress Control Number: 2021917433

CPSIA Code: PRV0422A
ISBN-13: 978-1-64543-694-2

Printed in the United States

In loving memory of my parents,

Joseph and Willadene Zedan

THE
SEARCH
for the
DRAGON'S
DAGGER

Daniel J. Zedan

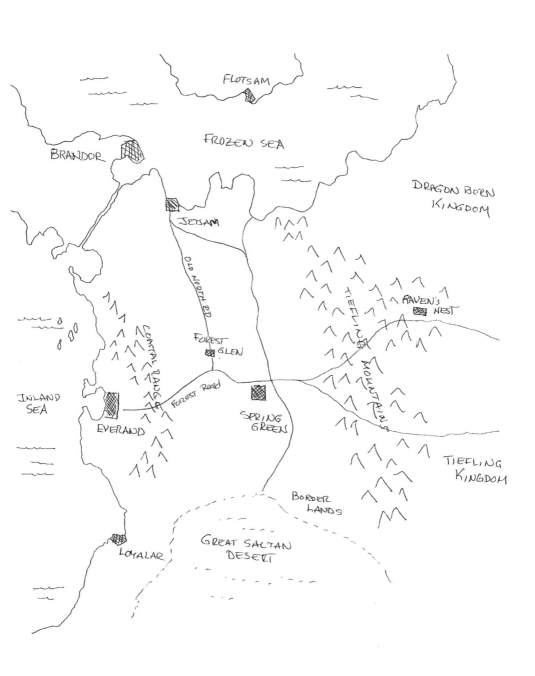

Contents

CHAPTER 1

SPRING GREEN

I t never ceases to amaze him. Every disgusting groggery or tavern that he has ever managed to find himself in reeks of the same repugnant odors: dust, burnt candle wax, urine, vomit, and cheap perfume. Why would anyone consciously decide to subject themselves to such an ordeal? After all, with few exceptions, the integrity of the individuals who usually frequent such establishments leaves little to be desired. Whether thieves, bounty hunters, adventurers, or the occasional local searching for a momentary escape from the hardships of daily life, these are not the kinds of people one would want to spend time with.

"You look like you've had a hard day," whispers the raspy voice of a working woman. "Can I help you wash away the dust of the day's journey?"

"No, thank you, I'm waiting for a friend," he replies. Then he shouts, "Loki, where's that beer you promised me?"

Seemingly unfazed by the attempted diversion, she retorts, "I could help your dwarf friend forget about the day's hardships as well."

Becoming agitated, he turns his head and tersely responds, "You look like a nice woman. Please don't make me ruin your day."

With that, she quickly saunters to the next table, where several travelers with large purses are partaking of the local brew while discussing the virtues of the various women working the room.

"Loki, what's taking so long?" Aramas asks. The obnoxious din of the slurred speech from around the room seems to engulf even the loudest of voices.

"Isn't this a great place?" Loki shouts as he jaunts across the floor. "I think it's the best pub we've ever been in."

Aramas just rolls his eyes as he grabs the lukewarm ambrosia from Loki's outstretched hand. "You think every pub is the best pub you've ever been in! What did the bartender say about getting something to eat?" Taking a long-awaited gulp from the tankard, Aramas impatiently stares at his friend as if his life depended on the answer.

"What did that beautiful creature want?" Loki asks.

Aramas again rolls his eyes and shakes his head. "The usual." After another gulp of his beer, Aramas then asks, "What is it with you and pubs? It's almost as if you have some mission in life to partake of every local brew in every corner of the land."

Loki replies, "The gods would not have put pubs on this Earth if they didn't expect us to make good use of them. I'm sure that even Moradin must have his favorite watering hole. Where else can one meet such interesting people while partaking of the local culture?"

Aramas and Loki have traveled together since meeting in a similar tavern only four years earlier. Aramas had only just entered the establishment when he happened upon the fubsy red-bearded dwarf cleric surrounded by several imposing drunken travelers. Without knowing what had caused the confrontation, and feeling a need to even the odds, Aramas joined the fray only to learn that Loki was more than proficient with a war hammer. In the intervening years, the two had become close friends, each willing to lay down his life for the other. Life has not been kind to either, but together, they share a common bond: a respect for their gods and a compulsion to help those who cannot help themselves.

"So now that we've returned the opal to Alissa, where do we head next?" Loki inquires.

The question, while innocent enough, unexpectedly thrusts Aramas back into the catacombs below the city as unspeakably gruesome memories are suddenly brought to the fore.

His mind replays the screams of his companions as, one by one, they succumb to the black beast. Blood-soaked tabards, armor dripping with death, the sound of a skull being crushed between the creature's jaws, brain matter oozing from beneath the crumpled helmet, and the sight of grown men tossed about like rag dolls all pass before him.

Jumping to his left, Aramas leaps over the sweeping motion of the creature's eight-foot-long tail. Before the beast can react to the danger now attacking its flank, Aramas's longsword finds its mark, and the force of the strike forces it to drop the body of another companion, entrails cascading to the stone below. The creature pivots to the left and swipes at Aramas, its sharp claws narrowly missing their target. Aramas counters the beast's attack and once again strikes true. The beast's left hind leg is now severely damaged, its movement severely impaired. Its focus is now squarely on Aramas, its shrieks of anger drowning all other sound, and as the creature exhales a stream of burning acid . . .

Tugging at Aramas's shoulder, Loki again asks, "Where do we head next?"

Surprised, Aramas regains his composure. He contemplates his next words, looking forlorn, before he replies. "I'm not sure. Those who helped us retrieve the opal did so at a very heavy price." Obviously shaken by what had transpired, an emotion rarely exhibited in the presence of others, he adds, "I thought the dragons had vanished hundreds of years ago, existing only in lore and legend. If that is so, how can one explain what happened?" Taking another drink, he continues. "There is a dark presence here, one that logic cannot explain. If unchecked, I fear that it will not be long before we are fighting for our very existence." Almost resolute, Aramas adds, "We will not find the answers we seek here in Spring Green, nor the legions of armies that will be required to defeat this dark power. That baby black dragon . . ."

Loki interrupts. "Let's not talk of this now. The bartender told me that the leg of lamb is fresh. After a good night's rest and a few more tankards of this fine brew, we will meet with Alissa tomorrow, claim our reward, and then head to the north. I am told there are some very fine pubs along the Frozen Sea."

Spring Green is a small outpost that rests at the base of the imposing Tiefling Mountains. Well-fortified, it is the only outpost within a hundred miles of anywhere where one can procure provisions, shelter, and protection from the barbarians that roam the nearby hills. The mountain range itself runs north and south and lies just to the east of town, a day's ride on a good horse. Hundreds of years earlier, shortly after the end of the Dragon Wars, the mountain range became the dividing line between the tiefling kingdom to the east and the domain of man to the west. One does not venture far into the mountains without a good reason and a very strong escort. Rumor holds that the mountains are protected by the spirits of the evil dragons destroyed so long ago. It is said that only the vilest of creatures dare to inhabit the area.

Two days to the south lies the vast expanse of the Great Saltan Desert, so named because of the extremely high salt content of the soil and the lack of any significant quantities of fresh water. It is widely believed that not many creatures can survive the two-week journey required to cross it. As such, only the most experienced traveler, or those under a wizard's protection, dare attempt it. While towns of vast riches lie farther to the south, the only safe way to reach them is to head due west to the Inland Sea and then proceed south along the coast.

Lush green rolling hills and vast plains lie to the north. The fields just outside of the outpost walls are dotted with a patchwork quilt of small farms and thatch-roofed homes. The soil in the area is rich and well suited for growing any number of fruits and vegetables as well as grazing livestock. A small stream, flowing down from the mountains, provides adequate supplies of water for both the outpost and the peasants who live in the area. While it is a good two-week's journey to the nearest town to the north, it is a relatively easy trip, and as such, is frequented by many as Spring Green straddles the only major road from the north to the west that traverses the Hinter Land.

Following the road out of town to the west requires one to pass through what seems like an endless dark forest, the canopy of which is so thick that even the rays of the sun, on the brightest of days, strain to touch the earth below. So dense is the forest that few roads traverse it in any direction. While there are several outposts and small villages along the way, it is a two-week journey to Everand, one of the largest ports on the Inland Sea. While well-traveled, it is not an easy journey. Further, bands of thieves are only too eager to relieve unsuspecting travelers of their possessions.

Only half-listening as Loki continues babbling about the virtues of the brew he is now enjoying, Aramas cannot help but wonder where the black dragon had come from. No one he knew of has ever seen a dragon, let alone fought one. Why had Alissa admonished him not to discuss the matter? What is the significance of the opal, and what makes it worth more than the lives of the five companions who had helped retrieve it?

Alissa, a tall brunette with long, flowing coal-black hair and a well-proportioned figure, is the great-granddaughter of Spring Green's founder. Strikingly beautiful and trusting of no one, she rules with an iron fist, commanding the loyalty of all around her. Adorning her svelte waist hang two gleaming scimitars, implements that she is not afraid to use and has often. Many a potential assassin and overzealous suitor have fallen to their adept use. Based on his observations, it is apparent to Aramas that she wants for nothing. Yet, only a month earlier, she had put great value on retrieving the opal. While beautiful and larger than most opals he had seen before, it did not appear to possess any unusual qualities.

"Aramas, are you listening?" quips Loki. "How long do you think it will take to get to Flotsam?"

Aramas pauses for a moment. "We may not be going to Flotsam right away. Something is wrong, and I can't seem to put my finger on it."

"It's none of our business," replies Loki. "Alissa hired us to do a job, and we did it. Now it's time to collect our reward and move on."

"I understand. But there is more here than meets the eye." Then, shrugging his shoulders as if to surrender, Aramas blurts out, "Well, are you going to get us a couple of those legs of lamb you spoke of?"

Loki quickly gulps the rest of his beer then stands up and moves over to the bar to order their meals.

As the bartender had said, the lamb is fresh and tender. This is certainly not the usual tough mutton they have become accustomed to. The beer too seems to taste a bit sweeter, more refreshing. It has been a while since they have partaken of such a good meal.

"My compliments, Loki! Let's have another beer and call it a night."

Loki nods affirmatively as he continues to gnaw at the remaining meat on the bone.

"Did the bartender say anything about a good place to hang our armor for the night?"

But before Aramas can get an answer, two heavily armed guards enter the pub and survey the room. Loki puts down the leg of lamb and turns to see what has caught Aramas's eye. They are two of the guards who had flanked Alissa when Aramas turned over the opal. Feeling the hair on the back of his neck slowly rise, Aramas quietly reaches for his longsword. He thinks this is not going to end well. The room has become eerily quiet, all eyes focused on the interlopers.

"You," shouts one of the guards, pointing at Aramas. "You and the dwarf are to come with us."

Grasping the hilt of his sword, Aramas asks, "Have we done something wrong?" Loki slowly reaches for his war hammer.

"I have been told to escort you to the keep's great room. I care not for what reason," the guard replies.

"May we collect our belongings?" asks Loki.

"I was given no instructions otherwise. Bring what you desire." Not wishing to get into a confrontation where so many innocents might get hurt, Aramas and Loki grab their belongings and slowly move toward the door.

"Hey, they haven't paid for their meal," shouts the bartender.

"Alissa will take care of what they owe," says the guard as the four exit the building. Once out on the street, the party is joined by four other heavily armed guards, all wearing Alissa's coat of arms.

It is dark, the night air damp. Oil lamps from the surrounding buildings cast a dim glow on the cobblestone street below. Other than the clip-clop of a passing horse and rider, the street is relatively quiet. Inquisitive eyes can be observed peering from many of the partially shuttered windows. It is not often that Alissa's personal guards are seen outside of the keep. As the party slowly moves toward the inner sanctum of the outpost, Aramas quietly analyzes the situation while planning for what could be a nasty fight and hasty escape. However, the guards, while imposing, do not appear threatening.

After a few minutes, the party arrives at the inner walls of the outpost. The guard turns to Aramas and says, "Proceed to the keep. From there you will be escorted to the great room. Alissa will meet you there," at which point, the guard turns and disappears into the night.

"What kind of trouble do you think we're in now?" asks Loki.

"I'm not sure," replies Aramas. "But I don't get the impression that we should keep our hostess waiting."

For an outpost, Spring Green is well built and expertly fortified. While the outer walls are made primarily of wood, the inner walls, as well as the keep, are made of heavy granite blocks cut from the nearby mountains. Guard towers, rising almost forty feet above the earth, flank both gates and protect each corner of the outer wall. Connected by deep parapets, similarly constructed towers are evenly spaced between each corner tower around the city's imposing outer wall. Twenty-foot-high iron bound oaken doors protect the outpost's two major entrances. The inner granite walls are connected by similarly spaced towers and, while not quite as tall, present a significant obstacle to any attacking army. Archer slots dot all of the walls as well as an intricate maze of channels leading to murder holes designed to direct the flow of hot oil or boiling water to any number of desired locations.

Strategically located within the confines of the inner wall stands the armory, a blacksmith's shop, the guards' quarters, a large stable, a kitchen with a deep well, a substantial provisions warehouse, and Alissa's compound and the keep. The entrance to the keep is also protected by two large ironbound oaken doors and a portcullis. Immediately in front of the doors and just behind the portcullis is a twenty-foot-wide wooden trap door that, when triggered, opens to a twenty-foot-deep pit lined with spikes.

Once inside the keep, a gray-haired, purple-robed official approaches them. "I apologize for the way in which you were brought here, but we did not want anyone to suspect the real reason Alissa requires your presence. I am Brevek, cleric of Tabor and Alissa's counselor. Please follow me." The three slowly move through a short foyer toward the great room, the entrance of which is flanked by two similarly attired heavily armed guards. Both Aramas and Loki survey their surroundings. Tight confines do not leave many options when faced with a superior force, and the only exit appears to be behind them.

While not decorated with extravagant gems and metals, the room is quite imposing. Rough-hewn oaken beams span a cathedral-style ceiling from which large candelabras made of elk, moose, and deer antlers hang. Shields of fallen heroes hang from the walls, illuminated by ornate sconces. At the far end of the hall, sitting atop a two-step dais and flanked by two large braziers, is Alissa's throne. Ornate woodland and floral designs decorate the tiled floor leading to the dais.

"Wait here. I will inform Alissa of your arrival," at which point the cleric turns and moves silently, almost gliding, through a small door to the left of the dais.

Surveying the empty room, the only noise is coming from the crackling fires in the sconces and braziers around them. Loki turns to Aramas. "I fear that it might be some time before I get to sample those pubs on the Frozen Sea."

After a short time, Alissa enters the room, followed by the cleric and two of her personal guards, both of whom are carrying small pouches. Aramas and Loki bow their heads momentarily to acknowledge her rank.

Alissa motions to the guards. As they approach Aramas and Loki, Alissa says, "Please forgive me for interrupting your dinner. I hope that the contents of these pouches will compensate you for any inconvenience my guards may have caused."

Without opening the pouch, Aramas responds, "You are very generous, but certainly, there is more here than the mere cost of our inconvenience?"

"Yes," replies Alissa. "I have also included what was promised for the return of the opal."

Aramas bounces the pouch once in his palm, glances at Loki, and then responds, "Due to the hour of the night and the manner in which we were summoned, I would suspect that there are other reasons for this meeting."

Alissa sits down and reaches her open hand to Brevek, who in turn approaches and hands her a rolled parchment. "I understand that the two of you were going to be heading north as soon as you had secured your compensation. If there is no urgent need for your services elsewhere, I would like to persuade you to remain here a little longer."

Looking briefly at Loki before answering, Aramas replies, "What does my lady have in mind?" Alissa motions to the guards to leave the room.

Shortly after their departure, and with a look of deep concern, Alissa says, "Two days ago a small caravan from Everand was attacked on the Forest Road. Only one of the caravan's guards was able to make it back. He died an hour ago. However, before doing so, he was able to deliver a message from the attackers. Two members of the party were taken hostage and are now being held for ransom."

"What makes these two worth the payment of a ransom?" asks Aramas.

"They are the sons of my armorer and blacksmith," she replies.

"This must be a very special armorer," retorts Loki.

"He was a very close friend and confidant of my father. After my father passed, he took me under his tutelage and taught me how to defend not only myself but the people of this outpost. He is an armorer with unique talents and abilities, and his weapons are favored over those of his contemporaries."

Pausing for a moment, Alissa glances at Brevek and then back at Aramas. "He will not allow himself to be commissioned by just anyone. You must be worthy, and if deemed so, the weapon is fashioned to take advantage of its owner's greatest strengths. He uses only the finest of materials from throughout the Hinter Land, and nary one of his swords has ever failed its rightful owner. It is as if the soul of the weapon is joined to the soul of its owner."

"So why ask us to remain?" inquires Aramas. "I would think that your guards are more than capable of dealing with the problem."

Alissa ponders the question, glances again at Brevek, and then back again at Aramas, all the while slowly tapping the parchment in her hand. "If I send my guards, the hostages will surely be killed. I need to send someone who will not draw suspicion." Standing up, she moves slowly toward Aramas. "There are many eyes within the walls of Spring Green. Your apprehension by my guards tonight, and subsequent departure from the city tomorrow, should deflect any suspicion of our alliance, thereby allowing you to ascertain the whereabouts of the siblings, free them, and then return them safely to their father."

"Is that the only reason your need our help?" asks Aramas.

Alissa's eyes show a fear not noticed earlier. "The discovery of the dragon must be reported to the Grand Wizard in Everand. Further, I am sure that he will want to see the opal. I cannot do either until I know that the Forest Road is again safe for travel."

"How many guards accompanied the caravan?" asks Aramas.

"Ten," replies Brevek.

"Ten guards were overpowered? How many attackers were there?" asks Loki.

Hesitating before delivering his answer, Brevek adds, "For almost two months, every caravan going to or coming from Everand has been attacked and robbed. Initially the attackers took only the valuables.

However, that has not been the case in the last two attacks. The thieves have grown more brazen in their assaults and have left no one alive to provide us with any details. Fortunately, questioning the guard over the past two days has allowed us to make certain assumptions relative to the robber band's base of operations."

For a moment, no one says a word. Then, pensively looking down at the parchment in her hand, Alissa offers it to Aramas. "This is a map of the area we believe to be harboring the robber band. We estimate their numbers to be less than thirty."

"Oh, this should be easy," Loki blurts out sarcastically.

Aramas looks over to his friend, then over to Alissa before slowly opening the parchment. After a few moments, Aramas looks over to Brevek and asks, "What else can you tell us about the thieves?"

Moving closer, Brevek adds, "From what we have been able to piece together, their base is about three days journey from here and about two leagues north of the Forest Road."

"I see nothing but what appears to be a cemetery in that area," observes Aramas. Loki moves closer to see to what he is referring.

That is correct," replies Brevek. "Years ago, there was a small outpost there that served as a waystation for those headed north. The road was not well traveled, as the terrain was very difficult for wagons. However, for those on foot, several days could be saved when headed to Flotsam. Then, without explanation, all of the outpost's inhabitants died. Upon hearing of their fate, a delegation from Spring Green traveled to the outpost, buried the inhabitants, and then erected a small temple to honor their memory. Due to their unexplained deaths, the road has not been used since. The locals believe that evil resides there."

"And does it?" asks Loki.

"We do not believe that to be the case, but you could not convince those that have traversed the area. They report a cold damp feeling when nearing the cemetery, almost as if death stalked their every move. You know how superstitious these commoners can be. However, the guard did indicate that from afar, while he was being given the terms of the ransom, he could see a hooded figure attired in red robes quietly observing the proceedings."

Aramas continues to study the parchment then looks over to Alissa. "Even if we wanted to help, two against thirty is no match."

"I have made certain arrangements to help with that. You will stay here tonight so as not to be observed by the locals. Tomorrow, you will go over to the blacksmith's shop, which is contained within these walls, to get a description of his sons. You will then return here to meet two who have agreed to join you in this undertaking."

"Four against thirty? That certainly makes a huge difference," Loki says sarcastically.

"I understand your hesitance," replies Alissa. "However, I can assure you that after your visit with the blacksmith tomorrow, you will feel a little less apprehensive."

"And what about compensation?" asks Loki.

"I think that the blacksmith will be able to address those concerns as well."

Aramas and Loki study the map for a few moments then, looking back at Alissa, Aramas replies, "May we have the night to consider your offer?"

"As you wish. However, I am sure that you and the blacksmith will be able to come to terms. Further, I think that you will find that I can be very appreciative."

"Very well. You mentioned a room for the night?"

"My guards will escort you to your room. Tomorrow they will meet you at first light and take you to meet the blacksmith."

The knock on the door comes early. It had been a restless night, one in which Aramas could not shake the feeling that Alissa is still withholding something from him. Brevek too seems to know more than he revealed— just too many unanswered questions for his liking.

"Loki, shake a leg. We have an appointment to keep and questions to get answered."

A gurgle followed by a quick gulp of air emanates from under the robe on the bed in the corner. "Please tell me that I don't have to leave this little bit of nirvana. It has been so long since I slept in such a fine bed. Can't we linger just a little longer?"

"I wish we could, but the day will not allow us such pleasures."

As Aramas continues to don his armor, Loki slowly extricates himself from the womb of the fine sheets that have enveloped him for the past few hours. Unlike Aramas, Loki had no trouble falling asleep. It is not very often that the two find themselves in such fine surroundings. Even the best rooms at the finest inns cannot compare to the comforts Alissa had provided. Once on his feet, Loki slowly begins the process of donning his armor. Although he does not have to deal with the heavy plate armor that Aramas sports, his chain mail and leather still keep him busy.

Suddenly, the voice on the other side of the door barks, "Sir, I have been directed to get you to the blacksmith's shop as soon as possible. I do not wish to incur the wrath of the mistress of the keep. How much longer?"

"Not long. Loki, let's get moving."

After a few more minutes, the two emerge from the room to join the waiting guard. Then, just as they start down the long hall, Loki remarks, "Wait a minute," before scampering back to the room. Then, just as suddenly as he had disappeared, Loki emerges from the room with an apple in each hand.

"You couldn't wait until later?" asks Aramas.

"Just when do you think we're going to find time to eat?" replies Loki. "Besides, the fruit was put there to be eaten. I certainly don't want to be a bad guest."

"Will you be needing anything else out of the room before we depart?" asks the guard.

Looking disapprovingly at Loki, Aramas replies, "No, I think we're fine now," at which point the guard pivots smartly and continues down the long hall with Aramas and Loki following shortly behind.

The three move down the long dimly lit stone hallway, past several heavy wooden doors leading to what are presumed to be additional guest rooms, to a spiral staircase that leads to the lower level. Once on the main floor, the guard weaves past the great hall to the foyer and then to the main entrance, where he gestures for Aramas and Loki to stay put while he speaks with the two sentries guarding the door. After a few moments, the sentries open the doors and allow the three to leave the keep.

The sun is just beginning to peek above the tall inner walls of the outpost; the sky to the east is turning various shades of red, orange, yellow, and then blue as the sun slowly begins its ascent in the heavens. There is a crispness to the air, the breath of passersby clearly visible. The smells of porridge and freshly baked bread waft through the narrow streets. Not unexpectedly, the streets are relatively empty. Only essential civilian personnel are allowed to reside within the inner walls, and with the exception of the changing of the guards, it is fairly quiet.

As if their lives depend on it, Aramas and Loki are expeditiously moved from the keep through the winding streets to the back door of what appears to be a shop of some sort.

"This is not a blacksmith's shop," remarks Loki.

"This is where I was instructed to take you," replies the guard, at which point he knocks twice on the door, waits a second, then knocks a third time. There is a moment of silence before the sound of boots crossing a wooden floor can be heard on the other side, followed by the sound of a metal bolt being thrown.

The door opens revealing a well-dressed middle-aged gentleman sporting a dark brown beard with steely blue eyes. Glancing momentarily at Aramas and Loki, he turns his attention to the guard and asks, "When are they to be back at the keep?"

"The mistress of the keep asks that you occupy them only as long as need be."

"I will do my utmost. Thank you for bringing them here." The gentleman motions for the guard to take his leave, and just as smartly as before, the guard pivots and departs.

"Please come in."

Aramas and Loki cross the threshold into what appears to be a metal shop. In the near corner sits a small forge and anvil, hammers, and other tools of the trade neatly positioned nearby. Hanging from the rafter to the left are several pieces of iron in various stages of being formed into swords. Just below is a work bench with various metal working tools scattered about. Directly across the room are various animal hides, pieces of wood, and barrels of scrap metal, brass, and copper. Suspended from the rafters are various sets of deer and antelope antlers, bull horns, and exotic snake skins. Two spools of sinew lacing sit on the floor.

"Welcome. My name is Adwin. Thank you for agreeing to meet with me." He motions to Aramas and Loki to follow, turns, and moves into the next room.

As he follows Adwin into the next room, Aramas cannot help but wonder who this gentleman is. He does not appear to be your run-of-the-mill blacksmith nor does he dress like one. His clothes are finely tailored; his hands are clean and callous free; there is no dirt beneath his fingernails. While the back room contains the tools used by an armorer or blacksmith, it does not possess the normal dirt, grime, soot, and acrid coal smell that most forges do. It is almost as if the room is a prop for a play.

Moving into the next room only adds to the questions. This is no ordinary armorer's shop. Cases of exquisitely crafted knives occupy the center of the room. On the far wall to the right are some of the finest swords Aramas has ever seen. Finely crafted short swords, longswords, greatswords, bastard swords, scimitars. Some decorated with gold, silver, and the finest gems imaginable. The blades gleaming in the morning light. On the wall to the left, halberds, axes, and war hammers of various shapes and sizes. On the wall just inside the room are armor and chain mail, the light dancing on each ringlet. Then there are several tables of fine cloth and linens.

"Can I get you anything?"

"No, we're fine," replies Aramas.

"Are you sure? The lady of the house has prepared some fine cheeses and freshly baked bread."

"Is that apple wine I smell?" asks Loki.

"You have a keen sense of smell. Yes, it recently arrived from a small village to the east. Are you sure I can't pour you some?

Aramas looks over at Loki and back to Adwin. "I suppose that if I don't say yes, my good friend here will never forgive me. We shall join you."

Adwin looks over to the open door to Aramas's left and shouts, "Please prepare a table for our guests."

"Your wife?" asks Aramas.

"No, my wife passed away years ago. Anya has been with my family for over twenty years. I do not know how I would have survived without her, especially when my business often requires my presence elsewhere. She has been the mother my boys lost so long ago."

"And how old are your boys?" asks Loki.

Looking over to Loki, Adwin replies, "Argon is eighteen, Arron sixteen." Pausing briefly, Adwin looks down then back up at Aramas. "They mean the world to me. I will pay whatever it takes to bring them home."

"Why not just pay the ransom? It is obvious that you lack for nothing, yet you live a relatively secluded life. While I can understand Alissa's reasons for not sending her guards, why us?" asks Aramas. "Until recently, she didn't even know our names."

"Alissa is a good child, one who has learned well the lessons of a very difficult life. Her father and grandfather before her, while not good fathers, were just lords, and as is the case with many of her position in life, she bears many shortcomings. However, her judge of good character is not one of them." Walking over toward the swords on the wall, Adwin stops just short of a gleaming longsword. Slowly moving the open palm of his hand down the blade, he turns to look at Aramas, and fixating squarely on his chest, he comments, "the holy symbol on your tabard is unfamiliar to me, a red cross-shaped star on a field of white. I know of no god that uses that symbol."

"My god is no business of yours. I did not come here to discuss my beliefs," replies Aramas.

Adwin removes his hand from the blade then slowly moves along the wall to an exquisitely crafted greatsword. "Young paladin, I meant no offense." Pausing for a moment, Adwin glances down at Loki. "I know of Moradin and the power that flows from him through you." Then looking back at Aramas, "I know not the alignment of your god, yet I can assume from your exploits that he is a just being." He raises his hand to the blade of the greatsword and then slowly strokes it as he did with the longsword. "I specifically asked Alissa to send you here. Meeting you now only confirms what I have seen. Your faith is strong, and from the aura that surrounds you, I can only conclude that you are favored by your god. Should you decide to accept this quest, that faith will be tested."

"What are you not saying?" asks Loki.

"My sons were not taken by simple robbers, and that black dragon didn't just coincidently happen to be in that cave. Dark forces have returned to the Hinter Land." Then looking directly into Aramas's eyes, he says, "I know that you understand what I am saying."

"Again, I ask why us?"

As he slowly removes the greatsword from the wall, Adwin continues. "The forces behind the recent thefts are not confined to the Forest Road. Caravans from the east have also been interrupted. Further, not every caravan has been attacked, only those where we are transporting precious metals or rare gems. The attacks are well coordinated and are no doubt connected. Hopefully, in the process of rescuing my sons, you will be able to ascertain who is coordinating the attacks and why."

Glancing back to the greatsword in his hands then back at Aramas, Adwin moves deliberately across the room. With his outstretched hands, he offers the sword to him. "Try this. What do you think?"

Aramas takes the sword with both hands; a tingling sensation runs up his arms. "It is so light, lighter than my longsword." Wielding it from left to right in a figure eight motion then holding it straight up, Aramas surveys every inch. "Exquisite weapon, perfectly balanced. Alissa did not exaggerate when she said that you were an extraordinary armorer."

"It is yours."

Stunned, Aramas looks back at Adwin. "I cannot accept such a gift. I have done nothing to deserve it."

Adwin turns and walks over toward the other weapons. "I cannot accept your refusal. This weapon was made for you. It is a part of you."

"How can that be? We have never met!"

"That may be true, and while I know not much about your past, when I was fashioning this sword, your image appeared to me from within the blade." Pausing for a moment in front of a large war hammer, he turns back toward Aramas and remarks, "Remain true to your beliefs and it will never fail you."

Reaching his outstretched hand toward Adwin, Aramas proffers the sword. "Again, sir, I must refuse. I have done nothing to deserve such a fine weapon, nor will I allow such a gift to bind me to the service of another."

With a brushing-off movement of his hand, Adwin remarks, "It binds you only to your god, whomever he or she is. My payment will be your effort to return my sons to me."

"How do you know you can trust me?"

"The sword knows. I need know no more."

Turning back to the large war hammer, Adwin reaches down, picks it up, and then turns back to Loki. "Master Dwarf, I would like to trade you this meager weapon for the one you currently favor. After a short pause he adds, "What is your pleasure?"

Loki looks to Aramas in disbelief. Aramas shrugs his shoulders then nods his head in approval, at which point Loki moves across the room to consummate the trade. Like the greatsword, it is lighter than one would have expected. "It floats like the clouds," remarks Loki.

Pleased with himself, Adwin strolls past the two toward the kitchen. "If you do not wish to incur Anya's wrath, please join me at my table," at which point the three move into the kitchen to break bread and consummate their agreement over a glass of wine.

As they return to the keep, the guard instructs the two to remain in the foyer until summoned. Having spoken very little since leaving Adwin's home, Loki looks up to Aramas and asks, "So what kind of dark force do you think Adwin was referring to?"

"I'm not sure." He then slowly picks his next words. "It is obvious that we are not being told the whole story. Maybe it is because they are afraid that if we learn the true reason for the thefts and kidnapping that we will refuse to help. Or, and I believe this to be the case, it may be that they too are not sure about what lies deep in the woods or the mountains to the east. Either way, we will get no answers from within these walls."

Loki shakes his head in agreement then glances at the war hammer. "I have never seen such a fine weapon. I expect that it won't be long before I get the opportunity to use it."

About fifteen minutes pass before the guard returns. "Follow me."

The three move through the foyer and into the great room. It is empty—no guards, no Brevek, no Alissa. Continuing to the far end of the room, the guard walks over to the small door to the left of the dais, opens it, and motions for Aramas and Loki to follow him. The open door reveals a long hallway. Six sconces provide enough light to reveal that the floor is similar to that of the great room, adorned by beautiful mosaics. On either side of the hallway are three intricately carved wooden doors bound with brightly polished bronze hinges. At the far end of the hall is another door. Other than the sound of boot heels striking against the tile floor below, all is silent.

Once at the far door, the guard pauses and says, "Alissa awaits you." Then, as if on command, the guard assumes a protective posture to ensure that no one else enters the room.

The door opens to what appears to be a private meeting room. A large rectangular table occupies the center, at the far end of which sits Alissa. Brevek is to her right. Seated immediately to her left are two other individuals: one a dragonborn and the other a female tiefling. Brevek and the two strangers rise to meet Aramas and Loki.

Alissa remarks, "We have been expecting you. I trust that your meeting with the blacksmith was enlightening?"

"It was. Thank you," replies Aramas.

Brevek introduces the two strangers. "This is Kriv," he says as he gestures to the dragonborn. Moving to the tiefling, he says, "This is Aria."

Aramas and Loki approach to greet the two. Stopping short, Aramas moves his right hand over his heart, nods, and then, returning his hand to his side, announces, "I am Aramas, and this is my close friend Loki." Glancing briefly at both, he adds, "I cannot say that I have ever been in the presence of a dragonborn and tiefling when they were not trying to kill each other. Have the stars realigned themselves?" Loki chuckles. Aramas quickly attempts to size up each.

Kriv is a young nineteen-year-old warlord marshal and stands well over six feet tall. He is of medium build but obviously still too young to have fully developed wings. Clad in chain mail, his weapons of choice appear to be a shield and flail. The numerous scars on his body indicate that he has been involved in more than his share of altercations. On his shield is the holy symbol of Moradin.

Aria, on the other hand, is a little more difficult to size up. Heavily clothed, hooded, and veiled, only her piercing red eyes and the dusky red skin around them are visible. She appears to stand about five and a half feet tall. As she bows slightly to acknowledge Aramas's salute, spiraling horns and a prehensile tail become visible. A crown of silver runes adorns her head, and her leather armor bears the holy symbol of Ioun. Hanging from a finely crafted waist belt hangs a wickedly curved pact blade of obsidian metal lined with archaic runes. From the many tattoos that spiral around her forehead and arms, Aramas surmises that she must be a demonkind warlock.

"Strange times require even stranger alliances," replies Kriv. "Besides, in the Border Lands to the south, humans, dragonborn, and tieflings peacefully coexist."

Aria remains silent.

"What's the matter, cat got your tongue?" quips Loki.

Aria glances briefly at Loki and then returns her focus to Aramas. "My reasons for joining this quest will be made known when it is necessary to do so. Until then, know that I am committed to this alliance." Looking over to Loki, Aria adds, "I commit my blade to you."

Suddenly annoyed, Alissa leaps from her chair. "There is no time to waste quibbling over one's intentions. I have chosen each of you for your skills, both in diplomacy and combat. Each of you has proven yourself to me in the past. Your word is your bond and can be trusted. I have instructed the captain of the guard to provide you with whatever provisions you require. So as to make it look like you are guarding another shipment to Everand, you will be given a horse and cart with which to transport a number of items. Once provisioned, you will be escorted to the gates of the compound to begin your journey. Unless you have further need of me, I will take my leave. Brevek will introduce you to the captain of the guard."

Then, Alissa turns and departs the room.

Motioning to the door at the left side of the room, Brevek adds, "Follow me."

As they move through several empty hallways, Brevek escorts the party to a small warehouse beside the guards' quarters. There they are met by the captain of the guard.

"These are the new guards we spoke of earlier. Please ensure that they receive whatever provisions they require. Once the cart is loaded, take six of your best guards and escort them to the main gate. Is that understood?"

"Yes, my lord."

With nothing further to say, Brevek nods to the party and returns to the keep.

As instructed, the party is allowed to gather whatever provisions are required. As soon as the cart is loaded, the party is joined by six guards.

After the captain has a brief discussion with his guards, he turns to the party and remarks, "It is critical that this shipment gets to Everand. Is that understood?"

Aramas nods. With Loki at the reins, the party is escorted out of Spring Green.

CHAPTER 2

THE FOREST ROAD

I t is a bright spring day, and while it is almost midday, the air still retains its morning crispness. The trees in and around the fort sport newly sprouted green leaves while an artist's palette of colored wild-flowers blankets the surrounding fields. Immediately outside the main gate, a myriad of fruit and vegetable stands flank the road, manned by farmers and traders vying to move their wares. Children run about oblivious to the comings and goings of those around them while the village beggar, hoping to score enough money to buy his next drink, weaves his way through the crowd.

Almost unnoticed in the routine chaos that surrounds them, the party moves slowly past the various stands toward the Forest Road. At this point, the road itself is well traveled and wide enough to allow two wagons to pass. While there are a number of people on the road, most appear to be farmers coming from the nearby farms or travelers coming from the road to the north. The road to the east and the Forest Road to the west appear hauntingly empty. Even the farms along the way appear to be less active than their counterparts to the north.

A tension hangs over the group as the party slowly moves farther from Spring Green. Nothing is said; each member contemplates what might lie ahead. Having only met a few hours earlier and with little in common outside of the task at hand, suspicion, rather than trust, permeates the air. Almost out of routine, Aramas walks ahead and to the right of the horse as he continuously scans the horizon for anything that might be out of the norm. Kriv, walking alongside the cart to the left, and Aria, walking behind the cart, maintain a vigilant watch to the sides and rear.

"Now that we can speak freely, what's the plan?" asks Kriv.

No one responds.

"I said, what's the plan?"

Glancing back to his left, Aramas replies, "I'm not sure. We only have a few more hours before it gets too dark to travel. I am familiar with a small meadow not far from here that is well suited for a camp. There is plenty of water, a field of tall grass for the horse, and because of its location relative to the stream, it affords the best opportunity for defense should we be attacked." Turning his head back to the road ahead, he continues. "We will spend the night there and discuss our options."

Kriv pauses for a moment then asks, "When can we expect to reach the forest?"

"The eastern edge of the forest is about a half day's journey from the meadow. While I do not believe that our adversary would be bold enough to attack us while in the open, the numerous fields between the meadow and the forest should allow us to enter the woods knowing whether or not our presence has been observed. If indeed there is a traitor within Spring Green's walls, I would expect to be attacked sometime after we make camp tomorrow evening."

Loki asks, "How do you want the watch set tonight?"

"I want it to look as if we're just four guards on a routine mission; we suspect nothing. Make no special preparations. Stake the horse in the field nearby and keep the campfire burning. After dinner and a game of cards, we'll each stand a two-hour watch. That way, if someone is watching . . ."

Kriv interrupts. "Wouldn't that invite an attack?"

Aramas turns again toward Kriv, hesitates, and with a sly grin answers, "If they do, we'll be ready."

Few words are spoken over the next few hours, each party member intently scanning the horizon for anything out of the ordinary. Other than the sounds of birds flying through the fields and the rhythmic clip-clop of the horse's hooves, the only other sound to pierce the silence is an occasional snort as the horse shakes its head in a vain attempt to dislodge a pesky fly.

With the sun slowly settling behind the trees, the party finally reaches the meadow. A tall oak, its branches reaching out over the landscape as if to gather all within its reach, occupies the center. The stream, which runs from northeast to southwest, meanders through the lush fields just to the west. While it is a relatively shallow stream, it is just deep enough to hinder the advance of an uninvited guest. The road itself continues on and crosses the stream through a shallow ford about one hundred yards farther west.

Loki positions the cart near the tree, unhitches the horse, and takes it down to the stream for a well-deserved drink. While Kriv and Aria move out into the field in search of firewood, Aramas sets about unloading the bedrolls and provisions for the evening meal. Once the horse has been watered and staked in the field nearby, Loki returns to help Aramas prepare dinner.

It isn't long before Kriv and Aria return with enough wood for the fire. Loki pulls out his flint and steel and, with a few quick strokes of the flint, soon has a roaring fire. After cutting up several carrots and potatoes, Aramas adds some fresh herbs to the dried beef and vegetable mix before placing the pot on the fire.

As the pot slowly comes to a boil, Aramas turns his attention to the assembled party. "Based on the information supplied by Brevek, I do not expect any trouble tonight. None of the attacks occurred outside of the forest." He pulls out the parchment that Alissa gave him and, pointing to the area of the map near the intersection of the Old North Road and the Forest Road, continues. "Most of the attacks have occurred in this area of the Forest Road to the east and west of the Old North Road. The outpost town of Forest Glen lies here, just to the north." He moves his finger a little to the east. "However, according to the guard who escaped, the most recent attack occurred only one day's ride from here."

"What do you make of that?" asks Kriv.

"Maybe they're getting bolder. Maybe because of the reduced traffic they've had to expand their area of operation. I don't know. Regardless, I expect that if there is to be an attack, the first opportunity will be tomorrow night."

"What about the cemetery?" asks Loki.

"If it is their base, we won't know until we get to Forest Glen. Brevek indicated that the outpost offers little in the way of a base for this type of operation. I would expect that the answer will be found in the cemetery."

"What do we know about the cemetery?" asks Aria, her fiery red eyes fixed on the map.

"Only what Brevek told us." Aramas points to the cemetery on the map. "There are no buildings large enough to house this type of operation. Other than the monument erected to the village folk, there are no other structures. Therefore, regardless of when the attack comes, it is going to be critical that we take a prisoner for questioning." Pausing for a moment to roll up the parchment, Aramas adds, "Keep your weapons close at hand and be ready to move at first light."

After dinner, and a quick game of chance, the party retires. As expected, the night passes without incident.

Awakened by the sun's rays glistening off of the morning dew, Aramas slowly surveys the camp. There is a chill in the air. Fog, reminiscent of a thick feather blanket, slowly rises from the fields surrounding the camp. Other than the babbling of the nearby stream, a few birds overhead, and the occasional whinny of the horse, all is silent. Loki and Kriv lie huddled beneath their blankets. Aramas stands, and to the east, about fifty feet away, is Aria. She is facing the sun, kneeling and praying.

Aramas walks over to Loki and lightly kicks him. "Let's move it. There is a lot of road to put behind us." Turning to Kriv, he adds, "Aria has a pot of herbal tea brewing."

Grumbling as they slowly roll to their feet, each quickly packs their bedroll in the wagon and then meanders over to the fire for some tea, dried fruit, and jerky.

Aramas turns to Kriv and glances over to a still-kneeling Aria. "Does she do this often?"

"When possible. It is a custom of Ioun."

"I am not familiar with her god," replies Loki.

"Nor am I, and I do not ask."

"She doesn't seem to say a lot," adds Aramas.

"I do not know much about her past, and she is not very forth-coming. It is as if she has been sent on some sort of sacred mission and nothing, or no one, is going to keep her from it."

As if aware of the conversation, Aria stands and returns to the fire. Looking over to Aramas, she remarks, "Someone has been watching us. I was unable to see them clearly, but just to the other side of the stream, very early into my watch, there was a presence."

"How long were they there?"

"Not long, but long enough to evaluate our position and strength. I did not let them know that I was aware of their presence, but we are not alone."

"Any idea how many?"

"Only that there was a presence, someone wearing a hood."

Aramas looks down at the glowing embers. "Let's make sure that when the time comes, we welcome our *guests* with an appropriate greeting."

Loki chuckles then adds, "Let's get moving."

As if on cue, camp is broken. Once the horse is hitched to the wagon, and everything aboard secured, Loki takes the reins and slowly guides the horse through the field back to the road. As before, Aramas takes the lead just to the right of the horse, Kriv walks to the left of the wagon, and Aria to the rear.

It isn't long before the morning sun has burned off the mist that once blanketed the fields. The air is warm, the sky a brilliant shade of deep blue. A light breeze moves the grasses in the fields as if waving to the interlopers. The road itself has narrowed to two well-trodden ruts. There are no homes or farms anywhere to be seen. Flies continue to harass the horse, and other than a lone hawk surveying the landscape for its next meal, everything is quiet. Hours pass, and other than brief spurts of light conversation, the party remains quiet and focused on the horizon around them.

Around midday, the distant forest slowly comes into view. Aramas turns back to Loki. "Keep a keen watch. We don't want any surprises."

Loki nods his understanding then looks over at Kriv and then back at Aria before refocusing on the road ahead.

The road continues to be void of any travelers, the fields empty and quiet. The party has not encountered anyone since turning west out of Spring Green, and with the exception of an occasional hawk or lone deer, even the wildlife seems to sense the inevitability of the conflict that lies ahead.

Moving steadily toward the forest, trees are becoming more common. The tall grasses of the fields slowly give way to lightly wooded savannahs and then lush dense greenery. It isn't long before the road ahead appears to be engulfed by the vegetation surrounding it. Even though it is still early afternoon, darkness soon replaces shadows as the sun strains to penetrate the thick canopy. The air turns considerably cooler. The chirping of birds has been replaced by an eerie silence. There is an uneasiness in the air.

For the next mile or so, no one says a word, each party member carefully surveying the woods around them.

"We are being watched," reports Aria.

"I don't see anyone," replies Loki.

"The presence is not among us. I sense scrying."

"Any idea from where?" asks Aramas.

"No, but someone is definitely observing our every movement."

"How long have we been observed?'

"Soon after we entered the forest." Aria pauses for a moment. "Whomever is watching is no ordinary thief. They are drawing upon powers that only a mage could master, dark powers."

Suddenly the silence is shattered.

"Help! Someone help?"

Looking ahead to the right, Aramas exclaims, "Loki, can you see where that came from?"

"No, but it could be an ambush."

Aramas draws his sword and calls out, "Where are you?"

There is a brief silence. He calls again, "Where are you?"

Then a surprised, anxious voice shouts, "About fifty feet north of the road, bound to a large oak."

Aramas again calls out, "We don't see you."

There is an almost immediate response. "Come to the clearing in the road then north about fifty feet."

Glancing back at the party, Aramas motions to move forward. A long bend in the road lies ahead. Pointing to the bend, Aramas adds, "If there is going to be an ambush, it will happen there."

Kriv moves to the front, just to the left of the horse, flail drawn. Aria remains in the rear.

Moving cautiously toward the bend, the small clearing comes into view. There is no evidence of anyone in the area. Loki pulls back on the reins. "Whoa."

They survey the area around the clearing; there is no apparent evidence of an ambush.

"Hurry, before they come back!"

Aramas glances to the right. "I see you." Then, turning to the party, he says, "Kriv, come with me. Aria, remain here with the wagon."

Running through the low brush, Aramas and Kriv reach the sequestered victim. With hands and feet bound, he is suspended about three feet off the ground from a branch ten feet higher.

"Quickly, cut me down. They may come back."

As Kriv wraps his arms around the waist of the hanging wretch in an effort soften the coming fall, Aramas moves quickly to sever the bonds. Within seconds, and a sharp snap of the now severed line, the exhausted captive is slowly lowered to the ground.

Gasping for breath he says, "You didn't arrive a second too soon."

Quickly surveying the brush around them, Kriv asks, "What is your name?"

"Riadon, but I . . ."

Aramas interrupts. "No time for pleasantries. We need to get back to the wagon."

Kriv picks up Riadon and throws him over his shoulder so he can quickly return to the wagon. Aramas protects their retreat.

As if he were no more than a bag of grain, Kriv flops Riadon onto the back of the wagon. "How many were there?"

Brushing the grass and dirt from his clothes, Riadon looks up and replies, "Seven, but I got the feeling that there were more nearby."

"How many more?"

"I don't know. I didn't see anyone else."

"Then what gave you the impression there were more?"

"Because they were talking to someone." He pauses for a moment and then points toward the west. "Someone back in those trees. They were about to start beating me when he told them you were coming."

Looking toward the west, Aria replies, "That is the direction from which I detected the scrying."

"Are we still being watched?" asks Aramas.

"Not at the moment."

Looking over to Riadon and recognizing the hood, Aria remarks, "This is the one I observed this morning." Loki and Kriv both turn to see the response.

"Why were you observing our campsite?" asks Aramas.

"I was traveling the road and noticed your fire. Having heard that there were bands of thieves in the area, I simply wanted to make sure that you posed no harm."

Closely evaluating every word, Aramas replies, "Your words do not ring true. Why should we not believe that you are one of the thieves you claim to be so concerned about?"

"I am just a simple trader. If I were one of the thieves, why not attack you while you slept?"

"Then why were you on the road so early?"

"Due to circumstances beyond my control, I found myself needing to leave Spring Green a little earlier than expected."

"He's a thief," remarks Loki.

"Thief is such a harsh word. I would prefer to be referred to as an independent contractor who happens to be in the procurement business. Unfortunately, the transaction I was working on did not go as planned."

Kriv chuckles. "We just rescued a thief who was about to be robbed."

"And had you not come by when you did, I do not believe they would have stopped at just relieving me of my valuables."

Pausing for a moment, Aramas asks, "Where were you headed?"

"To Everand. However, based on recent developments, traveling this road alone may not be the wisest of decisions." Looking down at the goods in the back of the wagon and then back at Aramas, Riadon adds, "It would seem that you too are not what you appear to be." Stopping for a moment to take a closer look at the goods in the wagon, he continues. "Perhaps there is an opportunity here for a mutually beneficial arrangement."

"What would you have in mind?"

"It would appear that you are capable of handling most any obstacle that might present itself. Due to my current situation, I would be willing to offer my services to you in exchange for your company to Everand."

Loki tersely interrupts. "We are not going to Everand." Then, looking over to Aramas, he adds, "I don't trust him. He probably intended to rob us this morning but decided not to when he saw Aria."

"I will admit that the thought had crossed my mind. However, I am no fool."

Loki again interrupts. "What would keep you from robbing us as soon as the opportunity presented itself?"

Looking sternly at Loki, Riadon replies, "I may be a thief, but my word is my bond." Then turning back to Aramas, he continues. "Should you allow me to accompany you, I pledge you my allegiance."

Shaking his head in disbelief, Loki protests, "Don't tell me you believe him?"

Aramas looks to Loki and then, after pausing for a brief moment, turns back to Riadon. "I believe him."

"Thank you. You will not be . . ."

Aramas stops him. "We are not going to Everand. While I am not at liberty to tell you where we are headed, or why, understand that we expect trouble. We need to know that when the time comes, you will do as ordered."

"You have my word." Then, after waiting a moment, Riadon adds, "After you accomplish whatever it is you hope to accomplish, where will you be heading?"

"Back to Spring Green."

Understanding that this is not what Riadon had expected to hear, Aramas adds, "I understand that the circumstances of your departure from the outpost may complicate your return. However, while I cannot make any promises, and as long as you didn't kill someone, should we be successful in our endeavor, I will intervene on your behalf with the mistress of the keep. If there are still problems, I will make sure that you are able to continue on your own. You have my word."

Shaking his head in agreement, and with a jovial tone in his voice, Riadon looks around at the others and exclaims, "Then what are we waiting for?"

Loki again shakes his head in disbelief. How could Aramas believe this fool? Then, as if resigned to his fate, he gives the reins a quick shake and mutters, "I hope you know what you're doing."

The next several hours pass without incident. Birds again can be heard. Occasionally, a deer darts across the road, or a grouse shoots into the air after being startled by the unexpected intruders. There is no shortage of wildlife. Water is also plentiful. The streams teem with fish and the ponds appear cool and inviting. While the forest continues to be thick with under-growth, there are numerous clearings along the road. Wildflowers, gleaming in the sun's rays, help to brighten the otherwise dark confines. Long since extinguished campfires are further evidence of the importance of the road.

"How much longer before we make camp?" asks Kriv.

"Soon," replies Aramas. "I want to make sure that we are ready when our guests arrive. After all, it would be impolite for us not to afford them an appropriate greeting."

"Guests? What guests?" asks Riadon.

"I would expect that they will include some of the same individuals who greeted you earlier today." Then, turning to Aria, Aramas asks, "Are we still being watched?"

"Not that I can ascertain."

With the sun slowly falling below the tops of the trees, Aramas finally finds a clearing that will suit the party's needs. With the exception of a small pond about one hundred feet north of the road, the clearing is surrounded by trees, and while the undergrowth is heavy, it is not so thick as to offer total concealment to someone trying to get into the camp undetected.

"We will stop here for the night." Perusing the landscape around him then pointing to an area just before the pond, Aramas turns back to the party. "Loki, I plan to put the fire over there. Tie off the horse to the left but not too far away. The wagon should be close to the center of camp and angled such that anyone entering the area from that side must either go over or around it to reach us." Motioning over to the right, he turns to Kriv and Aria. "Scout the perimeter for the best places to set some traps. Assuming that they will not have boats or can walk on water, I want to force them to come at us from across the road." Then turning to Riadon he adds, "You and I need to gather enough wood for a good fire."

Without further discussion, the party sets about their assigned tasks.

Darkness now envelops the forest. The sounds of crickets, bullfrogs, and a not-too-distant owl fill the air. A light breeze gently moves the campfire-lit, cathedral-like canopy of leaves above as embers from the crackling fire below slowly drift into the air. To the east, a crescent moon periodically peeks through the rustling leaves. The pond appears to almost vanish into the dark woods behind it. Long shadows are cast into the surrounding trees as the party slowly prepares to turn in for the night.

Aramas turns from the pond and walks toward the fire. "Loki, I want you to take the first watch. Riadon and I will take the second, Kriv and Aria the third." Then, looking over to Aria, Aramas asks, "Are we still alone?"

"If we are being watched, it is not from afar."

Nodding his head in affirmation, Aramas turns to take one final look at the area around the camp. Then pausing for a moment, he adds, "It will be tonight. Be ready."

As everyone else slowly settles into their bedrolls, Loki kneels next to the campfire and takes out his ivory bone pipe. Turning it upside down and tapping it on his left palm, he methodically removes the remaining ashes before placing it in his mouth; his red beard and mustache engulf its stem as he reaches into his pouch for a pinch of tobacco. After filling the bowl, he pulls a short stick out of the fire, its glowing embers, leaving a yellow trail through the night darkness as he maneuvers it to its target. With each quick puff, the flame seems to perform a sort of ritualistic dance until the sweet aroma of fresh tobacco slowly fills the air. Savoring each puff, he drops the stick back into the fire then stands to survey the camp, studying every shadow around its perimeter. Satisfied that all is well, he moves over to the wagon and sits down with his back to the wheel, war hammer close at hand.

As Loki stares at the flickering campfire in front of him, he sits transfixed, thoughts drifting to what Aramas had said back in the tavern. While the two of them have experienced much together, nothing compares to what had happened in the bowels of Spring Green. What had started out as a simple mission to retrieve some stolen coins and gems had turned into a battle with that black dragon, a creature not seen in almost three hundred years.

And then there was the opal. While Alissa had mentioned several large rubies, a diamond, and two emeralds that had been taken, no one ever mentioned an opal. Yet when the coins and gems were returned, it was that stone that Brevek hovered over. The dragon itself appeared to favor it over all of the others, but why? Aramas is rarely wrong when it comes to his intuition; his training as a gladiator has served him well. Apparently, if there is nothing more to the opal and the dragon that possessed it, then why the urgent need to have it seen by the Grand Wizard in Everand? Further, if there was a baby dragon, where was the mother? What about additional siblings?

Still contemplating the possibilities, Loki reaches down to put another piece of wood on the fire. Just as he does, a muffled sound comes from the perimeter of the camp, a whoosh followed by the thud of an arrow embedding itself in the side of the wagon. Loki turns just in time to see three hooded figures running from the woods to the east. Reaching for his war hammer, he yells, "We've got company!"

Without hesitation, Loki turns to the intruders and charges forward. With his hammer raised high above his head, he shouts, "By the power of Moradin." Then, as if possessed with a mind of its own, the hammer flies out of his hands and finds its mark squarely between the temples of the closest adversary. Then, almost as swiftly, the hammer ricochets to the next invader, knocking him to the ground before returning to Loki's outstretched hand. Advancing to the now prone adversary, he again raises his hammer, and then just as swiftly, brings it down on the head of the writhing body below him; pieces of shattered bone and mangled flesh scatter to the four winds.

As the rest of the party springs to their feet, weapons drawn, several screams can be heard coming from the undergrowth as the well-placed traps fulfill their intended purpose. However, four intruders are still able to evade them and join the fray. Almost simultaneously, six more hooded figures emerge from the woods to the west.

Another arrow flies through the darkness, striking true in Riadon's leg. "I've been hit!"

Aramas shouts, "Take cover in the wagon!"

Then, from out of nowhere, a voice calls out to Aramas, "To your left!"

Pivoting on his left foot, sword raised high, Aramas turns and parries the attacker's first blow. Then, feinting a strike to the legs, Aramas's sword cuts across the attacker's chest, opening a gaping wound, blood spurting everywhere. The attacker falls to his knees in excruciating pain; Aramas's second blow ends his misery.

Almost immediately, the voice is again heard. "Behind you!" Too late to avoid the attacker, Aramas suddenly feels the searing pain of a short blade cutting into his thigh. With pain burning through his leg, and moving quickly to his right, he avoids another strike. However, the lunging intruder has left his flank vulnerable. Without hesitation, Aramas's blade finds its mark.

As Aria moves over to the wagon, Kriv moves to protect Aramas's flank. Kriv intercepts three of the intruders and exhales a searing breath of fire and lightning, instantly killing two and severely burning the other. Then, with an upper cut to the chin, his flail removes a significant portion of the third intruder's face.

Finding himself outnumbered, and having witnessed the quick dispatch of five of his compatriots, the remaining intruder flees to the safety of the woods behind him. Aramas and Kriv now turn to assist Loki.

Aria leaps aboard the wagon and quickly surveys the situation. With Loki about to be surrounded, she stretches out her right arm, palm facing upward, and calmly recites a short ritual to call forth a large fireball. Then, as if flicking a fly from her hand, she gestures toward the incoming invaders and hurls the inferno. Flames shoot in all directions as the fireball finds its mark, severely burning two of the interlopers. Surprised by the unexpected attack, the remaining attackers halt their advance. Realizing that they have severely underestimated their prey, and with Aramas and Kriv now bearing down on them, they determine that the better part of valor is to make a hasty retreat.

As the attackers return to the cover of the woods, Aramas and Kriv join Loki to question the two severely burned intruders.

"Where did you come from? Who are you working for?" demands Aramas.

Other than screams of pain, neither attacker utters a word.

"It will not be long before you meet your maker. We can help ease your journey to the afterworld. Why not make it easier?"

"He sees us even now. He can make it much worse."

"Who can make it worse?"

As if summoned without warning, the two quickly look to the west. With a look of horror written all over his face and terror in his voice, one of the thieves screams, "No . . . please, no." His body begins to glow a bright red.

Grabbing at Loki's leg, the other thief begs, "Please help me." Looking down at him, Loki sees that he too is glowing, his terror-filled eyes wide open, piercing the black night. Suddenly, both give out a scream of excruciating pain and then expire. Within seconds their bodies burst into flames and immediately turn into heavy black ash.

Loki jumps back, speechless. Aramas and Kriv are spellbound. Looking at each other and then back at Loki, Aramas exclaims, "Brevek obviously knew more than he let on."

Witnessing what has just transpired, Aria jumps down from the wagon and rushes to join the others. "We are again being watched."

"From the same source as before?" asks Aramas.

"It would appear so."

"Can you determine from where?"

"Only that the magic is coming from the northwest."

"Hey, I'm bleeding here!" shouts Riadon.

Everyone quickly moves to the wagon as Riadon slowly climbs down to allow Aramas and Loki to examine the wound. While the arrow missed the bone, it is firmly entangled in the muscle.

"You're lucky. There is no major damage." Then pausing for a moment, Aramas adds, "This is going to hurt," at which point he grabs the arrow's shaft, breaks off the fletching and quickly forces the remainder of the shaft and its arrowhead through the leg.

Riadon screams in pain.

As Aramas moves away, Loki quickly intervenes. Joining his palms together, head bowed, he whispers something. A blue pulsating glow begins to emerge from between his palms. As he continues his chant, the blue light grows brighter. After a few moments, he turns his attentions to the heavens. Reciting another unknown verse, Loki then refocuses his attention on the wound before him. Placing his hands on the wound, one palm over the entrance point, the other over the exit, he again recites an inaudible verse. As with blood flowing through a vein, the blue light passes from one palm to the next through the path of the arrow. After a few seconds, the light dissipates, Loki removes his hands, and the wound is no more.

With Riadon attended to, Aramas turns away, worried about securing the camp. However, as he does so, he briefly stumbles before catching himself on the side of the wagon. The pain that had been subdued by the ferocity of combat now radiates through the torn flesh of his thigh. Kriv immediately comes to his aid and helps him to the ground.

Loki, realizing for the first time that Aramas has been injured, quickly comes to his aid. He examines the wound and exclaims, "You have lost a lot of blood, my friend." Looking to the heavens, Loki again joins his palms and begins the ritual. It is not long before his healing power is flowing between his hands and Aramas's wound. Upon completion of the ritual, Loki looks over to Kriv. "Help me get them to the fire. They will need some time to recuperate."

As Loki prepares some herbal tea for Aramas and Riadon, Kriv and Aria move the dead bodies from the campsite to a concealed spot on the other side of the road. Stacked like cordwood, they will be buried in a shallow grave at first light, a far better ending than they deserve, but one that Loki and Aramas feel is required by their beliefs. After completing the task, the two survey the area once more before joining the others around the fire.

Other than Loki's chant, little has been said since the skirmish. Whether contemplating what has transpired or what might lie ahead, no one says a word. The warm herbal tea not only soothes aching extremities but helps to fend off the chill of the night. Crickets can again be heard throughout the forest as can an occasional tree frog or the deep-throated moan of several bullfrogs from the other side of the pond.

Then, wincing slightly, Aramas asks, "Are we still being watched?"

Taking a moment before responding, Aria replies, "I no longer sense the presence."

Aramas peers into the burning embers of the fire, then turning his focus to the comrades seated around him, he says, "Whoever sent the greeting party tonight obviously underestimated our strength. These were not trained warriors, merely simple thieves. I can assure you that they will not make that mistake again."

"Do you think they will return before dawn?" asks Kriv.

"I do not believe so. Their miscalculation will require some additional thought and planning before they return. Whoever is directing their movements now understands that they are not dealing with simple guards. We need to be ready, as the road ahead has just become more dangerous."

After a short pause, Aramas turns to Loki and, with a gleam in his eye, jokingly comments, "Adwin is obviously more than a simple armorer. I have never seen you use your hammer as you did tonight. And my sword, it was as if it had become an extension of my senses. I am sure that it spoke to me as the skirmish progressed."

Loki nods in agreement. "The hammer flew from my hands. No command was needed."

Then, with a quick smirk and a short chuckle, Aramas turns to Kriv and Aria. "I must admit that first impressions are not always correct. I had my doubts when we were first introduced, but I am glad that Alissa selected you to join the party. You are obviously very skilled, and I thank you for protecting my flank this evening."

Loki nods in agreement and adds, "Together we make a good team.

They will not soon forget who we are!"

Aramas then remarks, "We will pick up the watch from where we left off. Due to our injuries, Riadon will now stand watch with Kriv, and Loki will remain with me. While I do not expect another incursion tonight, we must remain vigilant. Tomorrow will be a long day with many unfamiliar miles to cover before we reach our destination."

"And what might that be?" chimes Riadon.

"You will be told when it is appropriate to do so," replies Aramas.

A bit frustrated by Aramas's answer, Riadon adds, "I have traveled this road before. Perhaps I can be of assistance. However, it would be nice to have some idea as to where we are headed."

Pondering his next words, Aramas replies, "Okay, are you aware of the road that heads to the north that lies about three days from here?"

"Yes, but there is not much there. That road has not been traveled for some time."

"Well that's all you need to know for now. We can discuss it more tomorrow."

"Aramas, it's time to get up," whispers Aria.

In a low groan Aramas replies, "Is it that time already?"

With a little urgency in her voice, Aria continues. "C'mon. We need to be on our way. We've been under surveillance for the past hour or so."

Aramas slowly rolls over. Blinking his eyes, he puts up his hand to block the morning sunlight as he looks over at Aria. "Is it our host?"

"It would appear to be." Then, after a brief pause, she continues. "Everyone else is up. The wagon is packed and Riadon has prepared something to eat. Loki has some hot tea on the fire."

Aramas slowly rises to his knees, rolls up his bed, and quickly dons his armor, all the time surveying the forest around him. "Other than the scrying, have you seen anyone in the area?"

"No, everything else appears to be normal."

"Good. Then let's not give them any reason to believe otherwise."

Moving deliberately over to the fire, Aramas reaches down for a piece of bread, some bacon fat, and a cup of tea. "Riadon, how is your leg?"

"As good as new. Loki did a nice job on it. And yours?"

Before Aramas can answer, Loki walks over and interrupts. "The horse is hitched to the wagon. We should be going." Then with a bit of a chuckle, he adds, "I hope you got plenty of beauty sleep."

"Very funny. Maybe next time, I'll wait a little longer before I decide whether to join the fray or not."

"All right, women, we've already tarried too long," exhorts Kriv as he picks up the teapot, dumps it over the fire, and heads back to the wagon.

Grabbing another piece of bread, Aramas hastily downs the cup of tea while Riadon packs the leftovers and puts away the remaining utensils. After kicking some dirt on the smoldering embers, Aramas leans over and picks up a nearby stick to stir the now muddy concoction. Once he is sure that the fire is out, he picks up the rest of his belongings, as well as his greatsword, and heads over to the wagon.

"Loki, Riadon will ride with you in the wagon. The rest of us will assume the same positions as we did yesterday. Aria, let me know if you detect any change in the scrying. Let's move."

With a quick flick of the reins, the horse smartly returns to the road. The squeak of the wheels seems to counter the creaking of the seat as the wagon moves along. While the air is not as crisp as the day before, a dampness seems to hang in the air. The sky is a bit overcast; the low-hanging gray clouds almost prophetically signal the coming storm. While birds can be heard chirping in the distance, there does not appear to be as much wildlife as the day before.

The next few hours pass without incident. Since departing the campsite, no one in the party says a word; all eyes have been focused on the road ahead and the woods around them. Loki sits contently smoking his pipe—the horse seemingly knowing the way—while Kriv, Aria, and Aramas maintain a constant vigil. Riadon fidgets with a deck of playing cards.

Looking back toward the wagon, Aramas asks, "Riadon, based on several comments you made yesterday, would it be correct to assume that you are familiar with the Forest Road, the village of Forest Glen, and the area around it?"

As if to signal his appreciation for being included in a conversation, Riadon eagerly responds, "Yes, why do you ask?"

"Is the forest this thick throughout the length of the road?"

"No. The forest remains fairly dense until we reach the village of Forest Glen just north of the junction of the Forest Road and the Old North Road. The village got its name because it sits at the edge of the darkest part of the forest. From there, the forest is considerably more open. To the west of the village there even used to be a few small farms."

Not letting on that he knows of the village, Aramas continues. "Is this a place where we can find safe harbor for the night?"

"It used to be."

"What do you mean, *used to be?*"

"On many a journey between Everand and Spring Green, I would spend the night at the Black Bear Inn in the center of town. The food was good, the mead excellent, and the company the best along the Forest Road. Travelers from all over the Hinter Land would spend the night. It was a very busy place. Then, two years ago, while returning from Everand, I stopped for the night, only to find the town empty. Everyone was gone. There had been no plague, no battle, nothing. The people just vanished. Three days later, when I finally arrived in Spring Green, I was told that everyone in the village had been killed. Many believed that an evil mage had taken their souls. I understand that the bodies were buried in a cemetery north of town, where a small temple was built to honor them."

"Have you ever been to the cemetery?"

"No, and from what I understand, no one else has either. The village has turned into a ghost town and no one wants to go anywhere near the cemetery. It is said that evil resides there, but you know how rumors get started."

"What about the Old North Road. Is it still traversed?"

"No. The road has been almost totally abandoned. It is overgrown, full of ruts and washouts, and is even more difficult to traverse than before. Travelers from the north now take the longer route through Spring Green. Since I do no business in Flotsam, there is no reason for me to go that way. Personally, I do not believe the stories about the cemetery."

"How long do you think it will take before we reach the village?"

"At this pace, we could be there sometime this evening. Why do you ask?"

"Just figured it might be a good place to spend the night—you know, a nice roof over our heads."

Stuttering slightly, Riadon replies, "But it is out of our way. The buildings are overrun with rats. There are no provisions there." Looking around at the other members of the party in the hope of finding some support, he then adds, "There is a suitable camp at the crossroads. In fact, there is a great place about an hour to the west of the crossroads. Why not make camp there?"

Without answering the question, Aramas turns back to Aria, "Are we still being watched?"

"Not at the moment."

Looking back to Riadon, Aramas continues. "How many people used to live in the town?"

"I don't know, maybe fifty?"

"What do you know of the recent attacks?"

"I hadn't paid much attention until yesterday. I've been told that they've increased significantly in the past few months." Then, hesitating for a moment and realizing what has been going on, he adds, "Please tell me we're not headed to Forest Glen."

Loki chuckles, shakes his head, and gives the reins a quick slap on the horse. Quiet again descends on the party.

About midafternoon, Aramas directs Loki to stop at the next clearing. After finding a convenient tree to relieve himself, Aramas returns to the wagon and calls the party together. "I plan to make it to Forest Glen tonight."

"Why the rush?" asks Kriv.

"I don't know if you've noticed, but for a road that is supposed to have seen a significant reduction in travelers over the past few months, there are certainly a lot of fresh tracks around."

Leaning forward from his perch atop the wagon and peering at the road ahead, Loki replies, "I would agree, and not just simple foot traffic. Heavy wagons and horses!" Looking back to Aramas, he adds, "As we suspected, it would appear that Alissa wasn't as forthcoming as she represented."

"What do you make of the tracks?" asks Aria.

Aramas says, "We were originally told to expect less than thirty thieves in this supposed band. Since being told that, we have been under constant surveillance from afar, have been attacked, have saved Riadon from attack, and have continued to come upon an increasing number of tracks on a road that is supposed to be relatively unused. This is not a simple band of thieves, and I suspect that the attacks have been nothing more than a ruse. There are other forces at work here, and whatever the plan, they want to minimize the chances of detection; therefore, the attacks."

"So why the need to get to Forest Glen tonight?"

"Those that attacked us were not trained soldiers and they certainly weren't trained assassins." Aramas pauses briefly and looks to the west, cocks his head slightly to the left, left index finger stroking his upper lip, and then after a moment, looks back at Aria. "No, based on everything that has happened, I suspect that they were just trying to keep travelers off the road. This is a well-organized group, and before we march up to that cemetery, I want to get a better idea of what we could be up against. I think those answers lie in Forest Glen."

Stuttering again, and very surprised, Riadon interrupts. "Cemetery? Assassins? More than thirty? I figured you weren't traders but . . ."

Aramas turns sharply and tersely responds, "You're welcome to return to Spring Green whenever you'd like. I will not keep you." Then, touching the hilt of his sword, he continues. "Understand that once you leave, regardless of your intentions, you will not be allowed to travel to the west."

Surprised by the tone of Aramas's voice, Riadon looks around at the other party members. Finding no solace in their stern expressions, he looks back to Aramas and quietly responds, "I gave you my word. My blade is yours."

Nodding to Riadon, Aramas turns back to the rest of the party. "We have about four more hours of good light. I would like to reach the town before nightfall."

Without another word, Loki snaps the reins, and the party is again headed to the west.

CHAPTER 3

THE ROAD TO NOWHERE

As described by Riadon, the thick forest canopy disappears just to the east of the junction between the Forest Road and Old North Road. It is a large clearing with a small farm, a few outbuildings, an abandoned barn, and what were once productive fields, now empty and overgrown. A lone deer, grazing in a small orchard to the west, raises its head to scrutinize the interlopers as they approach the junction. After a moment, it turns tail and bounds into the shelter of the nearby trees. Shutters hang haphazardly from the farmhouse windows that have long since broken. Discarded and broken furniture lies strewn across the property. Near the barn, old tools lie rusting. No one has lived here for some time. Further to the west, the setting sun is clearly visible as it begins its journey below the horizon. It will not be long before darkness envelops the party.

As the party gets closer to the junction, the plethora of hoof prints and wagon tracks leaves no doubt that the Old North Road has become more than a simple foot path. Turning to Riadon, Loki comments, "For a road that leads to a ghost town, it is certainly getting a lot of use!" Then with a chuckle he adds, "Must be a lot of ghosts."

"I don't understand. It was not like this the last time I passed this way."

"How long ago was that?" asks Aramas.

"Maybe three or four months?"

Halting the wagon, Loki looks down to Aramas and asks, "So what's the plan?"

"I'm not sure." Then, walking ahead about fifty feet, he kneels, and with the tips of his fingers he studies the hoofprints in front of him.

After a few seconds, Kriv asks, "What do they tell you?"

Aramas quickly stands and then turns back to the party. "We're going to be staying at a very crowded Black Bear Inn this evening." Then, just as quickly, he motions to Loki to follow as he turns and proceeds up the Old North Road.

By the time the party reaches the village, darkness has settled in. The warm, inviting yellow glow of torches hanging along the road and from several buildings illuminates the area. Laughter can be heard throughout the town. While there are not many buildings, they all seem to be occupied. Small groups of men pass between them and from one side of the street to the other. Others can be seen gambling, sharing a bottle of spirits, or chatting with one of the few women brave enough to set up business in such a remote place.

Aramas motions to what appears to be a stable then walks over to the entrance. When he sees no one in the immediate vicinity, he pokes his head inside and asks, "How does one get some service here?"

From the back of the building, an older gentleman pokes his head out from behind one of the stalls and replies, "Give me a minute." Shortly thereafter he emerges from the stall stuffing his shirt into his pants. About the same time, a scantily clad, well-endowed middle-aged woman runs from the stall and quickly exits through the back door.

"How can I help you?"

"I apologize for catching you at an inopportune time, but my friends and I will be spending the night and were wondering if you could tend to our horse and watch over the goods in our wagon. We are willing to make it worth your while."

"I can certainly take care of your horse, my lords. A good combing down, feed, water, and fresh hay in the stall will cost you two silver pieces." Then, standing up on his tiptoes to look over Aramas's shoulder at the wagon, he asks, "What's in the wagon?"

Aramas deliberately pauses, looks around as if to imply he is hiding something, then replies, "The contents of the wagon are of no consequence to you, or anyone else for that matter." He looks the stable keeper directly in the eye and adds, "You look like an honest fellow, someone of above average intelligence who can be trusted." Then, placing his right hand on the stable keeper's left shoulder, he says, "We are willing to pay handsomely for that trust."

Initially caught off guard by Aramas's compliment, the stable keeper glances quickly at the hand on his shoulder, leans a little closer to Aramas, grins slyly, and replies, "Normally I would not be inclined to enter into such a transaction. As you can probably tell, the people in this town are not of the highest breeding. They would just as soon cut your throat than give you the time of day. I can assure you that you will find no honest people here, present company excluded, if you know what I mean." Then, after pausing for a moment, he mumbles softly below his breath while using the fingers on both hands to do some calculations. Once complete, he adds, "Being that we have something in common, one gold piece would be fair payment to ensure that no harm comes to your goods, horse included."

Nodding his head in agreement, Aramas takes a gold piece out of his pouch and hands it to the stable keeper. "You drive a hard bargain. Should anyone ask, you know nothing about us except that we are taking these goods to Everand. Do you understand?"

"Yes, my lord."

Loki and Riadon grab their bedrolls and backpacks then jump down from the wagon. Aramas, Kriv, and Aria retrieve theirs.

With gear in hand, Aramas turns to the stable keeper and remarks, "Please have the wagon ready by midmorning."

"As you wish," at which point he grabs the horse's harness and leads it into the stable.

It is not long before the party reaches the inn. While there are comings and goings in several of the other buildings along the main street, it is obvious that the inn sits as the focal point of everything. A cacophony of hoots, laughter, drunken singing, and wails welcomes the party as they enter the inn's main floor pub.

Inside, the scents of burning whale oil, candles, and mead permeate the air. A smoky fog-like haze hangs over the room. Six small tables, several surrounded by occupied chairs, line both walls. Opposite the main entrance is a large bar. To its left, a narrow set of stairs leads to the second floor. The sound of footsteps and creaking beds can be heard above.

As the party enters the room, there is a momentary pause in the discordant sounds as each member is carefully scrutinized by the menagerie of misfits residing within, but it does not last.

After he moves across the room to the bar, Aramas inquires, "Do you have a room for five weary travelers?"

The bartender replies, "You're early. I did not expect you until tomorrow."

Aramas is surprised. "You were expecting us?"

"Are you not the travelers who easily fended off twenty robbers last night?"

This is a piece of information Aramas had not expected. Hoping to learn more, he replies, "While we did run into a little trouble along the way, someone has given us more credit than is due. How is it you came upon this information?"

The bartender slowly pours a tankard of mead. Then, handing it to Aramas, he says, "There are few happenings that occur in these woods that we are not aware of." Wiping some spilled brew from the bar, he adds, "I know not your purpose in being here, but I would recommend that you not tarry long. You may not be as lucky the next time."

Aramas takes a few gulps from the tankard, all the while looking directly into the portly reddish face of the bartender. With a sternness of purpose in his voice, Aramas replies, "Luck has nothing to do with it. What about that room?"

A bit perturbed, the bartender asks, "Will the woman creature need a separate room?"

"One large room will do just fine."

"One silver per person, in advance. Food and drink is extra." Reaching below the bar, he takes a key and places it in front of Aramas. "First door to the left, at the top of the stairs."

While he reaches into his pouch for the five silver pieces, Aramas asks, "What else can you tell us about the thieves who attacked us last night?"

"Only that they have been very good for business." Then, pausing for a moment and looking around to see who might be listening, he quietly adds, "You ask too many questions. This room has many ears."

Nodding his affirmation, Aramas plops the five silver pieces on the bar and picks up the key. Then, after he joins the rest of the party, they meander over to the nearest open table and set down their gear.

Aramas comments, "Well Loki, this is another one you can cross off your list." Loki shakes his head in agreement, a large grin peeking through his thick red beard.

A bit puzzled, Kriv asks, "Have we missed something?"

Before he can answer, a rather comely middle-aged woman approaches. "The bartender said that you have just come off the Forest Road from Spring Green. What can I get you?"

Smiling, Aramas responds. "Four more tankards for my companions, a bite to eat, and some information."

"I believe we still have some venison stew and hard rolls. What kind of information?"

"Information about the road to the north."

She quickly glances at the party members around the table then nervously remarks, "I'll be right back with your drinks and dinner."

As she walks away, Loki sarcastically quips, "Well, that went well."

After a brief chuckle, Kriv asks, "Did you learn anything from the bartender?"

"No. He was too afraid to say anything. However, he did know about the attack and let it slip that there were twenty in the party." After a brief pause, he adds, "He also knew of our expected arrival but seemed genuinely surprised that we had arrived this evening."

"Do you think he is one of them?"

"No, I did not get the impression he was. Like the stable keeper, it would appear that he is only here to take advantage of the current situation."

"So what now?" asks Aria.

Before Aramas can proffer an answer, the barmaid returns with the four tankards of mead. Without a word, she moves around the table to distribute them. After placing the last in front of Loki, she remarks, "I'll be right back with your stew."

Then, before turning back toward the bar, almost as if she forgot something, she moves over to Aramas and puts her right hand on his left shoulder. She slowly bends forward, just enough to expose her firm well-contoured breasts, and quietly utters, "I'll be done at midnight. Is there anything else you might require of me?"

Aramas turns a bit red, embarrassed by the uninvited proposal. "While I might otherwise be so inclined, my current situation does not afford me the opportunity to take you up on your offer."

Undeterred, she moves closer, presses her mouth up to his left ear as if to nuzzle it, and with her left hand now slowly rising up Aramas's inner left thigh, she whispers, "I know of what you seek but cannot speak here. I will come by your room tonight." She then presses her moist lips to his in a warm, passionate kiss. After a few seconds, she moves away slowly, smiles, and says, "Until later!" at which point she saunters back to the bar to get the waiting meals.

"Should we be getting another room?" laughs Loki.

Kriv joins in the fun. "Isn't she a little old for you?"

Aria quips, "I certainly can't imagine what he sees in her."

"Oh, I think he saw plenty," chortles Loki. Everyone but Aramas seems to find the situation humorous.

Still laughing, Loki lifts his tankard to offer a toast. "Here's to nice bobbles!"

Kriv, Riadon, and Aria join the salute. "To nice bobbles!"

After several gulps of the long-awaited nectar, the others, almost in unison, slam the tankards to the table. Their red-faced partner does not appear to be the least bit amused at their humor.

After a momentary pause, Loki leans forward and quietly asks, "Well, what did she say?"

"Not what you think. She says that she knows of 'what we are seeking' but cannot speak right now."

"And what is it that we are 'seeking'?" asks Riadon.

Looking over at Riadon, Aramas replies, "You won't have to wait much longer to find out. She'll be coming by the room tonight, shortly after midnight."

The barmaid returns with the meals. After placing each one on the table, she again moves over to Aramas, cups her left palm around his chin, smiles, then moves back to the bar.

Obviously still amused by her flirtations, Loki asks, "Are you sure we don't need another room?"

Aramas smiles slyly, shakes his head, and without further comment, begins to enjoy his dinner.

The stew is warm, flavorful, and goes down easily. The few potatoes and carrots blend well with the fresh venison, which almost falls apart on the plate. There may even be a few scallions and wild herbs added. The gravy is thick and savory, and not wishing to waste a drop, Aramas breaks off a piece of bread and slowly swirls it around the plate until the dish looks as clean as if it had been washed. For the first time since entering the inn, there is silence at the table as everyone enjoys the dinner before them. For a few minutes, there is no thought of the task ahead, only on the moment and the simple pleasure it provides.

When Aramas finishes with his dinner, he lifts his tankard to consume the remaining brew then glances over at Loki, who has turned his attention to his pipe and tobacco pouch. Following his ritual after every dinner since the two have met, Loki lights up, takes a few deep puffs, and smiles with contentment.

After a brief moment of contemplation, Aramas turns to Kriv. "I want you and Riadon to head out to the privy, and while back there check the building for any alternate means of escape should one become necessary. We may have surprised them by arriving tonight, but they surely have had enough time now to modify any plans they might have had for us. We need to know our options."

Then he turns to Loki and Aria. "We'll set watches just as we did the other night. Aria, have you detected any further scrying?"

"No, none since we broke camp."

Loki interrupts. "Why would they? They know exactly where we are and where they can find us tonight. I rarely question your decisions, my friend, but I do not understand why we're here. It is as if you're looking for trouble, and I do not relish the idea of taking on an unknown number of assassins in such tight quarters."

Aramas turns to Loki. "I understand your concern. However, before departing Spring Green, we were told several things that have turned out to be far from fact. I do not know how much of that was deliberate or how much was simple ignorance. What I do know is that we need more information. By coming here, to the heart of their operation, I hope to get that information, and the barmaid may be able to provide that. Had we not come here, that wouldn't have happened."

"And if we're attacked?"

Aramas surveys the group and replies, "We will be ready."

While Kriv and Riadon head out the back exit to survey the area, Aramas orders another round of drinks. The conversation remains light, focusing primarily on the clientele in the bar.

Loki comments, "I figure maybe fifty, none of whom would appear to pose much of a challenge in a fight."

"Agreed. What we're looking for will not be found within the confines of Forest Glen."

By the time the drinks are delivered to the table, Kriv and Riadon return.

Once seated, Kriv leans toward Aramas. "Other than a few windows, and the stairs near the bar, there is no other exit from the second floor. It would appear that one of those windows leads to our room, but without a ladder, it would be difficult to enter our room through it."

Then, looking down at the table and using his finger as if pointing to a map, Kriv continues. "Behind the inn is a short alley between the barn and the main street. Fortunately, it is not a blind alley. However, the positioning of a small group of men here and here, at each entrance, could create problems for us should we need to exit that way. To make things even more interesting, one or two good archers strategically placed on the adjoining rooftops could really muck things up."

As they continue to discuss their options, three heavily armed burly men enter the inn, the shortest of which is wearing a bright red robe over his leather armor. As they proceed to the bar, Riadon slowly lowers his head and looks away.

Aramas notices and asks, "Have you encountered these men before?"

Riadon looks down as if he dropped something. "The tall one to the left, he is the one that seemed to be in charge of the group that robbed me. He is also the one who gave the order to leave when your party approached."

"I thought you didn't see the one who gave the order," remarks Kriv.

"I didn't. Someone behind the tree line shouted out to the tall one. The tall one then ordered the group to leave."

Glancing briefly at the three then back at Riadon, Aramas asks, "The tall one, was he the only one that was heavily armed?"

Riadon hesitates for a moment to ponder the question. "From what I can remember, the other six were clothed very much like the men seated around the room. The only weapons they brandished were knives and short swords. Two also carried bows, but they stayed in the background until I was tied up."

"Do you think they recognized you when they passed by the table?"

"I don't think so. They appeared to be too engrossed in their own conversation."

"What if they do?" asks Aria.

Aramas replies, "Unless forced to defend ourselves, we are to act as if Riadon remembers nothing about his attackers. As of yet, I don't think they realize we're here. It will be interesting to see how they react once they do." Then to Riadon he says, "Should they look our way, and should they recognize you, do not react! Simply smile as if acknowledging their presence and continue our conversation as if nothing has happened. Understood?"

"Sure, but what then?"

"Just follow my lead."

Meanwhile, the three men continue their conversation as the bartender pours their drinks. The one in the red robe does not appear to carry anything but a jewel-encrusted short sword and a small dagger. His leather armor appears to be well maintained and of the highest quality, his black leather boots brightly polished. Around his neck is a gold pendant. The other two are wearing chain mail, and each carries a longsword. The lack of heavy dirt on their boots would seem to indicate that they have not traveled far.

After a short toast, the three turn to face the crowded room. The tall one leans up against the bar as he takes another drink from his tankard until he gazes over at the party and a look of concern comes to his face. He leans over to his robed companion and nods in Riadon's direction while saying something. Obviously concerned, the other man quickly glances over. Then all three put down their drinks and move toward the table.

They stop across the table from Riadon, and looking directly at him, the tall one asks, "Do I know you?"

Doing as Aramas had instructed, Riadon looks up and replies, "I do not believe that I have had the pleasure."

"Are you sure? I could swear that we have met."

"I am sure that I would remember such an encounter," replies Riadon.

Standing up, Aramas glares at the tall one and asks, "Is there a problem?"

Before he can answer, the robed man steps forward and interrupts. "No problem. My friend appears to be mistaken." Then he pauses for a moment and comments, "It seems that your friend bears an uncanny resemblance to a thief he encountered on the Forest Road the other day. Unfortunately, he got away." He looks back at Aramas. "As I am sure you are aware, there have been a number of armed attacks in the area over the past few months. As concerned business owners, we have been forced to take matters into our own hands. I think you can understand. One can't be too careful." Then, looking at each of the party members, he adds, "Please accept my apology if we have offended you in any way."

At that point he turns and motions to his two companions to return to the bar. Turning back to Aramas, he asks, "So what brings you to Forest Glen?"

"We have been commissioned by Alissa of Spring Green to travel to Everand to attend to some business affairs on her behalf. Knowing of the recent problems, we felt it would be better to spend a night here in town rather than in the open on the Forest Road."

With a slight tilt of his head, the man replies, "A wise choice. However, looking at the five of you, it would appear that you are more than capable of handling any problem that might arise."

Then, placing his right hand over his heart, he bows slightly toward Aramas. "I have already taken enough of your time. My name is Craven. Should you need anything for your journey, please do not hesitate to ask. I own the mercantile across the street. After your return from Everand, should you be looking for employment, we could use men of your talent. With your permission, I will take my leave."

Aramas bows slightly in reply as Craven turns and returns to the men at the bar.

Aramas continues to observe Craven as he rejoins his companions at the bar. The three continue what appears to be a heated conversation, each periodically glancing over at the party. During the conversation,

Craven puts his left hand on the tall one's shoulder and nods as if motioning toward the door. Then, with one long gulp, the tall one finishes his drink and slams the empty tankard to the bar. Obviously not happy with what Craven has told him, he looks over to the party before leaving the room. After a few seconds, Craven and the other companion also depart.

Looking around the table, Aramas comments, "Well, if they didn't know we were here before, they certainly do now."

While the rest of the evening goes without incident, it is obvious that the presence of the party has not gone unnoticed. After the departure of Craven and his armed companions, an uneasiness permeates the room. Once-boisterous conversations are now more reserved, their participants careful about what they say and to whom. Passersby give the table a wide berth when going to and from the bar, and direct eye contact is deliberately avoided. An occasional glance in their direction, or a veiled nod of the head, only serve to add to the tension.

Surveying the crowd one more time, Aramas lifts the tankard and slowly consumes the last of its contents. He turns to his comrades and quietly remarks, "Finish your drinks. We have preparations to make." Then he stands, and after a brief moment, moves deliberately toward the barmaid standing near the end of the bar, feeling the eyes of almost everyone in the room now focused on him.

When she sees his approach, the barmaid puts down the two drinks that she was about to deliver and looks longingly into his eyes. Aramas reaches into his pouch and pulls out a single gold piece. Then, softly taking her left hand in his, he places the coin in her open palm and closes her fingers around it. Bending slightly forward, he gently kisses her left cheek then whispers in her ear, "I await your presence." He hesitates briefly then adds, "Thank you."

As if embarrassed by what he said, she slowly moves her hand over her heart, a faint smile coming to her slightly flushed face.

As if on cue, Loki approaches from behind, places his hand on Aramas's shoulder, and remarks, "Tomorrow will be a long day. We need to retire." Aramas nods slightly then turns and heads up the stairs.

The stairs are steep and narrow, with barely enough room for two to pass. Heavily worn, several of the steps have become loose and squeak loudly as the party climbs to their room. The hallway at the top is not much wider. Other than the noise from the customers below, all is quiet.

As Aramas opens the door to their room, Aria quietly drifts down the hall, stopping at each of the three doors to listen for anything unusual.

Their room is dark; however, from the light of the sconces in the hall, Aramas can see a small table immediately inside with a candlestick. He grabs it and lights it from the sconce in the hall then moves cautiously into the room. Inside are four beds, another small table with a candlestick, two chairs, and a window. While the room has obviously seen better days, it appears to be relatively clean. There is no indication of rodents, and the straw in the crude mattresses appears to be relatively fresh. Out the window, Aramas can see the alley and main street below.

"Any preference as to where you want to sleep?" asks Loki.

"No, but I think Aria should take the bed closest to the door. She seems to have the keenest hearing," replies Aramas.

Loki plops his bedroll on the mattress behind the door, stands his war hammer up against the head of the bed, and slowly begins to remove his chain mail.

"If Aria is to be nearest the door, I will take the floor next to the table," replies Kriv.

Riadon heads to the far bed on the inner wall.

Just as Aramas turns to place his bedroll on the remaining bed, Aria returns to the room. "Other than a couple obviously enjoying each other's company in the far room across the hall, we appear to be the only overnight guests."

"What about the window?"

"While I had no problem opening it, there is no easy way to get to it from the street. Anyone wishing to pay us a visit will have to come up the stairs."

"Good. With the configuration of the stairwell, we should be able to handle any unexpected visitors. Just the same, we need to be ready. I will take the first watch. Kriv, you and Riadon will take the second. Loki and Aria the third."

"Do you really think the barmaid will show?" asks Kriv.

Aramas replies, "I have no reason to doubt her sincerity."

Chuckling, Loki comments, "I'd say she's sincere. Nice kiss." The others join in the laughter.

Realizing that there is nothing he can say, Aramas shakes his head and begins to remove his armor. Without a word, as if performing some ancient ritual, Loki moves over to assist him. Over the years, Aramas had become adept at donning and removing his armor, and while wearing it was not something he enjoyed, his days as a gladiator had taught him to appreciate the protection it afforded. The numerous scars on his chest, back, and arms, received without it while honing his skills in the arena, were a testament to its effectiveness. Still, he longed for a time when it would no longer be necessary, a time when he could return to the lands unjustly taken from his family.

With back and breast plates now removed, Loki pats his friend on the shoulder and quietly moves back over to his bed. It has been a long day, and he too is looking forward to what he hopes will be an uneventful night.

It isn't long before the sound of his snoring companions permeates the room. Hoping not to wake them, Aramas moves quietly over to the door to await his guest, his sword at his side. The muffled sounds of the boisterous crowd below waft through the floorboards. Every so often the footsteps of a passerby can be heard moving between the stairway and the room at the far end of the hall, followed soon thereafter by footsteps moving in the opposite direction. Evidently business is very good.

Aramas cannot help but think of the two boys. How are they being treated? What must they be going through? Are they even still alive? He cannot shake the image of them being sold into slavery, tortured, or worse.

His mind soon turns into a trance-like hypnosis as he's transported to a time long in his past. His father, standing before him, is ordering him to remain in the small space between the temple's altar and the back wall. "You are not to come out, no matter what happens. Is that understood?"

"Yes, Father. But what about Mother?"

"I was unable to locate her. Her fate now rests in the hands of Bahamut. Remember, whatever happens, you must survive!"

From the small space behind the altar, Aramas can hear the cries of the people outside as they run in terror or fall victim to the invading marauders. His father, a high priest of Bahamut, moves slowly toward the sanctuary entrance, seemingly unfazed by the chaos outside.

Just before he reaches the temple doors, they are thrust open as five or six soldiers scramble into the sanctuary. Aramas's father calmly approaches them, halting their advance.

The leader slowly approaches the priest. "You dare stand in our way?"

"This is a holy place. You are not welcome here."

"I know not your god, and I certainly am not afraid of you." Then, without warning, the soldier plunges his blade through the chest of the priest. As the others laugh, Aramas can only watch as his father's body falls to the floor.

The soldier grins, wipes the blood from his blade on the priest's tunic, and commands to the others, "Take everything of value, then burn the place to the ground." As the others scramble to gather whatever they can carry, the leader takes one last look around the room, turns sharply, and rejoins the rest of his unit outside.

As the soldiers quickly gather whatever they can find, Aramas tries to force himself even further into the confines behind the altar.

Then, without warning, the commotion of the soldiers ransacking the sanctuary is shattered by the screams of a single woman, Aramas's mother.

A lone soldier drags the struggling woman into the room. As he throws her to the floor next to the body of her husband, Aramas hears the soldier laughingly remark, "Look what I've found." Peering out from the safety of the altar, Aramas watches as the others quickly surround her. Then, as they start to grab at her flailing body, unable to control himself, Aramas grabs a nearby candlestick and charges at the attackers.

The soldiers are taken aback when from out of nowhere, a young boy catapults his body into the closest attacker and thrusts the candelabra into his skull. Blood spattered, Aramas moves to defend his mother; however, before he can reach her, he is grabbed by the neck and thrown to the ground. Standing above him is the man who killed his father.

"It is a good thing I came back. Otherwise, I might have been too late to keep this boy from killing each of you." He asks, "How old are you, boy?"

"I have seen ten summers."

"Who is this woman, and what is she to you?"

"That woman is my mother, and I will kill anyone who touches her."

Laughing loudly, the soldier slaps Aramas's face, opening a large gash in his left cheek. He sarcastically remarks, "Put him with the others, and be careful. I would hate to have any more of you die at his hands."

Then he looks down at Aramas. "You seem to have no fear. That can be both a curse and a strength. It will serve you well in the arena."

The leader turns and strides toward the door. Without turning to look back, he says, "Once you are done with her, finish with this place and return to your unit."

Then, as if abruptly awakened from a deep sleep, come three faint knocks at the door. "Are you awake?"

Aramas quickly jumps to his feet; Aria and Loki follow suit.

The hushed and muffled voice from the hallway again implores, "Are you awake? I do not have much time!"

Aramas cautiously opens the door. As expected, it is the barmaid. Stepping slightly behind the door, he opens it just enough to quickly usher her inside. She appears very nervous, her hands shaking in the dim candlelight, her face taught and flushed.

"They told me to take no more time than necessary to attend to your desires, as there is still much for me to do before I am allowed to leave for the night."

"You said that you knew of what we were seeking," replies Aramas. "What did you mean?"

"The two boys! You came for the two boys."

"What boys?" asks Aramas.

"The blacksmith's sons."

"Why would you think that we are looking for two boys?"

"Because the older son told me of your coming."

Loki quickly interjects, "He foretold our coming?"

"Yes, the older boy told me so when I was bringing them their food. He said that six strangers would come looking for them, and that if I could help you in any way, I would be handsomely rewarded."

"He said six?" asks Loki.

"Yes, but where is . . ."

Interrupting, Aramas asks, "What else did the boy say?"

"Beware the Guardian."

"What does that mean? Who is the Guardian?" asks Aria.

"I don't know. I was simply instructed to repeat the warning word for word."

Kriv interjects. "How do we know she's telling the truth?"

Aramas takes her trembling hands in his and looks directly into her eyes. "I believe her." He then asks, "Where are they being held?"

"In the cemetery north of town. Craven and the two guards with him took the boys there shortly after they were taken captive."

"How many men are guarding them?"

"I don't know. But I've never seen more than a few dressed like them."

Loki asks, "What about the men below?"

"They're nothing more than hired thieves. They never go north of town. It would appear that their sole purpose is to rob anyone transiting the Forest Road and then deliver the stolen goods to Craven at the end of each day." Then, looking over to Riadon, she continues, "The tall one recognized you. Based on the conversation they had at the bar before leaving, they did not believe your story and left to warn the others of your coming."

"What others? Who are they going to warn?" asks Aramas.

"I don't know, but whomever it is, he is very powerful. He sees everything!"

"Why are they robbing all of the caravans?"

"I heard the other guard saying something about an ancient creature's skeleton."

"What ancient creature, and how is that related to the robberies?"

"That's all I know." She looks nervously around then says to Aramas, "I must get back. I have done what the boy asked. Where is my reward?"

Aramas reaches into his pouch and pulls out five more gold pieces. "If what you have told us is true, I will give you five more upon our return."

Taking the money, she lifts her apron to reveal a small leather pouch. Once the coins have been secured, she turns to the door and cracks it open slightly. The hallway is clear.

Then, just as she did earlier, she turns to Aramas, cups her hands to his cheeks, and presses her lips to his. However, before he can reciprocate, she pulls away and moves back to the door. As she is closing it behind her, she looks longingly back to Aramas and whispers, "I await your return."

CHAPTER 4

THE EVIL WITHIN

A s a nearby rooster announces the new day, the party slowly rises and sets about packing their gear and donning their armor. Not much is said as each member slowly prepares for what lies ahead.

Loki looks over at where his longtime friend hones a fine edge on the gleaming blade of his sword. He gets the feeling Aramas has been awake for some time. Then, turning his sights to the nearby window, Loki gazes past the wavy distorted pane of glass for some clue as to what might await them in the hours to follow. It is not a remarkable day. The sky is slightly overcast, the movement of the trees indicating a strong westerly breeze. As there is no early morning frost on the pane, he surmises that it must be fairly warm. On the window ledge sits a raven, staring into the room as if studying its inhabitants.

"Kind of eerie, isn't it?" asks Loki.

"What is?" replies Aramas.

"That bird. It's like it's watching our every move."

"It is. It's been there since sunup."

Surprised, Loki glances over at Aria. "Are we being watched?"

She replies, "Yes, and the presence is very strong."

Feeling somehow violated by the bird's presence, Loki stands, grabs his hammer, and swiftly advances toward the window. However, before he can raise it, the raven spreads its wings, screeches, and flies off toward the north.

Frustrated, Loki turns and strides back to his bed. "Let's get moving." As he picks up his bedroll and pack, he adds, "I don't want to give them any more time to prepare than we already have."

Chuckling, Aramas sheathes his sword and picks up his belongings. As he leaves the room he remarks, "Must be suffering from a bad case of bed bugs."

Except for a lone drunk sleeping it off on one of the nearby tables, the bar is empty and quiet. Chairs have been left strewn about the room exactly as they were when the last patron left. Many of the tables are littered with empty or partially filled tankards, dirty plates, and spilled liquor. On one of the far tables, a rat stops munching on what remains of a piece of stale bread just long enough to determine if either of the new arrivals is going to interrupt its morning meal. There has been no attempt to ready the room for the day's guests.

Aramas puts his hand on Loki's shoulder and asks, "Is everything okay? You seem unusually tense."

With a frown, Loki turns and replies, "This is not right. We know that we are walking into a trap, yet you do not appear to be concerned. It is as plain as the nose on your face that whoever has been watching us has seen through our ruse. Yet you seem to be acting as if this is some sort of game."

"No game. I just don't want to reveal our hand. They continue to observe because they don't know what to make of us or what to do next. If they were sure as to our true mission and felt confident in their ability to deal with us, they would have attacked long ago. Their hesitance indicates a lack of direction and therefore works to our favor. Every moment that passes affords us the opportunity to observe how they react."

Squeaky steps signal the entrance of the rest of their party. Aramas says, "If our hosts weren't sure of our intentions before, they soon will be." He then strides toward the door.

With the other party members close behind, Aramas quickly heads toward the livery stable. Like the bar room, what were bustling streets only a few hours earlier are now almost completely empty. Other than Craven's two companions from the night before, the town is devoid of inhabitants. Standing just outside the mercantile, the two watch intently as the party moves down the street.

At the livery, they find no evidence of the stable keeper, but their wagon is there, horse hitched up and ready for the journey ahead. Kriv inspects the cargo and notes that everything is just as they had left it. Nothing appears to have been touched. At Aramas's direction, Riadon goes out the back door to see if the stable keeper might be tending to the livestock. However, other than a few horses, a couple of goats, and a few chickens, there is no one around.

Riadon comments, "I hope no one expected a fancy send-off."

With a bit of sarcasm directed toward Aramas, Loki quips, "Not to worry. I expect that we'll be getting a proper send-off further up the road."

Aramas ignores the comment, grabs the horse's harness, and moves the rig out of the stable. He waits for a moment outside the stable door to allow Loki and Riadon to climb into the seat. With a quick snap of the reins, the party proceeds up the street, Aramas in the lead just to the right of the horse, Kriv to the left of the wagon, and Aria following.

As the party approaches the mercantile, they notice that Craven has joined his two companions.

"I thought you were headed to Everand?" he says.

"Change of plans," replies Aramas.

"I see. Sure hope that you don't run into any problems."

Aramas responds, looking directly at Craven. "Thank you for your concern; however, as a small group of visitors found out the other night, we're pretty good problem solvers."

The tall one, directing his comment at Riadon, adds, "The next time you may not be so lucky."

Aramas stops briefly and tersely remarks, "Someone else made that same comment just last evening. You would be wise to understand that luck has nothing to do with it." With that, and a slight nod of his head, he turns and rejoins the party.

As expected, the road ahead has seen more than its share of travelers, replete with the tracks of both mounted and dismounted travelers. Aramas stops and kneels to the ground to study an unfamiliar track.

Pulling back on the reins, Loki asks, "What is it?"

"I'm not sure. It looks like a bear's paw print, but it has an unusual shape and is much larger than any bear I've encountered."

Curious, both Kriv and Aria move to the front of the wagon, but neither is able to shed any light on the track's origin.

Standing up, Aramas turns toward Loki. "The track is fresh. The creature appears to be moving north, alongside the road, as if stalking prey."

Riadon asks, "What kind of prey?"

"Human."

With a puzzled look, Kriv remarks, "While I have encountered bears that have attacked to defend their young or their territory, I have never heard of a bear that prefers human flesh."

"Let us hope that I am wrong," Aramas says. Then he murmurs, "Let's hope I'm wrong."

For the next hour or so, no one says a word, everyone's attention focused on the road ahead and the surrounding woods. While the air has warmed considerably since leaving Forest Glen, intermittent gusts of wind blows leaves and dust across the deserted road. Every so often, the sun breaks through the clouds long enough to create a patchwork of light and shadow on the road ahead. Spring appears to have come late to this part of the forest, as many of the trees are just beginning to show their new buds, their swaying branches seemingly urging the party onward.

Pulling back on the reins, Loki asks, "What's that ahead, off to the left of the road?"

"It looks like a recent kill," replies Kriv.

As Kriv cautiously approaches, the sound of something farther ahead on the left can be heard amongst the underbrush. Stopping briefly to survey the area, Kriv draws his flail and slowly backs toward the group.

Drawing his sword, Aramas asks softly, "What is it?"

"The remains of at least two humans. Whatever killed them did not leave much behind."

Just as Aria moves to join Kriv and Aramas, a large bear-like creature explodes from behind the trees. Before he can raise his flail, the swift swat of the creature's paw knocks Kriv to the ground. Then, standing on its hind legs, it rushes toward Aramas.

Startled by the unexpected attack, the horse rears and tries to escape the impending danger. Drawing upon all the strength he can muster, Loki is able to prevent the horse from bolting, but in doing so, he is temporarily unable to help his fallen comrade.

As Loki steadies the horse, Riadon leaps from the wagon. Moving quickly toward Aramas, he extends his hand and calls forth a magic dagger. Then, just as quickly, he hurls it at the beast. As it leaves his hand, it morphs into multiple projectiles, all of which strike the creature but seem to be nothing more than a minor annoyance. Realizing that he will not be of much help in this fight, he grabs the horse's harness and shouts to Loki, "I'll take care of the wagon!" With a nod of acknowledgment, Loki draws his war hammer, jumps to the ground, and swiftly moves to join his friend.

Startled, the creature temporarily halts its advance, and in the brief respite, Aramas charges, his sword cutting a deep gash in the creature's thigh. It howls in pain and instinctively takes a swipe at the source. Unable to avoid the counterattack, Aramas is thrown to the ground.

As Kriv regains his footing, Aria raises her ashen rod and calls to Ioun. Almost instantly, the rod begins to glow. A powerful bolt of energy is hurled toward the beast, striking it squarely in the chest and pushing it back several feet. Aramas immediately rolls toward Loki.

From behind, Kriv's flail cuts deep into the beast's shoulder. As before, it swings wildly at the source of its pain. Kriv anticipates its moves and ducks, thereby avoiding another trip to the ground. The now enraged creature turns and takes another swipe at Kriv, this time inflicting a large gash across his chest and knocking him down. The creature focuses all of its attention on the wounded attacker and moves in to complete the kill.

As the beast lunges at Kriv, Aramas charges in, sword held high. With a ferocious swing, he thrusts his blade into the creature's lower back. Almost simultaneously, Loki's war hammer strikes the beast between its shoulder blades. Confused, and obviously in a great deal of pain, the creature releases Kriv and again turns to face its attackers. As it does, Aria unleashes another bolt of energy, temporarily stunning it. Aramas takes a quick step forward and plunges his now bloodstained blade deep into the creature's chest. As it slowly exhales its last breath, the creature slumps forward and falls to the ground.

Loki, Aramas, and Aria rush to the aid of their fallen comrade. Nearby, Riadon secures the horse and wagon before joining them.

As he attempts to get back on his feet, Kriv moans, "I'll be fine. Just got the wind knocked out of me."

"Sit still before you open your wound anymore!" commands Loki.

"I'm fine! The chain mail did as it was supposed to."

Kneeling next to Kriv, Loki quickly examines the wound.

"Do you need my help?" asks Aramas.

"No, I've got this."

As Loki tends to the wound, Aramas and Riadon walk back to the creature. It is an imposing sight, stretching over twelve feet in length. Kneeling next to the now lifeless corpse, Aramas slowly runs his fingers through the creature's thick brown fur, periodically rolling small clumps of hair between his thumb and index finger. It possesses a coarseness he has not seen before. Methodically he moves first to the creature's mouth, then its paws. The creature's canines are considerably larger than any bear he has ever seen—almost fang-like—and its claws longer than the largest bear he's ever encountered.

"It's huge. What is it?" asks Riadon.

"I'm not sure, but if I had to guess, I'd say it's a dire bear, a creature normally found in the Northlands on the other side of the Frozen Sea."

"How did it get here?"

"A good question."

Loki, finished tending to Kriv's wound, asks, "Aren't they normally found far to the north?"

"Normally yes. But with everything else that's happened over the past few weeks . . ."

Aria interrupts, "We're being watched again."

Aramas turns toward Aria. "From the same source?"

"Yes, and it is very close."

Looking to the north, Aramas adds, "I would suspect that many of our questions will soon be answered. Let's not keep our hosts waiting any longer."

Thirty minutes further up the road, the party comes to a fairly large clearing. To the left of the road is the cemetery. To the right, a solitary abandoned building overgrown with vines, its shutters clattering in the wind.

Aramas says to Loki, "We'll tie the horse up here and proceed on foot."

While Loki and Riadon tend to the wagon, Aramas, Kriv, and Aria walk across the road to survey the area. The cemetery sits on the side of a hill that rises to the west and is divided by a long north–south wall. Half of the cemetery sits above the wall, half below. Built into its center is what appears to be the small temple Brevek told them about. However, at the top of the hill sits a much larger temple, something Brevek failed to mention.

"So what's the plan?" asks Loki as he and Riadon join the others.

Aramas points to the temple at the top of the hill. "What we've come for is there. Since they know we're here, I see no reason to delay any longer." He pauses then turns to Kriv. "You and Aria come up on the right." Then to Loki he says, "The three of us will come up from the left."

As they move up the hill, the party finds nothing to suggest that this is anything other than a cemetery. With the exception of the wind, all is quiet. The woods around are still bare, and as such, afford little cover for a potential ambush.

At the top of the hill, the party converges on the granite and slate temple. The building appears to contain no windows and has only one entrance. Located at the front of the building, the massive iron-bound double oak doors overlook the cemetery and the abandoned dwelling below. With the exception of two words engraved in the granite above the doors, the temple is devoid of any markings.

Aramas asks Loki, "What does it say?"

"I am not sure, but if I'm correct, it reads, 'Raven's Haunt Mausoleum.'"

With some concern in his voice, Riadon asks, "Does that mean anything to you?"

Aramas replies, "I don't believe so. I've heard tales of a Raven's Nest Castle far to the east in the Tiefling Mountains, but that's all." He pauses for a moment then continues. "It's time you earned your keep. Check the entrance for traps!" Then, turning to Aria, he asks, "Do you detect any magic?"

As Riadon moves cautiously forward to examine the door and the structure around it, Aria, palms together and eyes closed, recites an ancient ritual.

Minutes later, Riadon turns to the party. "I can find nothing that would prevent us from entering the building."

Aramas turns to Aria. "Anything?"

"While there is some magic just inside the doors, I detect nothing of any significance. However, there is something below us."

"Can you determine what it is?" asks Kriv.

"Only that it is below us. I may be able to learn more once inside."

Aramas draws his sword and moves to the door. Turning to make sure that everyone is ready, he motions to Riadon to open the door to the right as he slowly opens the one on the left.

Inside is a simple rectangular room lit by three ever-burning flames on each side of the room. Below each is a sarcophagus adorned with an effigy of the warlord entombed within. Above each is a small niche carved into the wall with small statues of what appear to be deities of some sort. The niches in the left wall contain three statues of one deity; to the right, three statues of a different deity. In the center of the room is a ten-foot-tall obelisk, each side containing a number of inscriptions. There are no other decorations or engravings in the room.

Aramas slowly enters the room and motions to the others to fan out. "Do not touch anything!"

As the rest of the party moves between the sarcophagi, examining the effigies on each and statues above them, Loki moves to examine the obelisk.

Aramas asks him, "What does it say?"

"These are the names of twenty Kaius warlords," replies Loki. "Next to each is a brief list of their heroics." Looking around the room, he adds, "I suspect that the six sarcophagi contain the remains of the six greatest, each of whom is mentioned here."

"Anything else?"

Pensively, Loki replies, "I'm not sure," at which point he kneels to examine the base of the obelisk.

With everyone now focusing on Loki, Aramas asks, "Have you found something?"

"There are several small pieces of broken stone at the base." As the party moves around to see what he has found, Loki detects a slight breeze coming from below the obelisk's back panel. "I think I've found a secret door."

As Loki runs his fingers along the bottom of the obelisk, a deep raspy voice is heard from within it. "Interlopers, beware. If you trespass, you shall not realize the wisdom of my words. From entry sinister, the way becomes clear when son follows sire."

Jumping back, Loki's eyes remain transfixed on the obelisk. The rest of the party slowly backs away in anticipation of what might follow. Then, like steam rising from a boiling pot, a misty revenant slowly phases out of the obelisk.

As the party cautiously moves back toward the entrance, the spirit moves to the far end of the room, never taking its eyes off them.

Aramas returns his sword to its sheath, directs the others to stand down, then asks, "Who are you?"

There is no response.

Half glancing at Aramas, Loki remarks, "The Guardian?"

Without taking his eyes off the spirit, Aramas asks Aria, "What do you think?"

"I believe Loki to be correct."

"What does it want?" asks Riadon.

Taking a few seconds to study the spirit before answering, Aria replies, "I sense that it seeks our help."

"With what?"

Glancing around the room, Aria turns to Loki. "Besides the names of the warlords, what else is inscribed on the stone?"

"Only the names of the gods they revered."

"How many?"

Loki drifts back to the obelisk; the spirit remains motionless. Under its watchful eye, Loki again reads the various inscriptions. As he runs his finger across the names, he periodically looks over to the statues in the niches in the walls, first to the left then to the right. "Only two: Pelor and Bahamut." Then, to the party, he says, "The statues are of Pelor and Bahamut!"

"I am not familiar with either. Over what realms do they reign?" asks Aria.

"Pelor is the god of sun and agriculture, Bahamut the god of justice and honor."

Impatient, Riadon sarcastically remarks, "We've got some kind of spirit staring at us, and all you want to do is study religion?" He moves over to the closest sarcophagus. "Let's open one of these. If these guys were as great as the obelisk says, then there could be unimaginable treasures in each."

Before he can do so, Aramas shouts, "Don't move!"

Startled, Riadon looks back toward Aramas and finds that the spirit is now hovering just behind him.

"I told you not to touch anything! Now, move slowly back towards me!"

As he does, the spirit assumes a protective stance above the sarcophagi. No one else moves.

Placing his right hand over his heart, Aramas nods. "We mean you no harm. Our only mission is to rescue two young boys who were spirited away from their party not far from here. I give you my word that we will do nothing to dishonor those who rest here."

The spirit does not respond.

After a few seconds, assuming he has diffused the situation, Aramas turns to Aria. "Why the questions about the gods?"

"I believe that the riddle is the key to the secret door Loki found."

"How so?"

"*The way becomes clear when son follows sire.* What if 'son' is not a child but actually refers to the sun? I believe it has something to do with Pelor!"

Kriv interrupts, "Bahamut is the king of all metallic dragons. He could be the 'sire' referred to in the riddle."

Loki quickly looks back at the names inscribed in the obelisk. "Each warlord's name is followed by a picture of the god he worshipped." Looking again at the statues, then back at the inscriptions, he adds, "What if the statues above each sarcophagus are supposed to be the ones worshipped by the entombed warlord?"

"There are no names engraved on the sarcophagi. How are we supposed to know which is which since that thing won't let us open any of them?" asks Riadon.

Kriv interrupts, "*From entry sinister . . .* in another time, the word 'sinister' was oft used to mean 'left.' What if the riddle tells us to start from the left once we entered the mausoleum?"

Looking again at the statues, Loki adds, "I would think it fair to assume that the statues in the shape of a dragon's head represent Bahamut." He pauses for a moment. "It would appear that someone has placed all of the statues of Pelor in the niches to the left, Bahamut to the right."

"Does that mean they're on the wrong side of the room?" asks Aria.

As the party watches, Loki moves to the closest statue of Bahamut, picks it up, and starts toward the first niche to the left of the entrance. "Let's see. Switch all of the statues."

"Wait," shouts Riadon. "What about the spirit?"

Looking over to the spirit, Aramas replies, "It did not stop Loki."

Like ants scrambling to get out of the rain, each party member grabs a statue and moves it to the niche on the opposite side of the room. Once all of the statues have been moved, Loki moves over to the obelisk and tries to move the back panel. Nothing happens.

Puzzled, Loki asks, "What did we miss?"

Looking around, Kriv remarks, "Son does not follow sire! Pelor is not following Bahamut. Starting with Bahamut, the statues must alternate clockwise around the room. Switch the statues in the niches and alternate, Bahamut first!"

Aria and Aramas immediately comply. No sooner are the statues alternated when, without warning, the back panel of the obelisk slowly moves to the side, revealing a set of stairs leading to a lower level. As the party quickly moves to the now open stairwell, Aramas gazes back to see what the spirit is doing. However, it has vanished.

The stairs appear to go down about twenty feet to a lower hallway or chamber. The walls on each side of the staircase are adorned with carvings and inscriptions. The top of the archway leading into the chamber is inscribed with the word *Kaius.*

As Riadon studies the steps to determine if there are any traps, Loki studies the inscriptions. "It would appear that the lower chamber contains the bodies of the royal family."

Looking back to Aramas, Riadon remarks, "I do not detect any traps."

Pushing through the group, Kriv says, "I'll go first."

With the party close behind, Kriv moves quickly down the steps into the stone chamber, which is about half the size of the upper chamber. It is dimly lit; two oil-burning lamps cast a soft yellow glow throughout the room. At the far end sit two sarcophagi, one lamp atop each, blocking each of the two corridors that appear to lead out of the chamber. The floor here is littered with the rubble of broken and ransacked sarcophagi interspersed with human bones and rotted rodent-eaten garments. A heavy stench of fish oil permeates the air. Aramas redraws his sword and directs the others to be ready.

As the party cautiously moves toward the sarcophagi, Loki takes a few moments to examine the inscriptions. "If I am reading this correctly, there are two more rooms down here. One appears to be some sort of temple. Not sure about the other."

Aramas asks Aria if she can determine where the magic source is located. She points at the wall between the two corridors. "Somewhere on the other side of that wall."

Flail drawn, Kriv cautiously continues down the hallway. He observes that the two hallways seem to reconverge beyond the center wall and that a third sarcophagus blocks the exit just beyond. He can't help but notice the almost overpowering stench of fish oil.

Turning to the others, he comments, "The odor is too strong for two small lamps—"

Suddenly, two hobgoblins emerge from behind the two sarcophagi, releasing a hail of arrows into the narrow chamber.

With his flail swinging over his head, Kriv charges forward and attempts to leap onto one attacker. As he steps onto the sarcophagus, the lid shatters, causing the lamp to fall into the unseen oil within, sending flames in all directions. Unfazed by the inferno, the dragonborn quickly moves through the flames.

The hobgoblin drops his bow, grabs his battle axe, and quickly retreats toward the third sarcophagus with Kriv close behind.

With the unexpected retreat of his partner, the other hobgoblin drops his bow and attempts to remove the lid on the second sarcophagus in the hope of igniting the oil inside. However, just as the lid begins to move, Loki's hammer finds its mark, knocking the stunned attacker prone.

Realizing that he is about to be overrun, the hobgoblin rolls to his right and reaches for his battle axe, only to be stopped by the searing pain of Aramas's blade cleaving his shoulder. Covered in blood, the hobgoblin looks up in horror and attempts to fend off another blow. However, in the blink of an eye, Aramas raises his sword and thrusts its blade deep into the creature's chest. The blank stare of the hobgoblin's eyes and the shallow gurgling sound of air escaping through its now blood-clogged throat confirm that the creature will cause no more trouble.

As Aramas withdraws his sword, Loki leaps over the sarcophagus and advances on the remaining foe. Realizing that he cannot reach the sarcophagus, the hobgoblin turns, raises his battle axe, and awaits his fate.

"Throw down your weapon and we shall spare your life," commands Kriv.

For a brief moment, the creature contemplates the offer then sharply responds, "Death comes regardless. If you do not kill me, the Master will."

"Who is the Master?"

"The one who will ensure that you never leave this tomb."

"Where are the boys?" asks Loki.

In a shrill, high-pitched screech, the hobgoblin replies, "Where you soon will be." With the look of impending death in his dark black eyes, the creature charges wildly into the party. In a manner of seconds, it is over.

As Aramas turns to see what has happened to Riadon and Aria, the Guardian appears over a pile of bones near the now burning sarcophagus. Aria and Riadon remain motionless near the stairs.

"What do you want?" asks Aramas.

Like a mother protecting its young, the Guardian moves from one set of bones to the next, hovering briefly over each. Aramas again asks, "What do you want?"

With an expression of pain, the Guardian turns and slowly drifts toward Aramas. "You understand. Honor them." For a moment, nothing is said, all eyes focused on the exchange. Extending his hand, the Guardian touches Aramas's shoulder; a cold chill rushes through his body. The revenant, now an almost shimmering blue in color, again implores, "Honor them."

With his eyes pensively focused on the Guardian, Aramas reverently drops to one knee, extends his sword, hilt first, and bows his head. Hovering over him, the Guardian moves his hand to the top of Aramas's head. As he does, brilliant silvery sparks of light shoot throughout his being, changing color from shades of shimmering blue to white and then a silvery luminescence.

Aramas raises his head then turns to Loki. "Check to see if there is any oil in the far sarcophagus."

Without hesitation, Loki moves to the sarcophagus. Joined by Kriv, the two carefully remove the lid.

"It's empty."

Standing up, Aramas motions to the others. "Carefully pick up all of the bones and place them in the sarcophagus." Then he reverently takes a step back and bows his head slightly. "Sire, may your family now rest in peace."

As the others begin to retrieve the bones, the Guardian slowly drifts back toward the stairwell. Hovering momentarily above the bottom step, it turns toward Aramas and points to the step. "Seek within what will aid you on your quest." Then, as suddenly as it appeared, the Guardian fades away.

Aramas quickly moves to the stairwell to examine the bottom step. He finds nothing out of the ordinary, so he kneels and runs his fingers along the seams between the lower step and the walls and then the upper step and the floor. While running his fingers along the base of the step, he notices what appears to be a small vertical opening where the face of the step meets the wall. After he brushes away the dirt and particles of stone collected there, he inserts his fingers into the small opening. With a downward slide and a slight tug, he is able to remove a piece of the step's face to reveal a hidden compartment, inside of which rests a small vial of liquid.

As Loki turns to retrieve several more bones, he notices Aramas kneeling at the base of the stairwell. "What did you find?"

"I am not sure." Aramas opens the vial. "It appears to an odorless, orange-colored liquid." After a few more seconds, he adds, "It appears to be a healing potion." Resealing the vial, he places it in his pouch then moves to rejoin Loki and the rest of the party.

After they complete their task, Kriv turns to Aramas. "What now?"

Aramas gestures to the left wall. "Place both of the sarcophagi against the wall so as not to block our retreat." As he proceeds toward the end of the hall, he adds, "The boys are alive and are being held with another."

Riadon leans over to Loki and asks, "How does he know that?"

With a twinkle in his eye and a sly all-knowing grin, Loki replies, "You'll get used to it."

About twenty feet past the third sarcophagus, the stone hallway ends at the opening to a narrow tunnel that appears to have been carved out of the surrounding rock. It meanders about fifty feet before leading into a large natural underground cavern. While there are no torches, the glow of the greenish blue phosphorescence that clings to the walls provides more than sufficient light. Water droplets falling from the ceiling sparkle like emeralds as they melt into transparent mirror-like pools below. The air is warm, moist, and heavy; the smell of mildew hangs like the smoke of a dying campfire.

The cavern itself is half the size of the main chamber above, but its shape is odd, likely carved out of the earth many years earlier by the water. The tunnel from the hallway into the cavern is uneven and slick from the dripping water. However, based on the number of tracks, it has been well trodden.

At the entrance to the cavern, the party can see the glow of candles off to the right in what appears to be some sort of temple. A faint voice can be heard chanting. Shadows dance along the walls in the flickering light. To the left of the temple is a large rusted iron door; a large oaken beam bars it from being opened. In the center of the door is a carved likeness of a devil, its eyes glowing with a faint green light. The door is not guarded, but judging from the number of tracks leading to it as well as the scraped dirt along its base, it has been opened recently.

Aramas motions to the others to follow him. "I believe what we have come for lies beyond that door."

A few steps into the cavern, Aria whispers, "The scrying has stopped."

But before she can say anything further, a raspy voice calls out from the temple, "Do not stop now. I've waited a long time for this." What had earlier appeared to be a shadow dancing on the temple walls now takes the form of an elf humanoid in a long red-hooded robe. Silhouetted by the flickering candles, the figure moves into the open doorway. "I see that since our last encounter, you have been joined by some new companions."

"What encounter? I have no recollection of any such meeting," replies Aramas. "We have come for the blacksmith's sons. Release them, and we shall be on our way."

With a cackling laugh, the figure points at Aramas. "You took something from me; I want it back. Bring it to me, and I will release the boys. Do not, and I will kill them!"

"Old man, your mind is going much quicker than your age should allow. We have nothing of yours."

In a harsh crescendo, the figure shouts, "The opal. I want the opal!"

Looking up at Aramas, Loki asks, "How is it he knows of the opal?"

"Of what opal does he speak?" asks Aria.

Ignoring the questions, Aramas repeats, "Release the boys, and we shall be on our way."

"Enough! Once you have paid for killing my dragon, I will get what I want." Then, with a sweeping motion of his arms, four heavily armed skeletons appear before him, each wearing an iron helmet and bearing large scimitars and heavy shields.

The fey raises his outstretched arms and slowly ascends above the skeletons, drifting back into the temple before he comes to rest atop a ten-foot-high platform in the center of the chamber. A bright greenish-blue mist swirls around his feet as an eerie green light emanates from the numerous carvings of rampaging devils that adorn the platform's sides.

Glaring down from his perch, his eyes burning bright red, he motions to the skeletons to attack. Looking directly at Aramas, he adds, "Prepare to join those whom you have just interred." As they begin their advance, fiery beams shoot from the eyes of the fey, momentarily dazing both Aria and Kriv.

Loki extends one hand toward the skeletons and calls out, "By the power of Moradin." Like a bolt of lightning shooting earthward from the heavens above, a pulse of blue radiance shoots from his outstretched hand, striking the adversaries and hurling them twenty feet into the wall behind them with shards of bone flying in all directions.

Not wishing to waste the temporary advantage, Aramas rushes forward, sword held high. His greatsword smashes the shield of the nearest foe, pushing it away from the others. He then turns to the other two skeletons, and with a quick motion of his right hand, hurls them fifteen feet into the adjacent wall, each engulfed by a blue radiance.

Motioning toward the now-stunned adversaries, Aramas shouts, "Aria, Kriv, take care of them!"

The fey, surprised by the ferocity of the counterattack, calls upon his dark powers to rejuvenate the severely damaged minions. With a sharp motion of his hand, the skeletons rise from the floor and attempt to regroup.

As Aramas moves to press his advantage, Loki hurls his war hammer at the overwhelmed adversaries. He strikes the closest, smashing his war hammer through its chest, bones scattering in all directions. Then his hammer ricochets into the shield of the next, knocking the undead creature to the floor before returning to the hand of its master. As if possessed, Loki charges into the fray.

The skeleton turns to deflect the advance. However, before it can raise its sword, Loki's war hammer crashes through the creature's skull.

Aria and Kriv advance on the remaining skeletons as Riadon quickly moves to the right wall of the cave. He's experienced nothing like this and does not wish to draw the wrath of the fey, so he slowly moves from shadow to shadow toward the temple entrance.

Aria points to the nearest skeleton and unleashes a devastating bolt of dark crackling energy that explodes the creature's shield. At the same time, flail swirling over his head, Kriv charges the stunned foe.

However, before he can finish the attack, the second skeleton, with a sweeping motion of its hand, pushes Kriv away from his target and knocks him to the ground. Crawling backward, shield held high, Kriv attempts to retreat, but the skeleton's scimitar relentlessly smashes into Kriv's outstretched shield.

Aria unleashes another bolt of energy and temporarily halts the creature's advance.

Suddenly, from out of nowhere, the two skeletons are engulfed in a torrent of knives. As they turn to see who has attacked them, Riadon's longsword decapitates one of the attackers, allowing Kriv to regain his footing. Flanked and outnumbered, the remaining skeleton attempts to return to the safety of the fey.

Loki and Aramas move quickly to prevent its escape. As they pass before the opening to the temple, their advance is halted by a crashing sound behind them. They turn to see that the oaken beam that had earlier blocked the entrance to the other room now lies on the floor.

With eyes glaring at the intruders, the fey lifts his staff and strikes the floor twice. Almost immediately, the sounds of heavy footsteps and stone grinding on stone can be heard from behind the iron door.

Loki shouts to the others, "I think we've got company!"

As the fey's chant intensifies, so does the light emanating from the eyes of the carved devil on the door. The light grows from a faint greenish glow to a bright, burning yellowish-green that eventually engulfs the image but does not consume it. From behind the door, the sound of grinding stone grows louder.

With another sweeping motion of his right hand, the fey again pounds his staff on the floor; the iron door opens. Loki and Aramas stand in stunned silence as two large stone golems emerge from the room.

Loki again shouts, "A little help here!"

As the two prepare to engage the golems, Aria, Kriv, and Riadon corner and destroy the remaining skeleton. However, before they can rejoin Loki and Aramas, the fey conjures a bright yellow cloud that extends from floor to ceiling to block their advance.

"What do we do now?" asks Riadon.

"Hold your breath!" shouts Kriv, at which point he rushes into the cloud. He emerges on the other side apparently unscathed.

Looking over to Aria, Riadon remarks, "See you on the other side." However, upon exiting the cloud, searing pain suddenly shoots through his body. The flesh on his uncovered skin blisters and begins to turn gray.

Kriv shouts to Aria, "Cover your face and hands! The cloud appears to attack unprotected flesh!"

Within seconds Aria too passes through the cloud, and like Kriv, she does not appear to exhibit any ill effects of the gas.

Turning to Riadon, Kriv cups his hands around Riadon's and recites a short prayer. Within seconds, the pain dissipates and the color of his skin returns. "What doubts we may have had of you have been dispelled. Good work back there!" Then, seeing the golems, Kriv adds, "There is no time to waste."

Like the unspoken bond that exists between identical twins, Aramas and Loki have become capable of anticipating the other's every move; they can feel each other's pain. In combat, one's weakness becomes the other's strength, and together, their abilities exceed the sum of the two. Soldiers of fortune, with no obvious purpose, they have grown accustomed to wandering from town to town in search of adventure. Having experienced the plight of the oppressed, more often than not, they found themselves fighting for nothing more than a hot meal, a warm bed, and a roof over their heads, or in some cases, a grateful thank you.

In the intervening years, it was inevitable that the two would come upon several like-minded individuals: adventurers who have also experienced the taskmaster's lash or the bitter taste of servitude and were therefore equally inclined to offer their skills on behalf of those less fortunate.

As news of the party spread, more often than not, the lords of the province were not generally inclined to welcome the party into their realms. Having been denied entry into several small villages—and without a good payday in over a fortnight—the small band happened upon Spring Green. Whether by fate or the unseen hand of some omniscient being, Alissa learned of their presence and summoned them to the outpost's keep. She offered them the opportunity to recover a few stolen gems and gold pieces in exchange for a handsome reward and the promise of food and lodging as long as they were in her service.

The party gladly accepted the offer. Unfortunately, what had initially been presented as a relatively simple task ended with the loss of five members of the party and numerous unanswered questions. Until a few days ago, dragons existed only in tales spun by bards around campfires. Now they find themselves fighting creatures possessing powers beyond anything they had ever experienced.

Aramas shouts out above the entropy around them, "Kriv, you and Riadon try to flank them." Then, glancing back at the trio, he says, "Aria, try to keep the fey occupied!"

Moving quickly to the right, Aramas and Loki engage the first golem. They strike simultaneously, temporarily halting the creature's advance. The two quickly flank it and successfully strike a second time. Swinging wildly, the golem counterattacks and knocks Loki to the ground. As it turns to swing at Aramas, Loki attempts to regain his footing; however, before he can do so, the creature again smashes him to the floor.

With Loki dazed and unable to move, the golem again turns its attention to Aramas. Ducking to avoid a similar fate, Aramas shouts to Aria, "Distract him!"

Aria swirls her ashen rod over her head, creating a cloud of darkness that completely engulfs the golem. Within the impenetrable darkness, flying, swirling, fanged shadows chip away at the creature. As it attempts to escape the cloud, Aramas grabs Loki and quickly drags him out of danger. Kneeling beside him, he takes off his glove and places the palm of his hand on Loki's forehead. Almost instantaneously, a blue radiance shimmers from beneath his palm, its healing powers flowing into his motionless ally.

Then, almost as quickly, Loki opens his eyes. "Did we get him?"

From the left, Kriv and Riadon advance on the second golem. As Riadon maneuvers to get behind the creature, Kriv exhales an explosive blast of energy.

Stunned, but far from being immobilized, the golem continues its advance.

Kriv charges, using his flail to smash the creature's left knee and force it to the ground. As it attempts to stand, Riadon's longsword crashes into its neck. The golem swings wildly and strikes Riadon, propelling him into the nearby wall. Before it can direct another attack at him, Kriv delivers a decisive blow to the creature's injured knee, successfully separating the lower leg from the upper. Unable to stand, the golem panics and begins to swing uncontrollably at its attackers.

Realizing that its companion has been critically injured, the other golem turns and advances on Kriv.

With Kriv about to be pinned between the two stone giants, Aramas stands and charges. "Kriv, behind you!"

Unable to get out of the way, Kriv finds himself trapped and unable to maneuver. As the golem pummels him to the floor, Aramas's sword slashes into the creature's back. The golem turns to respond but is met by the crushing force of Loki's hammer. Reeling, the golem stumbles backward. It trips over its fallen companion and then comes crashing to the floor. Pressing their advantage, Aramas, Loki, and Riadon swarm over the fallen foe.

No longer trapped, Kriv attempts to stand, but a golem again smashes him to the ground. Having lost all feeling in his right leg, he claws at the rock floor in an attempt to crawl from beneath the creature's grasp. Kriv cries out in excruciating pain before finally drifting into unconsciousness. The golem slowly pulls his motionless body closer.

While Aria continues to fend off any attempt by the fey to assist its minions, Aramas and Loki, having reduced the other golem to a pile of rubble, now charge the remaining adversary. Before it is able to deliver a coup de grâce, Loki's hammer crashes into the creature's back. Surprised, the golem drops Kriv and turns to meet its doom.

Raising his sword, Aramas shouts, "Pull Kriv out of there!" before his sword slashes deeply into the creature's neck. Instinctively, the golem grabs his neck with one hand and attempts to extricate itself from the vicious onslaught, but the blows inflict greater damage with each strike.

Riadon wastes no time and pulls Kriv to safety and out of sight of the fey. Understanding that he has done all he can for his fallen comrade, he turns and rushes back into the fight to approach from the golem's blind side and plunge his dagger deep into its heart. The creature writhes in pain, all aimless flailing halted, before it slowly leans forward and slumps to the ground.

Aramas turns to Loki. "Tend to Kriv. Riadon, follow me!"

As if on cue, the fey halts his attack on Aria. From atop the misty platform he remarks, "You are formidable adversaries . . . but I still hold the two boys."

Aramas replies, "Release the boys, and we will spare your life. Do not, and I will send you back to the abyss that spawned you."

Laughing, the fey replies, "Foolish pawns. You have no idea who you're dealing with." He once again pounds his staff on the floor, and bolts of black energy surge from the misty cloud in all directions. "Give me the opal!"

Kriv moves into the entrance with Loki and responds, "We cannot give you what we do not possess."

With a sly chuckle, the fey looks back at Aramas. "You have not told them."

"Told us what?" asks Aria.

Again he directs his comments to Aramas. "It was wise of you not to tell them about the dragon and its gem. But then, based on your reaction, I suspect that Brevek did not tell *you* everything." He moves a little closer to the edge of the platform, fire dancing in his eyes. "There are many who seek the gem, greater and more powerful than even I. Like yourselves, I too am just a pawn, but unlike you, I have embraced what is to come."

He strikes his staff to the floor, and shrieks of tortured pain can be heard emanating from the other room. Then, slowly bowing his head, he drifts back into the center of the platform. After a brief pause, and the recitation of several nondescript arcane words, he again raises his head, his eyes now fully consumed by fire, and points his staff at the party. "I will be sure to send your condolences to Adwin."

No sooner have the words crossed his lips than a searing bolt of fiery energy shoots from the staff.

Almost instinctively, Aria swings her staff with a downward motion to the left, deflecting the bolt harmlessly into the chamber wall. She shouts, "You must get close enough to strike him. I cannot penetrate his aura!"

Kriv, Aramas, and Loki charge the platform. Unable to reach the fey, Aramas looks to Kriv. "Lift me onto the platform."

Loki interrupts, "You will be defenseless!"

He looks at his longtime friend. "It is the only way."

Acknowledging the response, the two propel Aramas upward. As he struggles to pull himself onto the platform, the fey attempts to take advantage of the opportunity before him. However, as he turns to attack, a misty hand reaches from within the platform and grabs his leg.

As Aramas pulls himself onto the platform, a familiar figure materializes, placing itself between the two combatants. "I will have my revenge!"

Once Aramas has regained his footing, the Guardian slowly drifts to the side. Raising his sword, Aramas hears a faint voice say, "Destroy the staff."

Aramas wastes no time and presses the attack. As he swings, the fey raises his staff to deflect the blow. At the moment of impact, the staff explodes, sending thousands of burning embers throughout the chamber and a wave of necrotic energy emanating outward. Eyes that were only moments earlier blazing balls of fire turn as black as obsidian. Flesh appears to begin to rot, eye sockets becoming hollow and sunken.

The fey draws a dagger and lunges at his foe, but as he does, Aria strikes him with a fiery bolt of energy. As he bursts into flames, the fey gives out a bloodcurdling scream then slowly sinks to his knees; the room is engulfed with the putrid smell of burning flesh.

Aramas again raises his sword, and with one swift motion, ends his misery. The fey's head falls to the platform and then the floor below. With justice served, the misty revenant disappears.

They regroup at the base of the platform. Aramas motions to the others. "Let's finish this!" They move swiftly out of the temple chamber and into the cavern toward the prison cell where muted cries of agony can be heard from within.

The room is not large, about forty feet wide by twenty feet deep, the air stale and moldy. Along each of the two side walls stand three stone statues similar to the two golems that emerged from the cell earlier, in between which are two empty spaces that apparently had once been occupied by the now-defeated foes.

In the center of the room is a large greenish glowing circle. Geometric runes adorn its outer rim, exuding a misty emerald radiance that slowly rises toward the ceiling. As Aramas had predicted, three prisoners lay shackled within, two humans and one dragonborn. While the dragonborn appears to be in fairly good shape, the same cannot be said for the two boys. Starved and tortured, they do not move.

"Come no closer," shouts the dragonborn. "The room is trapped."

Aramas extends his arms outward to make sure no one enters. "We have come to rescue you. What is your name, and how did you get here?"

"I am Patron. I, along with five companions, was sent here to rescue the two boys." Coughing and then spitting up blood, he adds, "I am the only one left."

"Who sent you?"

"Brevek!"

Loki looks up at Aramas. "Why that . . ."

Raising his hand to interrupt, Aramas continues. "Are the boys alive?"

"Barely. I fear that if they do not get attention soon, they will not see another day."

Riadon interjects, "You mentioned traps. What kind?"

"All I know is that any attempt to remove us from this circle will result in the demise of this chamber."

Turning to Aria, Aramas asks, "Can you determine what kind of magic protects the circle?"

Without answering, Aria closes her eyes and murmurs a ritual chant. After a few moments, she opens her eyes. "It appears to be an ancient warding circle created by those of my kind centuries ago. However, it appears to have been modified."

"How so?"

"It would appear that the circle has not only been converted into a holding area, but it can also be used as a teleportation circle."

Aramas interrupts, "There was a similar circle engraved in the surface of the platform in the temple chamber."

"That would seem to make sense, as I detect that the teleportation power is not very strong."

Turning back toward Patron, Aramas asks, "Can the boys help in their escape?"

"They will be of little help."

Aramas turns to Riadon. "Can you determine if there are any traps protecting the entrance to the room? I do not want to awaken any more of the golems."

Taking a few moments to study the area around the door and immediately inside the room, Riadon replies, "I can find nothing unusual." Hesitating for a moment, he takes a deep breath, motions to the others to stay put, and enters the room. Nothing happens. With a sly grin on his face, he whispers to himself, "See, that wasn't so difficult."

Riadon carefully examines the area between the entrance and the circle and then cautiously approaches. At its outer rim, he turns back to the party. "I can find no traps between the doorway and the circle.

However, it would appear that there are two traps protecting it. I'm afraid that both will need to be disarmed."

"Can you tell what kind of traps?" asks Aramas.

"No, and I'm afraid that if I try to do so, I may inadvertently set off one or both of them."

Patron interrupts, "Earlier, shortly after I was captured, the one boy said something about the ceiling."

Aramas turns to Loki. "Do you sense anything unusual about the ceiling?"

While Loki turns his attention to the ceiling, Kriv asks, "Now what?"

Pausing for a moment, Aramas looks back to Patron. "Are each of you shackled separately or together?"

"Separately."

"If we get you out of the circle, can you walk?"

"Yes, but not much more."

"What are you thinking?" asks Aria.

As Aramas is about to answer, Loki interrupts, "Whatever it is, you'll have to do it quickly. It wouldn't take much to bring the entire hillside down around us!"

Aramas looks up at the rocks above. "I suspected as much. There's far too much water finding its way down here. Kriv and Loki, you're with me. Aria, I need you and Riadon to make sure that this passageway remains open."

Then Aramas cautiously moves into the room and to the edge of the circle. He directs Kriv and Loki to take up positions on either side of him then motions to Patron. "I want you to move the boys as close to us as possible. I then want you to stand up and do the same." Pointing to where he wants each boy to be placed, he continues, "On my signal, Kriv and I will grab the two boys and attempt to make it out of here before we get buried. Loki will help you."

"I was blindfolded when they brought me down here. It might help to know where we're going."

"As you leave this room, off to the far right corner of the cavern, about forty feet away, you'll see a passageway. Head straight for that. Once in the passageway, follow it into the burial chamber."

Patron sarcastically quips, "Appropriate name."

With a smirk, Aramas continues. "Do not stop until you are up the stairs at the far end of the burial chamber, understood?"

Surveying the area one last time, Aramas calmly asks, "Is everyone ready?" Receiving no negative replies, he shouts, "Now!"

Almost in unison, Aramas and Kriv reach down and grab the limp bodies below them. As if loading sacks of grain, the boys are thrown over their shoulders, triggering the traps. The earth around the room begins to quake with dirt and small debris falling from every crevice. As Aramas and Kriv make their way toward the door, Loki grabs Patron around the waist and follows as closely as possible. The floor below them is heaving and shifting, the tremors increasing in intensity, dislodging large pieces of the walls and ceiling.

Aramas clears the threshold followed closely by Kriv. He exits the room in time to witness the destruction of the temple chamber. The central podium is now buried beneath tons of rock, timbers, coffins, and their skeletal contents. Like a large wave crashing against the shore, dust billows out of the chamber and engulfs everything within the cavern.

After what seems like eons, Loki and Patron finally emerge coughing and covered in dust. Looking up at Riadon, a panting Loki exclaims, "He's a little heavier than I thought!"

Without a moment's hesitation, Aria and Riadon lift Patron's arms over their shoulders and head toward the tunnel, Loki right behind. Before the party can reach the center of the cavern, the ceiling comes crashing to the floor. The dust is now so thick that the greenish luminescence that once illuminated the cavern quickly fades into darkness.

Drawn by the light still visible from the tunnel, Kriv reaches its entrance and then waits to ensure that everyone is accounted for. Aramas passes first, then Aria, Riadon, and Patron followed closely by Loki. Kriv turns and enters the tunnel just as the remainder of the ceiling in the cavern comes crashing to the floor. The choking dust, combined with the shifting and heaving wet floor, makes the way extremely difficult.

Aramas continues through the darkness and is the first to reach the relative safety of the torch-lit burial chamber. Proceeding past the two sarcophagi, he stops at the junction of the two corridors to ensure that everyone has made it out safely. As he peers into the tunnel's darkness, he momentarily drifts into a state of semiconsciousness, and scenes of what might have been had the sarcophagi not been moved flash before his eyes.

"What are you waiting for?" asks Loki. Jolted back to reality, Aramas looks down at his friend then to the far end of the corridor where Aria and Riadon are helping Patron up the stairs. "Did everyone get out?"

"Just waiting for you."

He places his hand on Loki's shoulder. "You are a welcome sight, my friend." With a nod of his head toward the stairwell, the two rush to join the others. As they ascend the stairs, billowing clouds of dust rush into the chamber as the remainder of the tunnel collapses. No one will enter these caverns ever again.

They emerge from the burial chamber. Aramas bends over and lies the young boy on the floor. To his right, Riadon is attempting to free Patron. To his left, Kriv attends to the other boy.

Aramas kneels over the lifeless body and places his ear just above the boy's mouth, listening for any indication of life. Sitting back, he turns to Loki.

"He's not breathing!" He places his hand on the boy's chest, blue radiance emanating from every finger as Aramas attempts unsuccessfully to revive him. He tries a second time, but again there is no response. "I cannot heal him!"

Loki kneels beside the boy, places his hands together and, as he has done so many times before, recites an ancient prayer, blue radiance growing brighter with each word. Placing one hand on the boy's chest, the other on his forehead, Loki again recites the prayer. Nothing happens.

He pauses for a moment then repeats the prayer. Again, nothing happens.

Staring down at the scarred and bloodied body, Loki slowly bows his head, eyes closed, right hand on the boy's forehead, and recites another prayer. After a moment of silence, he turns to Aramas. "He is gone. I cannot save him."

"Is there nothing that can be done?" implores Aramas.

"While I can prepare his body such that he slips no further into death, it will take someone with greater powers than I to bring him back from the other side."

"Then do so. It will be difficult to explain . . ."

Kriv interrupts. "I have been able to revive this one."

Coughing, and temporarily blinded, the boy grabs Kriv and tries to sit up. "Where is Argon?" Searching frantically with his other arm, he again asks, "Where is Argon?"

Moving to his side, and in a calm voice, Aramas replies, "You are going to be all right. Lay back and rest a moment."

"Rest can wait. Where is my brother?"

Aramas looks toward Loki, who has been quietly preparing the body, then back to the boy. "Your brother has crossed to a better place."

With anguish in every word, the boy replies, "No! It should have been me. He was the gifted one."

As Aramas supports the boy, Kriv places his thumb and finger over his eyes. In draconic, he recites a short prayer. Before it is complete, the boy's vision slowly returns.

Aramas asks, "You then are Arron?"

"Yes, youngest son of Adwin of Spring Green." Pausing for a moment, vision now fully restored, he looks over to his brother as Loki continues to administer to the body. "What is he doing?"

"He is putting Argon's body into a state of suspended animation."

"What does that mean?"

"It means that your brother's body will remain in its current state. For a period of time, it will not deteriorate or decay. While *we* cannot help him, there may be others who can."

He briefly rubs his eyes to wipe away the tears. "Is Sorac dead?"

He nods. "He will bother you no more."

As Aramas and Kriv help the boy to his feet, Riadon exclaims, "Success!" Then, they hear the clatter of chains falling to the floor.

A newly freed Patron stands. "Thank you. I feared that I would not see this day." After some congratulatory slaps on his back, Patron looks over to Arron. "I am sorry that I was not able to complete my mission."

"But you have," replies a raspy voice from the far end of the room. Standing just inside the mausoleum entrance, the Guardian stands erect holding two gem-encrusted scimitars and a gleaming set of armor. He offers the scimitars to Patron. "You may have need of these."

Patron hesitates for a moment then walks over to collect his weapons and armor.

The transaction complete, the Guardian drifts over to Aramas. "Young Paladin, your path was determined long ago; your destiny is incomplete. Do not shy away from what lies ahead."

Slowly turning to each in the party then back at Aramas, he nods his head and remarks, "Thank you. I can now rest in peace." The revenant crosses his arms over his chest then slowly disappears into a twinkling effervescence of silvery light that slowly drifts toward the ceiling. Silence fills the room.

After a few moments, Aramas turns to the party. "We have a long journey ahead."

Loki quips, "And a barmaid awaiting her reward."

CHAPTER 5

THE QUEST BEGINS

The journey back to Spring Green is not a pleasant one. Not much is said, and any questions concerning the gem or the dragon are ignored. Two days of torrential rain, heavy winds, and muddy roads do not make the journey any easier.

Aramas blames himself for their failure to bring both boys back alive. As his mind replays the confrontation with Sorac, the knowledge that Brevek was involved—and the possibility that Allissa may have deliberately withheld critical information—enrages him, a rage that is only intensified whenever he looks at Patron, the last remaining party member of an earlier ill-fated rescue attempt.

A dragonborn ranger, Patron had immigrated from the far south of the Saltan Desert after the passing of his parents. Like many of his kind who had been forced from their homeland during the Dragon Wars, safe refuge was usually nothing more than a temporary illusion. Although they had been welcomed, it seems that acceptance turned to discrimination, condemnation, and then persecution. Outnumbered and with no homeland to which he could return, self-preservation had dictated that Patron take up the sword. He became an expert swordsman, especially proficient wielding dual blades simultaneously.

Like Aramas and Loki, he had become accustomed to traveling from town to town, often offering his talents to the highest bidder. He'd met several like-minded adventurers along the way, and when his party came upon Spring Green a few weeks earlier, the offer to rescue the two boys seemed simple enough. The promise of one hundred gold pieces each made the decision even easier.

When they emerge from the forest onto the open plains, the party is greeted by their first rays of sunlight since they arrived in Forest Glen. Light filters through a dense layer of cloud cover to highlight the patchwork of fields and farms that lie before them. Unlike the trip west, which had been conspicuously devoid of any human activity, they spot a few farmers preparing their fields for planting and shepherds tending their flocks. Travelers too are again moving along the road with a chipper and upbeat demeanor.

It isn't long before the silhouette of Spring Green is visible on the horizon. Aramas turns to Loki and asks, "How is the boy doing?"

Loki quickly glances back at the boy. "He still hasn't said a word."

"What's he doing?"

"Just staring off into the distance."

Aramas shakes his head then, briefly closing his eyes, murmurs, "Father, help me find the words to tell Adwin."

Renewed activity appears all around the main entrance to Spring Green. Farmers, traders, and travelers of all ethnicities fill the road. Long lines form at the gate as an undermanned contingent of guards attempt to question the new arrivals and inspect the contents of their wagons. The congestion and chaos are made only worse by the quagmire of mud left by the recent rains. Not wishing to delay his burden any longer than necessary, Aramas directs the party past the lines, displeasing those who have been frustrated by the long wait. One of the guards responds to the ever-growing cry from the crowd and steps forward to prevent the party from entering. "What makes you so special?" he asks.

Not amused, Aramas replies, "We have urgent business with the blacksmith. Stand aside!"

However, before he can push past the guard, the captain steps forward. "We were told to expect you." Then motioning to the keep, he continues, "The mistress of the keep has directed that you be escorted to her chamber immediately."

"As I was telling the guard, we have urgent business elsewhere."

"I have my orders. You *will* follow me." Five of Alissa's personal guards immediately surround the party.

Just as Aramas reaches for his sword, a calm voice calls from within the gate, "That will not be necessary. I will ensure that they get to the keep."

Adwin steps through the gathering group of gawkers and approaches. "Captain, I can assure you that Alissa will not hold you responsible for any delay that I might cause by welcoming the safe return of my friends."

Taking a step back, the captain respectfully nods and sharply places his hand over his heart. "Please accept my apology. I was unaware of your interest in these travelers." Then, he motions for the others to resume their formation, he snaps his heels together, and he quickly retreats within the city walls, shouting to the crowd to disperse.

"Father!"

Adwin rushes to the wagon. "Arron, my son. Are you okay?"

Still weakened from his wounds and with tears streaming down his gaunt face, Arron falls into his father's arms.

Adwin pulls his son's shattered body to him. "I did not believe that I would see this day. Bahamut has answered our prayers. We are truly blessed!"

After an embrace that seems to last forever, Adwin turns to Aramas. "And what of Argon?"

Hesitating, Aramas moves to the wagon, reaches over its side, and slowly uncovers the lifeless body. The others reverently gather around.

Aramas quietly replies, "We were unable to save him."

Adwin lets go of Arron and slowly moves closer to examine the body. His eyes beginning to water, he leans forward, lowers his head, and places his outstretched palm on the boy's chest. After a moment, an expression of surprise comes to his face. Looking back at Aramas, he asks, "Who administered to my son?"

Loki briefly hesitates then replies, "I did."

He looks up at Loki, smiling. "You have done well. I will be forever in your debt."

Puzzled, Aramas responds, "I do not understand. We were only able to save one of your sons."

"I asked that you return my sons to me. You have done so."

"But . . ."

"Not only did you bring Arron back alive, but because of your friend's actions, I now have the opportunity to have both my sons back."

"How is that possible?" asks Riadon.

"There are those within our walls who possess knowledge of things beyond our comprehension. It will not be long before my son again walks among us."

Adwin places his hands on Aramas's shoulders. "Thank you." Then, after a brief embrace, and with apprehension in his voice, he adds, "Much has changed since your departure. We must talk before you meet with Alissa."

Adwin turns to the others. "You must be tired. First, we must take my sons to the temple. Then, once you have had some time to quench your thirst, and I have delivered what was promised for the return of my sons, we will talk." Then he looks at Patron. "Dragonborn, while we have not met, your aura appears bright and virtuous, your intentions honest and true. If Aramas has placed his trust in you, so do I."

Patron nods respectfully in reply.

Then with a look of chagrin, Adwin turns to Riadon. "You possess the lives of a cat. However, if not for the party with which you now travel, you would soon find yourself chained and shackled in the village square."

Aramas interjects, "Without his help, we would not have been able to return your sons."

Adwin glances at Aramas, then back at Riadon, then admonishes, "During your stay here, you would be wise to refrain from your trade and stay close to Aramas." After a brief pause, he adds, "You too will be rewarded for your help."

Figuring it would be best to say nothing, Riadon nods his understanding.

After he leaves his sons at the temple of Bahamut, Adwin leads the party to his home. As he walks through the door, with joyous exclamation, he shouts, "Anya, we have much to celebrate. Please bring whatever our guests desire."

With a twinkle in his eye and a boyish grin, Loki asks, "Do you still have any of that apple wine?" He looks over to Riadon and Patron. "It is the nectar of the gods."

Laughing, then turning to Aramas, Adwin replies, "Maybe it is good that Alissa awaits your return, lest your friend spend too much time partaking of his 'nectar.'" Everyone else joins in the laughter.

After a moment and in a serious tone, Adwin directs the party to be seated. "We do not have much time." Once seated, he addresses Aramas. "What do the others know of the dragon?"

Hesitating, Aramas replies, "Nothing."

"And the gem?"

"They need know nothing."

Interrupting, Kriv exclaims, "You mean, there really was a dragon?"

Riadon asks, "What about the gem?"

A bit annoyed, Aramas continues. "The fewer that know the better!"

Silence permeates the party; all eyes focus on Aramas and Adwin.

"Aramas, just as it was not by chance that you and Loki were brought to Spring Green, it was not by chance that this party has come together. Search your heart. You know that what I say is true."

Aramas bows his head and stares angrily at the table, his fingers nervously tapping.

Adwin turns to the others. "A few weeks ago, a party of seven entered the catacombs below the city in the hope of retrieving a substantial purse of gems that had been stolen from Alissa's treasury. Among the gems was a rather large opal. The existence of the gem is known only to a few, and while no one seems to know its significance, a small circle of trusted agents understand that it possesses some sort of magical power and have therefore sworn to protect it. While I do not know the gem's origin, I can tell you that it has been secretly held in the treasury since the time of Alissa's great grandfather."

"What does that have to do with a dragon?" asks Kriv.

"All in good time."

"May I interrupt to pour the wine?" asks Anya.

"Forgive me. Yes, please," responds Adwin.

Once the glasses have been filled, Anya turns to Adwin. "By your leave."

Adwin nods then continues. "For a time, and like the recent raids along the Forest Road, a small guild of thieves had been targeting local gem dealers and jewelers within the city's walls. After the theft from the treasury, Alissa's guards conducted numerous searches, all to no avail. Further, extensive searches of everyone entering and leaving the outpost yielded similar results. Dissatisfied with the lack of results, she hired Aramas, Loki, and five others to retrieve the gems and put an end to the guild. Without explaining, she let it be known that there would be a special reward for the return of the opal. Several weeks passed with no tangible results. Then, late one evening while following a couple of unfamiliar darkly clad individuals through the alleys of the city, Loki found the entrance to guild's hideout. He remained in the shadows and observed them climb down the main well in the village square. The two were soon followed by Aramas and the rest of his party. In the course of hunting down the thieves, the party stumbled upon the guild's stash. When they entered the large burial chamber, the party was confronted by a baby black dragon, the opal sitting at the base of its feet. During the battle that ensued, the dragon was killed. However, only Aramas and Loki lived to tell of the wyrm's existence. The return of the gem, as well as the existence of the dragon, was only made known to Alissa and Brevek, who in turn advised those within the inner circle. She also admonished Loki and Aramas to speak nothing of what had transpired."

"How does that tie to the thieves in Forest Glen?" asks Aria.

"We believe that the guild within the city had at one point been aligned with the forest guild. However, after they learned that the opal was of particular interest to Alissa, they decided to keep the gems for themselves. Once their betrayal was discovered and fearing that the thieves would try to smuggle the treasure out of the city, every party leaving the city was attacked and robbed by the forest guild."

"Where did the dragon come from?" asks Kriv.

"We still do not know. However, yesterday we stumbled upon someone who may."

Aramas raises his head and looks directly at Adwin. "Who?"

"Brevek. It seems that he had three visitors yesterday, all heavily armed, one wearing a bright red robe over leather armor."

"Craven!"

"You know of this man?"

"Let's just say that our paths crossed while in Forest Glen."

"The two men with him are probably the ones that were leading the raiding parties," remarks Riadon.

"Interesting." Then Adwin turns to Riadon. "Well they won't be raiding any more parties."

"What happened?"

Adwin pauses for a moment to take a drink then continues. "Three of Alissa's guards came upon the intruders as they tried to enter Brevek's quarters. When the alarm sounded, the taller of the three pressed his advantage, killing one of the guards and severely wounding the other before he himself was killed. Craven ran and was somehow able to get out of the city."

"And the third man?" asks Aramas.

Grinning broadly, Adwin chuckles. "Let's just say that as of this morning, he is a few inches taller than when he was taken into custody and has become very talkative."

"What of Brevek?" asks Patron.

"When he realized that his true identity was about to be discovered, he too tried to flee the city. Fortunately, he was cornered before he was able to do so."

"And?" asks Aramas.

"As of this morning, Alissa has been unable to learn the identity of the person to whom he has been passing information or what he knows about the dragon. Alissa may be able to tell us more, as I have not spoken with her since last evening." Adwin then gets up from the table and walks over to the kitchen door. "Anya, it may be a few hours before I return."

He turns back to the party. "We must go. Finish your drinks and I will accompany you to the keep." He points to Aramas's greatsword. "I trust my gift performed as expected?"

As soon as they arrive at the entrance to the great room, the party is met by one of Alissa's guards. Except for two lit sconces, it is dark and devoid of any activity.

Adwin remarks, "My lady is expecting us."

The guard motions to the party to follow and then briskly ushers them to her chamber. At the open door, he announces the arrival of Adwin, Aramas, and the rest of the party.

Other than Alissa, the room is empty. Unlike their earlier meeting, the room feels damp, the scent of mildew permeating the air. Alissa motions toward the empty chairs and invites the party to be seated. "Adwin, how are your sons?"

He nods respectfully. "I could not be more pleased. We are a family again."

Smiling, she in turn nods. "It is as it should be."

She then looks over to Aramas. "You have again proved worthy of my trust." Reaching into a small iron chest, she pulls out six money pouches. "While I understand that Adwin has fulfilled his promise to each of you,

I wish to express my gratitude as well. Loyalty is hard to find and should be rewarded handsomely. There is one pouch for each of you."

Aramas replies, "You have been most generous. Thank you." After placing the pouch in his bag of holding, he continues "Adwin has told us of Brevek's treachery. I would like to speak with him!"

"That may be difficult, as he did not take well to our questioning."

"Did he say anything about whom he was working for or from whence the dragon came?"

She pauses a moment then shakes her head. "Not exactly. Before he expired, he told us of a ritual that would allow the caster to bring back the long-banished dragons. To complete the ritual, certain elements would be required."

"What elements?" asks Aria.

"He did not appear to know. He indicated that his job was to steal as many jewels and precious metals as possible then report his cache each day. At some point, he was to be directed to deliver the spoils to 'the Master.' Once the ritual had been completed, he would be rewarded with lands and title, lands which included Spring Green."

With great interest, Aria moves slightly closer. "Did he say anything else about the elements?"

"Well, it wouldn't appear to matter," interrupts Loki. "The black dragon didn't just magically appear, and we certainly got the impression that it was real as it was killing our comrades."

Ignoring the interruption, Alissa redirects her comments to Aramas. "Brevek told of a burial site a weeks' journey east of here, high in the Tiefling Mountains. Further to the east is the long-abandoned Raven's Nest Castle. While he did not seem to know the significance of the burial site, he did indicate that its contents were somehow connected to the ritual and the castle."

Sarcastically, Loki again interrupts, "I don't like where this is headed!"

Alissa directs an admonishing glance at Loki before again directing her comments to Aramas. "Brevek's identity was known only to Craven. To ensure his safe passage into the castle when the time came for him to deliver his spoils, he was directed to respond to the challenge of the castle guards by stating, 'The journey to enlightenment passes through ignorance.'"

"How do we know that Brevek wasn't lying?"

"So, of what matter is it to us?" asks Loki. He turns to Aramas. "We should have been in Flotsam days ago. We have been misled, you know it to be so, and with every word that passes from her lips it becomes even more obvious that we are being played for fools!"

Aramas momentarily ponders Loki's frustration before calmly replying, "My friend, how long have we not questioned why it was our paths became intertwined? Surely we were not destined to simply wander from village to village offering our talents to the highest bidder?" He pauses briefly. "I cannot pretend to know what lies ahead, but what I do know is what I've felt since our encounter with the dragon; I said as much that night in the pub. There are unexplainable forces at work here, and while we still may not know our purpose, I think we both know what path we must follow."

Staring intently at Aramas, Loki asks, "Are you sure, because I am not."

Aramas replies, "If I wasn't, I would not be here."

Turning back to Alissa, Aramas asks, "What is it you require of us?"

Alissa addresses the party. "As I told you the last time we met, we need to advise the grand wizard in Everand of the dragon's existence. He will also want to see the opal. Now that the Forest Road is again safe for travel, I will dispatch an emissary tomorrow to do so."

Adwin steps forward. "No good can come of what we've learned unless someone travels to the burial site and Raven's Nest Castle. It will take two weeks to reach Everand to consult with the grand wizard. That time would be best spent trying to uncover our adversary's plans, and if possible, thwarting them."

For a moment, nothing is said. Then Riadon breaks the silence. "What's in it for us?"

"Half of all of the gold and gems that you are able to recover. Further, several of my supply trains were attacked while coming over the mountains. Return them to me, and half will be yours as well."

With eyes beaming, Riadon responds, "Seems fair to me. I'm in."

Aramas smiles then turns to Patron. "You did not start this journey with us. I would understand if you did not want to join us. However, you would be a welcome addition."

Patron nods his head. "I owe you my life. You have my allegiance."

Aramas turns back to Alissa. "We will need to replenish our provisions and get a hot meal and a good night's sleep. Also, the horse and wagon would be a benefit."

"Everything will be ready at first light. You will spend the night as my guests."

Looking over at Loki, Aramas smiles. "Flotsam will still be there when we return. But for tonight, I know of a great pub where the leg of lamb is said to be fresh."

Dawn seems to come earlier than expected. For most of the night, Aramas lies awake going over the events of the previous day. Brevek's treachery aside, Alissa's answers, or the lack thereof, resulted in only more unanswered questions. How convenient that Brevek had died during questioning or that Craven had been able to escape. After all, Brevek's quarters were deep within the confines of the keep.

"The guards are here to take us to the wagon. How much longer before you are ready?" asks Patron.

Shaking his head as if coming out of a trance, Aramas replies, "Shortly."

"Can I be of assistance?"

"No, thank you. I'll be along momentarily."

As he turns to leave, Patron stops then looks back. "I do not mean to pry, but you seem to be preoccupied."

Smiling, Aramas looks up at his inquisitor. "Not preoccupied, just concerned." He stops briefly, as if searching for the right words. "I know little of your past or why it was that our paths were destined to cross. However, if recent events foreshadow what is to come, there is a good chance that some within our group will not live to complete the task that lies ahead." Returning to his packing, Aramas adds, "I find no comfort in knowing that." Securing the strap on his haversack, he stands and moves toward the door. "When we get down to the wagon, please make sure that we have several sun rods. We cannot fight what we cannot see."

Patron acknowledges the order then turns and heads back to the others. Aramas hesitates, gazes momentarily toward the ceiling, then bows his head. After he recites a short prayer taught to him by his mother many years ago, he takes one last look at the room then heads down the stairs.

"What took you so long? Not enough beauty sleep?" asks Loki.

Chuckling, Aramas ignores the question, throws his haversack into the back of the wagon, and remarks, "You seem to be in good spirits."

"Why not? The sun is shining, we have a wagon full of provisions, we're headed to a castle that has been abandoned for centuries, one which is probably haunted, all to find out who, or what, is responsible for a black dragon that was not supposed to exist. What else could one ask for?"

"As I said, you seem to be in good spirits." Looking over the provisions, Aramas turns to Patron. "Do we have everything we need?"

Before Patron can reply, someone says, "You may need these."

Turning to the now familiar voice, Aramas replies, "And what might that be?"

Adwin steps through the commissary door and hands Aramas four small vials.

"What are these?"

"Healing potions. Hopefully you will not need them."

"Thank you." Aramas opens the bag, inspects the vials, then hands them up to Loki. "Please take care of these." Then he asks Adwin, "Is there anything else of which we should be aware?"

Adwin glances briefly around the alley. "We will only be a moment." Then, he pulls Aramas aside, and in a hushed voice, he says, "I could not speak candidly last evening, as there still may be traitors within the keep."

"Did the prisoner say something?"

"No, but Craven could not have gotten to Brevek's quarters without help." There is concern in his voice. "Alissa did not tell you everything about the castle."

"We suspected as much. What has she failed to tell us?"

"After the Dragon Wars, Raven's Nest Castle was erected as part of a vast network of outposts to protect the eastern entrances to the frontier and the inland seaports to the west. The main trade route from the Tiefling Nation to Spring Green ran directly below Raven's Nest. To protect the road and collect taxes on anything entering the frontier, the castle was heavily garrisoned and put under the command of Sir Lurgan the Red, a powerful paladin who had found favor with the warlords for his heroic exploits during the Dragon Wars. For years, the garrison performed as expected. Trade along the route was brisk, there was little or no crime, and monies from the taxes collected flowed at a steady rate into the treasuries of the warlords. Sir Lurgan was rewarded handsomely and eventually placed in charge of the castle. Soon thereafter, he took a wife and was blessed with a son."

"So what happened?"

"No one seems to know. However, what is known is that at some point, Sir Lurgan became dark and suspicious of everyone around him, falling into a state of depression and madness. Trusting no one, his madness became all consuming, and he was eventually driven to kill his wife and son. When confronted by the captain of the guard, he slew him as well as the two guards that had accompanied him. While little is known of what followed, based on accounts from several of the surviving garrison, Sir Lurgan went on a rampage, killing another twenty guards before he was finally overpowered. Soon thereafter, a cold pall seemed to fall over the castle. Haunting visions, some said to be Sir Lurgan himself, attacked anyone venturing into the lower reaches of the castle. Sure that evil now controlled the castle, the warlords ordered that it be destroyed, sealed, and abandoned. It has remained as such ever since."

Aramas looks briefly to the ground. "Is there anything else I should know?"

"Is everything okay?" asks Loki.

Aramas says to Loki, "I'll fill you in later." He turns again to Adwin. "Is there anything else I should know?"

Shaking his head, Adwin replies, "No." Then placing his hand on Aramas's shoulder, he adds, "May the gods be with you."

Acknowledging the reply, Aramas returns to the party. "We have much ground to cover." With a snap of the reins, the party begins their journey.

Once they are outside the main gate and clear of the many travelers entering and exiting the city, Loki directs the wagon to the Kings Road. Once a busy thoroughfare, the road has long since fallen into disrepair and is now not much more than two weed-covered wagon ruts separated by a patch of tall grass. The road that once hosted numerous caravans between the two kingdoms now only hosts an occasional adventurer. With the fall of Raven's Nest, and the rumors of the evil that protects it, most traffic through the mountains now traverses the area along a road further south. Those travelers who do venture along its worn path often report encountering strange creatures, of being attacked by roving bands of marauders, or of unexplainable supernatural occurrences.

As Spring Green slowly fades into the distance, everyone in the party quietly scans the horizon. In the warm spring sun, the fields around them sparkle in the morning dew with different shades of green shimmering like emeralds. A light wind wafts through the treetops, gently rustling newly sprouted leaves. As was the case along the Forest Road, wildflowers dot the landscape, bees bouncing from flower to flower collecting bright yellow and gold pollen. Other than the occasional whoosh of the horse's tail swatting a pesky fly, only the rhythmic sound of the squeaking wheels, the creaking of the wagon, and the clip-clop of the horse interrupt the bucolic scenery.

"So what was so important that Adwin had to pull you aside?" asks Loki.

Grabbing the horse's bridle, Aramas halts the wagon and in a half-joking tone replies, "Nothing much. Only that the castle may be haunted by an evil knight, one that first killed his wife and son, then proceeded to kill the captain of the guard and twenty-two of his men."

"Sounds like an engaging sort of fellow," quips Patron.

"Oh, and he may have been driven to madness by some unexplainable evil force." Then looking up at Loki, he says, "And don't tell me 'I told you so.'"

Loki begins to mutter something but is interrupted by Kriv. "Did he say anything else?"

"Nothing more than what we already know."

"Which isn't much," adds Loki. Shaking his head in frustrated disbelief, he makes a quick clicking sound and snaps the reins. "I still say we could have been in Flotsam by now."

"Just think of how much more you will have to spend when we do get there," laughs Aramas.

Hours pass as the party presses to the east, the large open fields slowly giving way to undulating hills. Trees, which were few and far between in the fields and farmlands outside of Spring Green, now occupy a greater portion of the areas to either side of the road. Small savannahs of large oaks and maples provide protection to a variety of wildlife, their large branches creating a cathedral-like ceiling over the road. Overhead, a hawk circles, looking for its next meal, periodically swooping to the ground but unable to ensnare its prey as the wily mouse darts from hole to hole. Creeks full of grayish-white, ice-cold water rush down from the mountains on their journey to Spring Green and the frontier beyond.

"Are you fellows always this quiet?" asks Riadon.

"Only when there's nothing to say," replies Loki.

"Doesn't that get a little boring?"

"Depends on what you consider boring."

Puzzled, Riadon fidgets a bit before continuing. "How long have you and Aramas known each other?"

Loki turns briefly to look at Riadon. "About four years."

"Where did you meet?"

Chuckling, Loki replies, "In a pub." He pauses briefly, a broad smile on his face. "If you ask him, I'm sure that he will tell you that he saved me from a group of drunken patrons. Considering that there were four of them, I can understand his concern. However, as he soon found out, I needed no help."

"What happened?"

"Well, I was discussing the virtues of the brew before me with one of the establishment's more attractive maidens when four travelers come stumbling into what was a very crowded room: no space at the bar and all of the tables occupied. It seems that one of them didn't much care for dwarves and figured that he should have my spot at the bar. For some reason, my refusal to move, and nonchalant request for him to look for another spot to park his fat ass, didn't go over too well. He exploded, grabbed my collar, and attempted to throw me out the door. Not having finished either my drink or my conversation, I was not so inclined. About the time he began to drag me toward the door, my war hammer crashed through his knee. As you might expect, he didn't much like that, nor did his three companions. While he was flailing on the floor, cursing in what I would suppose was excruciating pain, the other three jumped me."

Aramas interrupts. "Don't believe a word he's saying. The story seems to get better each time he tells it."

Loki replies, "You are still not ready to admit that I needed no help."

"No, you're not ready to admit that I saved your . . ."

"So what happened?" asks Kriv.

A bit befuddled, Loki momentarily hesitates. "Well, just about the time I'm about to extricate myself from what could have become a very precarious position, someone shouts, 'Let him go!' For a moment, there was silence in the room as everyone turns to see who would be dumb enough to interrupt what was fast becoming an entertaining brawl."

Aramas interjects, "Just skip to the part where I save you!"

Chuckling again, Loki continues. "There, standing about ten feet away, sword drawn, is some guy with a large target on his chest. 'Mind your own business,' shouts one of the travelers. 'Don't make me ruin your day,' shouts the young crusader. Turning to the guy holding me, one of the two travelers nearest the door shouts, 'We'll take care of him; you finish the dwarf.' With their attention now focused on Aramas, I regain my composure, break away, and resume my attack."

Aramas again interrupts. "Break away? You bit his leg!"

Loki rises up. "I didn't ask you!" Then, sitting back down with a bit of an aristocratic air, he continues. "No longer encumbered, I focused all of my attention on the task at hand." He drops the sarcastic tone. "Realizing that this young crusader was going to need my help and that there was no time to waste, I charged my would-be assailant and drove him into the bar. Just as he reached for his sword, I smashed a nearby tankard of ale into the side of his head. While he was trying to figure out what had just happened, I recovered my hammer and knocked him unconscious."

"What was Aramas doing all this time?" asks Riadon.

"Yeah, what was Aramas doing?" asks Aramas sarcastically.

"I'm getting to that!" shouts Loki.

"Please do," quips Aramas.

Playing to his captive audience, Loki continues. "I'm sure that by now the other two travelers are wishing they had minded their own business. Not only did they suddenly realize that this young crusader was nimble on his feet, he was also extremely adept at wielding a long blade. Within a matter of seconds, he disarms both and has them kneeling before him, his blade at their throats. Everyone in the room is staring in disbelief. Looking down at the two travelers, Aramas commands, 'Apologize to the dwarf, then take your two comrades, and leave us to drink in peace!' With blade still drawn, he turns to the others in the room and adds, 'Is there anyone else that has an objection to the dwarf drinking at the bar?' There was utter silence." Looking down at Aramas, Loki adds, "It was a display the likes of which I had never witnessed." Pausing for a moment as if to reminisce, then with a hearty quip, he says, "And we've been traveling together ever since!"

"Aren't you sorry you asked," remarks Aramas, at which point everyone in the party has a good laugh.

While the road continues to be nothing more than two weed-covered ruts, the fields to either side are increasingly less open. Stake-like rock outcroppings, pushed to the surface thousands of years earlier, become more prevalent, dotting the landscape in an almost enclosing, foreboding manner. Large expanses of aged forests slowly begin to replace the bucolic fields passed earlier. Full of dead rotting trees, they appear almost demonic, as if to warn interlopers to venture no further. The sky itself, while still clear and blue, is eerily devoid of any birds.

Aramas gestures to Loki. "We'll stop at the stream ahead. The horse could use a rest and some water."

Nodding, Loki stops the horse just shy of the stream, jumps down from the wagon, and leads the horse to the water's edge. The beast wastes no time lowering its head to partake of the cold water.

Riadon grabs several water pouches from the back of the wagon and slowly begins refilling them. As he wades knee-high into the heart of the stream, his sigh of contentment is only eclipsed by the slurping sound of the horse and the cascading water as it passes over the rocks below. Bending down, Aramas cups his hands in the rushing water then slowly lifts the cool water to his parched mouth.

As Patron and Kriv search for a suitable tree to relieve themselves, Aria, her eyes fixed on the road ahead, moves over to Aramas. "The road ahead has been traveled recently."

Aramas wipes his hands on his tabard then peers down the road. "What is it you see?"

"It is not what I see, but what I feel." She points to an outcropping about a quarter mile up the road. "Someone camped in those rocks last night."

"How do you know?"

"I can sense their aura."

Loki and Riadon overhear the conversation and, curious, move closer.

"How many?" asks Aramas.

"Maybe six to eight."

"Six to eight what?" asks Riadon.

"I am not sure, but the auras are not those of humans."

"Can you sense if they're still in the area?" asks Aramas.

Returning from the nearby woods, Patron interrupts. "Is something wrong?"

"Aria feels that we are not the only ones traveling this road," replies Aramas.

Kriv looks down the road. "I would not doubt what Aria says." Quickly surveying the surrounding area, he adds, "If there are others on the road, the surrounding rocks would provide ample cover for an ambush."

Aramas nods in agreement. Pausing momentarily, he turns to the west and raises his left arm as if to salute the sun, his hand clenched in a fist. Slowly moving the outstretched arm down to the horizon, he says, "We have about four hours of daylight left." He turns to Aria. "You should join me up front. Patron, take Aria's position behind the wagon. Loki, take Patron's place. Riadon can drive the wagon."

After he returns the now-filled pouches to the wagon, Riadon climbs into the seat and takes the reins, waiting for the others to assume their assigned positions.

Aramas asks if everyone is ready, then, hearing no negative replies, he grabs the horse's bridle and slowly leads it through the rushing water. Once on the other side, he adds, "When we get to the outcropping, we'll stop long enough to see if we can determine who, or what, might be joining us."

It does not take long to traverse the short distance between the creek and the outcropping. Stopping just short of the area, Aramas directs Riadon to remain with the wagon while the others search for any clues as to its prior visitors. Patron, Kriv, and Aria move between the rocks while

Loki and Aramas move up the road.

When they enter a small clearing within the outcropping, Patron calls out, "Someone was definitely here. There are tracks all over." As the rest of the party rushes to join him, he kneels and places his hand over what appears to be the partially covered remnants of a fire. Feeling no heat, he carefully examines several of the charred pieces of wood. "This fire was used sometime in the last two days." Then, pointing to several tracks near the abandoned fire, he asks Kriv and Aria, "Have either of you seen tracks like these before?"

Before they can answer, Aramas interrupts. "Kobolds, they're kobolds. I found a number of tracks just to the north of the road, moving east."

Loki interjects, pointing to the rocks on the oppose side of the clearing. "There are more tracks over here." Then, looking back at Aramas, he asks, "How many do you count?"

"As Aria predicted, no more than six to eight. Based on what Adwin said, probably a scouting party."

Riadon interrupts. "What's a kobold?"

"Reptilian humanoids with reddish scaled skin." Kneeling, Aramas points to one of the tracks. "They have four toes, three to the outside of the foot and one large one to the inside. The larger the separation between the large and smaller toes indicates the approximate age of the creature." Aramàs stands and turns toward the road.

"So what do you think they're scouting?" asks Riadon.

"Us," says Loki.

Aramas turns back to the party. "No, I don't get the impression that they know we're here." Looking down the road to the east, he continues. "If they are somehow connected to the castle, their sole purpose may be to scare away would-be intruders so as not to disturb the activities at the burial site."

"What about the robberies?" asks Kriv.

"Payment for their services?" replies Aramas. "Regardless, they are deliberately avoiding the road. Had it not been for Aria, we would not be aware of their presence."

Patron steps forward and gestures to the east. "They can't be that far ahead of us."

"No, and once they know that we're here, they will do their best to stop us."

Smiling, Loki remarks, "Don't they know who we are?"

Taking advantage of the remaining sunlight, the party continues east, only stopping to periodically check for additional tracks. Every so often, exposed remnants of the cobblestones that once dominated the road peer through the sand and weeds. While the wind has subsided, low-lying clouds now cover a large portion of the sky; the air becomes cool and damp. Thick forests, broken only by large cathedral-like boulders and rock outcroppings, dominate the landscape. There are fewer open fields the further the road progresses into the mountains. Looking back, the plains outside of Spring Green are no longer discernible; the road is a string-like snake weaving its way through the wilderness.

Three hours pass, and while the tracks continue to follow just north of the road, there is no indication that there are any more than six to eight in the party. Stopping, Aramas points to a large savannah of tall oaks about one hundred yards ahead and to the north of the road. "Make for those trees. They should provide ample cover for the evening fire and adequate protection should our presence be discovered." Acknowledging the order, Riadon pulls the reins to the left, slaps them once, and directs the horse to the savannah.

The area below the trees is spacious, covered by a blanket of thick grass and bright green ferns; the leaves above are thick, blocking out whatever sunlight still exists. Heavy weblike gray moss hangs from the higher branches, dangling, almost dripping toward the ground below. An acrid rotting smell wafts through the cool damp air.

Looking for a suitable spot to build a small fire, Kriv points to something on the ground and calls out, "What do you make of this?"

Riadon moves closer and quips, "Nothing more than cow dung."

"*Big* cow," replies Kriv. "Besides, I know of no cow that eats flesh."

As the others gather around to examine the pile of rotting dung, Aramas grabs a nearby stick, kneels, and slowly examines it. "I would agree with Kriv." The pile of dung is about two feet in diameter and approximately ten inches high. It is a dark blackish-brown in color, with a thin crusty surface and a mushy texture within. Using the stick to sift through the smelly goo, Aramas separates several hard objects from pile. "These are bone fragments."

"Human or animal?" asks Loki.

"I'm not sure, but whatever was here feasts on flesh."

"That would explain the smell," says Aria.

Dropping the stick, Aramas stands and motions to the others. "Spread out and check the rest of the area."

As they move throughout the clearing, several similar piles are found. However, all of them appear to be several weeks old.

Returning to the wagon, Riadon climbs into the seat and nervously exclaims, "Okay, let's get moving."

"Where are we going?" asks Loki.

"Anywhere but here!"

"I thought it was just a pile of cow dung."

"Cows don't eat flesh and I like mine just the way it is!"

Loki instead methodically unhitches the horse from the wagon then leads it over to one of the trees.

"What are you doing?" asks Riadon.

"What does it look like?" Loki secures the horse to a low hanging branch and then heads back to the wagon to start unloading the gear.

Obviously perturbed with the lack of urgency exhibited by the rest of the party, Riadon beseeches, "We need to go!"

"Go where?" replies Aramas. "Besides, it will be dark soon. I don't want to be caught on the road after dark."

"Well I don't want to be caught here by whatever left that pile of dung!"

As he takes out his bedroll and knapsack, Loki looks up at Riadon. "We'll have guards posted. Besides, this is a good, defensible position, with a good view in all directions. An intruder would be hard-pressed to get across the open field and into the trees without us noticing."

While Loki and Kriv search for firewood, Aramas, Patron, and Aria examine the various piles of dung.

Puzzled, Aramas remarks, "Based on the lack of tracks—or for that matter, any other evidence—it would appear that this creature has not been in the area recently."

"Any idea what left this?" asks Aria.

"None." He hesitates. "Hopefully, we won't be here when it comes back." Motioning to Patron and Aria, the three rejoin the others.

Aramas looks at Loki. "Keep the fire small, just large enough to boil some water. I don't know what left that pile of dung, but I'd prefer not to draw any attention to our position."

As Riadon starts to speak, Loki interrupts, "We know!"

The rest of the evening passes quietly. There is not much of a breeze; the smoke from the fire slowly wafts upward through the thick, leafy canopy. Where there are breaks in the overhead canopy, the yellow glow from the fire, reflected on the bottom of the leaves, is periodically broken by the twinkling stars of the clear sky above.

Dinner consists of dried meat, hard rolls, and sassafras tea. Soaking the meat in a cup of hot water yields a watery, gravy-like substance that adds significantly to the edibility of the rolls. Aramas forages in the scrub nearby and finds some fresh berries to round out the meal.

As Loki begins to pack items away, the others lay out their bedrolls. Having already done so, Patron grabs a small bucket of water and a handful of oats for the horse, who wastes no time in devouring them. While the grass is lush and sweet, the oats are a welcome treat. After placing the bucket of water near the tree, Patron runs his hands along the horse's flank as he passes behind to ensure that it is securely tied. "Rest well, my friend. We have a long day ahead of us." Slurping the cool water, the horse stops momentarily, as if to acknowledge Patron's comment, then continues.

When he returns to the campfire, Patron finds most of the party already stretched out, several party members already snoring loudly. Looking over at Aramas, he asks, "Do you want me to take the first watch?"

"Thanks. Wake me in about two hours." Within minutes, Aramas too is asleep.

Surveying the camp, all appears to be in order. The air is still; the only sound is the crackling of the small fire. While the area immediately around the fire is lit, out beyond the fire's loom, everything is black. Looking out beyond the trees toward the road, Patron's eyes slowly adjust to the low light. Fireflies can be seen over the field to the south; the sky is filled with stars. Beyond the road, the silhouette of the mountains juts upward like a vast wall separating one world from the other. Patron could remember many similar nights spent with his father while hunting game for his family; it was a simpler time in a world that no longer existed, one that had almost passed from memory.

Turning back toward the fire, he hears a gentle rustling of the leaves above. Initially thinking nothing of it, he picks up a nearby stick and slowly pokes at the glowing embers. As dancing embers slowly drift skyward, he notices that the rustling becomes louder, almost deliberate. Suddenly realizing that there is no wind to cause the rustling, Patron stands, grabs his swords, and quietly moves over to Aramas. As he does so, the horse whinnies, snorts, and pounds its hoof.

Tapping Aramas's shoulder, Patron whispers, "Aramas, we have company."

Having not yet drifted into a deep sleep, Aramas, sits up quickly. "What is it?"

"There is something in the branches above."

The horse whinnies again, snorts loudly, and tries to break away.

Aramas grabs his sword. "Everyone, get up. Intruders!"

As the rest of the party scrambles to their feet, Aramas and Patron rush toward the now frantic horse.

"Do you see anything?" asks Aramas.

"Nothing!" replies Patron.

A faint voice whispers to Aramas, "Above you!"

Without hesitation, Aramas looks up and wheels to his left, catching the sound of something that dropped to the ground in the space he just vacated. In the glow of the fire, Aramas can make out the silhouette of a very large hairy beast.

"Tree spider!" shouts Loki, his hammer smashing into the creature. Angered, it turns to attack him.

Patron, dual swords gleaming in the firelight, moves in from the right, his blades slashing deep gashes into the spider's torso; a banshee-like screech of pain pierces the air.

From the left, a broad sweep of Aramas's sword separates the beast from two of its legs. Stunned, it attempts to back away, temporarily falling to the ground.

"The horse!" shouts Kriv. "There is another one attacking the horse!"

While Aramas, Patron, and Loki continue to press their advantage with the crippled intruder, Aria and Riadon rush to join Kriv, the horse now whinnying uncontrollably as it tries to free itself from its captor.

Suddenly, the area is illuminated as Aria releases a phlegethon of fury upon the beast; the asphyxiating smell of burnt flesh and hair fill the air. Almost unfazed, the spider sinks its fangs into its prey, the once frantic horse quickly falling limp.

"Keep it from getting up into the tree!" shouts Kriv.

Aria and Riadon rush to cut off the only retreat. With arms out-stretched, Aria hurls another bolt of searing flames and energy into the defiant beast. Screeching, it drops the horse and thrusts itself toward Aria.

Kriv quickly takes advantage of the spider's now open flank and smashes the nearest leg with his flail.

As the spider attempts to back away from its tormentors, Riadon suddenly finds himself pinned beneath it. While Aria and Kriv continue their unrelenting assault, Riadon takes out his knife and plunges it deep into the spider's underbelly. Almost deafening screeches of pain fill the air. Riadon again plunges his knife into the beast then rushes to extricate himself from his precarious position.

The creature attempts to reach the tree. Stumbling, its life blood oozing from within, it slowly falls to the ground. Unable to move, its legs slowly twitch and retract. Death follows soon thereafter.

Pressing their advantage, Patron again buries his blades deep into the other spider's torso, a greenish-white viscous fluid oozing from each; searing screeches of pain echo through the surrounding trees.

As the spider again attempts to stand, Aramas amputates another of its legs. Its fate no longer in doubt, and unable to stand, it makes one last unsuccessful attempt to grab Loki. Pushing Loki out of harm's way, Aramas raises his sword high above his head then swiftly brings it down, its guillotine-like blow swiftly decapitating the beast. Its remaining legs slowly retract around its now lifeless body.

"Loki, you and Patron check on the others. I want to see if I can learn more about our attacker."

Rushing to the others, Loki asks, "Is everyone alright?"

"We are, but the horse isn't!" exclaims Riadon.

Kriv, who is kneeling beside the horse, looks up at Loki. "The poison was too strong."

Patron moves closer to the tree spider. "This one appears to be significantly smaller than the other. Do you think it's an offspring?"

"No, it's the male," replies Aramas, who joins the others and slowly moves closer to the corpse. Perusing the creature, he continues. "The larger one is the female. From what I can tell, she was soon to give birth."

A worried Riadon asks, "Do you think that there could be more?"

"If there were more, they would have attacked as well." He points to the gray, low-hanging moss above. "I found pieces of this 'moss' on the female. I think it is actually some sort of web." He rubs a small piece of the matter between his forefinger and thumb. "It is very strong and very sticky." Then, motioning to the surrounding trees, he adds, "This area was probably their nest. Anything coming into it would be attacked and then trapped in the web—a sort of food storage system. Like any predator, they would have defended their nest against any intruder."

"So when do we head back to Spring Green?" asks Riadon.

"Why would we do that?" replies Loki.

"Because we have no horse?"

"We need no horse to complete the task before us."

"Why not? Without a horse, how will we pull the wagon full of Adwin's recovered goods?"

Aramas interrupts. "Enough! Loki is right. I see no reason to return to Spring Green. The horse was merely a convenience, and our mission is not the return of the goods." He motions to the others. "We'll double the watch for the rest of the night. Patron, I'll take the first watch with you. Then tomorrow morning, we'll go through the provisions and collect only what is necessary. Kriv and Loki will take the second watch; Aria and Riadon the last."

From the tone of his voice, Loki knows that Aramas is upset, not so much with what Riadon said, but with himself. In hindsight, Riadon was right, but rather than listen to his suggestion to move on, Aramas let his fatigue and his inclination to discount suggestions from someone with little experience in the wild cloud his judgment. The horse is more than a convenience, and Aramas knows that. However, having traveled as long as he has with his friend, Loki also knows that Aramas would not make that mistake again.

CHAPTER 6

THE FUTURE BURIED BENEATH

The morning air is cool and damp, with a thick fog that blankets the meadow and obscures the nearby road. Other than the soft pitter-patter of dew hitting the canvas bedroll covers, all is silent. Like a dream playing out in slow motion, everything seems to stand still.

Peeking out from beneath the warmth of his bedroll, Aramas can tell that the sun will soon begin the slow process of burning off the curtain of fog that hangs over them. While he knows he needs to get up, for the moment he only wants to remain in the warmth. He is not quite fully awake, and it reminds him of his youth and the feeling of his mother's comforting embrace. It was during such moments that she would tell him stories of her youth, her struggles growing up, how she had met his father, and the importance of family. During his darkest hours in captivity, it was her voice that kept him from giving up. As if able to communicate through the veil of death, he could hear her promise that his god would be his armor, his faith his shield, right and justice the bite of his sword. If he kept his faith, he would never be given more than he could handle; she would always be with him.

"Aramas, we need to get the provisions sorted."

Looking up at Patron, Aramas begrudgingly replies, "I'll be right there."

Although still a young man, years of gladiatorial combat had not been kind to Aramas. While he had become an expert in his craft, the plethora of wounds and broken bones, and the aches and pains associated with them, were something that he had grown to accept. However, damp morning air had become the bane of his existence; each wound or broken bone remind him of the opponents that had fallen beneath his sword. As he stows his bedroll, he silently hopes that it will not be long before the sun burns off the source of his discomfort.

While Aramas and Patron sort through the provisions, the rest of the party packs their gear and begins to break camp. Breakfast will be kept to a minimum: hot tea, bread, and salt pork.

From the wagon, Aramas calls to Kriv, "Bring your bag of holding. We're going to need it."

"Are you going to need mine?" asks Loki.

"No, between Kriv, Patron, and myself, we should be fine."

With everything sorted and stowed, the party quickly finishes break-fast, extinguishes the fire, and resumes their journey. As they reach the road, Aria looks back at the wagon and corpses. "It won't be long before our presence is discovered."

Nodding in agreement, Aramas somberly replies, "I just hope that we're ready when they do."

It is several hours before the fog finally begins to lift. Hanging low, about midway up the trees, the clouds give off an almost ethereal aura. While the lumen of the sun periodically drifts in and out of view, the slow rolling mists overhead, like a thick curtain separating two plains, obscures everything else. What sound there is, much like the sun's light, is diffused, its direction almost undiscernible. It is eerily quiet. No chirping birds, no squirrels jumping from tree to tree, no visible wildlife. Other than small talk, the party too makes little noise, aware that there is at least one party of kobolds in the area.

The next several hours pass without incident. By noon, the fog has burned off, affording a clear view of the surrounding area and valley below. The road, which is now almost completely overgrown, has become considerably rockier. In several areas, the road passes along steep cliffs, revealing the valley floor over one thousand feet below. Spring Green, and the fields surrounding it, has long been out of view.

Stopping briefly, Aramas kneels to the ground and runs his fingers over the partially exposed soil.

"What do you see?" asks Kriv.

"It's not what I see, but what I don't see." He stands and looks back down the road. "For the past mile or so, I have been unable to detect any fresh tracks. While they may have turned further north and circled back, it is also possible that they have discovered our presence and are now stalking us." Studying the steep rocks above the trail, Aramas searches in vain for any indication as to where the kobolds might be.

With a note of concern, Patron remarks, "If they're in those rocks, we won't see them until they're on top of us."

"That's what I'm afraid of."

"Do you think they could have found our camp this soon?" asks Riadon.

"I don't know. We need to assume that there are more kobolds in the area than the small party we've been following. If another party stumbled upon our camp, they may have been able to communicate our presence to the party ahead of us."

"So what's the plan?" asks Loki.

"For now, we just continue as if nothing is wrong. While they may have learned of our presence, they have no way of knowing that we're aware of theirs. That is our advantage." Looking to the road ahead, he surmises, "While this would be a good place for an ambush, I don't believe they would have had enough time to stage one. However, we need to be ready just in case." He pulls out his water skin and takes a small drink. "Take a short break. Just in case they're watching."

After a few minutes, a few pieces of jerky, and a good swig of water, the party continues up the road. Not more than a mile past their respite, the road begins to level off and leads into a large mountain pasture, lush with tall grass and surrounded by tall pines. Where the road had been nearly unrecognizable earlier, it is now well defined and clear of most grass and weeds, as if untouched by the passing of time. Worn cobblestones are clearly visible and, in many places, freshly scratched by the passage of wagon wheels and horseshoes. Mountains surround the plateau on three sides, the ones to the east towering another two thousand feet toward the heavens. While the pines obscure their distance, Aramas estimates them to be another fifteen or twenty miles off.

Walking is easy, and the party is able to make good time. Unlike the trail leading up to the plateau, wildlife is more abundant; wild turkey, deer, and ducks are the most visible. About a mile ahead, a small lake is nestled just south of the road bounded by what appear to be aspen and birch trees still devoid of any foliage.

"What do you make of the marks on the road?" asks Loki.

"Like the Old North Road into Forest Glen, this road too has seen more use than expected."

"Any sign of our friends?

"Not yet, but something, or someone, was driving these wagons. Since there were no such tracks on the trail up here, I would expect that they've got something to do with the burial site and the castle."

Hours pass, and while Aramas continues to search for clues as to the whereabouts of the kobold scouting party, none are found. One open pasture seems to lead to another, and as the mountain range looms larger with each passing mile, a good campsite becomes the party's most pressing concern.

As they near the base of the high mountain range, Aramas scans the surrounding area for a secure campsite, ever mindful of what happened the previous night. Unhappy with the options presented, he directs the party to move into a small grove of cedars about a quarter mile further up the road. Situated near a small stream, it should provide adequate cover while affording a clear view of the surrounding area.

As the party approaches the grove, Aramas tells the others, "No fire tonight!" He looks to Kriv. "I want you, Aria, and Patron to check the area and establish a secure perimeter."

Then Aramas says to Riadon, "Take only what we need from the haversacks. The sun will be gone soon, and I don't want to be rummaging through them after dark. Loki, you and I will fill the water skins."

The sky glows a bright yellow-orange as the sun slowly dips below the western range with streaks of red highlighting purple clouds. Each passing minute mutes the bright colors, the sky growing darker, stars slowly piercing the dark canopy above.

When he returns to the others, Kriv reports that the campsite has been secured. "Anyone approaching from the north and west will be in for a surprise." He looks over to Patron. "There is a lot that we can learn from the newest member of our party."

With a nod of approval, Aramas points to a small open area nestled between the trees. "Riadon has laid out your bedrolls. Get something to eat. Loki and I will take the first watch."

Awakened by streams of sunlight filtering through the branches above, Aramas sits up, rubs the sleep from his eyes, and slowly surveys the area. A chorus of birds heralds the beginning of the new day. The air is crisp but not cold. A soft westerly breeze whooshes through the cedars. While it is dry under the protective cover of the branches above, the dew sparkles like diamonds on the tall grass of the surrounding pasture. To the east, the sky appears redder than usual, a portent of potential rain later in the day. As the others slowly extricate themselves from their warm cocoons, Aramas secures his bedroll and stuffs it into his haversack.

"Did you sleep well?" asks Patron.

"As good as can be expected. Anything unusual during your watch?"

"Other than a couple of bucks butting heads over a rather comely mate, all was quiet."

Smiling, Aramas replies, "A nice thick venison steak would go well right now."

"Did someone mention venison?" asks Loki.

Aramas chuckles. "Your hearing is as sharp as ever, especially when it comes to food or drink."

"My stomach is not amused," quips Loki. "A fine piece of meat, a few potatoes, and a tankard of that apple cider wine would go a long way to improving my disposition."

Nodding his head in amusement, Aramas turns to the others. "Let's get moving." Turning to look at the eastern sky, he adds, "It looks like we could get some rain. Finding any tracks after that will be almost impossible."

While the others don their armor and secure their haversacks, Patron moves to the camp perimeter and removes the various traps he had set the night before. Sure that he has left nothing behind, he returns to find the others removing anything that would indicate that the party had been there. After a final inspection of the area, and confident that nothing has been left to chance, Aramas motions to the others to move out to the road.

Hoping to reach the high mountains before the rain arrives, Aramas pushes the party. The good weather and clear road present few problems and allow the group to make good time, even as it slowly begins to ascend into the rolling hills at the base of the range. The open pastures that had flanked the road for a good portion of the previous day's journey once again give way to large expanses of trees, mostly pines and cedars. The plethora of wildlife seen earlier slowly vanishes. Other than the presence of a few birds and an occasional squirrel, the area is apparently devoid of anything other than the interlopers on the road.

By noon, the party has proceeded well into the rolling hills as the road continues its long winding path toward the summit. The large expanses of trees have given way to dense forests, the soil beneath black and damp, strewn with fallen trees, broken limbs, and large clumps of thick green moss. Brightly colored green and gray lichens engulf many of the tree trunks with an almost luminescence in the low light that streams through the canopy above. There are no low-hanging branches, and the area beneath the canopy is open; the open darkness is tunnel-like in appearance. Large roots, unable to penetrate the rock just below the surface, and rocks of various sizes make traversing the ground to either side of the road slow and treacherous. Large chunks of rock, exposed to years of rain and ice and dislodged from the cliffs above, dot the landscape. In some cases, trees have sprouted in their cracks and crevices.

While it is not uncommon for hours to pass with little or no conversation, since the discovery of the kobold scouting party, discussions of any sort have been kept to a minimum. Aware that with every passing hour the chances of detection increase dramatically, Aramas continues to search for any indication as to the whereabouts of the kobolds. However, the texture and nature of the surrounding area makes finding any tracks difficult at best.

The road itself has also become less accommodating; the increased number of dislodged rocks present additional challenges to passage. While for the bulk of the morning, it had been almost straight as an arrow, it now meanders through a myriad of natural obstructions, each presenting their own unique problems and hazards. Sightlines that had been miles in length now measure in yards. Throughout the area, rocks have come to rest upon each other. Covered by layers of moss, pine needles, and decaying branches, they form cave-like mazes, many concealed or invisible from the road.

"Well, I guess you were right," remarks Patron as small droplets of rain begin to fall on the party.

"Let's look for a spot to get out of the rain before we get soaked," replies Aramas.

Moving a little quicker, the party finds a stand of rocks that will provide adequate protection. Much like several of the stands passed earlier, the fallen rocks have created a narrow cave, dry and secure from the elements. Just as the party reaches the entrance, the rain increases in intensity. Streams of water cascade down the outside of the formation and surrounding hills, washing what loose surface soil remains toward the road.

Inside the dark cavity, Loki takes a torch from his haversack, recites a short prayer, and almost instantaneously, the torch ignites. To the surprise of Riadon, the torch does not give off any heat or smoke. Inquisitively he reaches toward the flame. It does not burn him. Staring in wonderment, he exclaims, "Handy little device."

The enclosure is long and narrow, about five feet wide, extending about fifteen feet before coming to a dead end. As Aramas looks out at the drenching downpour, he remarks, "You might as well get comfortable. We could be here for a while."

Wasting little time, haversacks are dropped to the floor, water flasks are retrieved, and small portions of dried meat and nuts are distributed.

"Aramas, you need to see this."

"What is it, Loki?"

"It looks like we're not the first ones to seek shelter here."

Aramas walks over to Loki. As the rest of the party looks on, Aramas kneels to examine what appear to be tracks. "Kobolds." Standing, he takes the torch from Loki and moves slowly toward the back of the cave. "Definitely kobolds, and not that old."

"How old are they?" asks Kriv.

"How many?" asks Patron.

"It's hard to tell because they haven't been exposed to the weather." He kneels again and turns to look to either side of the cave. "With all the tracks, I can't say for sure how many, but there was definitely more than one."

Standing, he turns to Aria. "Why is it that you did not see this?"

"It doesn't always work that way. Even now I do not detect their presence; I see no auras."

Puzzled, Aramas hands the torch back to Loki and walks to the entrance. Gazing out at the pouring rain, he remarks, "If they stopped here for the night, they cannot be that far ahead of us." Looking down at the ground just outside of the entrance, he notices several tracks headed toward the road. "Fate has again been kind to us. If not for this rain, we might have stumbled upon them. Loki, extinguish the torch."

Without hesitation, Loki does as ordered.

Kriv moves to the entrance. "It would not do us well to be discovered here."

"Agreed! However, if the rain has caused us to seek shelter, I would expect that the kobolds have done so as well."

"We can't assume that! If our presence has been discovered, there may be others coming up the road!"

Calmly, Aramas replies, "I don't disagree. However, even if they've learned that we're in the area, they have no way of knowing that we're here. If they did, they would have already attacked." Pointing to the torrents of rain soaking the forest outside, he adds, "The rain has removed any evidence of our movements, and as long as we remain vigilant, we maintain the upper hand." Moving back into the darkness, Aramas sits down, his eyes remaining fixed on the road. "I'll take the first watch."

The rain continues intermittently for the next several hours. Inside, the darkness conceals the intermeddlers, small rivulets of water making their way down the sides of the cave. Other than the sounds of dripping water from the surrounding trees, all is quiet, the air fresh and clean. A greenish-yellow glow permeates the forest as the clouds slowly disperse to reveal a rapidly disappearing sun, staining the sky just above the mountain ridge with bright yellow and red.

During his nap after his watch, Aramas is awakened by a few drops of water falling from the rocks above. He is momentarily startled, but it doesn't take long for him to remember where he is. Standing, he moves closer to the opening.

Loki, who has been standing watch for the past hour or so, turns to Aramas. "Everything is quiet. I would assume that we'll be spending the night here?"

He briefly looks to the west then again at the road. "No need to venture out now. We'll head out at first light."

No one has a restful night. The kobold scouting party is probably not too far ahead of them. Not sure if their presence has been compromised, they start preparations to leave their temporary sanctuary well before the first rays of the morning sun pierce the cave's darkness. With first light, any remaining gear is quickly stowed.

Hoping that Aria's ability to envisage a creature's presence will help the party anticipate a surprise attack, Aramas asks her to join him up front. While the heavy rains may have washed away any of the prior day's tracks, the newly muddied topsoil will make it considerably more difficult to travel the area undetected, both for the kobolds and the party.

The party heads to the road, unsure of what lies ahead yet filled with a sense of inevitability. While there is evidence of wildlife in the area, they too seem to sense the imminent conflict. The road continues to wind its way through the forbidding maze of trees, fallen timbers, and rock formations. Progress is slow and deliberate as every member of the party intently searches their surroundings for any hint of danger.

Not more than an hour into the day's trek, Aria abruptly stops. She points to three rectangular-shaped objects about one hundred feet ahead next to a large rock formation. "What do you make of those?"

Aramas replies, "They look like gravestones."

Motioning for the others to follow, the party cautiously approaches. While overgrown with weeds and covered by lichen, there is no doubt that they are gravestones, their surface worn smooth by time and the elements. What remains of the names and dates indicates that the occupants passed into the next world several hundred years earlier.

Looking around, Aramas notices what appears to be the almost undiscernible remnants of a small dwelling. Nestled between several large rock formations and surrounded by large areas of dense undergrowth, its original purpose long since forgotten, Aramas moves closer to investigate. Stopping short of the dwelling, he surveys the area. "We must be getting close to the castle. There can be no other explanation."

Before he can turn back to the group, two reptilian figures jump from the nearby underbrush, swords gleaming in the morning sun.

Simultaneously, three more emerge from the thick bushes behind the rock formation adjacent to the headstones, spears thrusting forward as they press their attack. Hoping to flank the party before they can respond, three more rush from the thick undergrowth across the road, directed by a fourth larger reptilian figure dressed in crimson hide armor and wearing a bone mask carved to resemble the head of a dragon.

Quickly moving back to back in a defensive circle, Patron, Kriv, Loki, Aria, and Riadon prepare to repel the advancing foes.

In Draconic, the crimson-clad kobold barks several orders. "Kill the two dragonborn!" Motioning toward Aramas, he adds, "Do not allow them to join forces! I want the paladin taken alive."

Then, raising his arm, palm open, fingers pointed toward the sky, he calls forth a nondescript orb and hurls it into the center of the party, acid spraying upon impact.

With no protective armor, Riadon screams as the liquid burns through his leggings. Almost simultaneously, Aria thrusts her hand forward and hurls a fireball, only to have it deflected by the swift sweeping motion of the kobold's shield, sparks flying in all directions.

Surprised, the kobold pauses, draws his sword, and shouts, "You are mine!"

Unfazed, Aria again raises her hand, points her index finger, and calls forth a stream of hellish flames. Again, the kobold's shield deflects the fiery burst.

Aramas, finding himself separated from the rest of the party, draws his sword just in time to deflect the first of two thrusts. Stepping back quickly, he parries the second. Then, in one fluid arc after another, blue radiant energy dancing from his blade, Aramas begins a blistering counterattack. His first strike shatters his closest opponent's sword.

Stunned, the kobold warrior steps back, trips into his comrade, and grabs for his knife. However, before it can clear its sheath, Aramas's next blow amputates the arm just below the creature's shoulder. With blood spurting everywhere, the kobold falls to the ground, writhing in agonizing pain, his life quickly draining.

Hoping to regain the advantage, the second warrior leaps over Aramas, coming to rest behind him. However, he lands only to find that Aramas has quickly pivoted, his sword colliding with what the kobold had hoped would be a crippling blow. He swings again, then again and again, only to have each foray deflected and followed by an even more forceful counterattack. Realizing that alone he stands little chance of defeating the paladin, he attempts to extricate himself from what has quickly become a futile engagement.

Aramas, however, has other ideas. Pressing his advantage, he finds a brief opening and plunges his sword deep into the chest of the bewildered foe. Then, just as quickly, he withdraws it and delivers another slashing blow, thereby ending the creature's misery. Turning to address his other attacker, Aramas finds nothing more than a trail of blood headed into the sanctuary of the rocks above.

Focusing on the three spear-wielding attackers, Kriv's searing breath temporarily halts their advance.

Patron, dual swords rhythmically swirling from side to side, focuses on the two kobolds to his right, hoping to force them to pivot away from their flanking allies.

Protecting Patron's flank, Kriv dodges the thrusting spear of the third attacker and counters with a broad sweep of his flail, making the chain wrap around the spear's shaft. However, before he can pull the weapon free, the blade of one of the flanking kobolds penetrates an opening in the side of his armor, and an intense burning sensation envelopes the area. Wincing in pain, Kriv continues his attack and yanks the spear from its master. As the frightened kobold grasps for his sword, Kriv charges forward, knocking him to the ground, his flail crashing through the kobold's skull.

Hoping to draw Loki and Riadon away from the others, the two remaining kobolds charge them. Aware that Kriv has been wounded and unwilling to give any ground, Loki sidesteps the first assault, redirecting the kobold's thrust into the ground. Off balance, it attempts a second thrust, only to again be repelled. As the creature attempts a third thrust, Loki's counterthrust makes him pay as his hammer crashes into the beast's shoulder blade.

Unable to hold his sword, the kobold stumbles backyards. With Riadon holding his own against the other attacker, Loki presses his counterattack, forcing the dazed creature back toward the road. However, before he can deliver a fatal blow, his advance is temporarily halted by the nearby explosion of another orb of acid; the momentary diversion gives the retreating kobold enough time to escape. Turning his attention to the source of the orb, Loki releases his hammer.

Blade drawn, Riadon moves to protect Loki's back, feigns an attack to the left, then suddenly appears behind the attacker. Surprised, the kobold halts his advance and turns to relocate his adversary. However, before he can do so, Riadon plunges his blade deep into the attacker's back. The kobold drops to the ground and falls lifelessly forward. Wasting no time, Riadon rushes to help Kriv, as his wound rapidly impairs his ability to defend himself.

With the sweep of his shield, the kobold caster deflects Loki's hammer and continues his advance on Aria. As he crosses the road, his advance is unexpectedly halted by Aramas, his sword slicing into the beast's exposed leg. Instinctively, the caster counters, his sword deflecting Aramas's next thrust. Pivoting to address Aramas, he is unprepared for Loki's charge, which nearly knocks him to the ground. Regaining his composure and surprised that his carefully planned ambush has quickly turned into a rout, he attempts to retreat into the thick cover across the road, only to find that Patron stands in his way.

"Going somewhere?" shouts Patron. "Drop your weapon, or join your comrades."

Hesitating, the caster surveys the situation. "What is coming is greater than you can imagine. It cannot be changed." Raising his sword, he charges Patron. Within seconds, it is over.

"Loki, see what you can do to help Riadon and Kriv," directs Aramas. He points into the underbrush and says to Patron, "See if you can track the one that got away."

Rushing back to the ruins, Aramas picks up the blood path of the wounded kobold and follows it back into the rocks. About fifty feet from the ruins, he locates the dying adversary.

The bloodsoaked creature attempts to lift his sword in an attempt to defend himself.

Aramas approaches, lowers his sword, and in Draconic says, "You have not long to live. Answer my questions and I promise to end your misery swiftly."

The kobold, eyes beginning to turn glassy, says in a raspy voice, "What is it you seek?"

"Where is the excavation site? How many protect it?"

The kobold struggles, his voice cracking with almost every word. "Another hour, a few hundred yards north of the road." He gasps. "Ten at the site. Many more at the castle." However, before another question is asked, the kobold reaches out and grabs Aramas's leg. "Please . . ."

With one swift blow, Aramas keeps his word.

"Aramas, the other kobold disappeared into the woods. Tracking him will be difficult."

Staring at the lifeless body before him, Aramas wipes his blade on the creature's tabard, sheathes his sword, then turns to address Patron. "He is sure to warn the others of what has happened."

"Were you able to learn anything from the creature?"

"Only that the force we might encounter at the excavation site will be small compared to what we can expect at the castle." He looks down the road. "If we are to minimize the chances of another attack, we have little time to tarry."

After tending to Kriv and Riadon, the party wastes no time in hiding the bodies as best as possible and moving up the road. They have a general idea as to the whereabouts of the excavation site but are unsure as to its exact location, so the party moves as quickly as possible, constantly alert to the possibility of another attack.

As expected, about an hour up the road, the party comes to a heavily traveled trail veering off into the woods to the north. Examining the nearby tracks, Aramas determines that the trail has been traversed primarily by humans, halflings, and goblins. "Unless there is another path to the burial site, it would appear that our kobold friend has not been here."

"So what's the plan?" asks Loki.

Surveying the surrounding area, Aramas turns to Riadon. "Scout ahead to see what you can find. Be careful! The kobold indicated that the site was only a few hundred yards up the trail."

Riadon nods in agreement and darts up the trail.

As he vanishes into the surrounding trees, Kriv asks, "Did the kobold say anything about how many guards were at the site? How many workers?"

"He indicated that there were ten guards. However, he died before relaying any more information."

"Ten is better than thirty," quips Loki.

Puzzled, Patron asks, "Where did you come up with thirty?"

Aramas chuckles. "That's the number of thieves Alissa told us to expect along the Forest Road."

After a brief discussion, and still concerned with the whereabouts of the escaped kobold, Aramas instructs Patron and Kriv to proceed up the road another hundred yards to verify that there is no other trail to the burial site and to rule out the possibility that the kobold crossed the road further to the east. "If you find anything, do not leave the road! Just get back here as quickly as possible." Acknowledging their instructions, the two proceed up the road.

"Aria, any indications that our presence has been detected?"

"Not that I can discern." Drifting a few feet up the trail, she closes her eyes for a few seconds then opens them. "This is a dark place. We should not dwell here longer than necessary."

Concerned, Loki turns to Aramas. "Should we be worried about Riadon?"

"We'll begin to worry if he has not returned by the time the others get back."

For the next several minutes, time seems to pass at a snail's pace, causing Aramas to become concerned with his decision to split the party.

The return of Kriv and Patron comes none too soon. "We found no other trail or any evidence of the kobold."

"How far did you go?"

Before Kriv can answer, Riadon comes running back and in a hushed voice says, "The site is just up the trail!"

"Did they spot you?" asks Loki.

"I don't believe so, but it is a lot closer than expected."

"So what are we in for?" asks Kriv.

Kneeling to the ground, Riadon picks up a nearby stick and begins to draw a map in the sand. "There is a steeply sloped long ridge overlooking the site, running from the south to the north and then to the west. The western edge of the site is open, overlooking a large pasture. The trail comes into the site from the southwest."

"How many guards?" asks Aramas.

"I did not have much time, but from what I could see, I counted three guards, about six workers, and an old friend of ours."

"Friend?"

"Craven is overseeing the excavation!"

Loki chimes in, "This should be interesting."

"Are the workers armed?" asks Aramas.

"There is a stack of weapons here at the end of the trail: short swords and a few spears. If we could surprise them, they would probably be unable to reach them. However, it will be difficult to surprise them unless we come in from the east."

"Where are the guards positioned?"

Using the stick as a pointer, Riadon continues. "One is positioned at the far southern edge of the ridge, one is here at the far northeast corner, and the other, a halfling, stands with Craven here, just inside the site about midway along the north ridge."

"How are they armed?" asks Patron.

"The two atop the ridge have short swords and shields. The halfling appears to carry only a knife and sling."

"What of Craven?" asks Aramas.

"A longsword."

Studying the map, Aramas asks, "What kind of cover is there?"

"Other than the pasture to the west, the forest runs right to the edge of the site."

"How far is the closest guard to the end of the trail?"

"About thirty feet."

"And the workers?"

"Most are well within the site, maybe fifty feet or so from the end of the trail."

"How high is the ridge around the site?"

"Ground level at the southern and western ends, about twenty feet in the middle where it turns to the west."

Running his finger along the south-to-north section of the ridge, Aramas asks, "What is this distance?"

"About two hundred feet."

"So unless the guard jumps down into the site, he will need to run the entire length of the ridge to engage us." Pointing to the area where the southernmost guard was observed, Aramas says to Riadon and Loki, "I want you two to take out the guard. Remain concealed until we rush the site. I would expect that he'll attempt to flank us. If we catch them off guard, we should be able to prevent the workers from getting to their weapons. Once the guard passes your position, come in from behind and take him out."

"What about the others?" asks Kriv.

"I would expect Craven and the halfling to immediately engage us. We'll deal with the other guard once we know what he intends to do."

Aramas draws his sword. "Riadon, you and Loki take the lead. Once you've found a good position to attack the guard, we'll move to surprise Craven and the others. If things go as planned, the closest guard will immediately attempt to stop our advance. As soon as he passes your position, take him out." He turns to the others. "It is imperative that we prevent the workers from getting to their weapons. If possible, we need to take a prisoner." The others nod in agreement and draw their weapons.

Following Riadon and Loki, the party moves as quietly as possible. About one hundred feet up the trail, Riadon pauses and motions the others to proceed along the trail while he and Loki move into the trees to set the trap. Aramas nods affirmatively and cautiously continues the advance.

As they approach the end of the trail, the open pasture comes into view. Aramas motions for the others to halt and then to move into the cover to their right. Concealed within the underbrush, Aramas drops to one knee and studies the area, the others close by. While the two guards are on the ridge, Craven and the halfling are positioned as expected, but the pile of weapons is farther to the east than Riadon had indicated. Further, it is guarded by two drakes and a gnome skulk.

Surprised, Aramas quietly turns to the others. "This is not going to be as easy as we thought." Looking briefly back to the pit, Aramas whispers, "Aria, I need you to keep the workers from getting to the weapons while the rest of us take out the gnome and his drakes."

"What about Craven and the halfling?" asks Kriv.

"The halfling won't charge. He'll attack from a distance. Craven, however, is another problem. Hopefully Riadon and Loki will have dispatched the guard before he can get into the fray. If so, they can help you here while I handle him."

"And if they don't?"

"Then you three are going to have to handle the gnome, drakes, and workers on your own. I will take care of Craven and the halfling."

"Maybe we should rethink this?"

"I'm afraid that if we do we'll lose the element of surprise. We don't know where that kobold is!"

There is a moment of silence.

"I agree with Aramas. We need to strike now," says Patron.

Kriv looks at Aria then back at Aramas. "Then let's do this."

From their positions, it is a good sixty feet to the pile of weapons; the drakes and gnome stand only a few feet away. Bursting out of the undergrowth, the four charge the unsuspecting gnome. From high above the site, the guard on the ridge shouts, "Intruders!" before sliding down the steep incline into the pit. The workers temporarily stop to see what has happened, then, realizing that they're under attack, they rush toward their weapons, picks and shovels in hand.

The gnome releases the drakes and shouts, "Attack!" as the short muscular creatures swiftly advance on the intruders.

As Aramas, Aria, and Patron charge forward, Kriv pauses long enough to exhale an explosive burst of fire. Startled and severely burned, the two drakes temporarily halt their advance. Before they can regroup, Patron hurls himself against the closest, his two blades cutting deep into its flesh; squealing screams of anguish fill the air. Aramas advances on the other while Aria extends her arm to release a dark crackling bolt of energy at the advancing workers.

While Patron continues his assault on the now crippled drake, Aramas engages the second as it lunges toward him. With a long, sweeping blow, his blade slashes deep into its right shoulder.

Sliding to the ground and temporarily stunned, it attempts to stand. With blood spewing from the nearly severed limb, it makes a vain attempt to resume the attack, using its razor-sharp teeth to grab at Aramas's leg.

Brushing aside the advance, Aramas plants his foot firmly on its neck and thrusts his sword through the creature's heart, its legs now violently twitching. With a gush of air, the beast exhales its last breath, its now life-less body pinned to the ground by Aramas's sword. Quickly withdrawing it, Aramas turns to address the oncoming workers.

However, before he can do so, he is violently knocked to the ground. Momentarily dazed, Loki helps him to his feet. "The halfling is pretty good."

Shaking his head to clear the cobwebs, Aramas replies, "I'm okay! Where did you come from?"

Loki smiles. "We had no trouble with the guard, so we figured we'd give you a hand."

Patron, having killed the other drake, turns back to Aramas. "We need to move!"

Directing his comments to Riadon, Aramas motions toward the pit. "Take out the gnome! Patron, stop the guard. Once he has been taken out of the equation, I expect the workers will turn and run." Aramas motions for Loki to follow then darts off toward Craven and the halfling.

While Aria continues to slow the advance of the remaining guard and workers, Kriv, joined by Riadon, advances on the gnome, moving to force the smallish creature away from his allies. Kriv thrusts his swirling flail at the gnome. However, just as he does, the gnome disappears. Surprised, Kriv slides to a halt, his head turning from side to side, hoping to locate his foe.

"Did you hit him?" shouts Riadon.

"I don't know. He was there and then he wasn't."

Without warning, the gnome reappears within a few feet of where it just stood. With a screeching high-pitched laugh, it delivers a cutting blow to Kriv's thigh.

Reaching for the wound with his off hand, Kriv again thrusts his flail at the small target. As before, the gnome disappears. Unsure as to where the creature will appear next, he slowly backs away, his head again turning from side to side, hoping to prevent another successful attack. "Where is it?"

Just then, it reappears. As it does, Riadon temporarily vanishes and immediately reappears behind the gnome. Flanked and temporarily confused, the gnome turns to address Riadon. However, before he can do so, Riadon thrusts his blade deep into the creature's back. As it reels from the searing pain, vainly attempting to reach the blade, Kriv's flail swiftly ends the encounter, causing the gnome's lifeless body to crumble to the ground.

"Are you okay?" asks Riadon.

"I'll be fine," Kriv says, grimacing. "We need to get to the others."

Patron, as directed, rushes toward the guard. The guard shouts at the workers to get to the weapons while he takes on the advancing dragonborn. Like two bull elks charging headfirst across an open field, the two collide just short of the pile of weapons; the sound of cold steel echoes off the walls of the pit, each collision of blades sending bright yellow sparks into the air.

For the first few seconds, neither combatant gives any ground. With each slashing blow of Patron's dueling blades, the guard counters with a sweep of his own, his shield deflecting blow after blow. Like a finely choreographed ballet, each maneuvers around the other, feigning penetration after penetration in search of any opening that might afford the opportunity to deliver a debilitating or fatal blow.

As soon as the workers reach their weapons, they quickly gather their swords and spears. Without hesitation, they rush toward Kriv and Riadon.

After withdrawing his knife from the gnome's back, Riadon quickly sheaths it and draws his short sword. Jokingly he shouts to Kriv, "I don't get many opportunities to use this!"

Moving to find a more advantageous position from which to launch her attacks, Aria hurls a ball of hellish fire into the advancing workers. The group's leader screams in agony as his body, engulfed in flames, falls to the ground. Stunned, the others stop momentarily, their brief hesitation allowing Kriv and Riadon to prevent them from joining the guard.

"Attack, you cowards!" shouts the guard.

Confused, the workers attempt to retreat, only to find that Riadon has suddenly appeared behind them. Swinging wildly and with little effort, Riadon kills two workers. Kriv's flail, like a sickle cutting through grain, systematically fells those that remain.

As the pair maneuver to assist Patron, Kriv shouts, "Aria, see what you can do to help Aramas and Loki!"

Sword drawn, Craven motions to the halfling to take up a defensive position amongst the rocks at the base of the pit's north rim. "Keep the dwarf occupied while I take care of the paladin."

Then, turning his attention to Aramas and Loki, Craven slowly drifts toward the open field. Finding a spot to his liking, he stops, points his sword at Aramas, then begins to tap the tip of his blade on the ground, each tap tauntingly inviting the advancing adversary. Then, as if welcoming a long-lost friend, he extends both arms, his steely eyes focused on Aramas, and calmly remarks, "I've been waiting for this."

Without taking his eyes off Craven, Aramas motions to Loki to advance on the halfling. Then, accepting the challenge, he begins to circle his opponent, each man sizing up the other, their focus on nothing else, their blades glistening in the first sunlight of the day.

"So nice of you to spare me the trouble of having to find you," remarks Craven. "I did not have the opportunity to take from you what is ours earlier." Then smiling broadly, he says, "You will not be that lucky today."

"As I once told you, luck has nothing to do with it."

With the swiftness of a rattlesnake, Craven lunges forward, his blade deflected by the sweep of Aramas's sword. Momentarily stepping back, the two combatants begin to circle again, slowly moving counterclockwise, each man looking for an opportune opening.

"You know that you cannot win," remarks Aramas.

"I have overcome worse odds," replies Craven.

Almost in jest, Aramas responds, "I guess you don't know who we are."

"No, you don't know who *we* are!" at which point Craven unleashes a feverish series of sweeping attacks. Giving only what ground he must, Aramas parries each.

As the two exchange blows, the sound of singing steel ringing off the ridge behind them, Patron, Kriv, and Riadon quickly dispatch the remaining guard. Stopping to survey the carnage around them, Riadon comments, "I thought that we were supposed to take a prisoner."

"It is what it is," replies Patron as he rushes toward the others with Kriv and Riadon following close behind. Realizing that it is not likely that Craven will surrender, Kriv shouts ahead, "We need the halfling alive!"

As the three fan out to reinforce Loki's position, their progress is temporarily halted by a rapid succession of sling bolts. Huddled behind a nearby rock, Loki sarcastically remarks, "Nice of you to drop by."

Kriv shouts back, "It would appear that you have matters well in hand." Then, after briefly surveying their position, Kriv shouts to Riadon, "Get behind him. Aria and I will try to keep him pinned down!" Almost immediately, he turns to Loki. "On my signal, you and Patron advance on his position."

Both Loki and Patron nod their understanding. Waiting to make sure that Riadon can achieve his objective, Kriv shouts, "Now!"

Like two sentinels, both Kriv and Aria stand, unleashing a hellish volley of arcane energy and fire, forcing the halfling to dive behind the nearest cover. Realizing that he can no longer hold his position and hoping to get to higher ground where he might have a chance to escape the inevitable, the halfling turns and rushes toward the wall. However, as he does, Loki's hammer slams into his back, thrusting him headlong into the surrounding rocks.

Kriv shouts to Riadon, "Check to see if he's alive. If so, bind him, and tend to his wounds!"

Sensing that the end is near, Craven halts his attack, his blade pointing at Aramas. "Your victory will be short-lived. We serve a power that you cannot comprehend, one that will not only engulf you but the world as we know it."

As the two continue their slow minuet, they are surrounded by the others.

"Stand your ground," shouts Aramas. Still focused on Craven, he asks, "Who do you serve?"

Without hesitation, Craven raises his sword and throws himself at Aramas. With one anticlimactic blow, Aramas wheels to his right, his blade waist high, parallel to the ground, as it slashes through Craven's midsection.

Craven drops to his knees, his entrails spilling onto the ground around him, then looks up at Aramas. "The rift awaits you."

With the gurgling sound of air slowly escaping from his lifeless body, Craven slumps forward, facedown in the tall grass of the meadow.

As if caught in a state of suspended animation, Aramas stands motionless before the defeated foe, his blood-spattered tabard testament to the carnage his sword has spawned.

"Of what power was he referring?" asks Patron.

Exhausted, Aramas replies, "You heard the same as I." Turning toward

Loki, and with a sense of resignation in his voice, he says, "I fear that our lot has been cast on a course that we cannot yet fathom." Loki quietly nods his acknowledgement.

Before the two head back to the rocks to check on Riadon and the halfling, Aramas says to Aria, "Check the bodies for anything that might indicate what we'll be up against at the castle."

Overhearing the conversation, Riadon shouts, "Don't forget to check for anything of value!"

With a slight chuckle, Patron shakes his head. "I'll give you a hand."

Directing his comment to Aramas, Kriv jokingly asks, "How's your head?"

"Better than your thigh."

"What are your plans for the halfling?"

"Depends on what he has to say."

"I hope you don't plan on letting him go."

"It depends on what he has to say." Looking over toward the pit, Aramas points to the excavation. "Loki, see what you can learn from the digging."

Moving into the rocks with Kriv, Aramas asks Riadon, "Is he able to talk?"

"He's able but not sure how willing."

Kriv interjects, "He'll talk."

Sitting atop a rather large rock, his hands and feet bound, the smallish creature is understandably nervous. He sports an elaborate braid of hair, his dark complexion is complemented by his forest green and brown clothing. The halfling exudes a tough countenance. "What's to be my fate?"

Aramas replies, "It depends on how you answer our questions."

"There's not much to tell. I am nothing more than a simple mercenary trying to scratch out a meager living."

Kriv asks, "How is it that you came to be here?"

"I was approached by two well-dressed strangers in Spring Green."

"Who were they? What were you offered?"

He motions toward Craven. "Him and some guy who wore long robes, some sort of priest or cleric."

"Brevek?"

"I didn't pay much attention and didn't ask any questions. I needed the money, and they needed someone to help oversee the excavation while providing some additional protection for the workers. Seemed like a good idea at the time. Besides, they caught me taking advantage of a certain friend of theirs during a business transaction. I wasn't given much of a choice."

"How long ago was that?"

"Maybe three or four weeks."

Aramas asks, "Did you ever see the cleric again?"

"No, and until a few days ago, I hadn't seen this guy either. I came here with the workers and guards and haven't left since."

"What do you know about the excavation?"

"Only that they wanted to recover as much of the dragon skeleton as possible."

"Did they say why?"

"Not my problem."

"Did they say who wanted the skeleton?"

"Again, not my problem. All I wanted to do was complete the job, collect my money, and get as far away from here as possible."

Aramas asks, "So you would have us believe that you know nothing more about the operation than what you've told us?"

"I've got no reason to lie. You're the ones that just made quick work of two drakes and close to a dozen men." He holds his bound hands out toward Aramas. "Besides, you've got me bound like a pig headed to slaughter. If I hope to get out of here alive, I'd better make sure that you like my answers."

Kriv interrupts. "What do you know about the castle?"

"Only that the guy in charge was having the bones transported there as quickly as we could uncover them."

"Did you ever go to the castle?"

"No. I was instructed to stay at the site. Each day, two goblins would show up with a small horse-drawn cart. We'd load it and they would return." He briefly hesitates. "I'm told that the castle is possessed."

Kriv turns to Aramas. "What do you think?"

"He appears to be telling the truth."

"How much were you being paid?" asks Kriv.

"Twenty-five gold."

Just then, Aria and Patron return. "Other than a few pieces of gold, a couple of gems, and three longswords, it was pretty slim pickings. Nothing to indicate what they were doing or why." Gazing at the bound halfling, Patron asks, "What do you plan to do with him?"

Kriv replies, "Hire him!"

Startled, Aramas replies, "What?"

"Hire him. You, better than anyone, can attest to his accuracy with a sling."

"That has nothing to do with it. Besides, we already have one thief in this party."

Kriv turns his attention to the halfling. "Since we have apparently deprived you of what you were owed, I'm willing to double what they offered in return for your allegiance."

"Have you gone daft? He tried to kill me!" exclaims Aramas.

"My point exactly. He did what he was paid to do even in the face of inevitable defeat." Addressing everyone in the party, he adds, "We don't know what to expect at the castle. Do you really believe that we couldn't use someone with his ability?"

There is a momentary silence. Patron replies, "Makes sense to me." Aria nods her agreement.

Just then, Loki returns from the dig. "What did I miss?"

Aramas points to the halfling. "Kriv wants to hire him."

"He is pretty good with a sling." Loki smiles. "You should know."

With a sense of frustration in his voice, Aramas says, "I know, Kriv already reminded me." He hesitates for what seems like an eternity then glares at Kriv. "His pay comes out of your share."

"That's fine."

"And if he doesn't do as expected?"

"He'll answer to me."

Looking at each of the party members, Aramas asks, "Is everyone else in agreement?" Each responds affirmatively.

"When do I get paid?" asks the halfling.

Aramas throws up his arms and brusquely replies, "When the job is done!"

Kriv draws his knife and cuts the halfling's bonds. "What are you called?"

"Slinger."

As he walks away, Aramas sarcastically murmurs, "It figures."

Chapter 7

Raven's Nest

Along with the other youth that had been spirited from his village, Aramas soon found himself moving from town to town. Having somehow found favor with his captors, he was not subjected to many of the tortures forced upon the others, particularly the girls. While he was still too young to fully understand, he knew by the anguish in their eyes that whatever it was, it was unspeakable.

As the months passed, the numbers of those he knew dwindled—most sold off, never to be seen again, and others beaten so badly that death became a welcome salvation. While the days were difficult, he most dreaded the nights. Not only were the girls taken at random, so were many of the youngest boys. By the time he reached his eleventh summer, none of those taken with him was still with the marauders; each was eventually replaced with others equally as unfortunate.

For the first few years of captivity, the days were spent gathering firewood, unloading the spoils of battle from the master's wagons, tending to the horses, cleaning weapons, and polishing armor. However, as he approached manhood, his responsibilities changed. The defense of his mother in the face of overwhelming odds had made an impression on his master, a man who loved gambling and pitting his stable of gladiators against all comers.

As his height approached six feet, Aramas was placed under the tutelage of Gastinian, the master's most decorated gladiator. A big burly man with dark hair, deep gray eyes, and bronze complexion, Gastinian was a master with a greatsword. Having won twenty-three matches, he had survived longer than any of his contemporaries. For his prowess in the ring, he had earned his freedom and proudly displayed his gladius. However, he had known nothing else, and with no family to whom he could return, he decided to remain in the service of the master. Acquiescing to his master's request, Gastinian accepted his new ward. He too realized that Aramas was somehow different.

Training was not easy. Each day started long before sunrise with exercises designed to build strength and agility. These were followed by regular examinations by the master's doctor or massages and rubdowns. No longer forced to live off gruel, scraps, or whatever else he could scrounge, his meals, three or four times a day, consisted of various grains, boiled beans, oatmeal, vegetables, ash, and dried fruit. Each meal was followed by instruction in various combat tactics or practice in developing one's sense of balance. While weapons proficiency was of paramount importance, so was one's ability to size up an opponent's strengths and vulnerabilities and take advantage of each. When weapons training did commence, it was with a wooden sword weighing twice that of the weapon he would eventually master.

While Gastinian was an unmatched ruthless warrior in the arena, one who neither gave nor expected any quarter, he was just the opposite in his private life. He was a disciplined taskmaster but also kind and understanding. "A great warrior not only knows how to deliver death, he also knows how to dispense mercy. Never allow vengeance or anger to dictate your actions," he would say. "They will only lead to your destruction." During many of the exercises, Aramas was blindfolded. "Don't rely on what you can see. Use all your senses and become one with your surroundings. Make nature, geography, and weather your allies."

"And religion?" asked Aramas.

Holding up his greatsword, Gastinian replied, "This is the only religion I know."

"But if I am to draw from all of my senses, am I to disregard what is the strongest within me?"

Having been caught off guard by the logic of the question, Gastinian hesitated before answering. "While I know not of what you speak, draw upon *all* of your senses."

"Aramas. What do you make of them?" asks Loki.

Returning from his thoughts, Aramas replies, "This dragon died in combat." He points to what appear to be ribs. "Judging from the discoloration, it was a fiery death."

Walking into the pit, Aramas runs his hands over the creature's bones then steps off the distance between its skull and the end of its tail. "Fifty feet."

Sarcastically, Loki quips, "Glad we didn't run into this fellow."

Moving toward what is left of the dragon's wing, Aramas kneels and carefully removes a shiny object from the soil.

"What did you find?"

"It would appear to be a scale."

As Aramas stands to study what he has found, the others arrive at the rim of the pit.

Slinger remarks, "We figured those to be scales."

Aramas looks up at Slinger. "Did you find many?"

"Several bags worth."

"What did you do with them?"

"We loaded the bags on the wagon. I figured they must be worth something; otherwise, why send them to the castle?"

Rubbing the scale between his thumb and fingers, he asks, "Was anything else sent to the castle?"

"We removed the horns from the skull and the tip of the creature's tail."

"Nothing else?"

"A few of the rib bones. Didn't make much sense to me."

Aramas spits on the scale and slowly wipes away the dirt. "If the lore is correct, this was a good dragon."

"I didn't know there were good dragons," remarks Loki.

"How do you know it was a good dragon?" asks Riadon.

"The scale is metallic in color, possibly bronze or copper."

Riadon gets a glint of hope in his eyes. "Are they made of bronze or copper?"

"No. Like feathers on a bird, the color distinguishes the type of dragon as well as its strengths and abilities."

"So what color were the bad dragons?" asks Loki.

Stepping forward, Kriv stretches out his hand. "May I examine it?" Aramas hands it to him. After a few seconds, Kriv hands the scale back to Aramas. "Evil dragons were chromatic in color: black, red, blue, green, and white."

"Good dragons were metallic in color: gold, bronze, silver, copper, iron, adamantine, and platinum," adds Patron. "Aramas is right. The color of the dragon could tell you where the dragon lived and what it subsided on. However, it also told you what powers it possessed."

"If what I was taught is correct, this dragon was probably killed by a red dragon."

"What tells you that?" asks Riadon.

"Red dragons breathed fire."

After they bury the bodies, the party gathers their gear and heads back to the road.

"How far to the castle?" asks Aramas.

"Not sure. I was never there. However, we would load the wagons early in the morning and the empty wagon would be back at the site later that night," replies Slinger.

"Why didn't we see a wagon today?" asks Patron.

"It was loaded and left before you attacked us."

"What about kobolds? Did you ever see any kobolds?" asks Aramas.

"No. Just goblins, although I did overhear Craven talking to one of the drivers about some a few days ago."

"Do you remember what he said?"

"Only that word had reached the castle about a small party from Spring Green that was being tracked by a squad of kobolds." Looking around, Slinger continues. "Based on what's happened, I would assume that you're the party and you've either taken care of the kobolds or they never found you."

Loki sarcastically remarks, "They found us." Nothing further is said for the next several hours.

Shortly after noon, as the road passes through a grove of dense trees at the top of a small hill, Aramas stops abruptly. There, about two miles ahead of them, standing like an ancient sentinel, is Raven's Nest Castle. Perched high atop a balding mountain overlooking the road east, its silhouette dominates the horizon. Crumbling towers and walls, surrounded by large piles of rock, are clearly visible. While the forest has slowly begun to swallow the fields outside the castle's outer wall as well as the road leading to the keep, most of the area is barren. From their current position, the road ahead is clearly visible, not only to them, but to anyone standing watch on the parapets two miles distant. While the main road continues its serpentine path past the castle to the east, about a mile ahead, another road veers to the north toward what was once the castle's main gate.

Staring at the ruins, Patron remarks, "Whoever picked that location knew what they were doing. There's no good way to approach the fortress without being seen."

Sarcastically, Loki replies, "Based on what Slinger heard, it won't much matter. They've known of our presence since we left Spring Green."

Silence again settles over the party as they survey the valley and the road to the castle. Breaking the silence, Aria warns, "It would not be wise to enter the castle."

Puzzled, Aramas replies, "Why? What do you see?"

In an almost foreboding tone, she says, "A power stronger than any that I have ever encountered."

"Is that worse than haunted?" asks Riadon.

Acknowledging the comment, Aramas briefly looks at Riadon then back at the castle. "I gave my word. But I will understand if there are those who would prefer to return to Spring Green."

For what seems like an eternity, no one says a word. Finally, Aria calmly replies, "I do not mean to question the purpose of our undertaking. I swore to defeat evil in whatever form." Then bowing slightly, she adds, "I have not traveled these many months to turn away now."

The others nod their agreement. Looking back to the castle, Aramas remarks, "Then let us waste no more time." Motioning for the others to follow, he moves over the crest of hill and heads down the road into the valley.

As the party continues into the valley, birds flushed from the undergrowth on either side of the road indicate that no one has passed by this area for some time. The sky, clear and blue with few clouds, hosts several birds of prey searching for their next meal. Fifty yards ahead, three deer emerge from the undergrowth, stop in the middle of the road momentarily to observe the intruders, then quickly dart to the other side. No one says a word, their eyes searching the surroundings for any hint of discovery or ambush. Arriving at the fork in the road, Aramas directs the party to proceed in pairs up the hill, himself and Aria in the lead, Patron at the rear.

Fifteen minutes later, standing in the ruins of the castle's outer wall, Aramas asks Aria, "What do you see?"

"Only what has been observed."

While significant parts of the outer wall remain, the area is strewn with rubble, large blocks of weathered rock, rusty armor, and broken weapons; weeds and small saplings slowly devour any remaining open areas. The large oaken gates that once prevented unwanted intruders lie splintered to either side of the overgrown road. Little remains of the inner walls, or the buildings that they once protected; however, the keep still towers above everything. Although the bulk of the front entrance wall has long since collapsed, exposing several of the building's upper floors, it is still an intimidating structure. A cool, almost foreboding breeze whistles as it passes through the holes, cracks, and crevices.

Kriv points to what appears to be a stairwell leading underground just inside what was the entrance to the keep. "This area is too open and exposed. If they have been observing us, I would expect them to wait for us to enter the keep. The stairwell would afford them the greatest advantage."

"I agree," says Patron.

Moving cautiously toward the stairwell, Aramas suddenly motions for everyone to halt. "Someone is coming up the stairs."

No sooner does he make the pronouncement than two short dark-skinned creatures emerge. "What business have you in this place?"

Aramas replies, "We bear a message from Brevek."

"Hmmm. Craven has always been our contact." Momentarily pausing to size up the party, he continues. "Give us Brevek's message, and we will ensure that it gets to whom it is intended."

"We were instructed to deliver it in person."

"I understand, but we have our orders."

"Brevek indicated that you might question our arrival. We were instructed to tell you that '*The journey to enlightenment passes through ignorance.*'"

Taking a quick step back, one of the goblins draws his sword and shouts to his companion, "Warn the others! Brevek is dead."

"So much for what Alissa got out of Brevek," remarks Loki as he draws his hammer.

"Take care of him. I'll get the other!" shouts Kriv.

As Aramas, Patron, and Loki make quick work of the goblin, Kriv charges down the stairwell. Stopping briefly at the bottom, he quickly surveys the open area before him. Directly in front of him is the intersection of four hallways: two directly ahead—one to each side of the main foyer—and one each to the left and right. All are well lit, with glowing sconces positioned every few feet along the corridors. The ceiling above the foyer is buttressed by four large columns, between which the floor is decorated with a large circular mosaic. Everywhere else, the floor, walls, and ceiling are constructed of finely crafted stone.

When he hears a laugh from the hallway directly ahead and to the left, he rushes forward. However, as soon as he steps onto the mosaic, the floor collapses, sending him twenty feet into the pit below. Wincing in pain, he slowly rolls over, sits up, and begins to survey the situation.

"Are you all right?" asks Loki, peering down from above. The others circling the pit's rim. "Don't move!"

Sarcastically Kriv replies, "I'm not going . . . " but before he can finish, the walls around him appear to move; rats pour out of every opening, their harsh squeals filling the air, their bites stinging. Drawing his flail, Kriv attempts to reduce their numbers. "Get me out of here!"

Patron quickly pulls a rope from his backpack and lowers it into the pit. "Grab hold!"

Kriv wastes no time securing the line around his waist. "Go!" With the help of Aramas and Loki, Kriv is quickly extracted from the pit, several rats still clinging to his legs and back. "Get them off me!"

Once the last of the rats is removed, Riadon chuckles. "So how was your trip?"

Unamused, Kriv gives Riadon a quick look of disdain then turns to Aramas and replies, "I heard one laughing down the hall ahead and to the left."

"Did you see any others?" asks Loki.

"No. I didn't actually see the one that laughed. I lost sight of the one I was chasing before I reached the bottom of the stairs."

"So we don't even know if it was the same creature."

Looking briefly down each of the hallways, Aramas directs his comment to Kriv. "From now on, we have Slinger check for traps before proceeding. We may not be as lucky the next time." Kriv nods affirmatively.

"So which way do we go?" asks Loki.

"It probably doesn't matter," replies Aria. "We must assume that the others have been alerted to our presence."

"Then let's not give them any more time to set up an ambush," adds Patron. "If the laughter came from the hallway ahead, they are probably waiting for us. I say we go to the right prepared to fight but do so on our terms."

Aramas asks, "Any other suggestions?"

"It makes no difference. Pick one," says Kriv.

Motioning to the hallway on the right, Aramas asks Slinger to take the lead. Checking for traps as quickly as possible, the party moves cautiously down the well-lit hallway, Aramas immediately behind Slinger and Patron protecting the rear.

Forty feet later, the hallway turns to the right. Peering cautiously around the corner, Slinger in a low voice reports, "The hallway appears to be clear."

Aramas peers down the hallway and asks Aria, "Do you sense anything?"

"There are creatures in all directions."

Loki interjects, "I could have told you that."

Closing her eyes, Aria clasps her hands and places them against her forehead. A minute later, she opens her eyes. "There is powerful magic directly below us."

"What kind of magic? How far below?" asks Kriv.

"I cannot be certain." She looks at Aramas. "There may be several levels below us."

The party continues down the long narrow hallway, the only noise coming from the crackle of sand beneath their feet on the stone floor. Doors are clearly visible at the end of the hall, one at the northern end of the hallway and one on the western wall. On the eastern wall, directly across the hallway, is a set of iron double doors. The hallway is otherwise devoid of any points of entry or escape.

Halting a few feet before the door at the end of the hall that has bloodstains clearly visible at its base, Aramas motions to Slinger. "Check the doors."

Quietly moving from door to door, Slinger checks for traps before peering through the keyholes.

"Any traps?" asks Loki.

"Can you see anything?" asks Kriv.

Briefly confused, Slinger replies, "No, and no. The room to the left is dark. However, judging from the smell of grain, canvas, and burlap, I'd say it is a storeroom. The room ahead is lit. I could see a rack, an iron maiden, and a firepit. I could also hear someone moaning in the background but could not see anyone moving around. The room to the right could be a problem. It appears to be the guards' quarters.

"Did you see anyone in the quarters?" asks Riadon.

"No, but I heard muted chatter. There are enough tables, chairs, and beds in there that a goblin could easily conceal their presence until we're well inside."

Aramas looks to Patron. "Guard the rear. Kriv, Loki, watch the other two doors." Then standing to one side of the storeroom door, Aramas motions to Slinger. "Open it."

Slinger does as directed. As expected, the room contains dried meat, dried fruits, grain, and several casks of mead.

Staring at the casks of mead, his mouth watering, Loki asks, "Have we got time to fill our skins?"

Aramas shakes his head. "Later." Looking back down the hallway, then at the double door, Aramas nods toward the torture chamber door. "Ready?" Hearing no objections, his sword ready, Aramas says, "Open it!"

Again, Slinger does as directed. However, no sooner is the door opened than three crossbow bolts zip over his head, splintering on the wall behind him. Wasting no time, Kriv rushes through the open door, his flail swirling above his head.

Behind the rack stand three goblins, two sharpshooters and the torturer. Another goblin, sword drawn, emerges from behind the iron maiden. The torturer, hot iron in hand, leaps over the rack hoping to halt Kriv's advance as the two sharpshooters attempt to reload their crossbows.

Loki and Aramas follow Kriv, Aramas taking on the warrior and Loki one of the sharpshooters. In the far corner, a previously unseen sharpshooter releases another bolt, hitting Patron in the shoulder as he dashes into the room. Briefly stunned, Patron pulls out the bolt, and with both swords rhythmically swirling in front of him, advances on the attacker with Slinger and Aria close behind.

However, before either can contribute to the melee, the fight is over. The five goblins are no match for the interlopers.

Surveying the room, Aramas asks, "Is everyone okay?"

Patron, blood running down his tabard, groans, "I could use some help."

"Loki, see what you can do." Moving back toward the open door, Aramas looks down the hall, louder chatter coming from behind the double iron doors. "Well, if they didn't know where we were before, they certainly do now."

From one of the cells off to the left, they hear a feeble squeaky voice. "Would someone please let me out of here?"

Motioning toward the cell, Aramas directs Kriv to investigate the cell-block, Aria close behind. As Loki tends to Patron's wound, Aramas stands guard in the doorway while Riadon checks the bodies for anything of value.

"Did you find anything?" asks Patron as Loki dresses his wound.

Almost giddy, Riadon replies, "Fifty-five gold pieces, fifty silver, and some hide armor that could be worth something."

"Nothing else?"

"A half dozen spears, a short sword, some leather armor, and three crossbows." Rummaging through the pile, he continues. "Nothing that we could use."

"Might I see the armor?" asks Slinger. He briefly studies it. "I'd say this is probably worth eight hundred to a thousand gold pieces." He looks over to Aramas. "I could use this. Would you mind if I wear it?"

Riadon interrupts. "I thought we were splitting all of the spoils."

Aramas replies, "All accounts will be settled once we get back to Spring Green." He briefly glances down the hall then back at Riadon. "I see no harm in allowing him to wear it. Besides, that's one less thing we have to carry."

"Look what we've found," exclaims Kriv. Firmly in his grasp is a pathetic-looking figure of a goblin.

"My name is Splug. I am forever in your debt for releasing me from my chains. If you allow me to slip down the hallway, I promise to tell no one of your presence."

"He claims to have been unfairly imprisoned because several casks of mead went missing," adds Aria.

"Everyone here thinks me a thief. I did not steal their precious mead, nor was I responsible for depriving them of their rations." He bows politely toward Aramas. "I am a simple creature who wishes only to serve. That was my lot, and I gladly accepted it. If you will not let me go, maybe I could lend you my services."

Staring suspiciously at the goblin, Loki remarks, "You're not going to fall for this."

"But Master Dwarf, I was unfairly charged. There was no evidence."

"If you stole *my* mead, I'd . . ."

"Enough!" declares Aramas. He focuses on the goblin. "What do you know of the castle?"

"Very little. I was not permitted to venture much beyond the walls of the barracks and entry corridor."

"How many guards are there?"

"I really don't know. Maybe five to protect the entry and fifteen or so in the quarters. Balgron the Fat was very secretive about such information."

"Who is Balgron the Fat?" asks Patron.

"The captain of the guard. He is so important that he has his own bodyguard."

"Where might we find him?"

"His room is at the far end of the guard's quarters behind a large set of wooden doors."

Pointing to the iron doors, Aramas asks, "Other than these doors, is there another entrance to the quarters?"

"Not that I am aware of. However, there have been several instances when Balgron was found not to be in his quarters after he was clearly seen entering them."

Looking back toward Aramas, Loki remarks, "A secret entrance?"

"Could be, but I doubt that we'll have time to find it."

"What kind of weapons can we expect to encounter?" asks Kriv.

"Spears, crossbows, and short swords."

"What does this Balgron look like?" asks Patron.

164

"Short, fat, thick, knotty fingers."

"That could be anyone."

"You'll know him when you see him. He favors a large, spiked club."

Directing his comments to Aramas, Loki asks, "What are we going to do with him? You aren't seriously considering taking him with us!"

"No, I'm not." He motions to Kriv. "Bind his hands behind his back, gag him, and put him back in his cell."

"But Master Paladin, I can be . . ."

"Oh, shut up," replies Kriv as he stuffs a rag in the creature's mouth.

While Aria and Kriv bind his hands, Aramas continues. "Slinger, upon my command, you and Riadon will open the doors. I expect a welcome like the one we just received, so remain low. As soon as their archers have released their bolts, Aria will hurl a fireball into the room."

Slinger interrupts. "The hallway into the room is about forty feet long. Can she throw it that far?"

Aria replies, "That should not be a problem."

Aramas nods. "Once the fireball is released, Loki, Patron, and I will charge down the hallway." He turns to Kriv. "Once we're into the room, you follow with Slinger and Riadon."

"What about our rear?" asks Loki.

"We'll take care of it," replies Kriv.

Looking around the room, Aramas asks, "Any questions?" Hearing none, he says, "Get him back into his cell."

As Kriv and Aria return the goblin to his cell, Kriv admonishes him. "Any attempt to notify your friends will not end well. Do you understand?"

Splug nods his head in agreement. With the clank of cell door shutting, Kriv withdraws the keys and throws them into the torture room's firepit. Splug, his eyes agape, squirms and moans to convey his displeasure.

Kriv looks back at the cell. "You'll be fine. If you're still here when we get back, we'll let you go."

After they position themselves just past the double iron doors, Kriv and Aria stare down the empty hall looking for any indication that the guards may be ready to launch an attack. Aria looks back at Aramas, who is standing with Loki and Patron just inside the torture room door, then motions down the hall and whispers, "There are others just around the corner."

Patron interjects, "Let's wait for them to advance and take them here."

Aramas quietly replies, "If we don't move now, we'll be trapped. No, we need to move before we have no place to go."

He motions to Riadon and Slinger, who are now positioned low and to either side of the doors. "On my signal."

After he checks one last time to ensure that everyone is ready, Aramas shouts, "Now!"

Riadon and Slinger push the doors open, both loudly slamming against the stone walls behind them. However, there is no volley of arrows, only silence.

Aramas shouts, "Throw the fireball!" Aria immediately responds, hurling the fireball down the long hall and into the main quarters. Striking what appears to be a large stone table in the center of the room, the fireball explodes, hurling hot embers in all directions. Thick acrid smoke fills the air.

As planned, Aramas, Patron, and Loki rush into the quarters, followed closely by Riadon and Slinger. Halfway down the hall, two warrior goblins emerge from behind the stone table, each hurling a javelin into the now smoke-filled hallway, neither hitting its intended target. However, as the three reach the main room, two more goblins leap from behind a wooden table to the left, joined by four from a previously unseen room to the right. As the sound of clashing steel fills the air, four more goblins emerge from another room to the left as well as two from the room directly ahead, one feverishly ringing a large bell.

Suddenly, from down the long hall, three crossbow bolts ricochet past Kriv and Aria and shatter into the wall behind them. As Kriv and Aria back into the quarters, Kriv shouts, "There are four coming up the hall! Three archers and a swordsman!"

Aramas replies, "Shut the doors!"

Closing the doors behind them, Kriv hastily looks for something with which to bolt them shut. Finding nothing, he shouts to Aria, "Help the others. I'll hold here."

"Are you sure?"

"Go!"

As Aria rushes down the hall, Kriv takes a few steps back and prepares for the coming assault.

Hoping to avoid being flanked, or worse, surrounded, Patron, Aramas, and Loki slowly back to the hallway entrance, Slinger and Riadon assuming positions ten feet behind. Two more spears pierce the smoke, one hitting Loki, the other Riadon. Seriously injured, Riadon falls to the floor.

Aramas shouts to Slinger, "We need to take out the two warriors!" However, before Slinger can respond, a powerful bolt of energy from Aria explodes atop the stone table, hurling the two warriors into the wall behind them. Each collapses to the floor, stunned by the unexpected turn of events. Before they can regain their senses, Slinger ensures that neither will again present any problems.

As the smoke slowly dissipates around the combatants, a short, grizzled figure emerges from the back room. "Do not let them escape!" He motions for the two guards at his side to attack.

Aramas and Patron continue to battle at the entrance to the hallway, each dispatching several attackers.

Unable to effectively continue the fight, Loki falls back to tend to his and Riadon's wounds. However, before he can determine the extent of the damage, he hears what sounds like a prayer of healing coming from behind him. Within seconds, both he and Riadon have been healed sufficiently to allow them to rejoin the fight. Surprised, Loki looks back toward the two iron doors: Kriv broadly grins back at him. Loki gives a quick acknowledging wave, stands, and rushes back down the hallway to rejoin the others. Riadon, still feeling the sting of the spear, is slow to get to his feet.

Suddenly the iron doors are thrust open, and three crossbow bolts zing into the hallway. While one zips past everyone, two find their mark, one lodging in Kriv's leather armor, the other in Aria's shoulder.

As Aria turns to face the advancing menace, Kriv exhales a powerful breath of lightning and fire. Two of the archers fall to the ground, writhing in agony. However, before Kriv can press the advantage, the swordsman charges, his sword held high above his head.

Shifting quickly to his right, Kriv parries the first blow then counters with his flail. While the two exchange blows, the remaining archer reloads. As he raises his weapon, he is suddenly thrust back into the hallway by a searing bolt of fire. Engulfed in flames, the putrid smell of charred flesh now filling the air, the archer falls to the ground and, within seconds, exhales his last.

Confronted by both Kriv and Aria, the swordsman attempts to withdraw into the long hall. As he backs through the doorway, his retreat is stopped by the searing pain of a blade being thrust deep into his back. Dropping his weapon, the swordsman stands motionless, as if suspended in time, then slowly collapses against the wall. Cocking his head slightly, he stares quizzically at the dragonborn before slumping to the floor.

Standing in the doorway, Riadon reaches down and retrieves his knife. As he wipes the blood from the blade, he looks up at Kriv. "I thought I'd return the favor."

Kriv quickly closes the doors and rushes toward Aria. "Are you all right?"

Her reply is wobbly. "I will be. Can you remove the arrow?"

Kriv quickly evaluates the wound. "You are lucky." Reaching into his waist pouch, he pulls out a clean piece of linen, then he places it around the base of the bolt and presses the palm of his right hand against Aria's shoulder. Then, grabbing the shaft with his left hand, he asks, "Ready?"

Aria nods. With one swift movement, Kriv extricates the bolt. While Aria does not scream, she momentarily reaches for the wall in an attempt to maintain her footing. With Riadon's help, she is gingerly lowered to the floor. Placing his hand over the wound, Kriv recites his prayer of healing.

Wasting no time, Kriv bids Riadon to stay with her then leaps to his feet to rejoin the others.

Realizing that their flanking maneuver has failed, the eight remaining swordsmen attempt to regroup behind the stone table, hoping to draw the invaders into the open. As they pull back, Aramas and Patron give no quarter, their blades continuing to extract a heavy toll. Once reinforced by Loki and Kriv, the four again press forward. One by one, the goblins fall before the advance, unable to prevent the inevitable.

Seemingly unfazed by the deteriorating situation, Balgron shouts from behind, "Hold your ground, for if they don't kill you, I . . . ," but before he can finish, Slinger's bolt silences the chieftain.

With no escape, the last of the guards drop their weapons. Aramas says, "Kriv, bind and gag them then throw them into one of the cells."

"That could be a problem."

"How so?"

"I threw the keys into the firepit."

Puzzled, Aramas pauses for a moment, then motions toward the door. "Figure something out."

While Kriv and Patron take the prisoners to the cell block, Aramas proceeds to the chieftain's quarters. "Slinger, see if you can find that secret door. Loki, you and Riadon check the other rooms. I'll check the chieftain's."

Passing through the double doors, Aramas enters the quarters of Balgron's personal guards. Other than two beds, a table, and one chair, it is devoid of amenities. In the far right corner, several large ornate tapestries hang from the ceiling, concealing what lies behind. Aramas moves to the beds and tosses the bedrolls. Finding nothing, he moves to the table. Other than some dried bread crusts, a small dagger, and two empty tankards, there is nothing to indicate what might lie ahead. Moving to the tapestries, he takes his sword and cautiously pushes aside one of them, revealing a small cot tucked neatly in the corner, the bedroll soiled and tussled, as well as a small chest hidden beneath it. Turning back to the double doors, Aramas shouts, "Slinger, Riadon, come in here!"

The two arrive momentarily, followed closely by Loki. Pointing to the chest, Aramas says, "Check to see if it's trapped."

The chest is not large, maybe a foot wide, two feet long, and fifteen inches high. Kneeling, Slinger cautiously examines it. "I see no traps. However, it is locked."

Aramas turns to Loki. "Check the chieftain."

Scurrying into the main room, Loki quickly searches Balgron's pockets. "Found them!"

"Found what?" asks Patron, having returned from the cell block with Kriv.

As he jumps to his feet and rushes into the other room, Loki replies, "Keys!" Kriv and Patron follow him.

Loki hands the keys to Slinger. "This should do it."

Glancing between the ring of keys and the small box, Slinger selects what he expects to be the correct key, slides it into the lock, and turns it to the right. With a large grin of satisfaction, Slinger cautiously places his hands on either side of the lid and slowly raises it.

A very impatient Riadon blurts, "So what's in it?"

With the chest firmly in his grasp, Slinger turns to the others and exclaims, "Gold!"

Quickly moving to the small table, Slinger sets down the chest with the others gathered around. Aramas motions to Patron. "Make sure that no one comes through the door." Then he says to Riadon, "See if you can find that secret door. I don't think it best that we exit the same way we entered."

Loki sits down at the table, and with Slinger, begins to count the coins.

Aramas then asks Kriv, "Did any of the prisoners say anything that could be of help?"

"Only that they were admonished never to enter the lower levels. We did not spend a lot of time questioning them, but it would appear that they were pretty much confined to this area of the castle."

"Nothing else?"

"One of them kept saying that while we may have gotten this far, we would not get past the Crypt of Shadows."

"Did they . . ."

Loki interrupts. "Three hundred sixty gold pieces and a wand of some sort."

Aria asks, "May I examine the wand?"

Aramas motions to the table and nods his approval.

"Did they indicate where the crypt is located?"

"No, only that they were told that if they entered it, a terrible evil would befall them."

"Did you believe them?"

"I saw no reason to believe otherwise."

"Well, we don't have time to interrogate them further. Did you make sure that they won't be getting out any time soon?"

Holding up a charred set of keys, Kriv smiles. "I think so."

Walking over to Aramas, Aria remarks, "The wand is magical and could be put to good use."

"Then consider it yours." Aramas turns his attention to Riadon. "Any luck with that door?"

"Still working on it."

"Slinger, Loki can handle the money. Give Riadon a hand."

While Loki and Kriv stow the gold in the bag of holding, Slinger and Riadon continue to search the walls.

When he returns to the party, Patron reports, "I've secured the door to the hallway. I would recommend we secure the doors to this area as well."

"Agreed, but before we do that, we need to find that door."

Riadon shouts, "Got it!"

About ten feet to the right of the bed and three feet above the floor, Riadon points to a nondescript stone.

"I don't see anything," says Aramas.

"The spacing is different."

"I still don't see it."

Moving closer, Aramas and Patron examine the surrounding stones. "Okay. What does it do?"

Smiling broadly, Riadon pulls the stone out of the wall, exposing a small key hole. Slinger bows sarcastically and hands him the key ring. "You should have the honor."

Patron immediately puts his hand over Riadon's. "We don't know what's on the other side." He looks back to the others. "We don't need any more surprises."

Aramas motions to the lock and says to Slinger, "Check first to make sure that it's not trapped."

After he finds nothing to indicate that the area is trapped, Slinger puts his ear to the wall. After a few seconds, he turns to Aramas. "I detect nothing on the other side."

"Okay. Patron, secure the double doors." With the help of Kriv and Loki, the task is completed in short order.

Checking one last time to make sure that everyone is ready, Aramas directs Slinger to open the secret door. No sooner is the key inserted and turned than the door silently slides open to reveal a stairwell leading to a lower level. The hallway at the foot of the stairwell is well lit and extends another ten feet to an intersection with a perpendicular hall. As with the other halls, the walls and ceiling are comprised of fine-cut stone with a flagstone floor.

Aramas puts a finger to his lips and motions Slinger to check the stairwell and the adjoining hall. Hearing nothing, Slinger cautiously drifts down the stairs, his back hugging the wall to his left.

When he reaches the intersection of the two halls, Slinger looks down the one to his right. Not ten feet away is a stairwell headed up to the main floor with a closed door at the top. To his left, he hears the muted sound of goblins and what sounds like picks and shovels. Looking back to Aramas, he motions for the party to quietly join him.

As soon as Aramas reaches Slinger, in a hushed voice he asks, "What is it?"

"While I can't make out what they're saying, it sounds like an argument between several goblins."

Listening intently, Aramas asks the others, "Does anyone understand

Goblin?" When he receives no positive response, he asks Kriv, "Well, what do you want to do?"

"We were told that what we're looking for is down below. The hall to the right goes up. I say we find out what they're arguing about."

"Loki?"

"I agree with Kriv. I just wish we knew what they were saying."

Cautiously peering around the corner, Slinger can see that the hallway opens into a large room. Further, while he does not see any goblins, he can see what appear to be large planks crossing a large hole. Studying the area, he turns to Aramas. "There is an entrance to what appears to be a lower level down the hallway to the right. However, the voices are definitely coming from the room at the end of the hall. I think they are digging up the floor."

"They're what?" asks Loki.

"They're digging up the floor."

"Why would they . . ."

Kriv interrupts. "Enough, we're wasting time." Motioning to the others to follow, he darts into the hallway and rushes into the room.

"So much for the element of surprise," remarks Loki as the party rushes down the hall.

When they enter the room, the party is surprised to find that much of the floor has been excavated. While large sections of the original floor remain, the bulk of the room is nothing more than a large ten-foot-deep excavation site. The remaining "islands" of floor are connected by narrow planks; ladders extend from two to the pit below.

Having caught the goblins unprepared for visitors, Kriv rushes to cross the first plank. However, before he reaches the next island, the plank breaks, sending him crashing to the dirt below. Temporarily dazed, he attempts to stand. As he does, a crossbow bolt strikes his arm. From the far corner of the room, sitting high atop one of the islands, a goblin archer fumbles to reload his bow.

Aramas shouts, "Aria, take out the archer! We need to give Kriv some cover."

Joining him, Loki shouts, "This one is obviously a slow learner."

Almost simultaneously, from behind two of the islands, two more goblins appear, one with a large drake. Swords drawn, they quickly move to flank Kriv.

Aramas rushes to the nearby ladder and shouts, "Slinger, give us cover! Loki, Patron, follow me!" After returning his sword to its sheath, Aramas proceeds down the ladder. However, before he can reach the bottom, a second drake appears from behind a nearby island and rushes toward Kriv. As Aramas scurries to reach the bottom, Loki hurls his war hammer at the approaching beast.

Kriv regains his footing, his flail swirling over his head, then moves on the advancing drake. As he does, the creature's advance is temporarily halted when Loki's hammer smashes into its shoulder. Taking advantage of this momentary respite, Kriv buries his flail in the drake's skull. Screeching in pain, it rears up on its hind legs, crashes against the island wall behind it, and falls to the ground.

"Behind you!" shouts Aramas.

However, before Kriv can turn, the second drake crashes into his back and drives him to the ground, its teeth tearing through the leather armor and into his flesh. Shaking Kriv violently from side to side, the beast attempts to drag the thrashing body back to its lair. It pauses momentarily then again buries its teeth into Kriv's back.

From above, Slinger hurls several projectiles at the advancing goblins, temporarily slowing their advance, while Aria continues to keep the archer occupied.

Upon reaching the bottom of the ladder, Aramas draws his weapon and shouts, "Patron, Loki, take out the two swordsmen. I'll take care of the drake." Wasting no time, he rushes the beast. With a long, broad sweep of his sword, Aramas cuts a deep swath in the creature's side.

Startled, the drake stumbles and releases its prey. Quickly refocusing its anger, the beast regains its footing and lunges toward the unexpected foe. Aramas moves swiftly to his left and avoids the attack; the drake slides to the ground. Before it can recover, Aramas delivers a severing blow to the creature's neck, blood spurting in all directions.

As Patron and Loki engage the two swordsmen, Aramas rushes to Kriv's now unconscious body. Placing his hands on the gaping wounds, a blue glow pulsating from each, Aramas attempts to stabilize his dying companion.

"Is there anything I can do?" asks Riadon.

Surprised, Aramas asks, "Where did you come from?"

"I figured you could use some help."

Smiling, Aramas replies, "I need to get one of the healing potions. Stay by his side." Picking up his sword, Aramas stands and rushes to join Loki and Patron.

Realizing that his position is too exposed, the archer drops his crossbow, draws his sword, and jumps into the pit. The goblin tumbles as he hits the floor, darts behind the nearest island to get his bearings, then rushes to join his compatriots.

Unable to continue her assault without potentially exposing the party to friendly fire, Aria shouts to the others, "The archer is on the ground!"

Aramas halts his advance and looks up at Aria and Slinger, both of whom are pointing to the island behind Patron and Loki.

A familiar voice exhorts, "To your right!" Instinctively pivoting to his right, Aramas crashes his sword into a goblin's blade before it can strike home. With the ferocity of a cornered animal, Aramas unleashes blow after punishing blow, each met by a similarly ferocious counterattack.

Having lost the element of surprise, and unable to reach the others, the goblin unsuccessfully attempts to extricate himself from a very untenable position, only to fall to Aramas's blade. Aramas turns to see how Patron and Loki are doing.

"What of Kriv?" asks Patron.

"There is little time," he says, extending his hand. "Loki, give me one of the healing potions!"

Loki reaches into his back of holding, takes out one of the healing potions, and hands it to Aramas. The three rush to join Riadon. Kneeling, Aramas lifts Kriv's head, places the vial between his lips, and empties it;

the bluish-green liquid slowly brings life back to the fallen comrade.

Looking up at Aria and Slinger, Aramas yells, "Make sure that we are not interrupted. We can ill afford any surprises." Then he motions to Patron. "See if there is anything we can use." To Riadon he says, "See if you can figure out what it is they were seeking."

As the others go about their assigned tasks, Loki tends to a now conscious Kriv. Carefully removing his armor to expose the severely torn and shredded flesh, Loki proceeds with the precision of a surgeon, his hands moving deliberately from tear to tear, slowly repairing each.

Unable to contain his frustration, Loki asks, "Have you learned nothing? After what happened earlier, why did you rush blindly into the room?"

Kriv does not answer.

"Don't you realize that not only did you nearly get yourself killed, you jeopardized everyone in the party? Had Aramas been unable to stabilize you …"

"I was not thinking."

"How is he?" asks Aramas.

"He'll live."

Looking down at Kriv, Aramas shakes his head then remarks, "I am glad you have returned to us. I trust that you will not make a habit of this."

Nodding his affirmation, Kriv takes a sip from Loki's wine skin.

When Riadon returns from his search of the area, he reports, "Other than twenty-two gold pieces and a holy symbol, I have been unable to find any reason for the excavation."

Aramas extends his hand and takes the holy symbol. After a careful examination, he says, "It is a holy implement of Bahamut."

"May I see it?" asks Loki. He carefully runs his fingers over the artifact. "To use this implement, the holder must be a follower of Bahamut. It has the ability to increase the effectiveness of its holder's weapon."

"Isn't Patron a follower of Bahamut?"

"I believe so."

Loki hands the implement back to Aramas. "Patron, you may have use of this."

Patron takes the glistening artifact from him. "Thank you. It will be used as Bahamut intended."

"Can you help me to my feet?" asks Kriv. With the assistance of Aramas and Patron, a wobbly Kriv regains his footing. "Thank you."

Looking up toward the entrance to the room, Aramas asks, "Anything to report?"

Slinger replies, "Nothing yet."

"Let's get out of here." Moving to the ladder, the party climbs to the main level and proceeds to the door.

Aria peers down the hall. "The source of the magic is ahead and below. I see nothing blocking our path at this time."

Before they proceed into the hallway, Aramas points to the entryway they passed earlier. "Is the magic coming from what lies below?"

"I do not believe so. The source appears to be well ahead of us."

Not wishing to find the party flanked, and hoping to clear the level before proceeding any further, Patron interrupts. "We need to make sure."

Aramas pauses briefly to contemplate his options, then turns to Slinger. "See what you can ascertain."

Without hesitation, Slinger proceeds to the entrance. While the sconces in the main hallway cast enough light to illuminate the first few stairs, there is no light at the bottom. He cautiously enters the darkness where the cold damp smell of mildew fills the air. Slinger listens for any sound that would indicate what lies behind the dark veil.

Hearing nothing other than the chatter of rats darting behind the cover of darkness, he quietly retreats up the stairs. "The darkness obscures what lies ahead. However, I did not detect anything that would lead me to believe that this is the path we should take."

Riadon looks at Loki. "What about that magic implement you used when we were in the cave?"

"You mean my ever-burning torch?" Loki hesitates for just a moment. "That might not be such a bad idea." He looks up at Aramas. "Who better to investigate?"

"Agreed. Aria and I will go with you." He motions to the others. "Remain vigilant. We should not be long."

Having been raised in a world of underground cities, caves, tunnels, and dungeons, Loki was at home below the surface. His father and grandfather, both chieftains in their own right, made sure that their prodigy was not only exposed to the best possible education but also to the martial and tactical skills that would serve him best long after their time had passed. An adroit student, Loki soon became a master, both with a war hammer and crossbow, as well as in the art of dungeoneering.

But that was not where his greatest strength lay. Throughout the arduous training regimen, it became apparent that he possessed a unique spiritual relationship with the god of their clan, Moradin. It was not long before the decision was made to send him to the city of Caladrene where he would be tutored by the high priest of Moradin, himself once a great hospitaler. For the next three years, Loki was schooled in the art of casting, religious fealty, and the sacraments required of a cleric.

While much of Loki's persona was chiseled in those years, it was a natural event that would change the course of his life. Early in the fourth year of his internship, word arrived that a great earthquake had opened a cavernous schism resulting in the complete destruction of his village; his entire clan was swallowed by the darkness below. Overtaken with grief, and having completed most of his training, Loki requested permission to leave the temple to search for his family. The high priest advised him that the search would be futile. However, Loki was determined.

Although he was unable to convince Loki to stay, he was persuaded to seek the guidance of Moradin before departing. For the next two days, isolated in the catacombs below the temple, Loki prayed, refusing all food and drink. On the morning of the third day, he emerged fully prepared for what lay ahead.

He would spend the rest of his life in service to his faith, a healer and protector of the weak, a guardian of the clergy, and an adversary of evil wherever it was found. After consulting with the high priest, and with his blessing, Loki left the temple in search of his lost clan. It was this chevalier who sauntered into a small village pub four years earlier hoping to have a quiet drink with one of the village's more attractive barmaids.

Loki removes the ever-burning torch from his haversack and recites a brief prayer. Loki asks, "Ready?"

Aria and Aramas nod affirmatively.

Loki's eyes search the outer reaches of the torch's light for any movement as the three descend into what appears to be a cave, the finely worked steps and flagstones giving way to an uneven floor of dirt strewn with stalagmites, debris, and broken rock. Stalactites hang from the ceiling, water drips into small pools, and the smell of mold, rat urine, and rotting flesh permeate the air. Beyond the torch's reach they hear rats.

They move a few feet further into the cavern, and as the debris becomes thicker, the clear paths become narrower. Glistening pairs of orange eyes, temporarily caught in the light, pierce the darkness as they appear and disappear between the debris.

Aria whispers, "I do not believe we will find what we seek here."

Moving the torch from side to side, Loki carefully examines the area. "Other than the tracks of a few rats and one or two goblins, no one has entered this area for years. I agree with Aria. There is no need to waste our time here." The three retreat to the stairs and return to the party.

"Well?" asks Kriv.

Extinguishing the torch and returning it to his haversack, Loki replies, "There was nothing of any consequence there. We need to proceed up the stairs back to the main level."

Aramas directs Slinger to check the door at the top of the stairs; it is neither trapped nor locked.

"Do you hear anything on the other side?"

"No. All is quiet."

With weapon drawn, Aramas motions to the others to proceed up the stairs. With everyone ready, Slinger cautiously opens the door. Directly ahead of them is the pit in which Kriv had fallen. Moving swiftly to the intersection, Aramas dispatches Slinger and Riadon to check the two converging halls.

On his return, Riadon reports, "The bodies of the goblins still lie where they fell outside of the torture chamber."

Slinger, having moved quietly into the next room, returns as well. "Two open doors, about fifty feet down the hallway and to the left, reveal a set of stairs to the lower level. The area is well lit and provides no place to hide. Evidently anyone we haven't killed has retreated below."

Aramas acknowledges the reports then leads the party through the connecting room. Pausing a few feet from the top of the stairwell, he motions to the others to stay close to the wall behind him as he peers into the level below. The stairs are discolored. While the light behind him is sufficient to see into the dark room, its floor appears to be comprised of the same finely laid flagstone as on the main level, the strong over-powering stench of rotting human flesh wafts through the open doors indicating that the stone is the only thing similar.

CHAPTER 8

SIR LURGAN

I n a low voice, Aramas advises the others that they will proceed
to the lower room in two columns on either side of the stairwell
remaining as close as possible to each wall. Riadon is to lead one
column, Slinger the other. At the bottom, once everyone is ready, Riadon
will be given the signal to ignite a sun rod.

"This may be the Crypt of Shadows of which the goblin warned,"
says Aramas. Checking one last time to ensure that everyone is ready,
Aramas motions to proceed into the stairwell.

Cautiously, the party slowly descends into the darkness, their eyes
straining for any hint of an ambush. With each step, the stench of rotting
flesh intensifies. However, unlike the cavern they entered only moments
earlier, all is silent. There is no smell of mold, no dripping water, no rats.

Detecting no traps along the way, the party slowly makes its way to
the floor below. When they reach the bottom, Slinger and Riadon listen
intently for any signs of life. Ahead and to the right, two long hallways
slowly come into view. Each hall is approximately ten feet wide, the
floors and walls crafted of the same fine stone and constructed in the
same manner as the floor above.

Glancing back at Aramas, Riadon quietly asks, "Should I ignite the
sun rod?"

Aramas nods, the bright light illuminating a labyrinth of hallways to the right and what appears to be a room to the left. After briefly studying both hallways, Aramas directs the party to proceed.

They proceed in single file until the party stops at the entrance to the hall on the left. Riadon cautiously peeks around the corner. After a few seconds, he whispers to the others, "There is a hall that leads into a larger room. From what I can make out, there is another hall on the other side of the room." Nervous, he then adds, "It looks like the hallway is protected by dead bodies."

Not sure what Riadon is referring to, Aramas motions to Loki. "Check it out."

Loki moves past the others to peak around the corner. Ahead and to the right are three humanoid forms, eyes closed as if frozen in time, rotting flesh hanging from their grayish green limbs. Directly ahead, two larger armor-clad forms block the entry to the hallway beyond. Like the other three, they too stand in a state of suspended animation or a very deep sleep. Looking back at Aramas, he quietly reports, "Zombies."

"How many?"

"I can make out at least five. However, there could be more around the corner."

Patron asks, "Why haven't they attacked? They must certainly have seen our light."

Loki answers, "There must be some sort of tripping mechanism in the hall."

"Is there any way to get past them?" asks Aramas.

"Not from what I can tell. What do you want to do?"

Aramas joins Loki and peers into the hallway. "This must be the way. They appear to be protecting the far hallway." He glances back at Aria. "Is this where you detected the magic?"

Almost immediately she replies, "It lies both ahead and to our right."

Puzzled, Aramas asks, "Where is it the strongest?"

"Directly below us."

Sarcastically, Loki interjects. "Well that was certainly helpful."

Looking down at Loki, Aramas asks, "What do you think?"

He glances down the hallway then back at Aramas. "We can take these guys."

Motioning to Slinger, Aramas directs him to the other side of the hallway entrance. "See if there are any other surprises around the corner."

Moving quickly, Slinger slides past the entrance. He takes a moment to look into the dimly illuminated room. "There are two more creatures waiting just inside the room. Like the others, they do not appear to know of our presence."

Aramas looks back at Kriv. "You, Patron, and Aria protect our rear." Then he looks across the hallway entrance at Slinger. "Once Loki and I clear out the immediate threat, you and Riadon see if you can somehow flank the two guards."

Aramas and Loki enter the short hall preceding it. Nothing happens. Moving in lockstep, they slowly step into the room. Almost immediately, each of the creatures come to life, emitting low, hungry groans as they slowly move toward the intruders.

Loki thrusts his free hand forward, palm facing outward, and sweeps his arm from left to right. "By the power of Moradin!" Arcing blue radiance flows in all directions, hurling four of the seven adversaries into the nearby walls. Their putrid bodies quickly dissolve into a fine black powdery mist that dissipates as it slowly drifts to the stone below.

Loki shouts, "Minions!" then, turning his attention to the two zombie guards, Loki extends his war hammer. A brilliant ray of radiant energy shoots forth into the closest of the two creatures. Then, as he pulls the implement back toward his body, the zombie, now immobile, is pulled closer to its fate. Its companion, hands outstretched and moving from side to side in an attempt to grab anything nearby, staggers toward the intruders.

Aramas rushes the remaining minion and, with one sweep of his sword, sends it back to the dark reaches from whence it came. However, before he can engage the other zombie, his attention is diverted.

"Aramas, there are more!" From elsewhere in the Crypt of Shadows, five more rotting apparitions and two armor-clad warriors emerge to flank the party.

With his advance temporarily halted, Aramas shouts, "Hold them at the entrance."

However, before he can finish, Loki shouts, "Take care of the minions. I've got this."

Aramas replies, "I'll return momentarily!" Then, without further hesitation, he rushes toward the crypt.

After they dispatch one of the zombie minions, Patron and Kriv position themselves to hold the entrance. However, these attackers appear to be stronger than the ones so easily dispatched by Aramas and Loki. As Aramas arrives, Aria unleashes a bolt of fiery energy, striking the lead zombie and causing its rotting garments to burst into flames. Fiery embers of charred material drift slowly into the air.

Aramas extends his hand, palm outward, and, like Loki, sweeps it from left to right; arcing blue radiance strikes the six remaining attackers. With similar results, four are immediately transformed into a pile of fine black powder on the floor below as the two zombie warriors are hurled into the wall behind, temporarily unable to move.

Looking back at Aramas, Patron jokingly remarks, "How do I get one of those?"

Chuckling, Aramas replies, "Take care of them. I need to get back to Loki."

However, before he can do so, he is greeted by a familiarly jovial voice. "I told you I had this." Surprised, Aramas is met by Loki, Riadon, and Slinger. "Must we do everything?"

"We could use a little help here!" shouts Kriv.

Wasting no time, the four rejoin the party; their combined power quickly dispatches the two remaining undead.

As they pause briefly to catch their breath, Slinger points toward the hallway entrance once protected by the two guards. "There is a strange light coming from down that hall."

Riadon remarks, "That was not there before."

Loki peers down the hall and then up at Aramas. "He's right. What do you make of it?"

Taking a moment to analyze the light, Aramas replies, "It does not appear to be from a torch. It is almost as if the light has a life of its own." He hesitates then adds, "The last time I saw something similar, I was very young, standing within the walls of an ancient temple."

"A good temple, I hope," adds Riadon.

For the moment, Aramas does not reply. There is complete silence, everyone's eyes focused on what lies at the end of the hall.

Finally, Aramas replies, "The light is not of this realm."

"Is that good or bad?" asks Riadon.

Aramas carefully contemplates his next words before he continues. "Several years into my captivity, my captors raided a small village high in the mountains to the east. Having found little of value, and after they consumed all of the wine they could find, two of the guards decided to satisfy their carnal desires with one of the local girls. Not much older than I, but much wiser, she convinced them that if they would spare her, she would lead them to riches beyond their imagination, riches that had been buried many years earlier in the remains of an ancient temple. Supposedly, the temple was not far from the camp. Not sure how much treasure they would find, she suggested that they take me along to carry the spoils.

"However, before we reached the temple, the wine had its way, causing the guards to fall unconscious. Hoping to seize upon the opportunity, she implored me to remove her bonds. Initially I refused. 'My master will kill me, or worse, flog me until all of the skin is peeled from my back.' Grasping my hands, she told me that this moment had been foretold to her, and that when it happened, I would remove her bonds. Once free, she was to lead me to the temple.

"While I had no reason to believe any of her rantings, having witnessed what happened to young captive girls, I reluctantly did as she asked. She took my hand and led me through the thick undergrowth to a large outcropping of rocks in the side of a nearby hillside. 'About thirty feet into the darkness, you will find an opening to the left. Enter it. The temple is down a narrow passageway into the mountain.'

"Suspicious and confused, I replied, 'I have no need of treasure.

Besides, I have no torch.' For a moment she said nothing, standing motionless before me, her eyes gazing into mine. Then, after glancing around to make sure that no one was watching, she added, 'If you are who I think you are, you will have no need of it.' Before I could reply, she quickly vanished into the night."

"Was there a treasure?" asks Riadon.

Aramas pauses. "Not of this world." He stares briefly at the glow ahead then back at the party. "I did as my curiosity dictated and entered the dark cold passage; my hands felt the damp stone walls on either side. As she had foretold, I found the passageway to the left. Well down the passage, far into the mountain, I could see the faint glow of what appeared to be a light. As I progressed further into the mountain, the passage became wider and the earthen floor eventually became finely crafted flagstone. The light, now illuminating everything around, revealed a small chamber. At the far end of the room, atop a short dais, was a white marble altar with a single unlit candle seated in an ornate gold candlestick; the candle appeared to have never been lit. The light was coming from the ceiling."

"How could that be?" asks Slinger.

"At that moment, I had no explanation. The ceiling glowed with a white-blue radiance I had never witnessed before. Looking around, the walls were comprised of polished white and gray marble. The only markings anywhere appeared on the altar. Carved into the center front panel was what appeared to be a cross-shaped star."

"The symbol on your tabard," interrupts Kriv.

Nodding affirmatively, Aramas continues. "Looking around, I could see nothing of the treasure of which the girl spoke. Figuring that it might be near the altar, I cautiously approached. As I did, a light breeze seemed to brush by me, moving toward the altar. Suddenly, a flame burst forth atop the candle. Fearing some sort of dark magic, I slowly began to back away. But then, from above, a voice called to me, 'Do not be afraid. Your parents prepared you for this moment.' Looking around, I could see no one else in the room. I asked how that could be, as my parents had died years before. The voice directed me to approach the altar.

"As I moved up the steps of the dais, I got the feeling that time had stilled, all the while I was being drawn to the flame, its radiance almost hypnotic. I moved my hand closer to the flame. It produced no heat, no warmth. Confused, I inquired as to how the candle could burn yet not be consumed. 'Rely on your faith. It has protected you, shielded you, kept you alive.'

"For several minutes, I asked question after question. How had my father prepared me for this, how would my faith protect me, how could it shield me in the arena? Then came a long silence. The only sound was that of the flickering flame above the candle. 'Your father taught you to believe in a higher power, to respect the beliefs of others, to believe in the goodness of man, to honor women, and to never tolerate injustice. Just as when you came to the defense of your mother, you came to the defense of a girl of whom you knew nothing. In both instances, you did so at grave peril to yourself. It is your adherence to the teachings of your father that brought you here, here to become my champion.' Puzzled, I asked how I could be anyone's champion as a young gladiator with little hope of living long enough to earn his freedom. 'Believe in me, take upon yourself the emblem of my faithful and never stray from my teachings. Do so, and my shield will be your protection.'"

"How were you able to escape? Surely your absence was noticed," asks Kriv.

"By the time I emerged from the temple, the sun was just reaching its apex. I did as the voice had instructed and returned to the camp, but it was not there. Further, there was no evidence that it had ever been there: no tracks, no refuse, no charred remains of the cooking fires, nothing. It was as if the earth had swallowed it. I was a free man."

"And the light ahead, is that of your god?" asks Patron.

"No. I am aware of but one temple to my god. However, this radiance appears to be very similar. I would not fear it."

"Then why is the entrance protected by undead?" asks Loki.

"I do not know." Pausing, Aramas again stares down the hallway before continuing. "But we will not find out by standing here. The answer lies beyond the next room."

When he motions to Slinger and Riadon to check for additional traps, the party slowly progresses through the small outer room to the hallway beyond. Like the walls of the Crypt of Shadows, the hallway is devoid of any decoration. The passage grows brighter the closer the party gets to the source of the light.

At the end of the hallway, the party stares into what appears to be a large T-shaped mausoleum. Far to their left, the area over the cross of the T is bathed in the radiant light. The room's entrance is not at the base of the T but rather halfway up the north wall. Along the two long walls stand ten massive granite sarcophagi, five on either side of the room, each standing erect as if guarding the passage to the large bronze double doors at the far eastern end of the room. From the entrance, four sarcophagi stand along the walls to the right, six to the left. Carved into the cover of each is the image of a different armor-clad knight, their swords held before them, tips to the ground.

Pointing to what appears to be writing on the sarcophagus immediately to the right of the entrance, Riadon asks, "What do you make of this?"

Aramas approaches and, after a few seconds, replies, "It appears to be an ancient form of Draconic."

Their interest piqued, Kriv and Patron move closer, each studying the writing before them. After a few seconds, Kriv moves toward the sarcophagus that stands to the left of the entrance. "This appears to have the same inscription."

"What does it say?" asks Riadon.

"I don't know. It is a form of the language with which I am not familiar."

Surveying the area, Loki turns to Aria. "You're awfully quiet."

In her usual unemotional manner, she replies, "Aramas is right. The light at the far end of the room is not of this world."

Aramas approaches her. "Where was the magic?"

Extending her arm, she slowly directs his attention to each sarcophagus. "It resides in each." Then, pausing briefly, she points to the bronze double doors and adds, "It is the strongest there."

"That does not sound good," remarks Riadon.

Aria moves closer to the first sarcophagus then suddenly draws near as if she heard something from within. With her ear hovering over the lid's seal, she detects the faint sounds of clicking and scratching Taking an abrupt step back, she exclaims, "Death has been reborn!"

"What does that mean?" asks Riadon.

"What did you hear?" asks Loki.

"Scratching, as if what is inside is trying to escape."

Riadon, silently questioning why he agreed to embark on this quest in the first place, sheepishly suggests, "Maybe we should go the other way."

Calmly, Aramas responds, "No, we did not happen upon this place by accident. We were directed here." Looking past the rows of sarcophagi, Aramas studies the lighted room beyond. "This was once a sanctuary, a place of contemplation, worship, and refuge." He points to the double doors. "The key to what we seek lies beyond them."

As he steps into the room, Aramas pauses to see if anything happens. All remains as before. He motions to the others to follow then proceeds to the center of the room and stops. Four sarcophagi stand sentry behind him, six before him. The rest of the party, having done as directed, congregates around Aramas, backs together, facing outward.

Sarcastically, Loki comments, "Okay, that was easy. What now?"

Without answering, Aramas moves toward the double doors with the party close behind. Everything remains quiet until he passes between the two sarcophagi halfway into the main chamber.

Large concussive blasts explode throughout the chamber as the lids of each sarcophagus burst open, their contents emerging to challenge the intruders. Ten skeletons, eight bearing longswords and crossbows and two in full chain mail with longswords and shields, slowly advance on the party. As soon as they exit their tombs, the lids slam shut with the same concussive blast.

Almost in unison, Aramas and Loki send waves of arcing blue radiance into the attackers: eight disintegrate into dark mists. However, the two chain mail-clad warriors, while now severely wounded, continue to advance.

Aramas directs the party to consolidate their position and focus on the two warriors. Before they are able to do so, the chamber again erupts with the sound of large concussive blasts; each sarcophagus again bursts open to disgorge another ten skeletons, two of which are warriors.

Standing next to Aramas, Loki shouts, "This is not good!"

Unable to release another surge of radiant energy, Aramas replies, "We need to focus on the warriors."

The party continues to extract a heavy toll on the attackers while sustaining minimal damage themselves. In the process, with each skeleton that falls, ten more are disgorged from the sarcophagi. Within seconds, the party is surrounded, the ranks of the attackers having grown to forty. With no possibility of retreat, Aramas shouts, "We need to get to the light!"

As had been the case many times before, Aramas and Loki advance as one, their holy implements singing with heavenly energy. One by one, the warriors are defeated, only to be replaced by another. There is no possible advance. For every skeleton killed, another immediately replaces it.

"Aramas, Slinger is down!" shouts Patron

"Circle around him! Kriv . . ."

Unexpectedly, Aria breaks from the others and leaps to the closest sarcophagus. "Cover me!" With several skeletons clawing at her garments, she slowly pulls herself atop the middle sarcophagus.

"What's she doing?" shouts Patron.

"I don't know," replies Kriv as he battles closer to the sarcophagus. Focusing on the five skeletons trying to drag her back to the floor, he exhales a searing blast of lightning and fire, temporarily distracting them.

No longer encumbered, Aria leaps to the next sarcophagus. As she does, several skeletons fall back, drop their swords, and load their crossbows. Before she can leap to the last sarcophagus, a flurry of arrows rain down upon her, three finding their mark. Momentarily stunned and nearly losing her balance, she leans back against the wall to regain her composure. Reaching over her shoulder, she extracts two of the bolts, the third unreachable.

From below, several of the warriors turn their attention to her demise as the archers prepare another volley. Hurling himself into the horde, Patron attempts to cut a path to the archers while Aramas and Loki continue to engage the warriors. Hoping to take advantage of Aria's momentary incapacitation, one of the warriors climbs to the top of the sarcophagus and grasps at her leg.

"By the power of Moradin." Loki's hammer crashes into the would-be assailant.

"Go!"

Drawing upon her last ounce of energy, Aria leaps to the last sarcophagus and then to the floor below. She staggers toward what appears to be an altar, rests her bloodstained hand upon it, and drops to her knee, hoping to keep from falling unconscious.

While the battle continues to rage on, none of the skeletons give chase. At the same time, the sarcophagi cease to open or disgorge additional skeletons. Raising her head, Aria wearily looks back at the party, blood oozing from her wounds. Wincing in pain, she turns back to the altar, her eyes drifting to a tapestry on the wall in front of her; the likeness of a metallic dragon dominates the cloth. Before she loses consciousness, she lowers her head. There in front of her, carved in the altar, is an inscription, it too in Draconic: "*The Platinum Dragon is my rock, my fortress, and my deliverer. He is my stronghold, my refuge, and my armor against the foes of life—I need only kneel and offer him my praise.*"

Almost inaudibly, Aria mumbles, "Great Dragon God, I beseech thee to intercede on our behalf. Without your intervention, our quest will fail."

Unable to continue, Aria slumps to the floor. As she does, the light above grows brighter, illuminating the entire chamber. Silence quickly replaces the sound of clashing steel as each skeleton disengages and slowly turns toward the sarcophagus that gave it birth. In reverent obedience, the sarcophagi open to receive their spawn.

Momentarily distracted, Aramas looks around at the now retreating adversaries. Pointing to Slinger, he shouts, "Kriv, tend to Slinger! Loki and I will tend to Aria."

Rushing to the altar, Aramas kneels and gently cradles Aria.

As he does, Loki examines the area around the remaining bolt. "It is very close to her spine. I cannot simply extract it without the possibility of paralysis," Looking over at Aramas, "I will need your help. Stabilize her while I stop the bleeding."

Aramas immediately places his right palm on Aria's forehead, closes his eyes, and recites a short prayer. As he does, Loki methodically places his hands over each of the other two wounds; radiant energy heals both, stopping the loss of blood.

As Aramas removes his hand from Aria's forehead, her eyes slowly open. Grinning broadly, Aramas remarks, "I thought you to be smarter than Kriv. Do you both feel some need to throw yourself into danger?"

Aria smiles. "I thought it to be a good idea at the time." Wincing in pain, she asks, "How bad is it?"

Loki replies, "I've stopped the bleeding, but the bolt needs to be cut out." Nodding her affirmation, Aria again drifts off.

"Keep her still."

Grasping her tightly, Aramas nods. "Ready!"

Loki draws a short dagger from his belt, opens his wine skin, and cleanses the blade. As he is doing so, Patron, Kriv, Riadon, and Slinger arrive. "How is she?"

Looking up, Aramas replies, "We'll know shortly." He says to Slinger, "It is good that you are able to rejoin us."

With knife in hand, Loki directs Kriv to help Aramas keep Aria still. They turn her slightly, then he slowly inserts the knife into the wound. "It appears to have lodged in one of her ribs." Gently probing around its base, he attempts to dislodge it. After a few seconds, he says, "Got it." Grasping the bolt's shaft with his other hand, Loki slowly extracts the intruder, blood oozing from the wound as he does. Quickly examining the bolt, Loki exclaims, "It did not shatter!" Then he tosses the bolt to the wall behind him and quickly heals the remaining wound. "She should be fine."

Removing his backpack, Kriv places it behind her head. "I'll stay with her until she awakes."

Standing, Aramas surveys the area. "Patron, I believe that this is a temple to the Platinum Dragon. Is he not the god you worship?"

Nodding his affirmation, he replies, "Many of the metallic dragons once worshipped him as the first of their kind. He was so venerated that to speak his name was considered a sign of disrespect."

"Then it is imperative that we do nothing to defile his holy temple."

Walking to the far altar, Aramas takes a few moments to study it, then looks back at the other. The altars appear to be mirror images, set to either side of the sanctuary. Atop each is laid an elaborate tapestry adorned with two gold candelabras. Centered between them is a gold chalice positioned directly above an embroidered shield. Behind each hangs a crimson curtain bearing the likeness of the Platinum Dragon. The ceiling above, now bright with silvery white light, is decorated with a beautiful mural depicting a regal silver dragon with sparkling scales flying across an endless sky. Inscribed on the walls to either side of the altars are depictions of armor-clad knights kneeling in supplication, heads bowed, their swords before them, tips to the ground.

While Aramas studies the inscriptions, Slinger begins to search the altar nearest him. "There appears to be a secret drawer over here."

Aramas immediately reiterates, "Do not touch anything!"

Holding his hands up in front of him, Slinger replies, "Understood."

Riadon, gazing at the candelabras and chalice, "But this . . ."

"I said touch nothing!" Then Aramas motions to the bronze double doors. "Check them for traps!" he says and walks back to the other altar to view the drawer.

Slinger asks, "What do you think?"

"There was nothing like this behind the other."

"Should I check it for traps?"

"No, not until we know more." He focuses his attention on the depictions of the supplicant knights. "They were protecting this place." Walking back to the center of the sanctuary, he gazes at the now closed sarcophagi, the altars, and then the double doors. "This is not a temple; it is a burial crypt!"

"Whose crypt?" asks Riadon.

Aramas says nothing until he moves to the double doors. "Are the doors trapped?"

"Not that I can tell."

Perusing the walls around each door, Aramas can find nothing to indicate what lies behind them.

"There is nothing of this world behind them." Startled, Aramas turns to find Aria standing behind him. "The magic is strong but is not of this world."

Aramas places his hands on her shoulders. "I am glad to see that you are better. Can you determine the source of the magic?"

"No, but it is not far behind the doors."

Loki grabs Aramas's arm. "Are you sure we want to do this? If those skeletons are bound to spend eternity protecting what lies behind, do we want to chance reawakening them?"

Hesitating, Aramas takes a moment before responding. "As long as we continue to respect this holy place, I do not believe that we will be harmed."

Shaking his head, Loki replies, "I hope you are right."

Smiling, Aramas jokes, "Besides, with Kriv and Aria at our side, what could go wrong?"

Without further discussion, Aramas opens the two doors; a gush of stale air rushes into the sanctuary. Behind them lies a small room illuminated by sconces that don't appear to be consumed. At the far end of the room are four steps leading to a raised dais. In the center rests a single coffin. Like the walls around each altar, carvings of supplicant knights adorn the three walls around the coffin, and the Platinum Dragon adorns a tapestry hanging above. Carved on the lid of the coffin is the likeness of a paladin warrior in full plate armor, his sword laid upon his chest, point toward his feet.

Motioning to the others to spread out, Aramas directs them to look for anything that would disclose the coffin's occupant. "And do not touch anything!"

Pausing at the base of the dais, Aramas gazes at the coffin then at the pictographs on the walls around it. He mumbles, "Forty knights. There are forty knights." He turns to the others. "Loki, how many skeletons did you count in the other room?"

Loki stops briefly to recall the battle. "I counted no more than forty at any one time. Why?"

As if having received a revelation, Aramas exclaims, "I think that this is the crypt of Sir Lurgan the Red."

Aramas walks back to the door and again peers out into the sanctuary. "What if the knights aren't protecting the body? What if their purpose was to prevent Lurgan's spirit from leaving this place?" He walks back to the dais and again studies the pictographs. "The forty were Lurgan's captains of the guard, the knights he killed in his rage." He turns back to the party. "We need to leave, *now!*"

Without hesitation, the party quickly moves toward the sanctuary. However, before they can exit, the doors slam before them. Almost simultaneously, the coffin's lid explodes.

Stunned, their advance halted, the party turns to face the now open coffin.

"Declare your intentions!"

Standing before them, partially concealed by the cloud of dust and smoke, stands an armor-clad humanoid skeleton, its longsword held high, ready to strike. In a croaking, raspy voice, it declares, "If you are grave robbers, prepare to meet your god!"

Dropping to one knee, his head bowed, Aramas replies, "My lord, we intend no harm to you or your resting place. We come to destroy the evil that lies within the bowels of this once great fortress." As Aramas is speaking, the others also fall to one knee.

"Young paladin, I am sworn to defend this keep from all interlopers. How do I know that you speak the truth?"

Looking up into the hollow eye sockets of the vision before him, Aramas replies, "I have sworn my life to defend the oppressed and helpless and to destroy evil wherever it resides."

The skeleton takes a moment to study each of the party members then lowers its sword and looks back at Aramas. "I recognize the holy symbols of those in your party. How is it that I do not recognize yours?"

"My god is an ancient god, a god that existed long before this realm was created."

"Are you saying that your god is greater than the Platinum Dragon?"

"I say only that he seeks the same truths as the Platinum Dragon."

Pausing, the skeleton looks to Kriv. "You present yourself to be a fearsome warrior. Are you really as formidable as you would have others believe?"

"Like Aramas, my powers are used only for good. Moradin commands it."

"If they are only to be used for good, why is it you travel with a tiefling?"

Before Kriv can reply, the skeleton turns to Aria. "If you trust your senses not to betray you, tell me what you see before you."

Slowly standing, Aria replies, "I see what remains of a once great warrior, overcome by guilt, destined to remain eternally imprisoned in self-imposed shame."

Silence eerily engulfs the room as the menacing stare of the skeleton seems to pierce Aria's soul.

It turns to Riadon. "You, thief. You dare to enter my crypt? Would you too expect me to believe that your intentions in doing so were honorable? Did you not intend to spirit away whatever riches you could carry?" However, before Riadon can speak, the skeleton addresses Slinger. "And you. Not only are you a thief, but you would sell your talents to the highest bidder. Am I to believe that your intentions are honorable?" There is no reply.

The skeleton rises above the coffin then slowly drifts to the floor and walks over to Patron. "You bear the symbol of the Platinum Dragon. Would you risk eternal damnation by lying to me? What brings you to this keep?"

"Our charge is as Aramas stated, to destroy the evil that resides within."

"Unnatural forces dwell within. What makes you believe that you are equipped to overcome them?"

Loki unexpectedly stands. "We are not sure we can, but we have sworn to do so."

Surprised, the skeleton moves closer to Loki and, with a bit of scorn in its voice, counters, "Brave words from a dwarf."

"My hammer is Moradin's. His will be done, not mine!"

Pausing again, the skeleton returns to Aramas. "A convincing answer, or one that was convincingly given. Can you attest to the truth of your comrade's claim?"

Respectfully, Aramas stands to answer. "I can attest to all that has been said." After a moment of hesitation, he continues. "If you are whom I believe you to be, then you know that our words ring true. Are you not Lurgan the Red, commander of Raven's Nest?" There is no reply.

"Over the past few weeks, we have encountered forces and creatures that were long thought to be the fabric of legend and folklore. Each soul standing before you here has, on numerous occasions, proven their commitment to our quest."

Again, there is no reply. However, without explanation, Aramas's sword, as well as that of the skeleton, begins to glow.

Perplexed, the skeleton looks down at its sword, then at Aramas's. "They are of similar origin." Then, looking almost forlornly into Aramas's eyes, it says, "Such a weapon would not be entrusted to someone unable to wield it as intended."

The skeleton again peruses the party. Then, looking toward the closed doors, it makes a shallow sweeping motion with its free hand. The doors open. It walks to the opening but does not progress into the sanctuary. "Yes, I am Sir Lurgan, commander of Raven's Nest." Turning back toward the party, he says, "When I first arrived here, the future was bright. Abundant commerce kept the coffers of my lord brimming. Those that settled around the castle walls prospered. In due course, I met the woman I would later pledge to honor and protect all of our days. It was not long before we were blessed with a strong son. With success came additional responsibility. Soon

I was entrusted with the security of the keep. Picking forty of the best knights in the realm, we ensured that the laws of the land were enforced, and those that would violate them, punished. What I did not know was that the castle had been built over an ancient rift, a rift between this world and one controlled by forces stronger than I could have ever imagined. When unexplainable things began to occur, I sought the guidance of one who was supposed to be a cleric of Bahamut, one whom I would later learn had been corrupted by the evil beyond the rift."

Walking slowly toward the party, he again addresses Aramas directly. "The corruption beyond the rift eventually touched me. If you are not careful, it will corrupt you and everyone in your party. It is a vile evil bent on total domination."

Sheathing his sword, Lurgan slowly walks back to his coffin and forlornly runs his fingers over the depictions of the forty. "I not only failed them, I betrayed their trust." Bowing his head, he stands silently before the tapestry bearing the likeness of Bahamut then continues. "I allowed the taint of the shadow rift to overtake me. I became blinded to my sworn oath and eventually driven to madness. It possessed me, drove me to kill my wife and son and then attack those sworn to my allegiance. Soon, men that had once sworn their lives to me were now convinced that I must be stopped. Like a crazed fiend, I continued to kill anyone that crossed my path. Knight after knight fell to my sword. However, even in my rage, I knew that I could not defeat them all, so I retreated to the bowels of the keep, eventually finding my way into this crypt." He raises his hand and points to the sanctuary outside the door. "It was there, when I walked into the light, that I realized the enormity of what I had done. I could never atone for my actions. With no place to retreat, I awaited my fate, but the remaining knights did not enter the room. Instead, they sealed it, trapping me in here for time and eternity." Extending his arms, he opens his hands. "The stain of their blood can never be washed from these hands."

"What of the cleric?" asks Loki.

"I do not know. However, the evil has grown stronger, and it could not have done so without his help."

"How is that?" asks Kriv.

"The evil beyond the rift was trying to escape its own imprisonment by entering our realm. It could not do so unless someone on this side of the rift prepared the way."

"Prepared the way?"

"Yes, to prepare the way, someone from this world needed to perform an ancient ritual, a ritual that required some unusual components."

Intrigued, Aria asks, "What kind of components?"

"While most of the components were still known to exist, two were not: the scales, bones, and teeth of a dragon and a particular gem. Once obtained, they were to be mixed with the blood of innocents."

"That would explain what Craven was up to," remarks Loki.

Nodding in agreement, Aramas asks, "Does the name Sorac mean anything to you?"

"How about Brevek?" asks Loki.

"I recall neither."

After a moment, Loki asks, "What was the name of the cleric you confided in?"

"Karell."

"If he is still within these walls, where might we find him?"

With a tone of resignation in his voice, Lurgan replies, "He is still within these walls. His power has grown far beyond what I remember; I can feel it." He looks again into the sanctuary. "You will find him at the rift, deeper below."

"How far below?"

"I do not know. I was not permitted to venture into the lower reaches; Karell would not permit it. It wasn't until I went mad and sought refuge from my men that I found this place."

"How many more of his followers can we expect to encounter?" asks Patron.

"Again, I do not know. What I can tell you is that other than an underpriest and a few goblins, Karell is protected by those who have not been able to enter the afterworld. The dark arts have become his greatest ally. It will not be easy to defeat him." He looks back briefly to the image of Bahamut then back at Aramas. "What lies beyond the rift can never be allowed to enter this world. What I failed to do, you now must."

"And what of you?" asks Kriv.

"I am beyond redemption, my fate sealed. My captains will never allow me to leave this crypt. You, however, may be able to succeed where I could not. The fact that you are here, in this room, gives me to believe that all may not be lost." Lurgan walks up to Aramas and places a hand on his shoulder, then pointing at his heart with the other, he says, "Trust what is in here. Your faith is strong."

Turning to the others, he continues. "Seek Bahamut's boon at the altar. If your quest is true, he will assist you."

"Are you sure that there is nothing else we can do for you?" asks Aramas.

"Finish what you came here to accomplish."

As he completes his statement, all becomes silent. A soft cool breeze drifts from the sanctuary into the crypt; Lurgan's remains slowly rise off the ground and back toward his coffin. Once above his final resting place, he places his hands across his chest before slowly descending back into the coffin. No sooner do his remains disappear than a new stone cover materializes adorned by the image of an armor-clad knight, sword laid upon his chest, the point toward his feet.

For the next few seconds, the party stands silent, mesmerized by what just transpired. Although there are no apparent drafts in the room, no movement of air, the sconces begin to flicker, their flames reaching toward the sanctuary as if to usher the party from the crypt toward the altars. Reverently, the party exits the crypt.

"Riadon, make sure that the doors are left as we found them," directs Aramas. Walking back to the altar with the secret drawer, Aramas motions to Slinger. "Check it for traps."

As he carefully examines the drawer, as well as the area around it, Slinger finds nothing to indicate that it has been trapped.

"Can you open it?"

"I am not sure."

As he continues to examine the area around the drawer, Loki moves closer to see if he can be of assistance. "For what are we looking?"

Aramas replies, "I am not sure. Lurgan specifically directed us to the altar to 'seek Bahamut's boon.' Other than the candelabras and chalices, I see nothing of value anywhere in this room and certainly nothing that could assist us in our quest. The only thing out of the ordinary is the drawer."

Frustrated, Slinger stands and points to the drawer. "I can find no latches, keyholes, or other ways in which to open it. Perhaps it is not meant to be opened."

Puzzled, the three discuss what Sir Lurgan had said to them as well as possible ways to open the drawer without desecrating the sanctuary. Suddenly, Aramas asks Aria, "Tell me what happened when you got to the altar earlier."

"What do you mean?"

"We were under attack, engaged in fierce combat. Somehow you managed to get to the altar. As you did, the skeletons ceased their attack. What did you do?"

"I did nothing. I was too weak."

"You did nothing, touched nothing? Think! Something caused those skeletons to return to their sarcophagi."

Pausing to contemplate what had transpired, Aria says, "I am not sure. I was struggling to remain conscious. Having reached the altar, I remember placing my hand on it and kneeling to keep from falling over. As I began to drift off, I noticed the inscription. I don't remember anything else after that."

Interrupting, Patron suggests, "Maybe it was the act of kneeling, an act that could be construed as a gesture of obeisance."

Kriv looks at the inscription and reads aloud the last few words. "I need only kneel and offer him my praise." He turns to Aria. "Did you say anything?"

"I'm sorry, but I don't recall anything after I read the inscription."

Patron walks to the front of the altar and kneels, placing one hand on his sword and the other before the chalice. As the rest of the party silently observes, Patron bows his head and prays aloud, "My lord, I have pledged my life to you, and while I do not presume to be worthy enough to ask for your assistance, those who stand here before you are. Our cause is just, to defeat the evil that casts darkness across this land and seeks to enslave all within. I beseech thee to look favorably upon our quest and, should you deem it so, to guide and protect us."

For the next several seconds, no one says a word, all is silent. As if waiting to receive some form of reply, Patron continues to kneel at the altar, head bowed, but nothing happens. Sure that his supplication has gone unanswered, he slowly raises his head and looks up at the image of Bahamut. Then, just as he places both hands on the altar to stand, the drawer opens. Inside are seven platinum and gold statues, each a miniature likeness of Bahamut.

"Whoa, those will fetch a hefty price back in Spring Green!" exclaims Riadon.

"I don't think that is why they were given to us," replies Loki. He gingerly lifts one from the drawer and begins to examine it; Aramas keeps the rest of the party from touching the others until he is done. After a minute or so, he places the statue upright on the altar. "They possess some sort of protective power. I'm not sure how it works, but from what I can tell, the power is confined to Raven's Nest Castle."

"Can you tell how to activate its power?" asks Slinger.

"It would appear that it only has to be in one's possession. It somehow reduces the impact of an attack, sort of like wearing additional armor."

Reaching into the drawer, Loki hands a statue to each of the party members.

"Are you sure we're not supposed to sell these?" asks Riadon.

With a look of disdain, Aramas replies, "We promised Sir Lurgan that our intentions were honorable. I intend to make sure that they remain so."

"Just kidding." Affectionately caressing the statue he's been handed, Riadon adds, "But they are beautiful."

As Loki removes the last statue, the drawer slowly vanishes, leaving no indication that it had ever existed. Looking up at Aramas, he asks, "What now?"

Taking a moment to gather his thoughts, Aramas addresses the party, "We have been through a lot today. I can think of no better place to seek refuge for the night and to discuss our strategy for tomorrow than right here." He points to the sarcophagi. "Anyone looking for us has to get by them first."

Taking his haversack off his back, Aramas walks over to the corner wall nearest the door to Lurgan's crypt, pulls out his bedroll, and begins to remove his armor. "Kriv, set the watch and wake me for mine."

CHAPTER 9

INTO THE BELLY OF THE BEAST

Waking early, Aramas quietly goes about packing his gear, his thoughts replaying yesterday's events. After securing his bedroll, he sets aside a few pieces of dried meat for his morning meal before stowing the platinum and gold image of Bahamut. Pondering its glimmering brilliance, his thoughts are interrupted by a voice from behind. "Is anything wrong?" asks Loki.

Startled, Aramas replies, "No. Why do you ask?"

"You appeared lost in thought."

Like a child that has just been caught with their hand in a sack of sugar, Aramas hesitates before replying, "I feel uncomfortable carrying the image of another god into battle."

While it is rare for Loki to offer an opinion when it comes to religion, he remarks, "There are many realms and many gods. I am sure that your god, if he is as wise and understanding as you believe, will not be offended should the unrequested assistance of another help to defeat the evil you swore to destroy."

Smiling broadly, Aramas replies, "You are a good friend." He ties off his haversack, grabs his morning meal, and joins the others. Addressing his next remarks to Riadon, Aramas jokingly asks, "So how did you sleep?"

Everyone pauses to hear his answer. "As good as could be expected under the circumstances." He points at the rows of sarcophagi. "How could anyone sleep well with *them* staring at you?"

Kriv chuckles. "The only thing that kept you awake was the value of that statue."

"That too," replies Riadon, smiling shyly.

After some additional ribbing, Patron asks Aria, "Do you detect any change in the magic below?"

She shakes her head. "It is still below and to the north."

Interrupting the conversation, Aramas remarks, "Finish up. We cannot afford to linger."

Motioning to Kriv, Patron, and Loki to join him, Aramas continues. "Karell is surely aware of our presence. We need to maintain a tight group. Kriv, crack open a sun rod, as I will want Loki to examine the stone at the base of the stairway to see if it might be possible to determine the more heavily used passage."

"Won't that be exposing our position?"

"Yes, but it will also minimize the chances of being surprised. It will be difficult enough fighting in such tight quarters. I would at least like to see what opposes us." He pauses momentarily. "Loki and I will take the lead with Riadon and Slinger as they check for traps. I want Aria to maintain her focus on the source of the magic. Patron, I need you to protect our rear. Understood?" The three nod their agreement.

With everyone packed, the party proceeds respectfully between the rows of sarcophagi and through the adjoining passage into the Crypt of Shadows. Sensing no danger, the party turns to the right and proceeds to the base of the stairway, the room above still well lit.

"Loki, what do you think?" asks Aramas.

Loki studies the hallway to the right of the stairwell, then looking back down the hallway from whence they came, he kneels to examine the finely crafted flagstone floor. He gingerly slides his fingers over the mortar joints between the stones then over the stones themselves and determines that, due to the wear patterns, the passage to the right is the most traveled. Standing, he points down the hallway. "This way."

With Riadon and Slinger leading the way, the party cautiously moves down the narrow corridor. The light from the sun rod reveals another hall branching to the left and the main hall also turning left a short distance further. As they enter the first intersection, both Riadon and Slinger abruptly halt.

Pointing to several pictographs inscribed into the floor directly before them, Riadon exclaims, "I don't think this is the way!"

Slinger turns to the others. "What do you make of them?"

Aramas steps forward and studies the inscriptions. "They appear to be runes of some sort. Possibly religious in origin. Loki, what do you think?"

Peering at the floor covered with the drawings, Loki comes to the same conclusion but adds, "Whatever their original purpose, they appear to have been altered."

Before them are four runes, the largest of which separates the other three and touches all four of the stones in a large Y-shaped pattern; the shaft runs in the grout seam between the two closest stones. Each branch at the top of the Y is flared and extends diagonally across the top two stones. Carved across these stones are two intertwined eye-like circles. The lower stone to the left bears a pair of crossed arrows, and in the stone to the lower right, an open hand.

Kriv points down the hallway to the left. "There are none this way."

Slinger replies, "Whomever put these here may have done so hoping to entice us to enter that hall."

"There's only one way to find out."

"Wait!" shouts Aramas. "Let's be sure. Slinger, Riadon, check the hallway for traps."

Doing as instructed, both Slinger and Riadon slowly move down the hallway, carefully examining each stone with Kriv close behind. Fifty feet down the hallway, the party comes upon another hall to the right.

Slinger stops. "There is another set of those things here."

"They are identical," Kriv says.

Loki asks, "Do you see any way to get around them?"

"Not that we can see."

Aramas motions for the three to return. As they do, Aria remarks, "Passage through this area is protected by a dark magic activated by touch. Unless we can determine the type of spell, we cannot defeat it."

Patron asks, "Can you do so?"

"No, it is beyond my abilities."

There is a short silence as the party stares at the runes. "What if we jump over them?" asks Riadon. He points back down the hall toward the crypt's entrance. "If we get a good running start, why not?"

Loki looks up at Aramas. "It's worth a try."

"I'm in full plate. Unless I take it off, it is not likely I'll be able to jump that far. And what of you? Do you really think that you can jump ten feet?"

Kriv chuckles. "Patron and I could throw you that far."

Loki immediately replies, "Oh no you won't! No one throws this dwarf."

Aramas asks Aria, "Can you ascertain what might happen should someone step on one of the stones?"

"The magic is terror based, that's all I can determine."

With a bit of anticipation in his voice, Riadon says, "Slinger and I can go first. Patron can follow to provide protection while the rest of you jump over the area. We'll grab each of you as you land to minimize the chances of falling back onto the stones. Loki comes next. Kriv will wait while you remove your armor and toss it to us. Once you are safely on the other side, he will follow."

"It is a good plan," Loki says.

Aramas, while hesitant, replies, "I can see no other way." He motions to Riadon. "It was your idea. Show us how it is to be done."

Smiling broadly, Riadon retreats back down the hall, turns, and rushes toward the runes as the rest of the party stands in the adjoining hallway. As predicted, he has no problem clearing the runes and lands several feet past the cursed stones. "Okay Slinger, you're next." With similar ease, Slinger clears the traps. In the meantime, Aramas begins to remove his armor, Loki assisting as needed.

As planned, Patron leaps over the obstacles. "Toss me the armor."

As each piece of armor is removed, it is handed to Kriv. "Don't drop this!"

Smiling, Patron chides him. "Just make sure you get it to me." Within a few minutes, every piece of Aramas's armor has been safely shuttled to the other side.

Looking down at Loki, Aramas remarks, "Are you sure you don't want Kriv and I to . . ."

"Don't even think about it!" at which point Loki backs down the hall, rushes toward the runes, and leaps to the other side. However, as he hits the ground, he lands on his heels, loses his balance, and begins to fall backward. Fortunately, Riadon and Slinger catch him before he touches any of the cursed stones. "Thanks." With a huge grin, he turns back to Aramas. "See, nothing to it."

Wasting no time, Aramas rushes down the hall, leaps, and easily clears to runes, Kriv close behind. Bending down to retrieve his armor, Aramas remarks, "Let us hope that there are no more such traps."

While Patron and Kriv stand guard, Aramas dons his armor. After a few minutes, Aramas motions to the others that he is ready to proceed. With Riadon and Slinger in the lead, the party moves to the end of the hall, turns left, and proceeds toward the next junction. As expected, this hallway is also protected by a set of runes. However, unlike the prior runes that blocked passage down the hall, these are located at the intersection of the adjoining hall and do not extend into it.

Pointing to the corner stone then drawing an imaginary line from the main hall to the adjoining one, Slinger comments, "If we jump diagonally over the corner stone, we should be able to clear the runes with little trouble."

"How do we know that the floor beyond is not trapped?" asks Patron.

"We don't. However, I expect that whoever created the traps never imagined that someone would get this far without stumbling upon one of the other traps, especially in the dark."

"Don't forget about the undead," adds Aramas. "We were fortunate to have been able to dispatch them in an area devoid of the runes. Had we not turned toward Lurgan's chamber, we would have most likely been flanked by the creatures in the long hall and forced into the runes." Looking into the adjoining passage, Aramas asks, "Aria, what do your senses tell you?"

"I sense nothing protecting the area beyond the runes."

"That's good enough for me," declares Kriv. Taking a few steps back, he rushes forward and leaps the runes. Safely on the other side, he looks back at Aramas. "You should have no need to remove your armor."

As the others leap into the adjoining hall, Kriv proceeds thirty feet farther to where the hall again turns left. He peers cautiously around the corner and sees that the hall continues through a small room to a set of stairs leading to a lower level. "There are stairs here."

As they move to the top of the stairwell, Aramas peers down into the illuminated passage. "Stow the sun rod. We may need it later. Riadon, take the left wall, Slinger the right. Everyone else will follow staying as close to the wall as possible."

"Any particular order?" asks Loki.

"No, half to either side of the stairwell as we did when entering this chamber."

Checking each step along the way, the party moves cautiously toward the bottom of the stairwell. About halfway down, Riadon warns, "We've got company."

At the bottom of the stairwell is a large torch-lit chamber, in the center of which sits an open well surrounded by ornate tiles. Standing to either side are two scale-clad human-sized creatures, each bearing flails and shields, pointed ears sticking out from under their helmets, and sharp long teeth glistening in their drooling mouths. In the far left corner of the room is a small door. Directly ahead is a ten-foot entryway leading into another room at the far end of which is a large cage containing a spider the size of a horse, its body covered with thick dark bristles of black and gray stripes. Two guards stand on either side of the entryway. To the far right is another passage. Before the party can reach the bottom of the stairs, one of the soldiers steps forward and shouts, "Shadow seeks shadow!"

Loki whispers to Aramas, "This isn't going to end well."

Hoping to buy some time, Slinger replies, "We come to speak with Karell. We have a message from Brevek."

The soldier again shouts, "Shadow seeks shadow!"

Slinger looks back at Aramas as if to ask what to do next. However, before he can ask the question, both soldiers rush the stairwell. "Intruders!"

Hoping to prevent the intruders from entering the room, the two hobgoblin soldiers charge the stairwell. As they do, the two guards that had been positioned to either side of the far hallway quickly rush into the room toward the cage. As the sound of steel crashing against steel fills the room, two more guards emerge from the far hallway. Pointing to the small door at the other end of the room, the one guard shouts, "Wake the others!" He then rushes to join his compatriots.

With their advance halted by the rushing soldiers, Patron shouts, "Remain in the stairwell! We need to consolidate our position and force them to come to us." As Aria, Riadon, and Slinger move back up the stairs, Patron and Aramas hold their stance at the bottom, Loki and Kriv immediately behind. Suddenly, from the small room to the left, emerge three more soldiers.

In the far room, Kriv notices that the guards are beginning to remove the ties that secure the spider's cage. Releasing a searing breath of fire and lightning, temporarily blinding two of the attackers, Kriv pushes past Patron and Aramas, charges the blinded hobgoblins, knocking them prone, and scrambles toward the cage.

"What's he doing?" shouts Loki.

Aramas replies, "Not what he was told!"

As he rushes toward the outer room, Kriv is met by two of the incoming guards. Unable to get past them, and cut off from the rest of the party, he is left with no choice but to stand his ground and swing his flail wildly at each. Soon thereafter, having unleashed the spider, the other two guards rush out of the room to flank Kriv.

With the spider's path out of the room blocked by the five combatants, it slowly climbs the wall to the ceiling, its large fangs dripping with a yellowish green venom. Unaware of the approaching danger from above, his attention clearly focused on his attackers, Kriv continues to hold his own. He pivots to the left and lands a fatal blow with his flail, exposing a brief opening back toward the rest of the party. However, before he can take advantage of it, he feels a sharp burning pain in his back. It spreads rapidly throughout his body then quickly turns to paralysis. Unable to move, he slumps to the ground with the blurry, rapidly fading image of a giant arachnid preceding his unconsciousness.

Aware of the impending danger above, Aramas shouts to Aria and Slinger, "Keep that thing at bay!" His sword makes quick work of the first guard. "Loki, as soon as we even the odds a bit, you and Riadon try to reach Kriv." Another guard falls before Aramas's sword.

Patron, not to be outdone, drops two of his attackers. The four remaining soldiers, each more proficient with a sword than the other guards had been with their flails, slowly give ground.

Aria and Slinger focus their attacks on the spider to prevent the creature from reaching the stairs, rapidly filling the room with the putrid smell of burnt flesh and hair. Not to be denied, the spider leaps thirty feet to the wall adjacent to the stairwell and again to the ceiling above the combatants. With their position compromised, Aria and Slinger retreat to the top of the stairwell to gain a better vantage point from which to continue their assault.

Now directly under the spider, Loki shouts to Riadon, "Follow me!" However, Riadon is nowhere to be seen. Wasting no time, Loki takes advantage of the small opening Aramas and Patron have created and charges through it toward Kriv's lifeless body. He reaches into his bag of holding and quickly withdraws one of the healing potions. Cradling

Kriv's head with one hand, Loki puts the vial to his mouth and pulls out the cork, then forces the vial into Kriv's, watching the orange liquid rapidly disappearing, some spilling to the floor.

"Loki!" shouts Slinger.

Quickly putting Kriv's head back on the floor, Loki stands and turns just in time to see the spider drop to the stairs and leap toward Aramas and Patron. Almost instinctively, Loki's war hammer flies from his outstretched hand and lands squarely between creature's eyes. Stunned, it stumbles to the ground then attempts to regain its footing. As it does, Riadon suddenly appears on its back, his glistening blade plunging deep into its back.

From the top of the stairwell, Slinger rushes to assist; he unsheathes his longsword and, with a long arcing swing, slices open the creature's abdomen. Greenish-white fluid gushes forth, engulfing not only Slinger but the stairwell around him. The spider collapses once again, its legs beginning to twitch and fold underneath it, but it makes one last futile attempt to extricate itself from the stairwell. Riadon again plunges his blade into the spider; its shrill screeching cries drown out the sounds of steel against steel only a few feet away. With one final thrust, Riadon ends its misery.

Outnumbered and with their hairy ally lying listless before them, the four remaining soldiers turn and rush toward the far hallway only to have their retreat abruptly halted by Kriv and Loki. Pressing their advantage, the two force the soldiers back toward Aramas and Patron. Within seconds, the battle is over.

Slinger climbs over the spider and slogs over to the well, Aria close behind.

Laughing, Riadon remarks, "Nice smell. It's going to take more than water to get that stench out of your clothes."

Unamused, Slinger lowers the bucket into the well. Before Riadon can continue, an angry Aramas motions toward the bodies. "See if there is anything of value." Turning to Kriv, Aramas shouts, "What were you thinking? Have you learned nothing?" Before Kriv can answer, Aramas continues. "You put everyone in this party in danger, not to mention the fact that you jeopardized the mission!"

"I am sorry, but I felt that someone needed to prevent the release . . ."

"That was not what you were told to do! You were instructed to take up defensive positions in the stairwell. We could not afford to be surrounded." Turning away, Aramas takes a few steps toward the empty guard room, stops, then turns back to Kriv. "Your reckless behavior has forced us to use two of the healing potions, potions that may well be needed before we extricate ourselves from this evil place. You . . ."

Before he can continue, Loki steps between the two. "Enough! It does us no good to fight amongst ourselves."

Aramas redirects his comments to Loki. "You defend him? I would have thought that he would have learned something by now. No one is invincible."

Patron, having heard enough as well, interjects, "He is young. He will learn."

Realizing that he has let his temper get the best of him, Aramas pauses before directing his next comments to Kriv. After a moment, he continues. "It was wrong of me to chastise you as I did." Saying nothing more, he quietly walks toward the hallway leading to the next room.

"Riadon, what did you find?" asks Patron.

"Only a few pieces of gold and silver."

"Slinger, how much more time will you need?"

"I will be ready shortly."

Loki notices blood streaming down Patron's arm and approaches him. "Let me take care of that."

Looking down at his arm, Patron comments, "I had not noticed."

As Loki works on Patron, Riadon continues searching the bodies and the empty guard's quarters. Slinger and Aria wash the spider's entrails from their garments.

Five minutes later, Aramas returns. Walking over to Patron, he asks, "Are you okay?"

"Just a scratch. Had it not been for Loki, I probably would not have noticed it."

Loki quips, "Surrrrre."

Smiling, Patron asks, "What did you find?"

Briefly gazing at Patron's wound, Aramas replies, "There is another well in the next room. To the left and directly ahead are three more guardrooms, all empty. Based on the number of provisions, beds, and tables, they probably housed ten to twenty soldiers."

Loki asks, "There was no sign of them?"

"There was fresh food and drink on several of the tables. Their departure was hasty, not planned. I would presume that, not knowing our strength and the fact that we had successfully reached this level of the castle, they fled to the lower levels hoping to consolidate their numbers."

"Anything else?" asks Patron.

"There is a long well-lit passage to the right, maybe fifty feet in length. It opens into a large room with a set of double doors at the far end. I dared not venture any further."

Looking up at Patron, Loki remarks, "There, that should do." Patron grasps one of his swords with the injured limb and swings it before him in a tight figure-eight motion. "Good as new." He sheathes the weapon. "Thank you."

"Slinger, are you ready?" asks Aramas.

"As ready as I can be."

Patron interrupts. "We cannot afford a repeat of what just happened. We must be able to fight as a unit, not as individuals. We must function as one with one leader." He looks around at the party then back at Aramas. "Unless there are objections, I would propose that you assume the leadership of the party."

Surprised, Aramas searches for an appropriate response. "But . . ."

Kriv stops him. "I agree. You are the most qualified." The others nod their agreement.

Moving into the adjacent room, Aramas points down the long hall. "Riadon, you and Slinger check for any traps. Patron, you and I will follow with Kriv, Loki and Aria in the back."

Riadon and Slinger, wasting no time, proceed into the long corridor with the rest of the party close behind. As they reach the end, the party stops to study the large room. Other than the sconces on the walls, the room is completely empty. As Aramas had mentioned, two large oaken doors rest at the far end of the room, the face of each etched with fine carvings of a large knight standing next to a pool of water. Around the pool stand four cherubs, each holding an urn pouring water into the pool. At the feet of the knight, bowing in submission, are the images of two large dragons. Approximately thirty feet along the wall to the right is another corridor proceeding off to the west.

Loki pushes past Aramas and Patron to the entrance of the room but does not enter. After he takes a few seconds to survey the area, he turns and looks up at Aramas. "Well?"

"Well what?"

As if pleased with himself, Loki smiles and asks, "Which way?"

While Aramas takes a few seconds to evaluate his options, Patron interjects. "I would not want to open the far doors only to have the missing guards shoot out of the hallway behind us."

Aramas, perhaps thankful for the suggestion, replies, "I agree." He motions to Riadon. "We'll proceed to the corridor. You, Patron, and Kriv proceed along the wall. Slinger, Loki, Aria, and I will proceed toward the center of the room to protect your flank."

Nodding their agreement, the party continues into the room. When they find no traps, Riadon, Patron, and Kriv proceed to the corridor.

Riadon peers around the corner and reports, "Another set of double doors."

From the center of the room, Aramas replies, "Check them for traps."

As the three cautiously move into the corridor, Aramas and the others assume defensive positions at the corridor's entrance. Riadon examines each door carefully. "There are no traps."

"Are they locked?"

"No, but there is something strange about them."

"What do you mean?"

"It does not appear that these doors have been opened for quite some time."

Puzzled, Aramas moves down the corridor, Loki, Aria, and Slinger staying behind. "Show me."

Pointing as he speaks, Riadon explains, "The cobwebs, the dirt, the rust all indicate that it has been some time since the corridor beyond was traversed." He hesitates. "The guards did not come this way. I see no reason to enter."

Aramas runs his fingers over the latch, the thick dust falling in clumps to the floor, then looks back down the corridor and motions to Aria. As she approaches the door, Aramas points to the disturbed dust and asks, "Riadon is correct. Do you see any reason why we should proceed beyond?"

She nods affirmatively. "There is magic beyond and below."

"Where is it the strongest?"

"Below."

"Then why enter?"

"Because I sense a magic item within that could assist us in our quest."

"How can you be so sure?" asks Patron. "If we proceed beyond the doors and the guards return, we will have no escape."

Shaking his head in agreement, Aramas asks Aria, "What kind of item? Can you tell?"

"No, but I sense some type of protective power."

"Like the platinum statues?" asks Riadon.

"I cannot be sure without examining it."

"If no one has been here, what is the risk?" asks Kriv. "Let's get in, retrieve the item, and get out."

"I do not like it," counters Patron. "There is a reason why no one has entered."

Without waiting for a reply, Aria opens the door, brushes past Aramas, and moves into the hallway beyond.

"What are you doing?" asks Patron.

Aramas directs Patron to follow her then motions the rest of the party to join them.

While the hall is crafted of the same stone as the rest of the area, there are no sconces, the way ahead lit only by the sconces from the main room behind them.

"Kriv, we are going to need that sun rod," remarks Patron.

Once he lights it, Aria is nowhere to be seen, likely disappeared further down the hall. The party rushes to the end where the hall turns to the left and stares down the now illuminated passage. There stands Aria in front of another set of double doors with a large board nailed across them with the words "Do not enter" scrawled across it in large letters.

Grabbing Aramas by the shoulder, Patron, obviously concerned, remarks, "It's close to one hundred feet back to the main room. If we are discovered, there is no way out!"

Aramas glances back toward the main room then again at Aria. "You and Loki wait here until I return."

Rushing down the hall, Aramas grabs Aria and spins her around. "What are you doing?"

Before she can answer, Kriv, Slinger, and Riadon gather round.

"The power of the item on the other side of that door is strong. I can sense it!"

Angered, Aramas replies, "There is a reason this hallway has not been traversed recently! If the item is so valuable, it would not have been left in a darkened hallway protected as it is."

"But that may be the reason it has been left as it is. Those entering the passage would be dissuaded from proceeding further."

There is a moment of silence before Kriv interrupts. "We are here now. Why not investigate?"

From the end of the hall, Loki whispers, "We need to leave."

"It will not take long. The item is not far past the doors," pleads Aria.

Aramas turns back to Loki and says, "We'll be only a minute," then looks down at Slinger. "Do you hear anything on the other side?"

After a few seconds, he replies, "I hear nothing."

"What about traps?"

"I can find none."

Aramas pauses then says, "Do so quickly!"

Wasting no time, Kriv and Aria pull the board from the doors, the nails making a loud squeaky sound as they do so. No sooner has it been removed than Aria thrusts open the doors. Beyond, the now-illuminated hallway appears very different from the area just traversed. There is no dust or dirt of any kind on the floor or walls, no cobwebs in the corners or on the ceiling. The stone is unusually clean, almost as if it had been scrubbed and washed recently.

Staring down the hallway to a T-shaped intersection thirty feet further, Riadon says to Aramas, "Have you ever seen anything like this?"

He shakes his head. "No."

"What do you make of it?"

"I have no answer."

Dropping to her knees in the doorway, Aria bends down as if to smell the floor.

Puzzled, Riadon continues. "What is she doing now?" Aramas says nothing. Kriv and Slinger watch with similar curiosity.

Remaining on her knees, Aria sits erect and sniffs the air. After a few seconds, she again bends down and proceeds to lick the floor.

"Taste good?" jokes Riadon.

Saying nothing, Aria again sits up then comments, "No, it burns."

"Burns?" asks Kriv.

"Yes, as if the floor had been washed with acid." She looks up at Aramas. "The item is not far down the hall to the right. May I?"

Hesitating momentarily, Aramas motions to Patron and Loki to stay put. "Quickly! We need to move."

Like a child who has just been given sweets, Aria smiles broadly, stands, and rushes through the doorway, Kriv close behind. Other than the sound of the two proceeding down the hall, all is silent.

When she reaches the intersection, Aria peers down each hallway. Both appear empty. Turning to Kriv, she whispers, "Wait here," before proceeding down the hall to the right. She goes no more than ten feet before the silence is pierced by the thunderous sound of two large objects slamming to the floor. Startled, Aria stops.

"What was that?" shouts Aramas.

Before either Kriv or Aria can reply, two rotting corpses appear before them. Stumbling backwards, Aria turns to run back toward the entry, but her progress is immediately halted when her body is suddenly suspended in midair, engulfed in what appears to be a large translucent gelatinous mass. Like a glistening invisible membrane, the mass occupies the height and width of the hallway. Suspended throughout the mass are bits of clothing and flesh, the translucent blob shimmering in the glow of the sun rod.

Surprised, and fearing the worst, both Patron and Loki rush to join the others. Kriv hastily retreats into the doorway.

"What is it?" asks Riadon.

Gasping for breath, Kriv replies, "I don't know, but it has Aria."

The gelatinous mass continues to move toward the two corpses. The party arrives just in time to witness it consume both. For a moment, it remains motionless, almost as if it was resting between courses of a meal. Clearly visible to the party, Aria struggles to escape, her attempts progressively slowing as she begins to lose consciousness.

"She's dying!" shouts Kriv as he rushes toward the nearly invisible foe. Stopping short of his target, his flail cuts a deep gash into the gooey mass. Aramas and Patron follow his lead, their swords striking true; large chucks of gelatinous goo fly in all directions.

Aramas says, "Kriv, Patron and I will try to cut a swath through the beast to Aria. As soon as you can reach inside, try to pull her out!" However, like trying to cut a hole in a bucket of water, with each mass of goo that is cut away, it is almost immediately replaced.

Patron shouts, "This is getting us nowhere!"

Then the creature begins to move toward the party. Slowly retreating, their swords continuing to send gooey mass in all directions, the party moves back down the long hallway toward the entrance.

"We must not allow this thing to get out of here!" shouts Patron.

"We cannot leave Aria!" shouts Kriv.

As the party continues their slow retreat, Aramas shouts, "Kriv, focus your breath on Aria!"

"What?"

"Quickly, do as I say!"

As directed, Kriv exhales a penetrating blast of fire and lightning. Like a hot knife cutting through butter, the blast cuts a swath through the mass to Aria. Without hesitation, Aramas thrusts himself toward Aria and grabs her outstretched arm. "Pull us out!"

Almost immediately, and before the mass can heal the massive wound, Patron and Kriv grab Aramas's legs. With all of the strength they can muster, they extricate the two from the gelatinous grave. Unwilling to so easily relinquish its prey, the angered mass pushes forward, attempting to reclaim its meal; the sucking slurping sound of air rushes through its still opened gash as it lunges forward.

With Aria in tow, the party avoids the counterattack and rushes to the entrance with the gooey mass bearing down on them. When they reach the doors, Patron and Kriv close and hold them shut while Loki replaces the wooden plank that once bound it, using his hammer to tightly secure it.

Aramas throws Aria over his shoulder and continues down the long passageway. "Riadon, Slinger, get to the entrance and make sure our retreat is not blocked!" Rushing through the next set of doors, Aramas continues toward the main room.

"All is clear!" shouts Slinger.

Clear of the hallway, Aramas lays Aria on the floor. "Is she still alive?" asks Riadon.

"Barely." Detecting only a flicker of life, Aramas lays his hands on her forehead. He recites an ancient prayer; his hands begin to glow a familiar radiant blue. Slowly, the energy flows from his palms into the near-lifeless body; Aria begins to regain consciousness. As she slowly returns to the world of the living, Aramas rolls her on her side, and almost as if she'd nearly drowned, Aria coughs several times, thick translucent spew gushing from her mouth. As she continues to regurgitate the putrid mass, the rest of the party emerges from the hallway.

"We have secured both sets of doors," reports Patron. "That thing should be of no further problem."

"How is she?" asks Kriv.

"She should be fine." Aramas stands. "From this point forward, we concentrate on our mission. We can ill afford needless risks. Understood?" Looking down at Aria, Aramas asks, "Are you able to continue?"

When she nods her affirmation, Aramas reaches down and helps her to her feet. As she wipes the remaining goo from her garments, she sheepishly remarks, "I guess there was a good reason why the relic was left where it was."

Aramas says nothing and walks to the large double doors to examine the engravings.

Standing quietly, Aramas slowly runs his hands over the carvings, fingers feeling through each cut as he studies the engravings hoping to decipher their meaning. "They are not religious in nature nor can I find any historical significance." Motioning for Loki to join him, Aramas continues. "I do not feel that these are simple adornment."

Followed by the others, Loki approaches the doors. As he does, previously unseen runes begin to glow around the door's outer edges. Loki stops abruptly and stares at the now visible symbols. "A dwarf crafted these doors."

"Is that good?" asks Riadon. Loki does not immediately reply. Before Riadon can again ask the question, Aramas's outstretched hand stops him.

Loki says, "Pick me up. I need to read what is at the top of the door." Kriv and Patron do as instructed. Loki's intense stare drinks in each symbol as they move him from left to right. After a short period, he motions to put him down. Walking before each door, he continues to study each new symbol as it appears.

After a few minutes, he points to the carving of the knight. "The dwarf that carved this was Karell's prisoner. He was taken shortly after Lurgan's fall." Moving his hand from one rune to the next, he continues. "Unbeknownst to his captors, while carving the images, he added the runes. They confirm what Sir Lurgan told us. At some time, Karell stumbled upon a portal, or rift, to another plain. Knowing that Sir Lurgan would not allow him to exploit his discovery, he drove Lurgan mad. With his demise, he was free to open the rift. However, to do so, he needed some very rare components. While the engraver is unclear as to the nature of the components, or the actual ritual, with Lurgan out of the way, Karell's singular focus became the acquisition of the components. With them, he would somehow be able to call forth what was trapped in the other plain and, in so doing, would be able to recall and control the long ago banished evil dragons."

Puzzled, Kriv asked, "If he has yet to succeed, how do you explain the black dragon?"

"Do we know that he hasn't?" asks Aria.

"I don't believe he has," replies Loki. "It does not appear that he can recall the dragons without opening the portal."

"Does it say anything else?" asks Aramas.

"There is reference to a guardian that awaits beyond to stop those who try to enter the lower reaches of the castle."

"What kind of guardian?"

"It is not clear, as the runes inexplicably end."

Silence overtakes the group as Aramas ponders Loki's words. Turning to Aria, he asks, "Have you detected any change in either the strength or location of the magic force?"

"No. It has not wavered."

Motioning toward the doors, Aramas directs Slinger to check them for traps. Finding none, the party cautiously opens them. The room, now lit by Kriv's sun rod, resembles a memorial. Devoid of any decorations, sconces, or other ornamentation, it is dominated by the towering statue of an armor-clad titan with a longsword in its outstretched hand. Standing in the center of the room, the figure's gaze appears fixed on the statues of two crouched dragons in the corners of the room's eastern wall. Diagonally across the room from the entrance, about twenty feet past the warrior, an entryway leads to the only other exit. In each of the entryway's corners stand four small statues atop ornate columns: cherubic figures holding vases above their heads. Except for a well-trodden path diagonally across the room, dust covers everything, the floor and statues alike.

"Well, I guess we know where the guards went," quips Loki.

With Riadon and Slinger leading the way, the party proceeds into the room along the exposed path. As Slinger draws to within fifteen feet of the titan, the doors behind slam shut, heavy bolts fall into place. Almost simultaneously, the grinding sound of stone upon stone fills the room as the giant statue swings its longsword in a deadly arc toward the two. Instinctively both drop to the floor, the titan's sword swishing just over their outstretched bodies. Caught off guard, and temporarily stunned, the rest of the party quickly regains their composure and backs to the wall behind them.

Patron, having been the last to enter the room, retreats to the doors. Searching frantically for some way to unlock them, he shouts, "We won't be leaving through these!"

Silence returns to the room; the titan again stares at the statues before him.

"Well that certainly went well," says Loki with a smirk. "What now?"

Hoping to get to safer ground, Riadon stands and attempts to run toward the others. No sooner does he stand than the titan, having apparently learned from its previous miss, swings his sword in a much lower arc. Unable to dodge the blow, Riadon is thrust into the back wall, his body crashing to floor. Taking advantage of the situation, Slinger quickly stands and scrambles into the corner.

"Riadon, are you alright?" asks Aramas.

Riadon groans, holding his rib cage. "I'll be okay. Just give me a moment."

Hugging the back wall, the party slowly makes its way to Riadon and Slinger.

Aramas motions toward the far entryway. "Patron, you and Aria see if you can reach the other doors while we tend to Riadon."

The two slowly move along the wall toward the entryway. The titan remains silent. When they reach the entryway, Patron cautiously peers around the corner; the exit is tantalizingly close. Unlike the rest of the room, there is no dust on the walls. Other than a small puddle of water immediately in front of the doors, the area is suspiciously clean.

"Something is not right," remarks Patron. "Check the other statue to see if you can find any traps." As directed, Aria cautiously proceeds toward the other cherub. Standing before the column, she carefully examines the cherub, the floor, and the adjacent wall. "I can find nothing out of the ordinary."

Although concerned, Patron reports the same. He looks back at the others for direction but receives none, so he motions his approval to proceed into the hallway.

As they pass between the two columns and enter the hallway, each cherub tips her vase, and water rushes to the floor below. Simultaneously, a shimmering wall of translucent arcane energy appears between the columns. Patron turns to exit the hall but is unable to progress past the two statues, water rapidly filling the hallway. Taking a step back, he attempts to break the wall with the full force of his two blades. Nothing happens.

Hearing the commotion, Loki nudges Aramas and points to the hallway. "We've got a problem."

The rest of the party rushes to the hallway. "Stand back!" shouts Kriv. Without thinking, he takes a step back and raises his flail. However, before he can execute the attack, he is thrown into the nearby wall; the long arm of the titan has struck true. Stunned, Kriv sluggishly sits up, shakes his head, and mumbles inaudibly.

Aramas says to Loki, "We need to destroy that thing."

From inside the hallway, Patron's muffled voice calls out, "There must be some sort of control device."

Loki replies, "I've got this," then rushes back along the wall and behind the titan.

"What if we destroy the vases?" asks Riadon.

Patron replies, "We need to do something quick! The water will be over our heads soon."

Drawing back his sword, Aramas strikes the closest cherub; stone shards from its vase fly in all directions. Almost immediately, the nearest dragon statue shoots a searing breath of fire twenty-five feet toward the hallway. While engulfing the cherub closest to the dragon, the flames do not reach the second. However, surprised by the attack, Aramas instinctively jumps back and into the path of the titan, and its blade thrusts him into the wall.

Groaning and holding his side, Aramas asks Patron, "Can you reach the vase? Until we can find a way to neutralize the traps, it may be difficult for us to do so from here."

Patron takes several swings at the vase hit by Aramas, each sending larger pieces of stone into the room beyond. With each strike, the area in front of the passageway is engulfed with fiery explosions from the dragon statue.

As the water continues to fill the hallway, Loki rushes the base of the titan. Anticipating the timing of the statue's swing, he slides underneath the arc of the sword to the ground; his momentum thrusts him along the shiny slick marble floor to the safety of the statue's base. The titan continues to try and knock Loki off its base, but it is unable to reach him.

Loki climbs up the three-foot-high base and presses his body as close as possible to the titan's calves. Searching the crevices of its sculptured chain mail and armor, he slowly ascends to the waist of the statue. Seeing nothing to indicate the presence of a control device, he continues upward.

Once he reaches the statue's neck, his one hand grasping the titan's helmet, he quickly surveys the area. He notices what appears to be a small indentation in the stone, so he runs his fingers along it, dirt and dust falling away to expose what appears to be a small cover. Unable to pry it open, he grasps his hammer and thrusts its massive head into the back of the titan's skull. As if struck by lightning, the thunderous crash of steel hitting stone sends large chunks of the statue's head crashing to the marble below. A temporary silence engulfs the room as everyone turns to see what has happened; the titan now stands silent.

Still grasping what is left of the statue's neck, Loki shouts down, "That should do it!"

Aramas stands, his attention again drawn to the hallway where the water is now five feet deep. Patron and Aria cling to one of the cherubs, both no longer able to stand. Suddenly, as if caught in a tempest, the water begins to swirl, the vortex in the center of the hallway growing wider and stronger by the second.

Running to the hallway, Aramas shouts, "Slinger, Loki, focus on the damaged vase!"

Unhindered by the now silent titan, Slinger backs into the center of the room and hurls several bolts at the still-standing cherub, each bolt inflicting greater damage, each successful strike prompting another burst of flames from the dragon statue.

Loki leaps from the titan and hurls his hammer at the severely damaged target. As with the titan's skull moments earlier, the hammer smashes what is left of the cherub and its vessel; the flow of water slows to a trickle almost immediately. However, the velocity and intensity of the whirlpool remains strong.

Patron and Aria, their bodies stretched horizontally toward the center of the vortex by the swirling torrent, frantically attempt to keep from being sucked to their demise.

Loki recovers his hammer and raises it above his head. "By the power of Moradin." Calling upon all of his strength, he hurls it at the nearest cherub, its steel head glowing a radiant blue. It strikes true, holy power unleashed, and the vessel disintegrates, leaving only a cloud of fine particles hovering above the pool of water.

No sooner is the cherub destroyed than the arcane wall of energy disintegrates, sending a torrent of water rushing into the room. All in its path are swept off their feet and into the base of the titan beyond.

Exhausted and soaked, Patron and Aria sit quietly on the wet marble floor staring blankly into the now quiet room as the rest of the party slowly regains their footing and retrieve any equipment that was washed away when the wall disintegrated.

As she wrings the water from her robe, Aria remarks, "Next time, let's wait for the others to find the traps."

Patron gives a half-hearted chuckle then slowly rises to his feet. "Good idea." He quickly looks at the door then back at the now approaching party. "Slinger, would you mind checking the door for traps?"

When he finds no traps, Slinger, with an exaggerated sweeping motion of his hand and a slight supplicating bow to Patron, takes a step back and sarcastically remarks, "Be my guest."

Not quite sure what to do, Patron looks around at the others as if seeking direction.

"Well?" asks Loki. "Are you just going to stand there, or are you going to open the door?" at which point the others chuckle.

Realizing he's been had, Patron moves to the door and, before opening it, asks, "Everyone ready?" Hearing nothing, he raises his sword and thrusts open the door, and the smell of rotting meat quickly fills the hallway. Wincing at the putrid odor, Patron turns his head in an attempt to avoid it then cautiously moves into the room. "Follow me."

The room is small and dimly lit, the only source of light coming from the bottom of a stairwell to the left. Death has resided in this room; humanoid remains, partially eaten corpses, and the skulls of those less fortunate litter the floor. A dry well occupies its center. At the bottom of the stairwell they can hear the footsteps of several beings scattering.

Moving quickly into the area, Patron silently directs half of the party to proceed around the well to the other side of the stairwell while he leads the rest. Once everyone is positioned to either side of the stairwell, he cautiously peers around the corner at the stairs below and sees a set of open double doors leading into the next level of the mountain's bowels. He motions for everyone to proceed below, hugging the walls as they do. The party does as directed and moves down the stairs to either side of the opened doors.

Before Patron can give additional orders, a voice comes from the room beyond. "We've been waiting for you. Please, come in."

Surprised, Patron looks across at Aramas. "What do you want to do?" He pauses briefly. "Let's not keep our host waiting."

They step through the doorway onto a large ornate, hand-woven carpet inside a huge temple that is over one hundred feet wide. A dull bluish-green light, emanating from four crystal columns in the center of the room, provides sufficient light to illuminate the entire area. Between the columns is a large hole in the floor, the outer perimeter of which is covered by a metal grate. The floor around the grate, like that in the titan's room, is finely polished marble. Carved into it is the massive image of a satanic-looking ram's head, its mouth surrounding the opening to the lower level. At the far end of the room is a raised dais from which streams of blood flow down its steps and over the polished marble into the hole.

Hanging from the ceiling through the hole to the lower level are four large chains, the flowing blood oozing down each. A tall humanoid figure stands on the dais in dark robes, the tattoo of a ram's skull emblazoned across his face. A sacrificial knife, dripping with blood, is in his outstretched hand. "You have proven to be worthy adversaries."

"Karell?" asks Aramas.

"You flatter me. No, I am only his underpriest." Stepping down off the dais, the humanoid glides toward the center of the room, stopping just short of the hole. "I do hope that you are planning on spending some time here. It is not often that we have the privilege of hosting such talented guests."

"The time of our stay will only be long enough to kill your master."

"Oh, I like your spirit. So brave yet so naïve. Almost makes me quiver. Unfortunately, while you have shown yourself adept at getting this far, much further than any before you, I am afraid that you will not have the honor of completing your quest."

"You obviously underestimate us," replies Loki.

The underpriest steps to the edge of the opening. "If you are who you believe yourselves to be, then join me. We await your arrival." Without further comment, he clasps the knife in both hands, raises it to his chest, takes one step forward, and disappears through the hole.

The party rushes to the center of the room and peers into the chamber below. Standing in the center of a large pool of blood, surrounded by twenty to thirty vampire spawn, skeletal warriors, and at least one wight, the underpriest looks up, spreads his arms in a welcoming gesture, then shouts, "Come, meet your fate!"

Stepping back, Patron remarks, "We need to find another way down there!"

Aramas looks around. "I see no obvious alternative."

Flustered, Kriv asks, "Did anyone see Karell? Is he even down there?"

Calmly, in an almost reverent tone, Aria replies, "He is there."

From near the chains, Loki comments, "With the amount of blood flowing down the chains, we should be able to slide down with little resistance."

"Sure, but fine targets we'll be. No better than fish in a barrel," replies Kriv. "We lost the element of surprise long ago. There will be no cover, no protection. We'll be cut down before we can reach the bottom."

"And this from the one who rushed down the steps of the keep, headlong into . . ."

"Enough!" declares Aramas. "This accomplishes nothing. Slinger, see if you can find another way into the lower level. Riadon, go with him." Aramas asks Patron, "Any suggestions? Kriv is right."

There is a long silence. Then, without explanation, Patron walks over to the hole and shouts into the room below, "Do not go anywhere! We will be right down."

Surprised, Loki responds, "What are you doing?"

Smiling, Patron replies, "I have an idea. Follow me." Walking briskly back toward the entrance with Aramas, Kriv, Loki, and Aria close behind, Patron stops next to the large rug. "Each of you grab a corner and help me move this."

Completely puzzled, Loki asks, "What?"

Bending down to grab a corner, Patron replies, "Just do as I ask." With no further questions, the others follow suit.

"So what now?" Loki asks sarcastically.

"We're going to put this over the hole."

"What? Do you know something about this carpet that we do not? If not, how does covering our only entrance into the lower chamber help?"

"I'll explain momentarily. Slinger, Riadon, come give us a hand."

As directed, the party moves the carpet to the center of the room and carefully stretches it over the opening.

With a look of satisfaction, Patron says, "Slinger, Riadon, did you find another way out of here?"

"No, but we didn't have time to complete our search."

"It doesn't matter. Kriv is right. We lost the element of surprise once we entered the keep. Regardless of whether there is another entrance or not, they will be waiting for us. We need to do something they won't expect."

"And that is?"

"Not long ago, Aria had a run-in with a very nasty invisible beast with a voracious appetite. It did not appear to care whether its dinner came from friend or foe. What if we could enlist its help with our current problem?"

Loki replies, "I'm not following you."

He smiles broadly. "What if we entice it into this room and onto the rug?"

"And how does that help us?"

Realizing what Patron is suggesting, Aramas replies, "Because if we can get the creature onto the carpet, it will fall into the pit, making it their problem, and in the process possibly reduce the number of those waiting to kill us." He pats Patron on the shoulder. "I like it!"

"And how do we get it to stand on the rug?" asks Loki.

"Leave that to me," replies Patron. "Aria and Kriv, you come with me. The rest of you be ready. When we come running through the door, I need you to be standing on the other side of the rug. Slinger, you, Riadon, and Loki attack it to draw its attention. If it does as it did in the passageway, it will follow."

"So I'm bait?" asks Aria.

"You could say that. After all, it seemed upset that we were able to spirit you away."

"Why not take all of us?" asks Loki.

"Someone needs to make sure that Karell and his followers do not escape. If the only way in is through that hole, then so it is to get out."

Smiling contently, Loki replies, "I like it."

Patron, Kriv, and Aria run out of the great hall and rush back toward the sealed passageway, careful to ensure that all of the doors are left open as they do. When they reach the passageway, Kriv takes out the still-activated sun rod before proceeding to the first set of doors. Hesitating, he directs the others to be ready just in case the creature was able to break through the other doors. On Patron's signal, he thrusts open the doors, the hallway behind as vacant as before.

Patron moves around the corner to the sealed set of doors and removes the recently reinstalled plank but does not drop it to the floor. He cautiously opens the doors, and with the area now brightly illuminated, the three slowly move down the hall. As if on cue, the intersection at the far end appears to shimmer; the remains of the two rotting corpses, still suspended within, are clearly visible as the creature enters the intersection.

Patron hurls the plank into the gelatinous mass and shouts, "Let's get out of here!" Wasting no time, the three turn and run back down the hall through the doors. As expected, the gelatinous mass quickly follows. They rush into the titan room, and Patron stops only long enough to pick up a few pieces of stone and hurl them into the angry mass, but its progress is unhindered.

As they run down the stairs and into the great hall, Kriv shouts, "Get ready!"

As directed, no sooner does the creature enter the room than Slinger, Riadon, and Loki unleash a devastating volley of ranged attacks. Surprised and temporarily stunned, the creature's progress is halted just long enough for it to heal. Although silent, it is obviously angered; the translucence within its form changes from clear to a pinkish-red color and shimmers erratically. Within seconds, it continues its advance, the entire party now waiting just beyond the rug.

As planned, it moves onto the carpet, and its weight causes it to fall through the hole to the unsuspecting fighters below. Chaos ensues as the party members gather around the now open entry to observe the results of their "surprise." As hoped, while the creature is eventually defeated, it succeeds in killing the underpriest and most of the other creatures.

Grabbing one of the chains, Aramas shouts, "Let's go!" then jumps through the hole, sliding down the bloodsoaked chain to the chamber below. The others waste no time following his lead.

As they come to rest in the large pool of blood, the thick viscous liquid reaching the top of their boots, the party finds themselves in what could best be described as a nightmare, streams of blood still pouring into the pool from above and the remnants of bones, body parts, and large globs of gelatinous goo strewn everywhere. Other than two figures, neither of whom seem to be concerned about the interlopers, they are the only fighters still standing.

The chamber, as large as the one they just exited, has two raised daises, one each along the eastern and western walls. In the center of the western wall stands a heavily armored human, his back to the party, holding a skull-capped rod; an open book sits before him atop a large altar. On the opposite wall stand two small statues of an unknown god flanking what appears to be a well. Before it, silently observing the party's every move, stands the wight, gaunt with pale leathery skin tautly stretched over its bones, its eyes glowing a bright red with sharp black claws extending from its fingers and toes. Like a skull devoid of flesh, the creature's nose is sunken, its lips appearing frozen in death's grip.

In the center of the north wall is a large gaping black portal, something dark and ominous straining within its confines, apparently trapped by a thin invisible dark veil. Before the portal, inscribed in the marble tiles, is a large circle of glowing runes. From across the room, sitting in a throne-like stone chair, the winged statue of the same unidentified god peers into the dark void of the portal, its head and face in the form of a satanic ram's head, the same as was inscribed in the marble floor above.

Turning toward the party, his eyes still closed, the armored human remarks, "Brevek did not exaggerate. Not only are you formidable, but your resourcefulness, your ingenuity, is impressive. Nothing like the others. Unfortunately, you are too late." Opening his eyes, he walks to the steps of the dais.

As the party slowly exits the pool of blood, the armored figure addresses Aramas. "So you are the knight that killed our child." He pauses, almost as if on the verge of tears. "Somehow it was able to traverse across the plains, ending up in Spring Green, perhaps through some sort of treachery or just unfortunate luck. Regardless, its mother still mourns. Have you ever heard the cries of a mother dragon? I suspect not, why would you. While much shriller, it is not unlike the mournful cry of a wolf that has lost its mate. Very sad."

"May I assume that you are Karell?"

"Oh, I do apologize. I should have introduced myself. Yes, I am Karell. And you are?"

"Aramas."

Karell takes a few steps to his left then stops and again faces the party. "Well Aramas, what is it that you want?" He smiles broadly. "Since none of you will be leaving here, and out of respect for the fact that you managed to get this far, I see no reason why I shouldn't let you die with at least some idea as to why."

Loki interrupts. "You said that the child's mother still mourns. Does that mean that there are other dragons?"

"Oh, this one is quick. And you are?"

"Loki."

Karell shakes his finger. "I suspected as much. Brevek spoke of an impish dwarf that travelled with the knight. Well Loki, there have always been dragons. They have just been out of sight."

"For over three hundred years?"

"It is a long story. Suffice it to say that once I have disposed of your miserable party, dragons will once again become a part of everyone's life, albeit an unpleasant one."

Puzzled, Aramas asks, "You've found a way to reincarnate dragons?"

"Not reincarnate—recall and control. While I may not have all the elements I need, I believe that what exists beyond the portal does, and soon, I will set it free. Together our power will be unmatched."

"We will not let that happen," Loki says.

Laughing, Karell replies, "Are you so naïve as to think that others haven't tried to stop me? Even Sir Lurgan, as strong as he was, could not prevent the inevitable."

"It's obvious you don't know who we are!"

As if seriously pondering Loki's remark, Karell answers, "Someone said that earlier." He turns to face Loki. "Oh yes, it was you." Waving his hand as if to flick away a pest, Karell motions to the wight. "Remove them from my presence. I've become bored. Besides, I have more important things to do." Appearing unconcerned by the presence of the interlopers, Karell turns a page of the book, closes his eyes, and begins a low chant.

Almost immediately, the sound of clattering bones can be heard around the room. The wight, with clawed fingertips glistening in the light of the sconces, slowly raises its arms toward the ceiling. As it does, scattered bones rise from the floor and drift toward the wight. Once all of the bones are floating before the dais, the wight begins to rotate both hands in opposing circular motions, sending the bones into four tornado-like columns that extend from the floor toward the ceiling. It claps its hands twice, and the bones quickly reassemble into four skeletal warriors, their imposing figures flanked on each side of the wight. With another movement of the wight's hand, four short swords emerge from the mass of gelatinous goo and fly to the waiting arms of the warriors.

"Well, that certainly complicates matters," quips Loki.

Aramas draws his sword and says to Loki, "You take the two to the left. The two to the right are mine. Patron, take the wight. The rest of you keep Karell occupied!" Moving in unison, Aramas, Loki, and Patron advance on the dais. At the same time, Kriv and the others move on Karell, still seemingly unfazed by the unfolding events.

As the four skeletal warriors advance down the steps, the wight moves back to the well. With a broad sweeping motion of its arm, a bolt of energy leaps from its open palm and strikes Patron, hurling him fifteen feet to the foot of the seated idol.

Countering, Loki extends his offhand in a familiar sweeping motion, and blue radiant energy shoots forth, striking the four attackers and thrusting them into the wall behind. However, unlike before, each immediately regains its footing and rushes back into combat. As they approach, Loki hurls his hammer, hitting his assigned foes and temporarily halting their advance. With the hammer's return, he raises it upward. "By the power of Moradin." A powerful bolt of energy shoots forth and strikes each.

Seemingly unfazed, they continue their advance in an attempt to flank their singular target. However, before they can do so, Patron's twin blades strike home, severing the offhand of the closest warrior.

With their focus temporarily diverted to the enraged dragonborn, Loki delivers two successive blows with his hammer, the first shattering the chest of its target, sending shards of splintered bone flying in all directions. The second shatters the pelvis of the other. As the warrior sinks to the floor, Patron separates the creature from its head.

To their right, Aramas parries the first thrust of his attackers, redirects the second, then quickly counters with two of his own, both striking true. However, before he can deliver another, he is suddenly thrust fifteen feet with the force of necrotic energy, temporarily stunning him.

Pressing their advantage, the two warriors rush forward, the sound of steel on steel echoing throughout the room. Aramas calls upon his faith, and radiant energy surges forth as he sweeps his hand to the right, thrusting the two warriors into the steps of the dais.

Aramas hears, "Beware the wight," just in time to parry another blast of necrotic energy. Regaining his composure, he pushes forward, and two devastating blows with his greatsword disintegrate the remaining two warriors. He rushes up the steps of the dais, joined by Patron and Loki, to cut off any retreat of the outmatched wight.

With each advance, the wight casts spell after spell, each repulsed by the combined power of the three. Cornered, the wight lashes out, its clawed fingertips tearing at its attackers. However, within seconds, the creature falls to the floor, writhes in pain, then vanishes into a fine powdery mist.

While Aramas, Loki, and Patron are dispatching the wight, the rest of the party focus their attention on Karell. Spreading out to minimize the chance that Karell will be able to retreat from the dais, Aria and Slinger's initial volleys are quickly repulsed by a simple wave of his hand.

Annoyed, Karell turns and, with a thrust of his hand, sends forth a wave of necrotic energy. Unexpectedly and without apparent intervention by the party, the wave is repulsed, hitting no one. Surprised, he sends forth another wave of necrotic energy. Again, the wave is dissipated without striking its targets. Hoping to capitalize on the situation, Aria, Slinger, and Kriv rush the dais while they simultaneously launch multiple ranged assaults; Karell easily deflects each.

His initial spells ineffective, Karell disappears and suddenly reappears in the circle of glowing runes at the entrance to the portal. With two hands clasped tightly together, he sends forth another wave of necrotic energy, but like the others before, it is repulsed by an unseen force. Infuriated, he raises his staff, swirls it over his head, then abruptly points it at Aria; brilliant reddish bolts of necrotic energy leap forth.

Thrusting her staff forward then rapidly sweeping it to the right, Aria successfully redirects the attack, and the deflected energy shatters the winged god seated across from the portal.

Before Karell can repeat the assault, Aramas's sword crashes into his outstretched staff. With a brilliant flash of reddish-white concussive energy, the staff explodes, temporarily halting the party's advance.

Instinctively, Karell sweeps his hand to the left, pushing Aramas toward the portal as its long black tentacle-like appendages lash out from within, attempting to ensnare its prey. Aramas regains his footing and rushes forward. A faint voice tells him that the mage is no longer able to stop him.

Surrounded by an unrelenting melee assault by Kriv, Patron, and Loki, and with his every counterattack mysteriously ineffective, Karell attempts to retreat to the protection of the beast within the portal. He shouts to Aramas, "Orcus will not be denied!"

With the sweeping thrust of his greatsword, Aramas replies, "Nor will I!"

Just as Karell reaches for an amulet around his neck, Aramas's sword slices through him; the two halves of his body fall to the floor, blood gushing in all directions and mixing with the blood from above.

"The amulet!" shouts Riadon.

As if drawing power from its dead host, the ruby within the amulet begins to pulsate, its brilliance increasing with the pool of blood from Karell's body. Fascinated, Riadon draws nearer as the rest of the party stands silently nearby, mesmerized by the gem's brilliance. He bends down and reaches for the gem. However, before he can grasp it, a stinging bolt of energy surges from the gem, knocking him to the floor. "He's still alive!" he yells.

Startled, the rest of the party quickly steps back. From within the portal, the black tentacle-like appendages quickly withdraw, accompanied by the sound of air being sucked into a dark void.

"Destroy the portal!" shouts Aramas. The urgency in his voice springs the others to action. Aria and Kriv send powerful blasts of lightning and fire into the dark void as Slinger and Loki concentrate their volleys on the stone surrounding it.

With its defender and liberator lying dead before it, the intensity of the creature beyond the veil grows dimmer with each assault. The sound of sucking air, like the last breath of a dying creature, decreases with each strike until it is no more. With one final blow from Loki's war hammer, the stone around the opening comes crashing to the floor, sealing the portal forever. Dust and small particles of stone billow into the room, temporarily obscuring everything.

Other than the sound of party members coughing, silence overcomes the room; the dust slowly settles on everything in the area. From within the cloud, Aramas finds his attention is again drawn to the amulet. Gazing at the still brightly glowing gem, he moves closer.

"I wouldn't do that," admonishes Riadon.

Aramas pauses momentarily, but the gem's hypnotic brilliance draws him closer. He kneels and extends his hand toward the amulet, the gem's intensity growing as his hand draws nearer. When he touches the gem, its brilliance illuminates the surrounding area. With the tenderness of a lover, he caresses the gem, then gently removes the amulet. He rises to his feet, eyes fixed on the artifact, then proceeds up the steps toward the well and stands between the two statues.

Confused, Loki asks, "What are you doing?"

Without responding, Aramas touches the amulet and is immediately teleported to the circle of runes. Standing in the center of the circle, he replies, "It is an amulet of teleportation." He steps back out of the circle. "While I try to ascertain what powers it might possess, check to see if there is another way out of this room. I do not relish the idea of having to scale those chains."

"And if there is anything of value?" asks Riadon. Aramas doesn't reply, so he joins the others.

While the others search the room, Aramas walks over to the dais and plops himself on the steps to study the amulet. It is a finely crafted artifact; the focal point is a brilliant ruby adorned with, and secured by, interwoven braids of gold and silver to form the main body of the pendant. One end of the silver chain takes the form of a dragon's skull, the mouth of which acts as a clasp to secure the amulet around the wearer's neck.

As Aramas gazes into the gem, a series of images appear momentarily and then dissolve into the next: the circle of runes, fine pieces of diamonds, sapphires, and quartz poured onto the floor by a robed figure, each component carefully crafted and then intertwined into the ornate circle. The images grow brighter with each pulse of the ruby, and the sequence repeats several times; the only difference is the area in which the circle is created. Then he sees the figure leaping from circle to circle, each time initiated with a touch of the gem. In one image, the figure leaps with several other robed individuals, each touching the wearer of the amulet.

"Aramas, you need to see this!"

As he comes out of his trance, Aramas's eyes are met by Loki pointing toward the well. "You need to see this," Loki says again.

Aramas stands, placing the amulet in his pouch and walks toward the others. "What is it?" The rest of the party is gathered in and around the two statues.

"Don't you see?" asks Slinger.

"See what?"

Pointing to the ceramic wall tiles behind the well, Slinger replies, "That."

"I see tiles."

"Look closer," says Aria. "The tiles move."

Looking closer, Aramas realizes that the tiles are indeed moving, almost shimmering. "What do you make of it?"

"A portal of some sort."

"To where?"

Riadon replies, "Maybe it's another way out of here."

Aramas turns to Aria, motioning toward the portal. "Is there a way to determine where it goes?"

"No, not unless one enters it."

"Is it here all the time?" asks Riadon.

"Its existence depends on who created it and for what purpose. Some portals are used once and then disappear. Others exist as a means to travel long distances or between different planes. They remain while needed or until dismissed by their creator."

"Between different planes? Which is this?"

"You ask questions I am unable to answer."

"So we could go through it and not be able to return?"

"It is possible." She looks briefly at the body of Karell. "I believe it was his creation. It is now frozen and will not close unless closed by someone more powerful than us."

Kriv interjects. "It must have something to do with whatever he was trying to release. Maybe we should investigate further."

"I'm not going through it," Riadon replies nervously.

"I made a promise to Sir Lurgan," says Aramas. "I will not leave until it has been kept."

"So who's going through?" asks Patron.

"I do not believe it prudent to split the party. Our strength rests in our numbers. Should we run into trouble, we will face it together."

There is no immediate response as everyone quietly looks at the others.

"I will go first," says Slinger.

"I will go next," responds Loki.

"Then it is settled." Then Aramas says to Riadon, "You are welcome to stay, but I hope that you do not."

Riadon takes a few seconds to compose a response then smiles. "I'm coming only because you need me."

Loki sarcastically adds, "It wouldn't be that you're afraid that those skeletons might return?"

Riadon ignores Loki's remark. "What are we waiting for?"

As agreed, Slinger steps into the portal first and exits onto a rock ledge easily one hundred feet above the desert floor below. Surprised, he sticks his head back through the portal. "Be careful. You are stepping onto a narrow ledge!"

He pulls his head through the portal again and, with his back against the rock wall behind him, slowly moves to his left to make room for the others as they come through. Before him is a vast desert, with barren mountain ranges on either side. In the distance, he sees an orange sky with two celestial bodies, one close to the horizon, the other high above it. While it is warm, it is not hot, and a dry wind gently blows along the ledge. Further to his left, he can see an opening in the side of the mountain, a cave of some sort. Once the others have emerged from the portal, Slinger points to the opening and presses his index finger to his lips asking for quiet. He then motions for everyone to follow him.

Moving cautiously along the ledge, the party slowly advances to the opening. Slinger peers around the corner then whispers to the others, "I can only see about forty or fifty feet."

"Can you hear anything?" asks Aramas.

"No, but there is a foul odor."

"What kind of odor?"

"Dung!"

Puzzled, Loki asks, "What would live at this elevation? A bear? Lion? There is no nearby food, no water."

Aramas carefully moves past the others to join Slinger. Peering into the cave, the foul odor almost overpowers him. He quickly withdraws his head. "That's no bear!"

"What is it?"

"It smells like the catacombs under Spring Green."

"You mean . . . ?"

"Yes."

"Yes what?" asks Riadon.

Aramas replies, "We need to make sure."

"Make sure of what?"

"Loki, you and Patron get up here." They do as directed, cautiously moving past the others to the opening.

Aramas says to Patron, "Slinger, Loki, and I are going in to investigate. You and the others remain out here. I don't want to be surprised should the occupant come back while we are still inside."

"Occupant? What are we looking for?"

Hesitant with concern, Aramas replies, "If it is as I fear, that's the smell of dragon dung."

Patron does not immediately reply. "And if it is . . . ?"

"We get back to the portal as quickly as possible!"

Loki interrupts. "Are you sure we want to go in there?"

Aramas nods. "Karell boasted that the dragons had never vanished, only hidden in another plane. He was certain that he had discovered a way to return them to our plane, control them, and with the help of whatever was behind the veil, subjugate the world under his power. We need to know . . ."

"What are we looking for?" asks Slinger.

"Anything that might confirm my suspicion: dung, a nest, scales, anything."

Patron replies, "Be careful."

Drawing his sword, Aramas motions for Slinger to proceed. They move stealthily along the inner wall, the odor becoming almost unbearable with each step. Twenty feet into the cave, Slinger abruptly stops, his hand reaching back to stop Aramas. Nodding toward a ledge on the other side of the cave, Slinger points to what appears to be another cave about ten feet above the floor. Aramas nods his understanding.

Moving quietly to the other wall, Slinger surveys the area, looking for a way that it might be scaled without dislodging any of the surrounding rocks. Satisfied that he has found a safe route, he quietly scales the wall to a point just below and to the left of the opening. As he carefully peeks over the ledge, he almost loses his grip, caught off guard by what lies before him.

Tucked neatly inside the opening, sound asleep, is a large black dragon, its tail, like swaddling clothes, tightly wrapped around three sleeping baby black dragons. Wasting no time, Slinger quickly climbs back down the wall and, as quietly as possible, makes his way back to Aramas and Loki. He says nothing, just directs them back to the opening where the others anxiously await their return.

"Well?" asks Patron.

"Get back to the portal now!" He looks back at Aramas. "It is worse than you expected."

"What do you mean?"

"A large black dragon with three babies." As he moves onto the ledge, he continues. "We risk waking them if we tarry any longer!"

While being as quiet as possible but wasting no time, the party retreats along the ledge to the portal, minutes later safely back in Raven's Nest.

Slinger, his hand shaking as he points to the portal, asks Aria, "How do we close this? Those things cannot be allowed to come through!"

"Only the one who created it can close it."

"That cannot be. There must be a way to prevent their passage into this realm?"

Aramas interrupts. "If they could have passed into this realm, why have they not? Was that not what Karell was trying to do?"

"Then how do you explain the dragon we encountered?" asks Loki. "It too was black and a baby?"

"I have no answer, only that Karell too was surprised. He said so when standing before us on the dais." Aramas walks toward Karell's body. "He had not yet accomplished his goal; his frustration was evident as he spoke. I too have more questions than answers. However, the ledge was too narrow to be traversed by the dragon we killed, and even if it had somehow discovered the portal, the dragon's size would have prevented it from doing so."

"I don't know," says Slinger. "We need to get back to Spring Green and warn everyone!"

"And be thrown into the dungeon as mad men? Who is going to believe you?"

"Alissa!"

"Will she? Other than us, no one has ever seen a dragon. For over three hundred years, they have existed only in myth and lore. Even if we were to be believed, what then? Panic, hysteria? No, we can tell no one of what we've seen here until we have more answers."

"And where do we get them?" asks Kriv.

"As I said, I too have more questions than answers." Walking over to the chains, Aramas looks up to the floor above, the flow of blood having ceased with the death of Karell, and remarks, "The answers we seek rest with the opal."

"And what do we tell Adwin? He is expecting news of his stolen shipments. We have seen nothing to indicate that the stolen goods were ever brought here."

"We will tell him the truth. We found just over three hundred gold pieces. As promised, we will give him half of what was recovered."

"And the wand and amulet?" asks Aria.

"I will advise him of their existence. However, I do not believe they were part of any shipment. Therefore, unless argued otherwise, we will keep them."

"But what if he sends his guards to search the area? They could discover the portal," asks Kriv.

"They could, but it is highly unlikely. After all, the castle is possessed by evil spirits and haunted by the spirit of a crazed knight, a knight that killed his wife, his son, his captain of the guard, and at least twenty of his best knights. Should that not dissuade them and they do enter the castle, they must then force themselves to ignore the smell of rotting flesh and the piles of bones from creatures they have never before encountered. I believe that our secret is safe."

Riadon pulls out the gold and platinum statuette. "Are we taking these with us?"

Patron replies, "I for one am returning mine to where we found it. It has served its purpose."

Surprised, Riadon asks, "What purpose?"

Pointing to Karell, Patron replies, "Why do you think he was unable to stop us, each spell thrust aside? Loki said as much when we found them. Sir Lurgan was bound by his fate, but through us, he could be avenged. These were given as his way of aiding us in our quest."

"I agree," says Kriv. "May he now rest in peace." Looking at Aramas, he asks, "And you?"

"Each must search his heart to know what is right. However, I fear that I might have need of it again. I expect that this will not be my last visit to Raven's Nest. It will remain with me."

Riadon stares at the statuette then looks at the others before replying, "It's probably not real gold anyway."

They search the area one last time for another way out, and finding none, the party scales the chains to begin their trek back to Spring Green, stopping only long enough to return the statuettes. Emerging from the lower bowels of the castle, the party exits the keep to the stench of rotting goblin flesh already fouling the air below.

Outside once again, the party is greeted by the fresh smell of a crisp morning breeze, the bright morning sun a welcome sight. Aramas pauses at the top of the castle steps and stands silently surveying the valley before him; the road to the west is inviting, beckoning him forward.

"What are you thinking?" asks Loki.

Putting his hand on his friend's shoulder, he replies, "I know not what lies ahead, but for the first time, I know what must be done." He looks down at Loki. "And together we will do it."

Turning to the others, he says, "Slinger, you were asked to join us with the promise of fifty gold pieces. It was not my choice, and not one to which I agreed. I now find myself admitting that Kriv was right. You have kept your part of the bargain. Should you decide that it is time to part ways, I will understand. However, I would hope that you might consider joining us as an equal partner. You have become a valuable member of the party, your skills invaluable." Looking around at the others, he adds, "I believe everyone here agrees."

Smiling, Slinger jokingly remarks, "I have nothing better to do."

"Then it is settled." Glancing briefly at the sun, Aramas starts walking down the trail toward the main road. "We should have a good eight hours of sunlight before we make camp. Let's make the best of it."

Following close behind, Loki asks, "Do you think Alissa will have received word from Everand?"

Looking back over his shoulder, Aramas replies, "We'll know soon enough."

CHAPTER 10

EVERAND

The days pass uneventfully during the party's return to Spring Green. The weather is favorable, with many of the trees now fully dressed in bright green leaves, some even sporting fragrant pink and white flowers. Like the fields outside of Spring Green on the outbound trek, the sound of humming bees fills the air as they flit from flower to flower gathering the tasty nectar. Birds in the sky transport bits of grass and small twigs to build their nests. Wildlife is abundant everywhere, oblivious to what had transpired only days earlier.

However, there is little conversation within the party, each member focusing on what they witnessed deep within the bowels of Raven's Nest Castle and, more importantly, what lies before them. Fortunately, the days pass quickly. By the time the party reaches the outer gates of Spring Green, the sun hangs low in the western sky, candlelight glows from many of the city's buildings, and the streets are growing quiet.

As they navigate the streets, the party slowly makes its way to the tavern hoping to quench their thirst and partake of the first warm meal they've had in weeks. Although the quiet of the evening is periodically broken by passing horse carts or the whispered conversations of passersby, their presence goes virtually unnoticed. Before they arrive at the tavern, Aramas again reminds the party not to say anything about what has transpired until they meet with Alissa and Adwin.

The party emerges from one of the side streets and then proceeds down Spring Green's main thoroughfare, beckoned onward by the warm glow of the tavern's interior. At their destination, Aramas steps into the hive of activity followed closely by the others to the loud boisterous clamor of satisfied customers and the almost seductive smell of beer and mead, fresh bread, and roasted chicken.

Pausing momentarily, Aramas surveys the room for a table large enough to accommodate the weary travelers. Spotting one in the far corner, he motions for the others to follow and takes the chair in the corner, affording him a clear view of the entire room.

No sooner is the party seated when four burly, heavily armed men leave the bar and approach the table. "You're sitting at our table."

Aramas replies, "I'm sorry, we were not aware that this table was taken. We have traveled a long distance. Would you mind if, just this once, we could impose on your hospitality?"

"Hospitality? Fancy talk. What if we don't want to be hospitable?"

"Sir, we desire no trouble, only a cool drink and warm dinner."

Before the stranger can answer, a voice comes from the direction of the bar, "Don't you recognize them?"

Surprised, the four turn to see who has interrupted what they had hoped would be a good brawl.

The stranger walks to the table and motions for the four to back off. "These are the ones who freed the blacksmith's sons, Alissa's champions." Startled, the four step aside as the stranger pushes past them. "Please forgive their ignorance." He points to Slinger but addresses Aramas. "While I do not recognize him, how could anyone forget you and your dwarf friend? There are not many who could have done what you did."

"I thank you for your kind remarks and intervention, but we did not act alone. To whom do I have the honor of addressing?"

"I am Trevor, the owner of this establishment."

"How is it that you know of what happened?"

"Adwin is a friend of mine, his sons like my own. Everyone knows what happened."

"Apparently not everyone," quips Loki.

"Never mind them. What can I do for you? Wine, women, what?"

Wasting no time, Loki replies, "Wine!"

Smiling, Trevor asks, "And the rest of you?"

Kriv answers, "Wine for all. How much will that be?"

"Because you honor me with your presence, the first round is on me."

"You are very generous," replies Aramas, "but not necessary."

"It would be my honor."

Smiling, Aramas asks, "Is that fresh bread I smell? And chicken?"

"The best in Spring Green."

"Then bring a plate for each of us."

"As you wish," Trevor says, at which point he turns and scrambles toward the bar.

As the evening draws on, several customers stop by the table, some to add their thanks, others simply to see what all the fuss is about.

Putting down her drink, Aria remarks, "It is not wise to remain here much longer. We need not the attention."

Having consumed more than his share of the gratuitous libations, and beginning to feel a bit drowsy, Loki replies, "I sort of like the attention."

Laughing, Patron remarks, "You like the free wine."

"That too."

Smiling, Aramas says, "I agree. We should retire for the night. I am sure that Alissa will be eager to speak with us." Motioning to the bar, Aramas summons Trevor to the table.

Drying a mug as he approaches, Trevor asks, "What is your desire?"

With a loud gurgling belch, Loki drops his head to the table and remarks, "I know what I desire."

Shaking his head, Aramas replies, "We need lodging for the night. Might you be able to accommodate us?"

"Sure. I have one large room with four beds and two with two beds each."

"Are they clean?"

"They don't have fine sheets or feather pillows, but they're clean."

"How much?"

"One silver each."

"We'll take the large room and one of the small."

"I'll see to it right away."

Just as Aramas is about to stand, one of Alissa's guards comes through the door and surveys the remaining customers. Lifting his head slightly, Loki remarks, "This cannot be good."

When the guard notices the party, he briskly approaches the table and snaps to attention. "My lord, Alissa requests that you meet her in the keep tomorrow morning about an hour after sunrise. Will you need an escort?"

"No, that should not be necessary. Please advise her that we will be there."

Clicking his heels, the guard nods and, as quickly as he entered, exits the room.

Loki sarcastically stands, snaps his heels, and nearly loses his balance. "Requested?" he slurs. "You mean commanded, don't you. I'd like to tell her a thing or . . ."

Placing his hands on his friend's shoulders, Aramas interrupts him. "We can discuss this tomorrow. Let's get you to bed."

The crowing of a nearby rooster comes far too early for Loki, his head pounding from the night before. With a low moan, his hand holding his head, he mumbles, "What day is it?"

Chuckling, Aramas replies, "Was it worth it?"

"Ugh. I'll let you know in a few hours."

"You don't have a few hours. Alissa is expecting us."

In a whiney tone of voice, Loki replies, "And we dare not upset Alissa."

"Someday you will realize that free does not necessarily mean without cost." Picking up his knapsack, Aramas heads to the door. "The others are waiting. Do not be long."

THE SEARCH FOR THE DRAGON'S DAGGER

A few minutes later, Loki gingerly descends the stairs; the rest of the party smirks as he approaches. "What is that banging?"

Patron laughs. "Rough night?" Everyone else attempts to muffle their amusement as Loki passes on his way to the door.

Outside, the pitter-patter of a soft spring rain fills the air. Passersby, their heads hung low attempting to avoid the rain, pay no attention to the travelers exiting the tavern as they try to navigate the myriad of puddles, piles of manure, and scattered bits of trash. On the corner, a beggar huddles beneath another overhang, his shaky hand outstretched, the smell of rotting garbage wafting through the streets. The sky above is gray, almost as if it was going to snow, but the warmth of the rain says otherwise.

They make short time of the distance between the bar and the gate to the inner walls of the outpost, until the party is stopped by two guards. "State your business!"

Aramas replies, "We have been summoned by the mistress of the keep."

Sizing up the party, the second guard walks into a small enclosure and returns shortly thereafter. "Let them pass. The night watch left a notation in the log that they were to be expected." He looks at Aramas. "Can you find your way to the keep?"

Nodding his affirmation, Aramas thanks the guard and motions to the others to follow, the rain now starting to fall a little harder. After they pass through the gate, the party wastes no time getting to the keep. A guard opens the doors and ushers the party past the portcullis and into the main hall. "Wait here. Alissa will be with you shortly."

"Wow! This is quite some place," exclaims Riadon. "Considerably nicer than the other places I've visited while in Spring Green."

Amused, Loki remarks, "That's because this isn't the jail." After a brief pause, he adds, "Be sure to touch nothing!"

Smiling, Riadon sarcastically replies, "You cut me to the quick."

Turning his attention to Aramas, Loki asks, "What are you going to tell Alissa?"

"Only what she needs to know."

"What's that?" asks Kriv. "Our stories must not deviate."

"Are we to speak nothing of the portal and dragons?" asks Loki.

"No, not at this time," replies Aramas. "These walls may still have ears. Other than Adwin, we are to trust no one."

"Even Alissa?"

"Especially Alissa," replies Loki. "She has shown herself to be very adept at the art of deception. She is not to be trusted."

Aramas comments, "While I do not believe that she has deliberately attempted to deceive us, I do feel that she was not as forthcoming as she could have been."

"All right, then what should we reveal?"

"She will want to know how Slinger came to join the party. We should tell her. We can advise her of Craven's death, Karell's, and what he was trying to do, but nothing more."

"What of the beast he was trying to free?"

"No. Brevek was a close confidant of Karell. We do not know if there are others within these walls who were members of their circle, members who need not know of the existence of other dragons. We give them no information that would either aid their efforts to reform the group or continue its purpose."

"What about Sir Lurgan?" asks Aria.

Wryly looking to Aria, Aramas replies, "The castle is haunted, possessed by evil. In our recounting of events, it should remain that way."

Before anything else is said, a familiar figure interrupts. "My friends, it brings me great pleasure to see you safely within these walls. I trust that you were successful?"

Turning, Aramas walks over to greet his friend. "Adwin, it is good to see you. How are your sons?"

He places his hands on Aramas's shoulders. "Doing well thanks to you." He looks at the others. "And to you as well." Then, realizing that there is a new member in the party, he asks, "And whom might this be?"

Slinger takes a step forward and bows slightly. "I am Slinger. The others have spoken highly of you. I am glad to hear that your sons are well."

Adwin turns back to Aramas. "We have news from Everand . . ."

Before he can continue, Alissa enters the room. She walks directly over to Aramas, her gaze drinking in every inch of him before she regains her composure and exclaims, "The success of your journey precedes you. You must tell me everything." She motions toward the far door, her comments directed to the entire party. "Come, join me in my chamber. There is much to discuss."

As directed, the party follows her through the main hall and down the inner corridor to her chambers. When they enter the room in which Aramas and Loki were first introduced to Kriv and Aria, she says, "Please, be seated." Smiling, she looks at Loki. "I am told that you have a palate for fine wine."

Laughing, Patron remarks, "He likes any wine."

Amused by Patron's comment, Alissa smiles before directing her servant to bring some refreshments. Then she takes her seat at the head of the table. Suddenly noticing the party's newest member, she comments, "You have me at a disadvantage."

Aramas interrupts. "The fault is mine. This is Slinger. His unique skills contributed to our success."

"Unique skills? I would not call thievery a *unique* skill."

Surprised by her sharp reply, Aramas attempts to quell her sudden concern. "My lady, as a young boy I remember being admonished by my mother not to judge the contents of a book by its cover. While I have often found it difficult to do so, it is advice that I have endeavored never to forget. I assure you that, without his help, our mission would have surely failed."

Alissa hesitates before answering, glancing first at Adwin then back at Aramas. Regaining her composure, she continues. "No, the fault is mine. If you have accepted him, then so shall I." As she is finishing her comments, the servant returns with a platter of various cheeses and fresh fruits as well as two bottles of wine. Waving her hand as if to shoo a fly away, she remarks, "Just set them on the table and leave us." Without hesitation, the servant does as directed, then backs out of the room.

As the party partakes of the refreshments, Alissa asks, "So what did you learn?"

"From what we could ascertain, Brevek worked in league with a high priest by the name of Karell. We believe they were followers of the ancient god Orcas."

Adwin interrupts. "The followers of Orcas were banned hundreds of years ago. It is said the Orcas himself was so evil that the other gods locked him in another plane, unable to ever return."

"Well, that explains the black thing in the tunnel," blurts Riadon.

Surprised by the comment, Aramas glares at Riadon then quickly tries to redirect the conversation. "There is no doubt that the castle is haunted by unholy creatures, the undead, and unexplainable visions, many of which appear to be from worlds beyond this one. While we know nothing of Orcas, we did learn that Karell hoped to find a way to return the dragons to this world."

"You say they were trying to find a way. The black dragon you killed would appear to indicate that they had succeeded," replies Alissa.

"No, our impression was that, while they knew of the dragon's demise, they were just as surprised as us of its existence. Brevek was the conduit by which they learned of its existence and death. When we confronted Karell, he spoke of it fondly but confirmed that he was not sure how it came to be. He was certain that the key to resurrecting the dragons lay in the gems Craven was stealing and the scales of the dragon skeleton they were excavating."

Concerned, Adwin remarks, "That may be why Nemo has requested your presence."

"Who is Nemo?" asks Loki.

"He is the grand wizard in Everand. I was about to tell you of him when Alissa entered the room."

"What has he been told?" asks Kriv.

Alissa answers, "Only how the gem came into my possession. Nothing else." She looks at Aramas, hands clutching each other nervously. "We received a dispatch by pigeon from Everand two days ago. Nemo has studied the opal but will speak nothing of it until he meets with you and Loki."

"He said nothing else?" asks Aramas.

"No. He will speak of it to no one but you." Standing, Alissa walks over to a nearby table and from a small drawer removes a rolled parchment. She extends the parchment to Aramas. "This will introduce you to the tower guards and Nemo." Aramas stands to accept it. "Adwin has readied seven of our fastest horses to take you to Everand." Then she glances at Slinger then Adwin. "We will need another horse."

Adwin steps forward. "It is important that you arrive in Everand as soon as possible. While Nemo's dispatch was short, its urgency was clear. Stop only as needed along the way and speak to no one of this."

Curious, Loki asks, "If you did not know of Slinger's presence, how is it that you readied seven horses, and why would we need another?"

Somewhat shyly, Alissa touches Aramas's hand. "There is a favor I must ask of you." She cups Aramas's hand in hers. "There is a young apprentice that I would ask you to take under your tutelage."

Loki stands and interrupts. "And why would we do that?"

"I am not asking you."

"Loki is right. Why would we do that?" asks Aramas. "What may lie ahead is no place for a novice. Who is this person to you?"

"He is my nephew."

Aramas is surprised by the request. "Why not have him remain here under the tutelage of his mentor, where he is safe?"

"Because Brevek was his mentor." Flustered, Alissa turns and faces the party, obviously angered by Aramas's hesitance. "This is not a request!"

"My lady, I cannot guarantee his safety, and I will not jeopardize the lives of the others trying to do so."

Aria interrupts. "I will take the responsibility."

Caught off guard, Aramas turns. "Are you sure? We know not what lies before us."

"I will take the responsibility."

Pleased with Aria's offer, Alissa replies, "Good, then it is settled. He will be waiting for you with the horses."

Aria asks, "What is his name?"

"Ghazbaren."

Having accomplished what she set out to do, Alissa turns to leave then stops momentarily at the door. She says to Loki, "The wine is from one of the best vintners in the valley. It would be a shame to let it go to waste."

Loki replies, "I have lost my appetite." After she exits the room, he picks up both bottles and places them in his haversack. Noticing that the others are staring at him, he adds, "I didn't say that I wouldn't have an appetite later."

As indicated, Ghazbaren is waiting with the horses. He is a good-looking young man, perhaps sixteen or seventeen in age and barely able to contain his excitement as the party approaches. He exclaims to Aramas, "It is a true honor. Thank you for . . ."

Before he can finish, Aramas interrupts. "Thank not me. Thank Aria. She will be your mentor." He stops abruptly before him. "You are to do as directed, no questions. Your life could depend on it."

"Yes, sir. I understand."

"No, you do not. This is no stroll in the woods. Understand that it was not my idea to be your wet nurse. You *will* do as directed, or not even your aunt will be able to save you." Saying nothing more, Aramas walks over to a large gray Percheron and begins to secure his gear.

As the others do the same, Aria walks over to Ghazbaren. "Do not mind his temper, only his words. He is a good leader and an honorable man. He spoke to you as he did only out of concern. You can learn a lot from him."

"Thank you." Gazing at Aria's dusky red skin and bright red eyes, he comments, "I have never met a tiefling before. Brevek told me of your race during several of my lessons, but I never figured I would meet one."

"Then you have a lot to learn." Walking over to her horse, she asks, "How do your friends address you?"

"Most simply call me Ghaz. Only my aunt refers to me by my given name."

"Then Ghaz it shall be." After mounting her horse, she looks down at her ward. "You had best get into the saddle. No need to invite another tongue-lashing from Aramas."

Smiling broadly, Ghaz mounts his horse and moves it alongside Aria's.

Seeing that everyone is mounted and ready, Aramas looks down at Adwin. "Is there anything I should know about the boy?"

"Only that he is young and eager to learn. While I understand your concern, he can learn nothing else here. Alissa has done her best to raise him, but what he needs now can only come from a strong man. I can think of no better." He glances at Ghaz, then back up at Aramas. "I meant what I said. Delay only as necessary, and tell only Nemo of what has been discussed. I am sure that Brevek did not act alone."

"And his apprentice?"

"There is no indication that he was in any way involved. He will not let you down."

Pulling his hood up over his head, he replies, "I hope not." As he adjusts his reins, he asks, "Where can we find Nemo?"

"That will not be a problem. He resides in the tallest building in Everand, a seven-sided jade-colored tower.

With a slight nod of his head, Aramas motions to the others to proceed then waves to Adwin. "Be well."

As the party proceeds toward the gate of the inner wall, Aramas turns briefly to take one last look at Adwin.

Standing in one of the windows high in her compound, Alissa watches as the party disappears through the gate.

Other than several days of heavy rain and roads in some areas made almost impassable by flooding, deep mud, and a few downed trees, the journey to Everand is uneventful. Eight days after leaving Spring Green, the immense Inland Sea becomes visible, its shores extending from horizon to horizon. As they stand atop the vast rolling hills to the east, the party looks upon the largest city any of them have ever seen.

· The largest port on the Inland Sea's eastern shore seems to stretch forever in both directions. Protected by a labyrinth of snakelike outer walls, its massive parapets would discourage all but the gods. Outside, the landscape is dotted with farms, ranches, and dairy farms busy plowing and planting. Other than the Forest Road, there are major roads converging on the city from both the north and south, pushing commerce of all types in and out of the city's massive gates. The harbor is dotted with ships at anchor, its piers filled with activity. Between the inner and outer walls, streets stretch like a patchwork quilt in all directions, smoke wafting skyward from the myriad of chimneys, smokestacks, blacksmiths shops, and other buildings. The hum of the city, like that of an active beehive, can be heard even from where the party now stands.

As Adwin had indicated, Nemo's tower is the city's most imposing structure, even taller than the fortress' keep. Staring in amazement, Ghazbaren remarks, "Have you ever seen anything like it?"

Patron replies, "And to think that Falls Deep is said to be at least twice the size."

"Where is Falls Deep?"

"I am told that it is on the far northwestern corner of the Inland Sea."

Loki dryly adds, "Not a place I would like to live. Too crowded and dirty."

"But think of all the pubs," laughs Kriv.

Unable to contain his excitement, Ghazbaren asks Aramas, "Will we be there before nightfall?"

Smiling, Aramas replies, "Judging from the sun's position, we should have plenty of time to find suitable lodging, and if the gods are willing, a good meal."

Pleased with the answer, Ghazbaren slaps the rein on his horse's hindquarter. As it lurches forward, he shouts to the others, "Come on. Everand awaits."

Not sure how to handle the exuberance, Aramas shakes his head than calls to Aria, "Remember, he's your responsibility."

Aria laughs, gives her horse a kick, and takes off at a quick gallop, Kriv, Patron, Slinger, and Riadon close behind.

Smiling broadly, Loki looks over at his friend. "Well, are you just going to sit there? I for one do not intend to let them drink all of the wine."

Taking up the challenge, Aramas kicks his horse and shouts, "Last one to the gate buys!"

Following suit, Loki replies, "That's not fair!"

When they reach the outskirts of city, the party stops to ask a nearby farmer where they might find lodging for the night and a good meal near the wizard's tower.

The farmer wipes the sweat from his brow and shields his eyes from the bright sun. "I would recommend the Sleeping Bear Inn. It is run by my sister and brother-in-law. If you let them know that we spoke, they will give you a good rate. From there it is only a short walk to the tower."

"Where might we find the inn?" asks Kriv.

The farmer walks to the center of the road and points to the main gate. "Through the gate. Once inside, there is a perimeter road that follows the wall. Go to the left and proceed about one-quarter mile to the blacksmith's shop. I would recommend that you use his stables to bed your mounts. He takes good care of the animals in his charge, and his fee is reasonable. From the stable entrance, take the street to the right toward the inner wall. The Sleeping Bear is no more than fifteen minutes down that street. It will be on the right."

After they thank the farmer for his time and information, the party continues toward the main gate. As they move closer to the city, the number of people on the road increases dramatically. In addition to the local traffic and normal myriad of travelers, there are also heavily loaded wagons teaming with goods destined for the port. To either side of the road are various small tents and vegetable stands, their boisterous proprietors hoping to sell their wares at inflated prices but more than willing to negotiate or barter for the best possible deal.

When they arrive at the gate, the party is stopped by one of the guards. "What brings you to Everand?"

"We have business on behalf of the Lady Alissa of Spring Green," replies Aramas.

"Business? What kind of business?"

"That is no concern of yours."

"I have been directed to make it my concern." He sizes up the party. "If you're looking for trouble, you have come to the wrong place. The town fathers do not look favorably on troublemakers."

Wondering what the holdup is, the sergeant of the guard approaches. "Is there a problem?"

Aramas replies, "There is no problem. Your friend was just explaining some of the city's ordinances."

The sergeant looks at the other guard then back at Aramas. "Move along!"

Once they enter the city, the party does as the farmer directed and takes the perimeter road to the left, arriving at the blacksmith's shop a few minutes later. Before the party can dismount, a large burly soot-covered man drops his hammer, takes off his gloves, and walks over to greet the newcomers. "Can I help you?"

Aramas replies, "We have been on the road for almost two weeks and require a good place to leave our mounts. Your stable comes highly recommend."

"I do my best." He looks over the horses. "How long will you be in town?"

"Only as long as necessary," relies Aramas.

"Do you have lodging for the night?"

"The Sleeping Bear Inn has been mentioned."

"I am told they do a good job." He takes a few seconds then points to the corral outside the stable. "For three pieces of silver, they'll get a good rub down, fresh hay, and a bucket of oats."

"That seems a fair price."

Turning back to the forge, the blacksmith calls to a young boy, "Jacob, please make sure that you take good care of these horses." The boy, who had been standing behind the anvil, sets down a bar of iron and rushes out to meet his boarders. As the party dismounts, he eagerly takes the reins from them, then leads the horses to the water trough.

Aramas hands three silver to the smithy and asks, "Can you direct us to the inn?"

He points down the street toward the inner wall. "A few minutes' walk on the right. You can't miss it. A large sign of a sleeping bear hangs over the door."

"Thank you. We will return tomorrow once we know how long we will be in town."

Even though it is late in the afternoon, the sun still sits well above the horizon. Like bees hopping from flower to flower, villagers and travelers clog the street as they move from shop to shop. Unlike the main road into the city or the perimeter road within it, there are no horses and wagons on this narrow street, only pedestrians. For a large city, the streets are relatively clean, and the preponderance of shops are well-maintained.

When they arrive at the inn, the party is greeted by the pleasant smell of broiled chicken intermingled with fine tobacco and a mellow hint of wine. The party wastes no time entering the establishment.

Loki jubilantly remarks, "I think I'm going to like it here."

From behind the bar to the left, an attractive red-headed, middle-aged woman dries a recently washed tankard. "You're welcome to sit wherever you like." She steps from behind the bar, places her clenched fists on her hips, and asks, "Your first time in Everand?"

Not sure how to interpret either her posture or the question, Aramas replies, "Yes."

Smiling broadly, she remarks, "I'm surprised the city guards let you pass. They generally don't take kindly to adventurers, especially ones as heavily armed as you."

Before Aramas can reply, Kriv interjects. "We do not intend to remain long."

"Oh, don't take me wrong. It matters not to me. I just don't want any trouble here."

Riadon sarcastically remarks, "Not one of the friendliest towns I've ever been in."

"There will be no trouble," replies Aramas.

"Traveled far?"

"We left Spring Green eight days ago."

Surprised, the woman remarks, "You made good time. This time of year the roads can be impassable." She walks back to the bar. "So what can I do for you?"

"We're looking for lodging and a good meal. This place comes highly recommended."

"Oh yeah? By whom?"

"A farmer outside of town on the Forest Road."

With a loud chuckle, she quips, "So you met my no-good brother." Smiling, she adds, "It's been a while since I've seen him. Running this place doesn't afford much time for visiting, if you know what I mean. Did he look okay?"

"He seemed to be doing fine."

Thankful for the news, she replies, "Well, it will be a silver piece each for the room and dinner. We start serving in about an hour."

"And the wine?" asks Loki.

"That's extra."

Aramas pats Loki on the back. "You'll have to excuse my friend. It's been almost a week since his last drink."

"I am familiar with his kind and their affinity for strong drink." She points to several kegs behind the bar. "One of the best selections in Everand." Then she looks at Loki. "Be forewarned, don't get sick in my establishment. If you do, you either clean up your own mess or sleep in the street."

Turning to Riadon, Loki grumbles, "I agree. Not very friendly."

Tersely, she replies, "No, just tired of cleaning up after those who can't hold their drinks." Stepping behind the bar, she puts the tankard on the shelf, leans over the bar, and asks, "Well, what will it be?"

Aramas replies, "Do you have any large rooms?"

"Unless you don't mind sleeping on the floor, I have only one large room. It has four beds. All of the others have two."

Without hesitation, Slinger interrupts. "We'll give you six silver for the large room and eight meals."

Sticking her tongue in her cheek, she smiles. "Okay, six it is." Reaching under the bar, she proffers a rather large brass key and motions to the back of the room. "The privy is out that door. The room is at the top of the stairs. Dinner will be served in an hour. Don't be late."

Slinger sarcastically salutes. "Yes, ma'am." Then he takes the key and heads toward the back stairwell.

Aramas smiles. "I'm looking forward to it." As the party proceeds toward the stairs, he abruptly stops and asks, "How far to the jade tower?"

Thinking for a moment, she replies, "Maybe ten minutes."

"Thank you."

After a large breakfast of eggs, potatoes, fried pork, and cider, the party gathers their belongings and heads out the door. On their way out, Aramas thanks the innkeeper for her hospitality and gets directions to the tower.

"Will you be returning later?" she asks.

"Probably not. I suspect that once our business is concluded, we will be on our way."

"Should you happen this way again, you will be welcome."

Smiling, Aramas nods and joins the others.

When they turn the corner two blocks from the inn, the massive tower complex explodes into view. Still several blocks away, the impressive wall surrounding the area dwarfs the buildings around it, its jade tower glimmering in the morning sun. Leading to the complex's entrance is an expansive open-air mall replete with finely manicured shrubbery, ornamental trees, and colorful beds of spring flowers. Finely crafted jade sculptures flank the bronze double doors leading into the complex, as do two muscular splendidly attired guards stopping all hoping to enter.

Within minutes, the party joins the short line of those hoping to gain entry. However, the wait is not long, as the guards appear to be very adept at turning away the curious or those with no bona fide reason to meet with the grand wizard.

"What is your business?" asks one of the guards.

Reaching into his tabard, Aramas takes out the parchment given to him by Alissa and hands it to the guard. "This should explain."

The guard studies the document's contents then hands it to his part-ner. He too carefully examines it. Then, rolling it up, he hands it back to Aramas. "You are to leave your weapons with the guard inside to the right. Once you have done so, you will be escorted into the tower." Before anyone can object, the other guard assures them that there is no safer place in Everand. While not enamored with the idea, the party does as directed.

After securing their weapons, they are met by an older gentleman adorned in a fine hooded tunic. He bows slightly as he approaches. "I am Themos, acolyte to Nemo. I have been asked to accompany you into the tower. I understand that you have traveled from Spring Green."

Aramas replies, "That is correct. We are to meet with the grand wizard, Nemo."

"We had not expected your arrival for several more days. I trust your journey was uneventful?"

"Other than the rains."

"The gods be praised. Your arrival has been highly anticipated."

Once inside, the party is whisked through a long green marble foyer;

emerald-encrusted sconces illuminate the finely polished stone. Beyond the foyer is a large open atrium with vaulted ceiling and polished walls. In the center is a beautiful fountain surrounded by several large jade vases of flowering plants.

They stop briefly at the fountain when Themos is approached by two men. In a hushed conversation, the three speak briefly before Themos turns. "Nemo has been advised of your arrival. I have been asked to take you to his quarters where you will be attended to."

The party is guided through a set of large iron doors, down another sconce-lit hallway adorned with exquisite tapestries and fine woven rugs, and into what appears to be a library, its walls almost hidden by the hundreds of books and rolled parchments that line its shelves. A second-floor balcony encircles the room, shelves of books and parchments covering those walls as well, and above it is another level, each connected by a circular iron stairwell.

Stopping just inside the room, Themos points to a small table with fresh fruit, assorted cheeses, and a decanter of wine. "Please, make yourself comfortable. Nemo will be with you shortly." Then, just as quickly as he appeared, he exits the room, closing the doors behind him.

The room is suddenly quiet, each party member standing in stunned silence. For a few seconds, nothing is said as they study their surroundings.

Loki proceeds to the table and picks up the decanter. "Is anyone going to join me?"

Patron replies, "If you are pouring." Joined by the others, Loki pours eight cups of wine.

Aramas takes a sip of wine, picks up a piece of cheese, and walks over to a nearby table, atop which sits a large parchment map. After studying it, he calls to Loki, "What do you make of this?" Curious, the others follow Loki to the table.

After perusing the map, Loki innocently replies, "It is a map of Everand and the surrounding area."

Sounding exasperated with the answer, Aramas replies, "I can see that. Don't you think it odd though?"

"Why? I am sure that there are hundreds of maps contained within these walls."

"Wizards rarely travel outside the walls that surround their compounds, and when they do, they rarely venture outside the confines of the city." He sweeps a hand over the map. "This is a map of all the lands to the north, east, and south of Everand."

"Okay. And that is important why?"

He points to several marks on the map. "Don't you think it interesting that marks have been placed on Forest Glen, Spring Green, Raven's Nest Castle, Everand, and *Brandor?*"

Taking a closer look at the map, Loki replies, "That is interesting." He takes a sip of wine. "Have you ever been to Brandor?"

From the balcony above, a voice interrupts. "It is my understanding that none of you have." The figure walks over to the stairwell and descends to the main floor, his exquisite emerald green, gold-trimmed hooded robe surpassed only by the elegance of his gold sculpted skull cap. "I am Nemo."

He walks over to the party. "Your party is larger than I was told." Perusing the group, his eyes stop at Aria. "We don't see many of your kind here," then gazing at Kriv and Patron, he says, "and with dragonborn." Turning, he picks up the decanter and pours himself a cup of wine. "What stroke of fate brought the three of you together?"

Agitated, Kriv replies, "I did not come here to be insulted."

Stepping forward, Aramas intervenes. "We came at your behest. Alissa advised that you had stressed the urgency of our arrival. If we were mistaken, I apologize for taking you away from more *important* matters." Aramas puts down his cup of wine. "With your permission, we will take our leave."

Raising his hand, Nemo replies, "Please, please. I meant nothing by my remarks. It was simply an observation and not meant to insult." He picks up Aramas's cup and hands it back to him. "May we start again?"

Briefly hesitating, Aramas takes the cup. "Are the people of Everand always so unwelcoming?"

Nemo moves over to the table with the open parchment, carefully contemplating his next remark. "You must forgive us. For the past several months, unexplained occurrences have put the city on edge, so much so that our citizenry has become suspicious of any newcomers." He speaks directly to Aramas. "And from what Alissa has told us, you may have answers to some of them." Pointing to the map, he continues. "For several months now, in addition to the Forest Road being closed, roving bands of marauding goblins have attacked villages and outposts further to the north near Brandor, Flotsam, and Jetsam. To the south, near the Saltan Desert, entire caravans have disappeared." His finger lands on the center of the map. "Then there is Spring Green."

Removing his hand, he sets down his cup of wine, then walks across the room to a small table beneath a tall ornate stained-glass window. Sitting atop the table is a gilded metal box flanked by two burning candles. He opens it, takes something out, and turns toward the group. "And then there is this." In his hands is the large opal Loki and Aramas had recovered when they killed the baby black dragon. "Tell me, how did you come upon it?"

Before Aramas can answer, Kriv interrupts. "Something is wrong." Almost in a state of panic, he frantically reaches for something around his neck hidden under his garments. As he pulls what appears to be a necklace from behind his tabard, it is vibrating violently and stretches forth as if reaching for the wizard.

Almost immediately, the opal begins to glow, bright rays of brilliant white light encircling the gem. Suddenly, strong surges of electrical energy shoot from the gem into the wizard. Startled, he drops it; however, it does not fall. Suspended in mid-air, the bolts of energy increase in intensity, rays of blinding light beginning to shoot in all directions, illuminating the room.

Unexpectedly the gem shoots across the room toward Kriv. Releasing his grasp on the necklace, Kriv's head turns to avoid the bright light, his hands raised to prevent the gem from striking him. When they collide, there is a silent explosion of light and energy as the gem appears to melt into the necklace, the force knocking Kriv to the floor. Spellbound, the rest of the party watches in horror. Then, just as quickly, the light appears to be sucked back into the gem, everything almost immediately returning to normal. There is an eerie silence. No one speaks.

Rushing to Kriv's side, Aramas and Patron attempt to sit him up while Loki examines him for any injuries. From across the room, in hushed awe, Nemo whispers, "the Dragon's Necklace."

"What did you say?" asks Aria.

With a look of astonishment, Nemo replies, "the Dragon's Necklace."

Around Kriv's neck is an exquisite gold necklace with what appears to be seven slots for gems of various sizes, but the slot immediately to the left of the bottom center is now filled by the opal.

As he helps Kriv to his feet, Aramas asks, "What is the Dragon's Necklace?'"

As if coming out of a trance, the startled wizard replies. "The Dragon's Dagger." Moving closer to Kriv, his eyes transfixed on the necklace, he continues. "Legend says that it was destroyed centuries ago." He stretches his hand forward as if he wants to touch the necklace, but apprehensive about doing so, he asks Kriv, "How did you come upon this?"

Putting his hand on Kriv's shoulder, Aramas directs him not to answer. Aramas again asks, "What is the Dragon's Necklace or Dagger?"

Nemo's eyes are still transfixed on the necklace as he answers, "I am told that the necklace was used to control the dragons before the Dragon Wars. The evil dragons referred to it as a dagger, the most powerful artifact in existence."

"Control?" asks Loki.

"Yes. Before the Dragon Wars, there were two types of dragons, good and evil. You could tell which was which by their color. The good dragons possessed brilliant metallic-colored scales such as gold, bronze, and platinum. The evil dragons had scales of red, blue, white, green, and black."

"Aramas mentioned that at the excavation site," blurts Riadon.

"Excavation site? What excavation site?"

Obviously perturbed with Riadon's comment, Aramas intervenes.

"What has Alissa told you?"

"Only that a band of adventurers had found the opal amongst a number of other gems and valuables recovered on her behalf." He looks at Riadon. "What excavation site?"

Aramas again interrupts. "Did she say nothing else?"

Perplexed, Nemo replies, "Only that it appeared to be protected by a powerful form of old magic. When her advisor studied it, he felt that the gem was created using an old form of dragon magic. Not trained in the ancient arts, he advised her to send the stone to me. However, I too could not unlock its secret."

Loki remarks, "I knew Adwin was no mere blacksmith."

Looking again at the gem, Nemo remarks, "The stone now raises more questions than it answers."

Aramas replies, "No, it does answer several questions. The Forest Road was closed with the express purpose of finding this stone. Fortunately for us, they did not know what they were looking for."

"Why were they seeking the stone, and what does it have to do with an excavation site?"

"All in good time." Glaring at Riadon, Aramas continues. "You were telling us of the necklace when someone rudely interrupted."

"I am not familiar with all of the details, but from what I understand, for centuries the dragons enslaved all of the other races. Led by the humans, rebellion broke out against their rule, humans, elves, and dwarves leading the fight. During the war, the demon race, afraid of being ruled by the evil dragons should they prevail, revolted and bred with captured humans to create tieflings. Realizing that the balance of power was shifting in favor of the humans, the dragons mated with enslaved humans to create dragonborn. In the end, the evil dragons were defeated." He glances between Aria, Kriv, and Patron. "That is why I asked about the presence of both in your party. Your races were created to destroy each other."

"What about the empty slots in the necklace?" asks Kriv.

"They were for the other stones."

"Other stones?" asks Loki.

"Yes, each stone possessed a unique power or quality. In and of itself, the stone was only worth the value of a like stone, but combined, they became the most powerful known artifact capable of controlling all dragons."

"So what happened to the other stones?" asks Aria.

"I do not know. After the war, all dragons were banished and the necklace supposedly destroyed." His glance firmly fixed on Aramas, he asks, "I have told you what I know. What of the excavation site?"

Unable to avoid the question any longer, Aramas answers. "The robberies along the Forest Road and the excavation site were part of an elaborate plan to somehow return the dragons to this realm. We now suspect the robberies were to retrieve the gems and the excavation was to retrieve the essence of the dragons. Unfortunately, the death of their leader deprived us of the opportunity to understand by what process they hoped to achieve their goal."

"What was in the excavation site?"

"The skeleton of a long since deceased metallic dragon. Based on my evaluation of the remains, it was killed in combat with a red dragon." He motions to Slinger. "Slinger worked at the site."

"And now he stands with you?"

Smiling, Slinger bows politely and replies, "A mutually beneficial relationship."

Nemo looks back at Aramas. "Did you find any evidence that they were close to succeeding?"

Believing it unwise to mention either the baby black dragon or the black dragons on the other side of the portal, Aramas replies, "No. It was apparent to me that they possessed neither the required elements nor the knowledge to do so."

"What of the other conspirators?"

Riadon proudly replies, "We killed them all!"

Looking back at Kriv, Nemo again asks, "How did you come by the necklace?"

Unsure if he should answer, he looks to Aramas, who nods his assent. "It was given to me by my father."

"And how did . . ."

"I do not know how it came into his possession."

Aramas again intervenes. "We may have killed all involved in this venture, but we did not kill everyone involved in the enterprise."

Walking back to the map table, Nemo picks up his cup of wine and takes another drink. "I agree." Taking another, he places the now empty cup on the table. He looks first at Kriv, then back at Aramas. "Thorac must be advised of this."

"And who is Thorac?" asks Patron.

"He is the high priest of Moradin in Brandor." Walking over to the door, Nemo opens it and calls out, "Chavere, please bring me the document we prepared yesterday." He walks back over to the map table. "I'm sure that you still have many unanswered questions. Unfortunately, there is nothing more I can do to be of assistance. My knowledge in this area is limited." He looks again at the necklace. "When I received the opal, I knew it was no ordinary gem and immediately advised Thorac. After numerous conversations, it was decided that you should transport the gem to Brandor." He points to the necklace. "This is not how I envisioned it would be transported."

A knock comes at the door. "Sir?" The door swings open and a short gray-haired man hustles in, bows, and hands Nemo a parchment.

"Thank you; you are dismissed."

The old man bows again, backs out of the room, and closes the door behind him.

Nemo hands the document to Aramas. "This will introduce you to Thorac. I will secure passage on a vessel departing this afternoon for you and your party."

Loki sarcastically remarks, "Have we already overstayed our welcome?"

Smiling, Nemo replies, "No, but the answers you seek will not be found in Everand. Thorac has knowledge of the ancient magic and what transpired before, during, and after the Dragon Wars." Pausing briefly, he points to the necklace. "Besides, he will want to see this."

"What of our mounts?" asks Kriv.

"Before you leave, advise Chavere where they are stabled. He will ensure that they are returned to Spring Green."

Nemo places his hand on Aramas's shoulder. "Other than Thorac, speak of what was discussed here with no one." He glances over at Riadon then back at Aramas. "No one can speak of this. Understood?"

"I understand."

Turning to the rest of the party, Nemo directs his first comment to Kriv. "You were wise to keep the necklace hidden. I would recommend that you continue to do so." Then, he says to everyone, "May the gods favor you with their divine protection during the journey that lies before you."

While their meeting with the wizard Nemo had been enlightening, it left far more questions unanswered than answered. The fact that Kriv, who had been in possession of the necklace for most of his life, just happened to be in Spring Green when Aramas and Loki were being asked to recover the gem, had to be more than mere coincidence. Further, judging from Kriv's response when the gem melded with the necklace, he knew nothing of its origin or significance. Was it the Dragon's Dagger? Nemo seemed to think so. How else could one explain what happened? However, if it were the long-lost artifact, why not pass it on to someone who understood and could harness its potential powers, powers far beyond those of its current bearer? Why was Nemo asking the party to transport it to Brandor? Was the high priest that "someone" who could wield its power?

As the party gathers outside the library, they are approached by Themos. "Nemo has asked that I ensure that you have the provisions required for the journey to Brandor. Whatever you need, I am to provide."

Having never been to Brandor, Loki asks, "How long is the journey?"

"Depending on the weather, about five days. Other than your bedroll, you will need little while aboard the vessel. They will provide your meals and a hammock. I am to provide you with clothing, additional arrows, bolts, sun rods, and such other things as you deem necessary."

Fidgeting, Loki asks, "Oh, vessel? What if we were to travel by land?"

"A day or two short of two weeks," he said, clearly puzzled by the question. "Why do you ask?"

Looking around at the expressions on the faces of his companions, Loki hesitates before replying. "Just wondering."

Knowing his friend, Aramas asks, "Is everything all right?"

Still fidgeting, Loki replies, "Well . . . NO! It is not."

"What is not?"

Exasperated, Loki motions toward the Inland Sea, the large body of water to the west. "That!" Pausing briefly, he continues. "It just isn't natural."

"What isn't natural?"

"Getting on a ship. Ducks and seagulls are made for the water, not man. Besides, there are huge beasts hidden beneath the surface capable of swallowing entire ships."

Themos attempts to allay Loki's concerns. "Such beasts only exist in myth and legend. I assure you that travel by sea is both safe and expeditious."

Joking, Kriv laughs. "You see, there is nothing to worry about. Besides, you can swim, can't you?"

"I am glad that you are amused." Picking up his knapsack, Loki asks Themos, "Which way to the pier?"

Author's Note

In 1987, while visiting a Toys-R-Us store near our home in Glen Ellyn, Illinois, my oldest son, Daniel, purchased a book by Gary Gygax entitled *Oriental Adventures*. It cost $9.99, a relatively expensive purchase for a twelve-year-old, and it was my first exposure to *Dungeons and Dragons*—a purchase that would impact not only Daniel's life but mine. Not long after, while visiting relatives in Cincinnati, my oldest nephew, learning of Daniel's purchase, gave him two of his *D&D* books, *Fiend Folio* and *Deities and Demigods*. Daniel was hooked. Soon Dan's love of the game would be passed along to his siblings and eventually his own sons.

Over the years, I watched the kids playing this new kind of game. They referred to it as "role-playing." Unlike your typical board game, this game had no board, used a minimal number of pieces, and took hours to play. It was not unusual for a session to go well into the night and early morning. As a Scoutmaster, I recall many nights at summer camp where the boys played as long as I would let them, Dan serving as the Dungeon Master. However, it wasn't until 2005 that I played for the first time. My middle son, Tonas, and his wife, DeAudra, were living with us at the time. One evening, both Dan and Tonas approached me to ask permission to have a session at our house the following Saturday, hoping to utilize the dining room table. I told them that if Judith (my wife) approved, it was okay with me. Judith has always been willing to try new things, especially if it involved the kids, so she agreed. She had no idea that the game could go on for hours. As part of our agreement to play, Dan created two characters, one for her and the other for me. Before creating them, he asked us questions about what race we wanted our characters to be, what type of character, what religious deity we followed, our physical characteristics, and so on. Growing up, one of my favorite television shows was a western, *Have Gun—Will Travel*. The lead character, a gunfighter for hire who always turns out to be a champion of the downtrodden, carries a business card with a picture of a chess knight prominently displayed in the center. His name: Paladin. Once Dan told me there was a paladin character type, the choice was simple. Then I needed a name. Unexpectedly, I found it one morning on a bottle of cologne: Aramas. My father had given me the bottle years earlier, a gift from his sister who worked at Saks Fifth Avenue. Aramas was born.

Over the next two years, we played only intermittently; Tonas and DeAudra moved out, one player joined the military, and Judith decided that each session went on far too long. Then, in 2007, Dan asked if we could start again with a new group of players, people he had met and played with while attending Southern Illinois University. I would keep my character, now a level two paladin, Tonas would keep his (Loki), now a level three dwarf cleric, and the new players would create their own level one characters. Dan would continue to serve as the Dungeon Master. Based on the rules of the game and the way players level up, it would not take long for the characters to reach the same level. We have been playing ever since.

As the sessions went on, it became apparent that someone needed to take notes. There were just too many things to keep track of or recall months, and now years, later. I decided to take on the task. Today, those notes fill a three-ring binder. During one session, someone mentioned that if I added dialogue, my notes were good enough for a book. Besides, years earlier, the *Dragonlance* series was just that, a series of books based on a compilation of adventure notes from actual games. *The Search for the Dragon's Dagger* is a compilation of notes from the first three adventures our group played, beginning with that first session in 2007. Over the years, players have come and gone, but four of our original group are still playing: my son, Daniel; Brian; Ryan; and me.

It has taken me a little more than four years to finish my first attempt at being an author. Why did it take so long? Because during the first three adventures, no one kept an extensive set of notes. As such, much of what is written is based on my memory. Going forward, that should not be a problem.

I want to thank everyone who has been a part of this journey. In particular, the original group: Daniel Zedan III, Tonas Zedan, Brian Dugan, Ryan Mulvaney, John Filicaro, and Waleed Abbasi. I also need to thank the many players who, for a variety of reasons, have come and gone. Without their characters, the story would not have progressed.

Finally, I want to thank my wife, Judith. Without her love and support, none of this would have been possible. In addition to putting up with a bunch of grown-up kids for eight hours a day several times each month, she has been my proofreader, my sounding board, and, as an avid reader, my inspiration. I sincerely hope that this book brings as much pleasure to the reader as books in general have brought her.

ABOUT THE AUTHOR

A 1973 graduate of the US Merchant Marine Academy, Dan retired from the US Coast Guard Reserve in 2001 as a captain, is a Desert Shield/Desert Storm and Operation Uphold Democracy veteran, and is the founder and president of Nature's Finest Foods, Ltd, a Chicago-area food brokerage, marketing, and consulting firm. A lifelong member of the Boy Scouts of America and avid model railroader, Dan has a love of gaming that developed at an early age with his first chess set, eventually expanding into various card and board games. In 2005, at the behest of two of his sons, he participated in his first *Dungeons & Dragons* adventure and has been playing ever since.

Dan and his wife, Judith, still reside in the Chicago area and have five children, twenty-one grandchildren, and two great-grandchildren.